THE
CHAIN

THE SECRET OF
SPELLSHADOW MANOR
— 3 —

BELLA FORREST

THE
CHAIN

THE SECRET OF
SPELLSHADOW MANOR
3

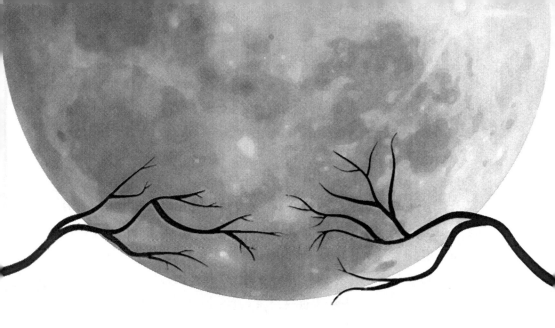

CHAPTER I

I N THE EERIE DARKNESS, THEY SEEMED TO RUN FOR HOURS. Alex's muscles strained and burned as he helped Natalie along. She could hold herself up, but at times, he felt her crumple against him with a wince, so he held onto her. The last thing he wanted was for her to fall, after what she had just done for them. Right behind, Jari and Ellabell flagged beneath the weight of carrying Aamir.

What had seemed like a reasonable distance from the vantage point of the Head's office in fact stretched away into an apparently endless field with a dense forest running alongside, filled with the peering eyes of unknown perils. The lake still glittered on the ever-present horizon, but it did not seem to get any nearer as they soldiered on across foreign territory. It was far bigger than Alex had expected. The gleam of it seemed to go on

forever beneath the twinkle of the night's stars. Alex kept looking back, certain they were being pursued, but the ground they
had already covered remained empty behind them. So far, nobody was following.

"How much farther is it?" Jari wheezed.

"Not much," said Alex, for what seemed like the hundredth
time. He had just as little idea where they were headed as the
others, yet he seemed to have fallen into the role of 'guide.'

"Do you think we'll get there soon?" Jari pressed.

Alex tried not to lose his temper. He knew they were afraid;
he felt it too. "Hopefully," he said.

He could have sworn the lake was much nearer, and he
wondered if the crackle and buzz of magical energy all around
him had something to do with it, altering the perspective of the
view from the Head's window, like the stickers on car side-mir-
rors that said, 'objects in mirror are closer than they appear.' It
was frustrating, to see their destination and still be so far from
it. He wanted to stop and take shelter in the forest to the right of
them, but there was something unnerving about the deep shadows within it that he didn't trust. Not that he knew the lake itself
was safe. In this peculiar place they had landed, all bets were off;
he had no idea what might be hiding over the next rise. For all
he knew, the forest *might* be their safest bet, yet he was drawn to
the glitter of the lake like a moth to a flame.

Finally, as he felt the blood pulsing in his ears and the heave
of his chest threatening to give in, the lake came slowly within
reach. Listening intently, he thought he could hear the susur-
ration of waves gently lapping against the shore, although the
sound of his rushing, overworked blood sounded a lot like that

too. He hoped it was the former.

The sight of it coming closer gave him a sudden surge of energy, and Natalie hopped along wearily beside him. She was relying on his strength to hold her up more and more as the minutes ticked into hours.

"We're almost there," murmured Alex, glancing down at the exhausted face of his friend. She gave him a tired smile as they covered the last few hundred yards.

The crescent moon shone down with a thin beam of pale light as they arrived at the lakeshore. Alex paused for breath, certain now that the soothing sound was coming from the water lapping against the beach, which was formed from glistening white pebbles that shone strangely in the moonlight. Alex felt a prickle of unease; he couldn't be sure whether the odd pebbles were made of rock or bone.

The very presence of the lake itself, so close now, also made Alex uneasy. It was as if he could feel his ancestors watching him from beneath the shimmering surface. Standing beside it, he couldn't take his eyes off the vast expanse of deep, dark liquid as he remembered what lay under the water. The lake made him think of the macabre beauty of a cemetery. He supposed it was one, in its own way. Somberly, taking in the stretch of water, so much larger than he had ever imagined, he wondered just how many bodies were buried there. Impulse compelled him to mouth a silent prayer as he looked upon their final resting place.

Setting Natalie on the ground, he glanced behind once again to check for pursuers. There were none, only Jari, Ellabell, and Aamir bringing up the rear.

Holding his sides as he dragged oxygen into his searing

lungs, Alex turned and gazed outwards. A gentle breeze, smelling slightly of ozone, washed over his face, cooling it. Squinting slightly, he tried to make out the other side of the lake, but he couldn't see it in the faint light of the moon; it was too far away. He shifted his gaze toward the shore they were standing on, which he could see a fair way up, until it disappeared again in a line of twinkling water. In the overhanging shadows of the thick forest that ran alongside, Alex could make out a shape among a thicket of trees. It jutted out slightly, catching the eye.

"Wait," announced Alex.

Jari and Ellabell had been about to put Aamir down, and their groans were irritated at the sound of Alex's instruction.

"What is it?" Jari asked, re-shouldering Aamir's arm. His forehead was slick with sweat, and his sweatshirt was drenched. Ellabell wasn't faring much better.

"A building, I think," replied Alex, pointing to the manmade shape within the thicket of trees.

It wasn't too far from where they stood, which seemed to curb Jari's annoyance. Their current location was too out in the open; they could all feel it. There was an unnerving sense of being watched, or that they would be snuck up on in their sleep, if they stopped where they were, just on the edge of the lake.

"Fine," muttered Jari. They set off toward the hidden structure in the tree line.

As they reached it, Alex could see it was a tumbledown shed of sorts, set back in a secluded clearing. A thin line of trees stood in front of it, giving it some camouflage. Behind it spanned the same dense forest, but it did not seem as menacing here, where the moonlight glanced in and brightened the place. It looked as inviting as any spot they were likely to find.

The door to the ramshackle hut was locked with a rusted padlock, and, though it would have been nice to sleep indoors, Alex wasn't sure they should risk the noise of breaking it, just to sleep inside a dirty shed. Besides, it was a clear, warm night— the perfect kind for sleeping beneath the stars.

Setting Natalie and Aamir down against two sturdy tree trunks, Alex and the others began forming a makeshift camp in the clearing, making sure they picked well-hidden sleeping places. From within the clearing, they had a good view of the lake and the surrounding area, in case anyone tried to sneak up on them.

Alex looked around at the tired faces of his friends; every single one of them was at their limit, their eyes flitting about, their nerves set on edge, wondering if a search party was coming after them. He knew, because he was thinking exactly the same thing and could not take his eyes off the path through which they had come. Natalie had successfully moved the portal, allowing them to escape, but Alex suspected it had taken far more out of her than she was willing to let on. She was barely able to sit unaided, her body tipping to one side from sheer exhaustion. Her breathing was shallow too, and her face was pale and waxy, but she pushed Alex away when he tried to help, claiming to be fine though they both knew she was not.

Aamir, leaning up against the tree beside Natalie, was still in a bad way too, as if cutting the band on his wrist had released something foul within him that had sickened him physically. His temperature was rising, and he was sweaty and feverish, calling out in his unconscious delirium about golden monsters and shadows that clawed at him. His voice was tight and on the edge of a whimper, laced with an undeniable tremor of fear. It spooked Alex, and he could see fear on the others' faces with each garbled cry, but no scream was as terrifying as the next words that came from Aamir's mouth.

"It will come... a plague will sweep the land... no escape... coming for us!" Aamir cried, lashing out in his unconscious state. Jari rushed to him, trying to soothe the sleeping figure as he twisted and turned beneath the hands of imaginary monsters.

It reminded Alex of dark biblical stories he had heard as a child, sending a snaking sensation of fear through him. The words were ominous ones, and Alex wished Aamir were lucid enough to shed some light on their meaning.

Eventually, after some calming words, Jari managed to get Aamir to settle and maneuvered him into a fetal position on the grass. After that, the crying out seemed to stop, and a calm slumber took over Aamir's body, marred only by a few jolting spasms.

Watching Aamir, Alex hoped that, *if* their friend got better—with the golden band gone—he would be able to talk more about what he learned when he became a teacher and the secrets bestowed on all the faculty. Glancing around, he could see he wasn't the only one. Even Jari's eyes seemed curious, as they flitted toward the now-empty spot on Aamir's wrist where the crackling band of golden light had been.

"I'll take the first watch," insisted Alex, refusing the protests of Jari and Ellabell, the only two still awake.

Natalie had shimmied down the tree trunk and was nestled into the ground, curled in a similar position to Aamir.

Wandering over to her with an air of concern, Alex checked that she was breathing and sighed with relief as he heard the quiet rhythm of sleep. Jari was frazzled, his blond hair sticking up, and Ellabell looked dead on her feet. It *had* to be Alex who stayed up. The others were in dire need of sleep, and he knew he at least had something left in the tank, whereas they were running on empty. Carrying Aamir had taken its toll on them, and, though they tried not to show it, Alex knew they were close to collapsing.

"Get some rest. I'll be fine." He managed to smile at them, gesturing to the ground.

The pair fell asleep almost as soon as their heads hit the grass. Ellabell was curled up in a shady corner, and Alex moved quietly over to where she lay, careful not to disturb her as he knelt on the grass and tucked his sweater loosely around her sleeping figure. It was chillier in the spot she had chosen, and he didn't want her to get cold as she slept. Feeling the brush of the soft fabric, she mumbled something in her sleep. Alex found there was a smile playing upon his lips as he watched her nuzzle the edge of his sweater and pull it closer around herself.

Not wanting to risk waking her, Alex stood and walked back across the clearing, taking up a position at the edge of the tree line, facing out toward the lake. He watched, mesmerized by the tiny waves that rippled on the surface, creating the sparkle he had become so familiar with. It was a spot he imagined would be peaceful in other circumstances, but there was too much on his mind for such things. Anxiety raced through his body. There was a lot resting on him, and he couldn't help but feel responsible for the sleeping figures in the clearing behind him, who were looking to him more insistently for a leadership he hoped he was ready to give. Guilt racked him too, riding alongside the anxiety for good measure. He knew he was the one who had gotten his friends into this mess, and he wanted to make sure they didn't regret their decision to come with him. Glancing back, he knew he would protect them in any way he could. They had put a lot of faith in him by leaving Spellshadow, and he was determined not to let them down.

His thoughts drifted to the school they had left mere hours before, wondering how the other students were doing after the half-successful uprising. Professor Gaze sprang to his mind, so ancient and fearless, and he hoped fiercely that the old mage had managed to keep the other students safe from harm. She had told him of her plans to scramble the hallways, but Alex knew such spells were only temporary where the Head was concerned, just as the displacement of the portal was. The Head would find a way through and come looking for his lost prey—Alex had no doubt about that. It was only a matter of time.

As recent memories raced through his head and his eyes came to rest on the glittering lake with so many bodies beneath, Alex couldn't help but be reminded of those who hadn't made it. The ones he had failed. The vacant eyes and stilled lungs of the dead students haunted him, and he felt a deep pang of sorrow at the tragedy of their passing, knowing the potential they might have had and thinking of the homes they would never go back to. So much needless loss at the hands of a power-hungry Renmark. It made the burn of vengeance glow ever brighter in his heart, though the sensation made him curious—hatred was proving a powerful fuel for the fire within him.

His gaze was drawn back across the water to the unseen shore on the other side, the shadows making him wonder what lay beyond it. The lake was huge, and there did not seem to be a settlement or building in sight, save for the old hut beside them—though at the center of Alex's mind blinked the idea of 'Stillwater House.' Here was the still water, but where was the house? He knew it was out there somewhere; he could feel it in his bones.

It was up to them to find it, but even that held a flicker of uncertainty for Alex.

What are we supposed to do when we do find it? he thought anxiously, staring out into the darkness that hid his goal from him. He thought again of Spellshadow, and wondered if they were simply out of the frying pan and into a much worse fire. At least at Spellshadow there had been glimpses of the real world, but this alien land did not feel like the real world at all. The magic that crackled in the air around him like static electricity reminded him of that fact. Yes, they had escaped Spellshadow, but not into the real, human, non-magical world he longed for.

Pushing away a looming sense of worry, Alex looked back at his friends in the clearing, who were resting easy because he had promised to watch over them. That promise, he knew, went beyond that night. It was his duty now. His stoic gaze rested on each one with fondness, despite any former misgivings, though it rested a little bit longer on the curled-up figure of Ellabell. There was a dogged determination within him to make good on his promises and his responsibilities.

Turning back to the distant, shadowed shore, somehow it no longer seemed quite as frightening. Instead of being filled with the unknown, Alex shifted his perspective, trying to see it instead as a land of untapped possibility. Beyond that darkened horizon was a way out. Alex didn't know what form it would take, but he knew he had to find it, whether it be another portal to another land, leading them home, or a person or thing along the way that might help them, or a bargaining chip that would keep his friends safe and maybe, just maybe, lead them out of this magical realm and back into the normal world.

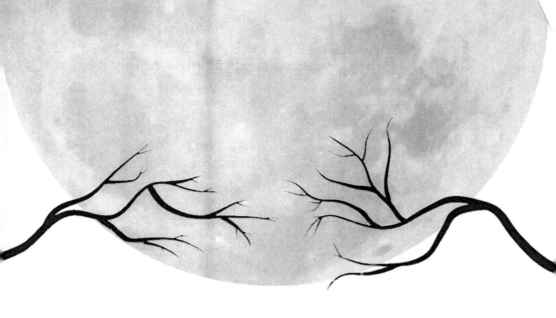

CHAPTER 2

ALEX TURNED SHARPLY AT THE SOUND OF A TWIG crunching underfoot, but it was only Jari, coming to relieve him of his watch. Looking up, Alex could see that it was almost dawn, the starry black of the night's sky diluted to a hazy mauve.

"How did you sleep?" asked Alex.

Jari gave him a groggy thumbs-down. "Not good."

"Go back to sleep if you want," Alex said, but Jari shook his head.

"No, man, it's your turn. You look like hell." He grinned, plucking a stray leaf from Alex's hair, which had taken on a mind of its own.

Alex grimaced and stretched out his arms, feeling the stiffness in his spine from staying in one spot for too long.

Jari sat down companionably beside him and gazed out at the lake.

"It's beautiful, huh?"

Alex nodded stiffly. "It's definitely something."

"Weird that the Head had it there all along, though. He must have really liked the view," mused Jari as he stretched out his limbs too.

"I suppose he must have," replied Alex, trying to keep the bitterness out of his voice.

"Hey, I meant to thank you last night, for what you did for Aamir," Jari said. "I was too beat to say it before." He looked over his shoulder at the sleeping figure of Aamir.

"How is he?"

Jari shrugged. "Not good. I don't know what that band did to him, but he's in a bad way. He's strong, though. He's a fighter... He'll pull through."

Curious, Alex got up and walked over to where Aamir was lying on the ground, with Jari following close behind. Resting his hand against Aamir's forehead, Alex was shocked by the blazing heat that came from his friend's skin. He was burning up, and there was a sheen of sweat across his face, though his lips seemed to tremble as if he were cold.

Alex tore a strip from the bottom edge of his plain t-shirt and jogged to the edge of the lake to dip it in. As soon as his fingers made contact with the water, a ripple of ice-cold energy snaked up his arm, and, as he looked down, he noticed a pulse of silver seemed to glow beneath the skin. When he removed his fingers, the cloth thoroughly drenched, the glow ebbed as the water dried on his hands. Frowning but undeterred, he made his way back over to Aamir and placed the dampened compress on the young man's forehead, letting the cooling water soothe the heat of the fever. It seemed to help, as the furrow of Aamir's brow relaxed slightly.

Sitting nearby, careful to keep their voices low in respect for the other sleepers, Alex and Jari fell into easy conversation. There was plenty to talk about, after all, but one thing in particular seemed to be on Jari's mind.

"So, what are we going to do next?"

"We find Stillwater House and see if we can get some help finding a way out or overthrowing the Head and rescuing those we left behind," replied Alex, hoping Jari didn't hear the big *ifs* in his plan.

Jari frowned. "*Is* there a Stillwater House?"

"It says so in that note I found, and the Head did mention it once." Alex grimaced, realizing the basis of his evidence was somewhat fragile.

"What are these havens, anyway?"

By now, the words were etched in Alex's brain. "*Of our havens, nine remained. Of those nine, we now have four. If you are magical, seek these places. Kingstone Keep. Falleaf House. Stillwater House. Spellshadow Manor*," he recited.

"What the hell does that mean?" asked Jari, gawping at Alex in exasperation.

Alex tried not to laugh at the confused expression on Jari's face. "They're schools or places of magical relevance."

"Meaning?"

"They're full of mages and magic."

"And?"

"And mages might be able to help us," said Alex. "Or if there aren't any people willing to help us, I'm sure there will be something we can *use* at Stillwater."

Jari lapsed into a span of silence, mulling over Alex's words.

"I'm gonna get some sleep," Alex muttered.

He found the most comfortable-looking patch of grass he could and lay down in the shadow of hanging branches. He slept poorly, all the sounds and scents unfamiliar to him, keeping him on a high alert that woke him briefly every hour or less.

When he awoke to the sun higher in the sky, the warmth of it pleasant on his tired face, he gave up on the hope of more sleep and rose to find that everyone else was awake too, except for Aamir, who twisted and turned on the grass in the throes of a fitful slumber. His skin was glistening with sweat, but the compress had been changed, the material of the new one matching the shirt Jari wore.

Approaching the rest of the group, Alex could see that the night's rest hadn't removed the broken, exhausted look from their faces. They were still tired, hungry, and thirsty. He knew because it had been hours since they had last eaten or drunk anything, and his own stomach ached with emptiness, his throat dry.

One pleasant surprise was seeing Natalie awake, though she didn't look much better.

"How are you feeling?" he asked as he sat down on the grass beside her.

She smiled weakly. "I am much better."

Alex wasn't convinced. "What did you do for us, back there?"

"I moved the portal, as you asked," she replied, her voice faint.

Her words left a bitter taste in Alex's mouth as he recalled that it was indeed him who had asked her to do that. Glancing at her, he sorely regretted it. She was pale and her fingers still trembled, though he could see she was trying to be brave.

"How? What magic did you use?" he pressed, wanting to know what she had risked.

"I told you, it was only big magic—it has taken a lot of my strength, but I will be fine. There is no harm done, I promise," she said. Her dark brown eyes were earnest.

"Is there anything we can do, to make you better?" he asked. He didn't like to see his friend this way, so exhausted and shattered. It reminded him too much of the worrying time she had spent beneath the gripping, sapping curse of Derhin's making.

Natalie shook her head, wincing slightly. "I just need rest… though perhaps some water might help. I am quite thirsty," she whispered, her voice choked up.

Alex nodded. "I'll go and hunt down some supplies for us," he said, standing.

Gazing around at the gathered group, Alex knew Natalie was too weak to be left alone with Aamir, who needed his compress changed frequently to keep his fever down, but he'd need some company collecting enough food and water for all of them.

"Do you mind if I stay here?" asked Jari. "I've gotten into a rhythm of changing compresses!"

"Okay. Ellabell, will you come with me?"

She was standing by the tree line, staring out at the lake as it shimmered in the morning light. There was a slump in her shoulders that hadn't been there before, making Alex's brow furrow with concern. Waiting a few moments for her response, he was surprised when it didn't come. It seemed the view had absorbed her entire focus.

"Ellabell?" he repeated, moving closer.

She jumped as he gently touched her shoulder. "Alex! You scared me," she gasped.

"You were off somewhere else." He smiled.

"It's so beautiful… I had forgotten there could be so much color in the world. The grass, the trees, the flowers." Lifting her face to the sky, her eyes closing, he heard the soft intake of breath as she drank in the cool, crisp air. He wasn't sure he had ever seen her look prettier. "Did you need me for something?" she asked, turning back to him.

"I was going to go hunt for food and water—want to come with me?"

"Sure, if you need someone."

"Cool, well, we'll start with water I guess." He gestured toward the gleaming shoreline with its eerie pebble beach. "Don't suppose anyone knows any spells for buckets, do they?"

With no readily imparted knowledge on bucket spells, Alex and Ellabell stepped out of the safety of the clearing and walked toward the lake. Racking his brain for inspiration, he had an idea that might work.

Slowly, he held out his hands and began to feel the familiar ice-cold of his anti-magic beneath his fingertips, dancing in silver and black tendrils across his skin. Focusing intently, he let the anti-magic spill out into the air before him, forging it into a disc-shape, similar to a shield. Ellabell watched him with curiosity as he poured another layer of energy into the curved barrier, solidifying it as he had done with anti-magical weapons before. Reaching out, he grasped the firm object in his hand and turned it ninety degrees until it looked more like a giant bowl than a shield. He grinned, pleased with himself as he carried the newly made bowl to the water's edge.

As he approached, however, he began to have second thoughts, remembering what lay beneath. A shiver rippled up his spine. It had been decades since the last body had been placed in its watery grave here, but Alex wasn't sure that meant it would be safe to drink. Had the years cleansed the lake of former sins? Looking closer, he noticed there was a strange quality to the water, the liquid darker than it should have been.

"What's wrong?" asked Ellabell.

"I'm not sure if it's drinkable," he explained, feeling a wave of disgust as he scooped the bowl into the water and filled it.

"Well, we don't have many other options right now. Maybe just take a small sip to see," encouraged Ellabell, licking her dry lips. The thought of even a small sip turned Alex's stomach.

Lifting the bowl, he watched the dark liquid slosh around the crackling, thrumming container. Cautiously, he cupped his hand and dipped it into the water, raising the contents to his mouth with trepidation. He drank it in one go, pushing down the rising sense of nausea as he felt the water run down the back of his throat. It tasted strange and metallic on his tongue, the trickling droplets prickling his mouth and throat like sour ice, at once bitter and freezing cold. He frowned, worried that it was poisoned—contaminated by the bodies submerged beneath it.

"Is it okay?" Jari asked, appearing behind them.

"I'm not sure," Alex replied hoarsely.

"Let me try," insisted Jari, holding out his hands for the anti-magic bowl. The blond-haired boy winced as his fingers touched the edge of the thrumming shield, sharply pulling his hands away, as if it had burned him.

"Can you make one?" asked Alex, forgetting the problems his anti-magic caused for his magically endowed friends.

"I can try." Jari grinned as he spun the first strands of golden magic from beneath his hands, creating the shape of a shield, as Alex had done. Jari was one of the only group members who still had some strength remaining, and Alex was relieved to see a mostly solid bowl of gold beginning to take shape in Jari's hands. It took a few tries, but, eventually, he got there, holding his vessel aloft.

Carefully, Alex tipped the bowl of his shield toward Jari's, making sure the edges didn't touch and cause any unwanted explosions. The last thing they needed was to draw attention to themselves. He watched as the peculiar, dark blue liquid poured into the golden bowl, half-expecting it to react with the magical vessel. Instead, it seemed to grow paler, looking closer to normal water than it had in Alex's bowl. Alex frowned, waiting anxiously as Jari lifted the shield-bowl to his lips and drank deep.

Jari gulped the water down and gave a satisfied sigh. "Tastes great!"

He passed the bowl to Ellabell. "It's delicious!" She smiled, nodding eagerly in agreement before taking another sip.

Alex took another sip of the remaining water in his bowl, but the liquid tasted just as bitter as before, and was almost unbearably cold in his mouth. Confused, he waited on the shoreline as

Ellabell forged a bowl of her own under Jari's instruction and the pair of them filled their containers to the brim.

Jari took his dish straight over to Aamir, kneeling as he held his friend's limp head in the crook of his arm and trickled the cool water into Aamir's mouth. The liquid seemed to stir Aamir from his fitful sleep for a moment, his lips parting just enough to slake his thirst. Meanwhile, Ellabell passed her bowl to Natalie, who guzzled the water eagerly.

"That water is so good!" exclaimed Natalie with a hint of a smile. "Do you mind?" she asked Ellabell, gesturing toward the rest of the water in the bowl.

"Go ahead, there's plenty more where that came from," Ellabell joked.

Alex was pleased the water had seemed to perk Natalie up, though he sorely wished he could quench his own thirst. The water had done something to ease the dryness of his throat and the arid texture of his tongue, but it was not quite the satisfaction he had hoped for. There was a lingering thirst that the lake water did not seem able to appease.

"Let's see if there's anything to eat around here," said Alex, suddenly eager to be away from the lake. He turned toward Ellabell. "You coming?"

Ellabell nodded, her golden bowl evaporating into a fine mist.

"See if you can find any pizza!" Jari shouted after them as they disappeared into the shadows of the dense forest.

The spongy undergrowth was thick underfoot, snagging at their shoes and pants as they walked, the two of them trying and failing to navigate the gnarled roots that twisted up suddenly from the ground. Across a tangled thicket of bracken, Ellabell stumbled, but Alex was there to catch her. She blushed, peering at him curiously from behind her spectacles as he propped her upright again. Smiling, he removed his hands, careful not to let them linger too long on her arms.

The air around them was heavy with the rich, earthy scent of damp soil and fresh vegetation that, for Alex, brought back childhood memories of damp hikes in the countryside. It was true what Ellabell had said—he had forgotten too, how colorful and textured the world could be. In the forest, life blossomed all around, filling every sense. Although he didn't know what this world was, or where it was, he had to admit it was beautifully crafted.

"How are you feeling about everything?" asked Alex, a little out of the blue, as they wandered along in a companionable silence, listening to the soft murmur of the wind in the treetops.

She shrugged. "I'm not sure yet."

"Why did you want to come with us?" he asked, shoving his hands in his pockets.

"I told you," she muttered, not looking him in the eye.

Sensing her unwillingness to talk, Alex didn't say anything else as they continued on through the trees, though there were a great many questions running through his mind. He remembered her saying she didn't want to leave him, as they had stood at the corner of the corridor, not knowing what dangers lay ahead, but he wasn't sure what she had meant by that. He realized there had been a tiny glimmer of hope on his part that a mutual affection existed between them—and now, alone, he wanted her to enlighten him on why she hadn't wanted to leave, but Ellabell didn't seem keen to share. Alex frowned, confused by her. Perhaps it wasn't the right time, or maybe he had read into something that simply wasn't there.

The sunlight dappled the forest floor, lighting the way.

"What are they?" asked Ellabell suddenly, pointing toward a cluster of large bushes that bunched up from a dim clearing in the woodland to their right.

Alex moved across the twisting undergrowth toward the plants. On closer inspection, he saw that among the waxy green leaves and spiny branches, the bushes were full to bursting with plump, shiny, blackberry-like berries. Tentatively, he plucked one from its barb and squished it beneath his fingers, letting the dark, burgundy juice run across his skin. Dropping the berry to the forest floor, he plucked another and popped it on the end of his tongue. He let it sit there for a while, hoping that if it were poisonous he would sense it before he swallowed the berry.

Slightly more confident that the fruit was edible, he chewed it, tasting immediately the sugary sweetness of the berry as it danced on his taste-buds. It was delicious, and there were bush-es and bushes full of them. Not an ideal diet, but enough to start with.

"Are they good?" asked Ellabell.

"Really good." He plucked a handful for her.

She tasted the first one, and her whole face lit up. "Delicious! Everything here is delicious!" She stuffed the handful into her mouth. Licking her fingers clean, she held them up to Alex with a delighted chuckle rippling in the back of her throat. He could see where the deep red juice of the berries had stained her skin, and couldn't help but laugh too; it made him happy to see her smiling again.

A tension had been broken between them, and before long, Ellabell seemed to feel easier again in his company. She hummed as she stretched out the fabric of her jacket, the arms tied around her waist for maximum fruit volume, and picked as many berries as she could. Alex couldn't place the song, but it was oddly familiar. A high, sweet tune that Alex enjoyed listening to, getting lost in the rhythm and cadence of it as he worked.

"Who is Elias?" asked Ellabell suddenly, taking Alex by surprise—and confusion. Where had the question come from?

"What?"

"Who is Elias?" she repeated, peering at him around one of the large bushes. Her mouth was now as stained by the sweet red fruit as her hands, the trickling streaks of dried juice giving her a slightly sinister quality.

"Elias is Elias," replied Alex warily, giving a shrug.

"You're going to have to do better than that," she warned. "Who is he? How do you know him?"

"It's… It's a long story."

"We have time," she insisted, her voice catching slightly in her throat. Alex frowned; the mere mention of him seemed to set Ellabell on edge.

"Elias is my shadowy advisor, I guess," he began, not knowing how to describe the shadow-man. "He appeared to me on the first day at Spellshadow, while I was waiting to be enrolled. He was a cat, and then, later on, he was a man—he sort of changes shape as he pleases, and though he can look human when he wants, I'm not exactly sure how human he is." He looked at Ellabell to see if she was following. There was confusion on her face, but curiosity too.

"Then what is he?" she asked. It was the very question Alex would love to have known the answer to, and his ignorance was not for lack of trying.

Alex shrugged. "I don't know. I only know that he changes shape and is made up of shadows and is very good at stealing things."

"Stealing things?"

"Yeah, he steals things and gives—well, gave them to me, back at the manor... I don't suppose he'll be doing that any-more," said Alex with a hint of regret. He wasn't sure where Elias was, after his last battle with the Head, or if he had even made it out alive—could Elias even be killed? Alex didn't know. The only thing he was sure of was that he had expected Elias to show up in the office with his sharp wit and silver tongue, claiming victory over the Head, but he had not and had not appeared since.

"Can I tell you something?" Ellabell whispered.

Alex frowned. "What?"

"I know I told you I fell into a bookcase... and I know you didn't believe me," she said, her voice trembling slightly.

"I believed you," he lied.

She raised her eyebrow at him, flashing a wry smile. "You didn't believe me. I know you didn't."

"Is that not what happened?" asked Alex as an understanding passed between them. She was ready to tell him what had really gone on in that room—the piercing sound of her scream still haunted him, the knowledge he hadn't gotten there in time. He felt a flutter of anxiety in the pit of his stomach, as if bad news were coming. Of course, he had known she was lying when she told him she had fallen into a bookcase, and even when she sidestepped his question of her being attacked, but he had never expected her to tell him the full truth.

She shook her head. "You were right, when you asked if somebody attacked me in the Head's library… Somebody *did* attack me, and I think that somebody was Elias," she admitted quietly.

"What?" Alex breathed, hardly able to believe it. "I can't imagine him doing that."

"I didn't see my attacker properly, but I am fairly sure it was your shadowy advisor." Ellabell looked at him earnestly, and he could see the honesty written there on her open face. As much as he wanted to defend Elias's honor, something held his tongue—a niggling feeling in the back of his mind that Elias *was* capable of doing what Ellabell said he had done. But Elias did everything for a reason.

"What were you doing at the time?" he asked.

Ellabell frowned. "I'm not sure."

"Think back. What were you doing when he attacked you?"

She paused, a thoughtful expression crossing her face. "I was reaching for a book… It had a bronze spine, dotted with red jewels. I remember because I was drawn to the glitter of it. Yes—I was about to pick it up when something swooped down from the shadows and hit me hard in the side of the head. Everything was dark, and I thought I'd gone blind, but then something tried to claw my tongue from my mouth. I remember the pain of it and feeling very cold… I saw strange, starry black eyes glaring at me from the darkness and could hear whispers all around, warning me to stay away from things that weren't mine and

24

seeking secrets that weren't for me to know, but I couldn't see the person who was speaking—there was only shadow."

Silence stretched between the two of them as Alex struggled to find the right words to say. Her description couldn't be of anyone but Elias.

"I'm sorry," he murmured, moving toward her.

"It wasn't your fault." She smiled sadly.

Alex longed to reach out and comfort her, but his hands were holding the edges of his jacket, filled with berries for the others. She moved toward him in a similar motion, only to glance down at the spoils in her makeshift apron, seemingly coming to the same conclusion.

"I should have been there with my anti-magic," he said, his mouth set in a grim line. "I should have stopped him."

"You got me out, Alex... and I'm the one who told you I didn't want to leave you on the mission. I meant it." A small smile played upon her lips, and Alex felt a glimmer of hope flicker once more inside him, though he wasn't sure what to say in return. All his previous questions evaded him, his tongue uncharacteristically tied.

"I need to get better at protecting my friends," he said finally. "I will do my best to keep all of you safe here, wherever 'here' is."

A look of disappointment flashed in her sparkling blue eyes, the smile vanishing. "We should be getting back with these," she announced hastily.

"O-Okay," he said, wondering if he had said something to offend her.

"They'll be wondering where we've got to." She turned and

led the way back to the clearing, suddenly more surefooted among the undergrowth.

As he followed in Ellabell's footsteps, listening to the thud of her shoes ahead, his mind was full of Elias and what she had told him. Leander Wyvern's notebook was still in Alex's back pocket, seeming to burn against his skin as all ill-gotten gains were wont to do. Repulsion at the shadow-man made his skin crawl, knowing how much trust he had put in Elias, only to find out what vile, reproachable things he was capable of. There had always been an uncertainty about Elias's moral compass, but Alex had never thought him an evil creature.

He thought back to the disposal of Finder and the retrieval of Elias's long-sought life essence, held captive by the Head. He thought of the uprising at Spellshadow, causing the Head untold trouble in regaining control, not to mention the anti-magic that had helped in the fight, only learned because of the books Elias had given him. Elias had made them seem like gifts intended to benefit Alex, and yet all of those things had helped Elias achieve selfish goals, in one way or another. The question Alex couldn't answer, however, was why—why did Elias need Alex to do the dirty work?

Walking back into camp, he wasn't sure he'd ever have the chance to ask.

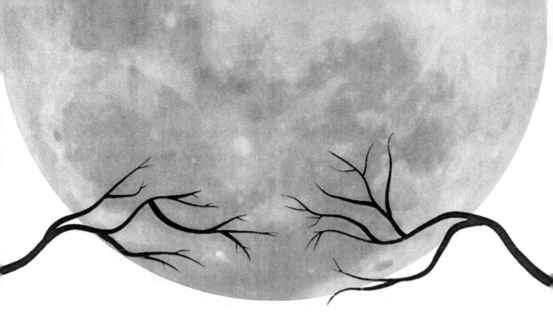

CHAPTER 3

THE OTHERS WERE PLEASED TO SEE THE FORAGERS, AS they returned with their jackets full of berries. It was a meager, plain meal, but it was better than nothing.

As Alex chewed, he turned his attention to Jari, who had tried to mash up some berries to feed to Aamir. The older boy had become worse during Alex and Ellabell's absence, and his skin was covered in red blotches that felt boiling hot to the touch. His whole body was on fire, sweat drenching every fiber of his clothes. Every few minutes he would lash out, his muscles shaking uncontrollably as his limbs jerked.

None of them had much of a grasp of healing magic, and nobody had volunteered to try in case they made him worse. It was uncharted territory, but if Aamir didn't get help soon, there was no telling what could happen to him.

Taken by a sudden impulse, Alex walked over to Aamir and settled down on the grass beside him. Jari looked on nervously as Alex laid his hands on Aamir's shoulders, sending tendrils of silver and black through the blotchy layers of Aamir's skin. Eyes squeezed tightly shut, Alex searched through the interior of Aamir's body until he touched upon the glinting, golden shape of a snake, coiled around the inside of Aamir's aura. There was no telling how long it had been there, but it was savage, snapping viciously at the intrusion of Alex's anti-magic. The cutting of the band, Alex realized with a twist of guilt, must have released a potent curse that was gripping onto Aamir like a vice, sapping him of his health and vitality far quicker than Derhin's curse had done to Natalie.

"What is it?" asked Jari, edging closer.

"He's cursed. It's a strong one," said Alex reluctantly. "It must have been the band."

"I can try and break it," Natalie said, but she still looked weak.

"No, Natalie—you're still not fully recovered. You shouldn't be doing any strong magic for a long time."

Turning back to Aamir, Alex wondered if he should try to break the curse himself. His powers had improved leaps and bounds since Natalie's curse, but this one was far stronger. Testing the waters, he pushed the very edges of his anti-magic against the burning curse, feeling it repel him forcefully as it attacked the silver and black tendrils that were running through Aamir's veins. He tried again, pushing the shimmering strands of his anti-magic closer to the glowing core of the curse, but it was no good; the coiled creature only gripped tighter to its host in retaliation.

Removing his anti-magic as swiftly as he could without hurting Aamir, Alex saw that the attempt had only made his friend worse. On the shady patch of grass, he was writhing violently, mumbling in his delirious state as he tossed and turned. Alex could no longer make out any of what Aamir was saying, but there was a note of fear still, within the fevered gibberish, that unnerved him.

Across the clearing, Jari was running like a madman to fetch cold compresses, his panic evident as he dipped strip after strip of torn-off material into the lake. The blond-haired boy's fear started seeping into the others like an infection, making everyone tense and snappish, until Alex wasn't sure he could take the anxiety anymore.

Alex rose, feeling the urge to step away from the situation to get some headspace. His throat felt as if he had swallowed thorns, his thirst still unquenched.

"I need to go and find some water I can drink," he announced.

Nobody objected as he headed through the woodland, keeping the tree-line in sight so he wouldn't get lost. He listened for the quiet babble of a stream nearby. He was certain he had heard something similar on his earlier trek with Ellabell.

A few minutes later, he found what he was looking for. A clear, inviting spring bubbled up from a cluster of rocks, meandering from the source, down through the undergrowth in a gurgling stream. He almost ran toward it, sliding down into the mossy forest floor on his knees as he reached for the crystalline liquid; he was so thirsty and desperate to feel cold water on his skin. It did not disappoint. Cupping his hands to catch the cool, crisp water, he drank deep, delighted to feel the liquid run down his throat without scalding it. He went back again and again, drinking the pristine water and washing his face in it, sloughing off the dirt and misery of the past day until he felt like himself again, some calm restored.

He stayed there awhile, sitting up against the damp rock, feeling the cool of it against his spine as he rested in the shade of the treetops. The buzz and crackle of the magic in the air seemed less noticeable in the silence of the forest, blending into the background as he grew accustomed to it, causing no disturbance to his quietude. If he closed his eyes, he could almost believe he was at summer camp, in the normal, non-magical world of home, pausing on a trail in the mountains somewhere…

He couldn't stay for long, or the others would grow worried. But as he rose slowly to his feet, a strange sound in the near distance snatched his attention. It was the soft, padding sound of stealthy feet, creeping close by. Squinting toward the direction of the lake, he caught sight of unknown figures walking just beyond the tree-line, moving with a deliberate slowness to keep their noise to a minimum.

Fear gripped Alex as he tore off through the forest toward the camp, the spongy, mossy undergrowth deadening the sound of his feet as he ran, hoping to beat the figures he had just seen. Bursting out into the clearing with very little time to explain, he ignored the stunned faces of his friends as he charged over and picked up Aamir.

"We need to go! Follow me!" he hissed, beckoning them into the woods as he tried to keep his voice as low as possible.

Staggering back into the forest, Alex headed toward a denser part of it, not too far from the clearing, where the trees were at their thickest. He could hear the footsteps of the others behind him as they moved into the more camouflaged cover of the forest. Desperately, his eyes scanned for a suitable hiding place in the undergrowth. Just off to the left there was a hollow in the ground, mostly hidden by a spiny-looking bush and a stack of fallen branches that had crumbled from the rotting tree above. Seeing the prime spot, Alex stepped down into it and maneuvered Aamir against the far side. Jari, Natalie, and Ellabell jumped in behind, helping Alex to pull the branches over the top of their hiding place, just in time to see a group of four people arrive in the clearing.

As Alex peered through a small gap in the branches, he saw that they were four of the most beautiful people he had ever seen—perfect beyond description. There were two young men and two young women, each of them more stunning than the last. One of the young women had silky, flawless hair down to her waist, the color and texture of spun gold, with porcelain-white skin that didn't seem natural. The other woman had long, flowing black hair held back behind her ear with a delicate lotus flower and the most exquisite, deep-toned skin Alex had ever seen, seeming impossibly smooth. The men were no different, one with perfect, curly warm brown hair that swept across a face of unnaturally chiseled bone structure, his coloring similar to Aamir's, the other with a jet black crop and glowing, pale skin. Dressed in a uniform of black well-tailored pants, military boots, and white t-shirts, they did not look real to Alex, more like photoshopped supermodels, but he knew that they were, in fact, very much real and looking for them.

They seemed to be scanning for any signs of habitation, scouring the area and talking in low voices that Alex couldn't quite make out. Trying to get a better look, Alex saw them check the padlock on the door of the shed. It was still locked. Alex breathed a quiet sigh of relief, glad he hadn't tried to break the lock on their first evening. The sight of it, still attached to the hut, seemed to reassure them somewhat that nobody had been there.

Just then, Aamir, in his delirium, jerked suddenly, the weight of his body cracking a large twig beneath him. The snap of it rang through the silent forest like a gunshot. Jari's eyes went wide with panic as he reached across for his friend, smothering his mouth with a hastily conjured silencing spell, in case Aamir cried out. Alex, still peering through the gap in the branches, watched in horror as the four beautiful people turned sharply in his direction, searching for the cause of the loud crack.

Alex felt the collective pause of everyone's breath being held as the four scouts crept closer to where the five of them were hidden. After hurrying to get as much detritus over them as possible, Alex hoped fervently that the thick blanket of moss and branches and gorse bush would be enough to keep them from sight. He didn't know what these unearthly creatures were or what their mission was. Were they friendly? Alex wasn't sure.

Edging ever closer, the scouts were almost on top of them. Nobody dared to move. One of them, the brown-haired young man, walked right beside Natalie's head, but he failed to make her out among the camouflage of the undergrowth. Beside Alex, Jari clung tightly to Aamir, holding him still and keeping him silent as the scouts continued their search.

For almost half an hour, the scouts came and went. Each time Alex thought it was safe to come out of the hiding spot, he would catch sight of them again, creeping around the back of the ramshackle hut or appearing once more through the tree-line. A few times, they came close to discovering the five fugitives. One kicked a branch, watching it skitter away, not realizing he had unearthed a small portion of Ellabell's curly brunette hair. Another almost trod on the back of Aamir's head, where he sat up against the earthen wall of the hollow, missing him by mere centimeters. A third, the one with the flower in her hair, reached down to pick up a miniature wildflower that had fallen from one of the bushes, almost coming eye to eye with Alex himself. If her focus hadn't been on the flower, he was fairly sure they would have been toast.

Finally, after doing one last lap of the area for good measure, as if to make sure the fugitives' heart rates stayed up, the foursome departed. Alex watched intently as they walked back the way they had come, disappearing from sight. He waited a while longer, just to be sure they had definitely gone, before he clambered out of the hollow and crept across the ground, following the four scouts as closely as he dared.

He tailed them for quite a way up the shoreline, before ducking behind a thick tree trunk as they came to a halt. From behind a rocky outcrop, they dragged a sleek blue and white rowboat they had pulled up onto the beach. Alex peered cautiously from his vantage point, watching them step into the boat and set off across the lake toward a faint rise of ground in the distance.

He hadn't been able to see it from the clearing, but it was more visible from where he now stood. There was definitely something out there, looming on the horizon, and he wanted to know what it was that called to him from beyond the glittering waters of the lake.

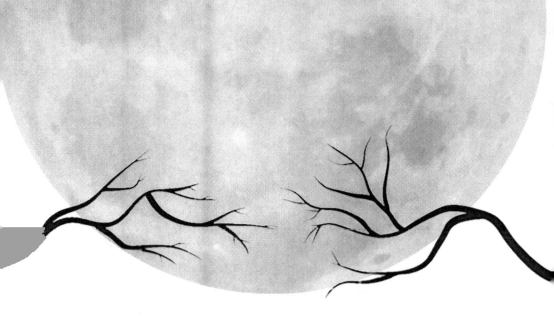

CHAPTER 4

ALEX REMAINED BESIDE THE TREE, STARING OUT AT THE water, wondering how they were supposed to get over to where the four people had disappeared. He wasn't sure what had spurred him into following the scouts, after the near miss of discovery, but the compulsion had at least pointed him in the right direction. It was becoming abundantly clear that they were going to need a boat of some sort, and, as far as he knew, there weren't any boats just lying around willy-nilly for strangers to hop into and use as they pleased, as much as he might have liked there to be.

He was almost certain now that it was Stillwater House that lay on the other side of the lake, drenched in shadow. It had to be. Yet the only way to get there seemed to be by water. He supposed they could walk around the lake to reach the shadowy rise on the other side, but that would take days, by Alex's estimation, if not longer. It was no good—they needed to get there sooner rather than later, if they were to stand any chance of reaching it undetected. Already, he could feel time slipping away from him. Even as he was standing there, he thought, the Head might have found a way through the portal and be in hot pursuit.

The sight of the rippling expanse of water frustrated and astounded him; it had all seemed so much smaller from the office window.

The vast distance made him think about magical travel for a moment, wondering if he could transport himself to Stillwater House via anti-magical means. Glancing back along the shoreline, he knew he couldn't just leave the others, especially with Natalie and Aamir in weakened states. Then again, perhaps this world didn't have the same barriers against travel that Spellshadow had.

Curious, he held his hands up to the empty air and fed his anti-magic upward, toward the atmosphere. There were some small sparks of resistance from the thrumming magic all around him, but it didn't have the same cold, deadening feel as the ivy at the manor. It didn't try to stop his energy—it merely seemed inquisitive. His interest was piqued, but he knew he'd have to get one of the others to test for an actual barrier, just in case it wasn't responding to his particular brand of energy. After all, he hadn't been able to sense the one that had sent Natalie tumbling from the sky, and he didn't fancy a repeat of that. However, he knew he'd have to shelve the idea for a while, until everyone was functioning at full capacity; they couldn't very well leave Aamir and Natalie behind.

Mulling over their options, Alex returned from the shore-line. As he neared the clearing, he saw that the others had moved back into the main space, though their eyes looked up in alarm as his shoes crunched on the pebble beach, signaling his arrival.

"They're gone," Alex announced, as his friends sighed in relief. "I followed them to see where they were headed—there is something on the other side. Only thing is, it's pretty far away, and the only way over seems to be across the water."

"Do you think we can do the shield trick and make a boat instead of a bowl?" asked Jari.

"I think that'd be a pretty tall order... I was thinking we could build something," Alex replied. "I mean, we have a forest, right? And forests have trees. We can... cut some down, strap them together with vines, or something."

"There might be something in the hut," suggested Ellabell, pushing her spectacles back up the bridge of her nose.

Alex looked from her to the ramshackle hut, which was still locked. Even if nothing was inside it, they could try to do something with the wooden planks it was made of.

He made his way over to the structure. The padlock was a beastly thing, covered in flaking red rust. He fed silvery tendrils of energy through the inner mechanisms, opening his hand sharply to explode the decaying metal with a loud crack. What remained of the padlock fell to the ground with a heavy thud.

As he pulled the creaking, rotting door open to see what was inside, he became aware of Ellabell next to him, standing close.

It was dark inside the shack, but the sunshine glancing in through the cracks in the wood shed some light on the cave of wonders within. It was full to the brim with things. There were stacks of crates to one side and coils upon coils of fraying rope. Hanging from the disintegrating walls on the far side were a variety of lamps in different shades of stained glass, with bulging canvas bags hanging below them. On the other side of the wall were several shelves stocked with a multitude of rusting tins and cans in all shapes and sizes, their labels long since peeled away.

Alex stepped farther into the musty-smelling hut. Other knick-knacks and bits of random wood lay strewn about, not much use to anyone. There was one shape, however, nestled beneath everything else, that grabbed Alex's attention. He could make out curved sides and chipped paint, poking through the dusty edges of a moth-eaten tarpaulin. Alex waded through the sea of debris, heaving boxes and crates and heavy bags from on top of the hidden structure and shoving them haphazardly onto the unstable piles of junk around him. Ellabell followed suit, moving around to the other side of the object, where she began to remove the bric-a-brac, stacking it neatly behind her.

Within a few minutes, their hands were filthy and their faces were streaked with dirt, but they had managed to clear the object of scrap, revealing the undeniable shape of a boat beneath. The tarp that lay across it had done little to keep the boat protected, however, as its state became apparent. It was more the skeleton of a boat, in dire need of work.

"What do you think?" Alex asked Ellabell, whose logical mind he knew would come in handy.

"It's a bit of a mess."

"Fixable though, I think..."

It was on casters, equally rusted and rotten, but there was enough integrity left in the wheels to get the boat out into the fresh air and space of the clearing.

"What's that?" Jari mocked.

"A boat," replied Alex, not taking the bait. Though, seeing it in stark daylight, he realized it really did need a whole load of work. He headed back into the shack and rummaged through the tins on the shelves. A few moments later he emerged triumphant, wielding a hammer, several tins of varnish, various types of glue, and a large container full of screws.

Armed with what they needed, the group set to work—Alex assuming the role of project manager. They toiled away through out the day and deep into the night.

It was only when a snore from Jari pulled him awake, the sunlight shining in his eyes, that he realized he had fallen asleep at some point. They all had. The last thing he remembered was seeing the first hints of daylight overhead.

Alex quickly turned back to what he had been doing, and as the hazy glow of sunset bathed the shoreline in a dim orange light, he put the finishing touches on the boat. Surveying their masterpiece, Alex felt a slight glimmer of pride at what they had achieved. It was mostly held together with glue and varnish, but it was as seaworthy as it was ever going to be.

He nudged the others awake.

"So, what do we do now?" Jari asked groggily, crawling over to inspect the vessel.

"We wait until it's dark, using it as cover. Then, we row."

As the last few rays of bronzed light disappeared into the horizon, giving way to the darkness, Jari and Alex lifted Aamir into the boat, making him comfortable near the bow. With the last remnants of creaking functionality from the wheels, the four friends pushed the boat on its casters toward the lake's edge.

As soon as it had edged into the shallows, Jari and Ellabell hopped up onto the benches, taking up the oars as Natalie jumped in behind, leaving Alex to push it the rest of the way into deeper water. Having forgotten momentarily about the lake's strange reaction to him, he was startled to feel a sudden burning sensation against his skin as he waded in deeper, at one moment boiling hot, the next sub-zero temperatures. Holding out his hands to the others, he let them haul him out of the odd lake and into the safety of the boat, where the sensations instantly stopped.

On the underside, small leaks had begun to spring, much to Alex's dismay. He pressed his palms onto either side of the boat and allowed the silver-black tendrils of his anti-magic to run along the wood, forging a barrier over the hull to keep the water out. The leaks ceased, but the freshly conjured barrier seemed to have a curious reaction to the lake itself. It began to glow with a blinding silver light that was almost bordering on white. Naturally, the sight of this reaction alarmed Alex—not wanting them to be seen in the darkness. However, before he could remove his energy and have one of the others put up a barrier, the glow ebbed enough to ease his fears, though he still couldn't shake the knowledge that it was a risk.

For some reason, the lake didn't seem to tolerate him. Why? Alex couldn't say. It didn't seem fair to him that he was the one it rejected, when the bodies of his ancestors lay buried beneath. Something didn't sit right with Alex, and, as he listened to the steady slap of oars cutting through the pitch-black water, he felt a familiar shiver of fear. What if they were headed somewhere far worse?

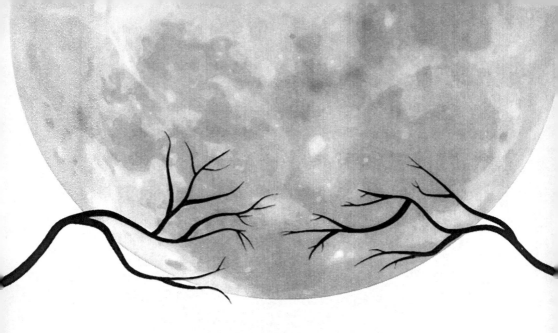

CHAPTER 5

THE STARS TWINKLED OVERHEAD, AND THE BLACK WATER glittered back as Alex and his friends made the long voyage across the lake. The shadows shrouded them from sight, though every so often the boat would glow dimly with silver as it sliced quietly through the mirror-like surface, disturbing the darkness. Around them, the world was deathly silent, interrupted only by the steady slap of oars cutting through the water. Natalie and Alex had taken over the rowing duties for a while, but Jari and Ellabell were once more at the helm, moving in unison.

Clambering over to the stern of the vessel, careful not to lose his footing, Alex sat down on the narrow bench at the very end of the boat, leaning sideways against the blunt wooden edge so that he could gaze back toward the side of the lake they had come from. Not that he could see much by the pale moonlight. He could just make out the frothing lines of their movement through the lake and the spreading ripples that showed the path they had followed.

The rowboat glowed again for a moment, and Alex peered over the edge, down into the inky water below. Staring into the still surface, Alex at last understood why the anti-magic was reacting to the liquid with such volatility. Beneath the water, illuminated by the dim glow of the boat, pearlescent skulls stared up at him with dead, empty hollows. Silvery gray vines twisted around the sickening gleam of bones, pulsing faintly.

Anger twisted inside Alex as he watched the gruesome scene, unable to tear his gaze away. There were too many to count, scattered thoughtlessly and shamelessly on the lake bed, jumbled together in a terrible mass until no skeleton could be separated from the next. And those were only the ones he could see beneath the muted light. It pained him to see that there were skulls and bones of all shapes and sizes. Gripping the edge of the boat tightly, he closed his eyes only when his vision trailed across a heartbreakingly small skull, tangled among the wreckage of so many Spellbreaker lives.

The glow of the boat ebbed away to nothing, returning the grim frieze to the darkness.

It made sense now—the lake's fierce reaction. It was his anti-magic responding to that of his dead ancestors, sensing the twisting vines of their silvery gray lifeblood within the water, feeling their loss connecting with the beating heart of his still-living body. Of course he couldn't drink it or stand in it or touch it without feeling the agonizing effects of such overwhelming loss.

How could he have even brought himself to do so?

As the boat skimmed through the water, he felt their ghosts all around him. There were eyes, following him in the darkness. Alex's skin prickled, giving him the disquieting sense that they were trying to warn him—these phantoms, moving invisibly in the air all around him. Shivers ran up his spine as he felt them reaching out for him, brushing his skin with cold, unseen hands.

Every so often, the rowers would exchange places, Natalie switching more frequently. For hours they rowed, skimming easily through the night. Those who weren't rowing tried to sleep, using the soft sound of the water lapping against the boat as a lullaby as they drifted off beneath the glitter of stars. Alex couldn't, though. Every time he found himself with a break, he would move to the back of the boat and gaze out over the edge, desiring bitterly to see a glimpse of the sunken depths and foul secrets the dark waters held. He hoped the sight might spur him on, fortifying his purpose through whatever trials may come.

It was a long night, with the finish line unknown. Every time Alex was certain they must be close to land, he was met with mile upon mile of endless water and a sinking feeling in the pit of his stomach. Refusing to be beaten, he took up the rowing seat once more and dug deep, chasing the oncoming dawn.

Just as the velvety black of the night sky was softening to a deep bluish hue, a small island appeared in the near distance. Sunrise was on its way, but they had yet to reach the opposite shore and whatever lay beyond it. It wasn't the objective Alex was after, but the island seemed like the only feasible compromise.

"Should we stop here?" asked Jari, who had been Alex's rowing companion for the last few hours. Glancing to the boy beside him, he could see dark circles around his eyes. Each pull of the oar was becoming more difficult, and, with the sun coming up, Alex didn't want them to be left out in the open.

Alex nodded. "I think it's the safest bet."

As the island grew closer, Alex could see there was a tower of sorts in the center of it—a lighthouse, almost, though the light at the top wasn't flashing down onto the water below, as it ought to have been. Running the boat aground through a narrow inlet, listening to the crunch of the wood on gritty sand, Alex thought the whole island seemed deserted. No shadows moved across the ground or through the glass dome at the summit of the lighthouse. Nor did their arrival send anyone running out.

"Stay here," whispered Alex as he jumped lightly from the boat and tied it to a stubby tree at the opening to the inlet.

"I'll come too," insisted Jari.

"No, stay with the others. I just want to check it's safe—no point waking them if it's no good," Alex replied, nodding toward the curled-up figures of Ellabell, Natalie, and Aamir.

"Shout if you need me," pouted Jari, his face showing his disappointment.

"I will." Alex flashed his friend a smile before turning to the lighthouse.

It wasn't far, but Alex still felt uneasy as he crept toward the towering structure. He could make out an overgrown path beneath his feet, leading from the inlet, but it had long since been reclaimed by weeds and delicate wildflowers that poked up in a myriad of surprisingly bright colors. Within a couple of minutes, he had reached the front door of the lighthouse, which had definitely seen better days. The hinges were brown with rust, and the painted door was chipped and cracking. However, there didn't seem to be a padlock or a lock of any sort on the front, and when Alex pulled the metal handle toward him, the door gave instantly with a rush of stale air.

He waited for someone to come running at the loud crack of the door opening, but nobody did. There was only silence beyond.

Alex moved quickly back to the boat.

"It seems safe," he said, moving around the side of the vessel to gently shake Ellabell and Natalie awake.

They gazed around in confusion, their eyes becoming accustomed to the gathering light. The deep blue sky was now shot through with the first bolts of pale pink and hazy orange as the sun began to force its way up through the inky shadows.

"Where are we?" asked Ellabell in a quiet, sleepy voice.

"Somewhere safe. Do you need a hand?" he asked as she stood to step out of the boat.

"Okay." She smiled shyly.

Alex's hands lightly encircled her waist, and her hands rested on his shoulders as she jumped from the side of the vessel. Their eyes locked for a moment as he placed her carefully on the ground, but it was only afterward that he felt a wave of elation run through him, making an unexpected smile play upon his lips. He knew very well that she could have jumped from the boat herself, but he had wanted the chance to help—to make up for not holding her back in the forest.

Natalie flashed a knowing smile at him as she vaulted the side of the boat with ease, showing him up for his unnecessary gallantry. He flushed a little, hurrying to help Jari get Aamir out of the boat and onto dry land in a vain attempt to hide the blush of his cheeks.

Aamir groaned as the two boys carried him toward the lighthouse and in through the broken door that hung awkwardly from its damaged hinges. Settling him down on the dusty floor, they returned to the boat and dragged it as high up the island as they could to hide it among some spiny bushes, intending to keep it out of sight from anyone who might pass by. For good measure, Alex tore down a few branches from a nearby tree with palm-like fronds and draped them across the top and sides of the boat, camouflaging it in the surrounding greenery.

Only then did he return to the lighthouse, where everyone else was now gathered. Inspecting the interior, he confirmed it was definitely abandoned, with grimy sheets over what furniture remained and everything else covered in a thick blanket of dust. A narrow set of curving stairs hugged the circular wall, leading up to another floor.

"These places usually have a bedroom for the keeper, right? We should get Aamir up there," suggested Alex, pointing through the gap in the ceiling.

There was a grumble of agreement. Jari and Alex knelt to pick Aamir up by his armpits and legs and carried him in an un-gainly fashion up the creaking, questionably stable staircase. The others followed. On the next floor, there were even fewer signs of habitation, but the circular room wasn't nearly as grim as the one below. Another curved staircase led up to a floor above, but Alex indicated for Jari to carry their friend over to the far wall of the first floor and set him down.

"Blankets!" exclaimed Ellabell, poking her head around a cupboard built into the curved wall. In her arms, she held a stack of soft-looking blankets, only slightly moth-eaten. They smelled musty, but they would keep them warm.

Jari took two, pulling one over Aamir's sleeping body before settling down nearby to get some rest of his own. It seemed like a good plan, and everyone else followed suit. Even those who had slept on the boat were still weary, their slumber having been often interrupted by an oar bashing the sides of the vessel or a sudden jolt in its movement.

Alex took a blanket too but knew sleep would take a while to come.

As the others drifted off to different sections of the run-down lighthouse in order to lie down for a while, Alex began to explore. Despite the ache in his muscles and the itch of his dry eyes, he wasn't tired. And so, he distracted himself with the tower. Moving stealthily past the sleepers on each floor—Natalie and Ellabell tucked away on the floor above Jari and Aamir—he investigated, though there wasn't much to be found. There were a few tables and chairs and empty bookcases. The odd cupboard with an ancient jar of beans in it. Mostly, the four floors of the lighthouse were empty.

However, as he reached the fourth floor, the narrowest room by far, he saw there was a trapdoor in the ceiling above his head. There were grooves in the stonework where ladders had been removed, but that only served to increase his curiosity as to what was up there.

Glancing around for something to use, his eyes settled on a bookcase, pushed up against the banister of the stairs. It looked a little suspect in terms of stability, but it was the only thing that would reach. Heaving with all his might, he hauled it over to the side of the room, just below the trapdoor, and climbed stealthily to the top. It bowed beneath his weight as he reached up and pushed against the wooden slats of the trapdoor. To his delight, it gave, flipping open with a creak before crashing down onto the stonework of the floor above.

Excited, he pulled himself up through the gap and into the very top floor of the lighthouse, where the light itself was kept. Alex grinned as he stood up in the stunning room, which reminded him so much of a greenhouse. The walls and domed ceiling were made of glass, separated by slim lines of white-painted metal, and on the very top, Alex could make out the turning shadow of a weathervane.

At the center of the room was the fitting where the light should have been, though there was no longer a lantern within it, to warn sailors on the black lake. It still had the curved blinker that would fit around the lamp, causing the flash that would let sailors know of rocks and treacherous waters beyond, but there was no longer a glow. It had gone out some time ago, Alex thought, from the looks of the place. Regardless, it was a work of mechanical art that made Alex smile like a schoolboy; the mechanisms beneath were brimming with cogs and clockwork to make the mind race.

Beyond the strange, hexagonal glass dome, which was all still intact save for a few cracks beginning to appear in some of the panes, the warm glow of the sunrise was streaking through the sky. It was beautiful. Alex walked toward it, his eyes catching sight of a narrow metal platform that ran around the outside of the dome. It was then that he noticed one of the panes in the hexagon was a door and not a window.

Gently, he pushed down on the handle and opened the door with a grating squeak, careful not to shatter the fragile glass as it swung wide. The breeze that whipped against his face was fresh and cool, dancing up from the sparkling water beneath.

He tentatively pressed his foot down on the outside platform, checking its integrity. Satisfied it wasn't going to crumble and send him plummeting to his death, he stepped out fully and walked along until he found a good spot to watch the sunrise. Sitting down, his legs dangling between the metal bars that acted as a barrier, he gazed with contentment as the kaleidoscopic sunrise shifted from rich pinks and fiery reds to burnished bronze and bold oranges, finally settling upon a golden yellow as the sky brightened to a beautiful azure that told of a warm day to come.

The daylight brought to life the world around him, the shadows falling away. In the surprisingly near distance, beyond the island, an exquisite, grand white building appeared, set back into the rise of a lush, green hillside. Along the shoreline, it sprawled like an Italian villa, with spires rising up from gleaming domed roofs, almost cathedral-like in their beauty. It caught the bright sunlight in the most stunning way, taking Alex's breath away.

There were walls surrounding it, but they were not the grim, gray walls Alex was used to. These were of the purest white stone, adorned with elaborately carved statues that stood atop the battlements in measured intervals, reaching up toward the sky with delicately sculpted golden hands. There was nothing ugly and unforgiving about this place. Not like Spellshadow

Manor. Everything here was beautiful and somehow welcoming. There was none of the insipid gray ivy, either, as far as Alex could see. The only plants he could make out were bouquets of roses, luxurious cream and deep red, surrounded by sprays of much smaller white flowers, set among vivid dark green leaves that hung from baskets against some of the walkways he could see in the brightening daylight.

There were figures, too, moving around the open piazzas of white marble and clustered in the beautiful, sunlit courtyards. He watched them for a while, mesmerized—seeing their glossy, perfect hair shining in the warm daylight. From nowhere, a choir raised its voice to the heavens, as angelic as Alex had ever heard. The music lifted from within the grounds and soared toward him. Tears prickled his eyes as he realized it had been months and months since he had heard proper music, and this song was like nothing he had ever heard before. He couldn't put into words the way it made him feel.

Alex sat, helpless to do anything but watch and listen from his solitary spot, as he felt his worries slip away, if only for as long as this dream lasted.

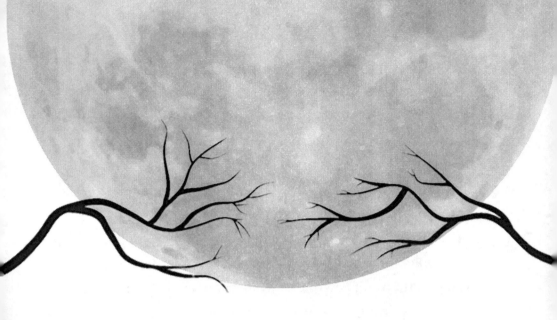

CHAPTER 6

ALEX HAD DRIFTED OFF FOR A TIME, IN THE QUIETUDE of the lamp-room, though it had grown too hot as the sun burned brighter. It was late afternoon by the time the others awoke, looking more refreshed than Alex had seen them in a long time. There wasn't any food left, but everyone had gathered on the first floor to share a bowl of water Natalie had fetched from the lake. Alex declined the offered dish as he leaned against the staircase banister, though his throat was fiercely dry.

"We found it," he announced, once everyone had quenched their thirst.

"What do you mean?" Jari asked.

"Stillwater House—I'm pretty sure it's Stillwater House, anyway. It's not too far. And believe me when I say it's beautiful."

"It exists?" Jari frowned in disbelief.

Alex nodded. "I'm fairly certain."

"It's… beautiful?" Ellabell sounded unsure.

Alex nodded again. "It's stunning. I saw it while you were sleeping. We couldn't see it in the dark, but it's there, I promise."

He took his friends up to the top of the tower so they could see it for themselves. A weight seemed to lift from the atmosphere as they gazed upon the view. There was still a short way to go, but Alex was confident they could do it without being detected. Even Aamir seemed more peaceful, no longer contorting in his fevered state.

As the sun set and darkness fell once more, the weary but hopeful quintet closed the door of the lighthouse behind them and pushed the rowboat back into the water, hopping aboard with a refreshed lightness in their step. Now that their destination was in sight, the rowing seemed much easier. Alex took up his position at the oar once more, with Jari beside him. There was still some light to see by, but enough darkness to keep them covered as the boat made its way over to the shoreline.

Within the hour, they had reached the shallows, though they docked a fair distance away from the glowing torchlight of the villa. As it ran aground on the same eerie, pale pebbles that had defined the beach on the other side of the lake, the four able-bodied friends hoisted Aamir from his sleeping spot and carefully set him down on the grass above the beach. Once he was safely to one side, they dragged the boat right up onto land, turning it sideways and hiding it in a cluster of densely packed trees.

A short distance from the cleverly camouflaged boat, Alex

spied a quaint cottage-like building, set into a semi-circle of thin trees, the glistening walls surrounded by a perimeter of plump bushes made up of tiny, waxy leaves. The structure was built of the same pure white stone as the villa but looked as abandoned as the lighthouse on the island. The door had the same ancient quality to it, as did the faint blue paint that had all but peeled away from the sills of the boarded-up windows.

Ushering everyone inside, Alex waited until they were all comfortable before announcing his next plan of action.

"I'm going to go and explore the outer wall of Stillwater, if anyone wants to come?" he said. After seeing the walls from his vantage point on the outer platform of the lighthouse, he was curious to know whether it had any of the same sort of barrier magic that Spellshadow had. If it did, it could make life harder for them. If it didn't, it might make things much easier, especially in terms of getting help for Aamir.

Jari's hand shot up. "Me! I'll come."

"Anyone else?" asked Alex, but the faces staring back at him didn't seem too eager. "Last chance?"

With only Jari in tow, Alex crept along the shore, the pair keeping tight to the trees to avoid being seen as they made their way toward the villa wall. It rose up before them from the emerald green grass, glistening white even in the dim evening light.

Alex approached it tentatively, glancing up to make sure there weren't any guards looming down at him from above. Confident nobody was watching, he pressed his palms carefully against the stonework, feeling for a barrier. To his surprise, it did not push back against him, like the ivy-covered walls of Spellshadow would have done. It was simply stone; there was nothing else laced within the fabric of it.

"Anything?" Jari hissed.

"It's just rock," whispered Alex.

Despite the wall's size, the hefty rectangular stones it was built from were staggered, making it more climbable than Alex had dared hope. Keeping flat to the wall's surface, they climbed it with ease, the edges between the blocks giving perfect hand and footholds for a swift ascent.

Once on top of the battlement, Alex made sure to keep low, gesturing for Jari to do the same. Surveying the landscape ahead of them, Alex saw there were indeed a few guards set in small lookouts along the walls, but they seemed almost ceremonial. The guards themselves weren't even looking up from where they sat, flipping through books or dozing off in the glow of cozy torchlight, and they certainly hadn't noticed the appearance of two strangers on top of the ramparts. Seizing the opportunity, Alex scurried along the wall and halted at the lip of a wide, open courtyard. Jari almost knocked Alex off the edge as he bumped into him, not quite able to see properly in the dim light.

"Sorry!" he whispered.

Alex frowned, glad Jari hadn't been running faster. As he turned his attention back to the villa below, Alex saw a few people moving across the wide courtyard, holding burning torches as they strolled through the grounds. There was no urgency, no pressure to the way they were moving. There was laughter too—bright and bubbling and genuine. A sound Alex hadn't quite anticipated. As the groups chattered, Alex tried to make out what they were saying to one another, but they were talking too low for him to hear anything much. The only thing he could decipher was the cadence of their voices, which was as crisp and polished as they looked. Alex could hardly believe it: every single one of the people passing below was of the same caliber of beauty as the four scouts they had seen in the clearing.

Suddenly, Alex heard the surprising sound of a low, loud whistle behind him, as Jari's eyes fell upon a particularly stunning young woman loitering beneath one of the archways that lined the courtyard. She was tall and slender, with pale, porcelain skin and gleaming hair that seemed almost silver beneath the torchlight. The pair quickly ducked down as the whistle drew the attention of the woman, who turned and squinted into the darkness, trying to make out where the sound had come from.

Scrambling swiftly back down the side of the wall, the pair collapsed on the grass, laughing until the tears rolled down their faces. It was the first time Alex had belly-laughed in what seemed like forever, and it felt good.

"I knew you were terrible at flirting, but I never thought it'd get me killed!" gasped Alex, clutching his ribs.

"I admit it—that wasn't my smoothest moment," Jari cackled, holding up his hands.

"What possessed you?" Alex asked.

"Did you *see* her? I had to!"

"For a moment, I thought someone was whistling at *me*!" joked Alex as he lay back in the grass, staring up at the stars twinkling overhead.

"You wish." Jari grinned, doing the same.

It was the closest to being an ordinary teenager Alex had felt in ages.

Although they had risked being seen, the close shave had

put them in good humor as they returned to the lakeside cottage, joking and teasing one another along the way. It was a balmy evening, and, had it been an ordinary lake, Alex would have waded in for a nighttime swim, but his knowledge of the lake kept him away from the tempting water's edge. Still, it was a nice walk back, with the buzz of laughter still fresh in the air.

At the cottage, everyone was asleep except Ellabell, who had waited up for them.

"Hungry?" she asked, passing each of them a loaf of crusty white bread.

Alex looked at her in shock. "How did you—?"

She smiled. "Let's just say I used my time wisely, instead of watching pretty girls," she teased, though there was a strange undertone to her words that sounded almost like jealousy.

He wanted to deny it, wondering how she had seen them, hiding up on the battlements. He hadn't seen her.

She is just full of surprises, he thought wryly.

"We weren't watching pretty girls," he said finally, trying to keep his voice as even as possible.

"If you say so." Ellabell smiled triumphantly. "Either way, we have food now."

"How did you get it?" Alex tried again.

Ellabell tapped the side of her nose. "I have my ways."

"But how?" Jari chimed in.

"It was easy," she whispered in a low, conspiratorial tone. The two boys listened intently. "I just found out where they chuck the food away at night." Laughter rippled from her throat, bringing a smile to Alex's face.

"I still think it was better to watch pretty girls." Jari grinned as the three of them moved outside the cottage and sat up against the outer wall.

As the moonlight made the tiny ripples of the lake dance and shimmer, they chatted and watched the lap of the waves on the shore. The two boys ate the pilfered bread, tearing it off in great, hungry chunks, and Jari regaled Ellabell with the brief tale of his ill-timed whistle, gaining an eye-roll from behind her spectacles.

"You really need to learn subtlety, Jari Petra," she said.

"Hey, I am the king of subtlety!" Jari exclaimed.

She raised an eyebrow. "Kittens—that's all I'm saying."

Alex laughed, nearly choking on a piece of bread as he remembered the first time Ellabell had told him of Jari's less-than-welcome flirtations. Alex had barely known her back then. In fact, all of that seemed like a lifetime ago now.

"Who doesn't like kittens?" Jari muttered.

"*Nobody* wants a room full of them. I still have the scars."

"All right, so I was a little heavy-handed," Jari sulked.

"A little?" Ellabell prodded.

"Fine, a *lot* heavy-handed. What are you bringing that up for again, anyway?" asked Jari. "That's all in the past. I have my sights set elsewhere now!"

"Poor girl."

"At least I let a girl know I like them!" Jari smirked, flashing a look at Alex.

Alex felt his throat drying up as Ellabell eyed him curiously. It certainly *did* feel like a long time since he had first met her. Back then, he had thought he might have feelings for the cute French exchange student whom he had followed blindly into a spooky old house. How times had changed; he certainly didn't see Natalie in any sort of romantic way now, leaving his path clear to consider other girls, and yet he found it difficult to put the affection he felt for Ellabell into words. With everything else that had been going on around them, he had been too distracted to really think about romance in a serious way. And yet, here was Jari, throwing him under the bus in front of the one girl he thought he might actually like.

He wondered if she was, in fact, waiting for him to put those feelings into words, as she continued to look at him strangely. Even Jari seemed to want him to say something.

Alex cleared his throat. "You just scare them away, Jari," he said, knowing how lame it sounded as Jari visibly winced.

Ellabell, however, showed nothing on her face. If she had been waiting for him to say something, she gave nothing away. It was only her sparkling blue eyes that showed the merest hint of disappointment, but Alex wasn't sure if that was him reading too much into it. It wasn't that he didn't want to say something to her—he just didn't have the right words.

"Right, well, I'm off to bed," announced Ellabell, with a forced brightness in her voice, as she got to her feet. "Goodnight, boys."

"Goodnight," they chorused. Alex watched her retreat back into the shadow of the cottage. For a brief second, she paused in the doorway, as if about to turn back around, but the moment passed and she disappeared into the darkness without another word. Whatever it was Ellabell might have wanted to say, she must have thought better of it.

"You blew it, man," murmured Jari, patting Alex on the back.

I know, Alex thought. *I know.*

CHAPTER 7

THE NEXT DAY, THE SUN ROSE TO REVEAL ANOTHER warm, beautiful morning. For once, Alex had actually slept, despite thoughts of Ellabell racing through his mind as he had lain down to sleep. He and Jari had stayed up a while longer, enjoying the pleasant warmth of the evening as they finished off their supper, until exhaustion had finally claimed Alex.

Rested and refreshed, he awoke to find that Aamir had deteriorated in the night. The slick sheen of sweat had returned to his forehead, his face screwed up in a permanent expression of agony. His body twisted and turned in all manner of unnatural positions beneath the exertions of the curse within him. Jari hadn't left his side, trickling water into his mouth every couple of minutes so he wouldn't be thirsty.

Seeing the decline of his friend, who had seemed much better the previous day, Alex decided he was going to try and find an infirmary or a pharmacy or something of that ilk within the villa itself, if he could find a way into the building in broad daylight. He was about to leave the cottage when Ellabell called him back.

"You need to eat something," she insisted, handing him more bread and a handful of dried apricots.

He took them gladly, eating quickly. "Thanks," he murmured, hoping she had forgotten the awkwardness of the night before.

"I'd like to come with you, if you don't mind," said Natalie, picking up some apricots of her own.

"Me too," Ellabell added.

Alex shook his head. "I have to do this alone. Too many people will arouse suspicion," he explained. Not for the first time, Ellabell seemed disappointed by his response. Natalie too.

"Nobody will notice us," insisted Natalie.

"We're pretty useful—you should know that by now," Ellabell chipped in.

Alex nodded. "You are both two of the strongest mages I know, but I *have* to do this alone. There are guards along the walls, and one person might slip past them in broad daylight, but three is too many. Plus, if there are magical barriers and things inside the villa, some of them may not even affect me, but they'll affect you. I just want to go and test the waters a bit."

The two girls frowned at him, making their displeasure known, but he was certain things would be simpler if only he went. If there were barriers and magic obstacles within Stillwater

House, as there were in Spellshadow Manor, he knew he stood a greater chance of avoiding them, simply because of what he was. Magical security, as far as Alex was concerned, was set up in magical schools to keep mages in line, but not Spellbreakers. After a frosty few minutes, the girls' resolve thawed and they relented.

With a full stomach and a focused mind, Alex moved stealthily along the shoreline toward the white side-wall of the villa, keeping once more to the shady tree-line. Nobody seemed to see him as he clambered easily up onto the top of the broad battlements and scurried along it, skirting beneath the lookouts so as not to be discovered. He pulled himself up onto a higher wall that looked across one of the piazzas, tiled intricately in ter-racotta and cream-colored squares. Staying low to the wall, he moved toward the very edge and watched the goings on beneath him. The piazza itself was busy with people going about their business—too many people for him to dare drop down into.

However, as he scanned the archways that led to other sec-tions of the villa, he saw a sign that gave him some hope. On a large square of stone embedded into the brickwork beside the arches, Alex saw, against all odds, a symbol he recognized. He had seen it so often, on all the trips he had taken to the hospi-tal with his mother, that it was instantly familiar. The *caduceus*, with its two snakes twisting around a rod, and a pair of wings at the top—the symbol for medical assistance. He just hoped it meant the same thing here as it did back in the non-magical world.

Despite his discovery, it looked as if it was going to be tricky to get into during the day. Not once had the piazza been empty enough to venture across. Once again, his endeavors would have to wait for the cover of darkness, but the sight of that symbol had brought him untold optimism. If it *did* mean the same thing it meant back home, then maybe they would have something to help Aamir.

Spurred on by his finding, Alex returned the way he had come. As he reached the far wall, curiosity got the better of him. He wondered if he could get through to the piazza, and thus the infirmary, from a different entrance. Mulling over the possibilities, he changed course and crept furtively across to the courtyard they had peered down into the previous night, hoping it would be empty. Lying flat on his stomach, he crawled toward a parapet built in the wall and peered around it, looking down.

To his horror, it was as far from empty as it could possibly be.

The courtyard was full of students, more than the whole of the Spellshadow student body put together, doing drills of some kind. To one side of the yard, big circular targets made of compacted hay, much like the ones used for archery practice back in the ordinary world, were set up against the wall for the students to practice their aim against. He watched in awe as time after time, thin darts of glittering gold shot through the very center of the board, never even a millimeter off the mark. Other students were grouped in threes, practicing shielding on one another. One would take aim and fire at another student, while the third put up a shield to protect their partner. Every time they successfully created a thrumming shield that rebounded the fired magic, they swapped places.

It was mesmerizing, to see them all so in sync, working

like cogs in a well-oiled machine. Not to mention that each and every student was as athletic as they were beautiful, and undeniably skillful. There was not a dull pupil among them. Magic seemed to flow effortlessly from their hands, doing their bidding without so much as a creased brow or a drop of sweat.

At the helm of these classes were teachers of equal youth and beauty. There were three in the courtyard, instructing the students and, while they were definitely slightly older than their charges, old age and ugliness did not seem to be permitted within the walls of Stillwater House. Alex listened as these instructors barked orders in crisp, clear voices, the students setting to their given tasks immediately. He was in complete awe. These students were no older than Alex, but they were conjuring complex spells he had never seen before as if they were the most basic of skills, sending them rippling across the courtyard with ease. Before long, the whole place was lit up with a fine mist of glittering gold—the magical fallout of their intricate conjurations.

At the far side of the courtyard, sparring fluidly with a young man twice her height and width, was the supremely stunning young woman from the previous night—the one who had caught Jari's eye. Not only was she sparring with this huge man, but she was winning too, flooring him with deft movements and expert magic. Alex watched as she ducked and rolled away from her partner's retaliations, moving as lithely as if she were made of liquid. Soon, it was not her exquisite beauty that kept Alex watching, but her skill. It was like nothing he had ever seen before. Even Natalie's magic, which was impressive in its own right, wasn't nearly as powerful as this young woman's. There was a fierce, fiery crackle to it that bristled with untold strength.

As her sparring partner stepped back to take a breather, the young woman's gaze snapped toward Alex, who ducked sharply behind his parapet. After a minute, he dared to peer back around, but her gaze was still focused in his direction. Shielding her eyes from the glaring sun, she had clearly seen him. Realizing there was no use in hiding, Alex's eyes locked with hers in a strange, mutual curiosity. There was surprise, too, and although she was some distance away from him, he was almost certain he could see the curve of a small smile playing upon her lips.

Cursing himself for his mistake, he crawled back across the broad width of the wall and clambered down, dropping the last few meters into the flowerbeds below with a heavy thud. He knew he had just done something that could put them all at risk.

Guiltily, he returned to the small cottage, wishing he had better news. He had intended to go to Stillwater to get something useful for Aamir and had come back essentially empty-handed. True, he now had an inkling where the infirmary might be, but he also had news of potential detection. It wasn't exactly a worthwhile exchange.

Jari looked up as Alex entered. "Did you get something?" he asked eagerly.

Alex sighed. "I have good news and bad news."

The others gathered around.

"What's the good news?" pressed Jari.

"I think I found out where the infirmary is," Alex replied.

Excitement spread across Jari's face. "You did? Did you see it?"

Alex shook his head. "There were too many people around."

"Is that the bad news?" Jari frowned.

"Sadly not." Alex grimaced.

"So, we go there after nightfall?" Natalie chimed in.

Again, Alex shook his head. "That's where the bad news comes in."

"What is it?" Jari was losing his patience.

"I think the students at Stillwater House might know there are some vagrants on the loose," explained Alex.

"What do you mean?" asked Natalie, suddenly worried.

"I went to the courtyard to see if there was another way in, to reach the infirmary, and… I think I was seen. The girl you saw last night, Jari—I think she saw me," sighed Alex, hating that it had happened.

"What?" gasped Jari. "How could you let that happen?"

"It was an accident."

"Well, what are we supposed to do now?" Natalie said, her voice tight with alarm.

"I say we stay put," Alex replied.

"What? You're insane!" yelled Jari. "How can we be safe here?"

"We're as safe here as we are likely to be anywhere else around here—including the lighthouse. At least here we're well hidden and have a good view of the lake and the wall, if anyone comes looking for us," he said evenly.

There was a rationale in what Alex had to say. It was true, they were well positioned. And who knew what the young woman he had seen was going to do? She might not say a word. Even if she did, nobody had followed him, and nobody had seen where he had gone.

His words seemed to calm the group as they weighed their

options—not that they had a great many at their disposal. In the end, a decision seemed to have been made to stay put, though nobody spoke the consensus aloud. A tense atmosphere bristled in the confined space of the cottage throughout the rest of the day, with the slightest noise setting everyone on edge. Even the soft whisper of the lake lapping the shore sounded like voices approaching.

So it was a surprise when the sound of actual feet approaching evaded their notice entirely.

The sun had just begun to go down when Alex heard the soft pad of a stealthy approach beyond the boarded window behind his head. Whoever they were, they had made it almost to the front door of the cottage undetected.

"Someone is outside," he whispered to the others. They looked at him in sudden panic, pausing what they were doing. "We need to make a run for it. Surprise whoever is out there, okay?"

They nodded.

"On my count, we run. Jari, you and I will get Aamir."

Another nod.

"Ready? Three, two—"

Just then, a voice called out. "Please don't run." It was a distinctly female voice, musical and clear. "It's only me out here, and I don't mean you any harm."

A look of panic flashed between the inhabitants of the dimly lit cottage. Alex couldn't be sure the feminine voice wasn't at the head of a hundred-strong army, though that seemed unlikely; he would definitely have heard that many people approaching.

"Stay where you are," warned Alex as he crept toward the door.

"Very well," replied the woman's voice. Alex stepped out of the cottage.

He was mildly surprised to see that it was the beautiful, powerful girl from the courtyard. The one who had seen him. Only now, instead of wielding ferocious magic, she was holding a basket in the crook of her arm, and there was a wide smile playing upon her lips.

"You?" whispered Alex.

"Me." She nodded, grinning.

Close up, she was even more beautiful. Alex could see she had striking pale eyes that were the same shade as that of raw magic, with a dark black ring around the iris. They were peculiar and mesmerizing, as much as Alex tried to look away. Her porcelain-smooth skin was almost unnaturally pale, but somehow it suited her, making her stand out from the other perfect people he had seen within the walls of Stillwater House. Naturally, her bone structure was second to none, with high cheekbones, a delicate jawline, and arched brows of a darker shade than her hair, which was long and silvery blond, held off her exquisite face with a dusky coral-colored rose. She was dressed in the black pants, boots, and white t-shirt all the Stillwater students seemed to wear, but it looked different on her tall, willowy frame.

Alex became aware of Jari standing beside him, staring agog at the stunning young woman as words failed him. The blond-haired boy's eyes were as big as saucers.

"I came to welcome you to Stillwater House," the young

woman announced. "Please don't be alarmed. I'm not here to hurt you."

"So this *is* Stillwater House? My friend Alex here thought it was, but he wasn't sure," said Jari, finding his voice again as he chattered happily. Emboldened, he ushered the young woman toward the secluded patch around the back of the cottage. The others followed reluctantly, a flash of amusement passing between them; they all knew of Jari's ineptitude when it came to women, and this one was an exceptional beauty.

"I didn't mean to startle you, only I saw your friend today and thought I would come and introduce myself. I figured you might be hiding somewhere around here. I have also brought food and drink for you, as is the custom here, and I thought you might be in need of refreshment," she explained, handing the basket to Natalie.

Inside were all kinds of delicious-looking treats and large bottles of colorful liquid that Alex secretly longed to taste, despite the suspicious place it came from. He was so thirsty.

"Who are you?" asked Natalie.

"How rude of me." The young woman smiled bashfully. "I am Helena."

It was a befitting name that made Alex think of the ancient Greeks they had learned about at school, though it wasn't quite the same name as the woman he was thinking of. Helen of Troy—the face that launched a thousand ships. He could certainly see men going to war over a woman like this one.

"How did you know we would be in need of refreshment?" Ellabell wondered, frowning.

Helena looked embarrassed for a moment, her gaze

lowering. "The truth is, there was some gossip going around the school that there were outsiders in the area. We don't get outsiders around here very often, and I was curious. We've been making bets on whether or not it was a hoax." She smiled shyly, causing Jari to look at her with utter adoration. Alex wasn't sure it was possible for the boy to get more smitten, but it looked like he was wrong.

For a moment, Helena had lulled Alex into a false sense of welcome, but suddenly, he felt his hackles rise again. He thought instantly of the scouts, searching for them in the woods; somebody had sent them to look for him and his friends. This girl had seen him on the battlements. Had she told anyone? If she had, their hopes were ruined. It was hard to gauge whether her intentions toward himself and the group were honorable ones or not.

"What do you intend to do with the information you have on us?" asked Alex coldly.

Helena looked surprised. "What do you mean?"

"Have you told anyone about us?" he pressed. Instantly, the atmosphere changed as all eyes focused with suspicion on Helena—even Jari's eyes seemed to narrow slightly.

She shook her head, her sleek hair glinting. "No, I haven't told a soul about you. I swear," she said earnestly. "It is not our custom. You are guests here. If you desire it, I will continue to bring food and drink to you in secret each day, until you decide what to do next—whether you wish to stay here or move on. But I will not tell anyone of your presence here unless you wish it."

Alex could not deny she seemed genuine. There was an honesty in her strange eyes that he could not ignore, and yet she had come from within the villa walls, from the unknown.

"We don't want anyone else to know," Alex said.

She dipped her head in a kooky curtsey. "Very well. Do you still wish me to bring food and water?"

Alex thought about the lake water and the burn in his throat. "If that isn't too much trouble."

She smiled. "Absolutely not. It is my pleasure. It is so very exciting to meet new people. You must tell me all about where you are from and what has brought you to our fair shores."

A wary look passed between the others at this request.

"Perhaps you could tell us something of your fair shores first. An exchange of sorts," suggested Alex.

"Yeah—why don't you sit and share some food with us? Tell us all about yourself," Jari encouraged as he sat down on the grass against the cottage.

Guardedly, they sat in a circle and shared out the food Helena had brought. Alex had his eye on the drinks, desperate to quench his thirst, but there were all kinds of foodstuffs in the basket. There were honeyed cakes that oozed with syrup and delicate pastries filled with a strange jam that was both sweet and sour at the same time. There were doughy white buns, soft and heavenly, with a melted cheese filling that was delicious, topped with crisp salad leaves and a shredded radish-type vegetable. Savory pastries too, with hearty, warming centers, delicately spiced with almost Moroccan flavoring that tickled the tongue for just a moment, before giving way to a comforting heat. They ate hungrily, satisfied sounds making their way across the group.

The drinks were strange and wonderful too. Alex popped open the top of a red-colored one and drank deeply. It slaked his thirst almost immediately, tasting of watermelon and strawberries mixed together, cool and refreshing on his tongue. It beat any soda he had ever tasted.

"So, tell us about this place," Alex said, after polishing off half of the red drink.

"Well, where to begin? It is a school for magical students." She paused thoughtfully. "Are you magical?" she asked.

"We are." Natalie nodded, biting into one of the pastries.

"Are you from a school?" she ventured.

"We are," confirmed Jari.

Alex frowned, not sure if they should have given that much away.

"You are from a school? Oh, how wonderful! We hardly ever get students from elsewhere around here. I thought I should check in case you weren't and I had just bamboozled you! Can you imagine if you were non-magical and I had just told you I was magical—you'd think I was mad!" She giggled. "Now, where was I?"

"Stillwater House," encouraged Alex.

"Ah, yes. So, this is a very ancient, very well-respected magical school for magically gifted students. It is much like any other magical school, only this one is for the children of noble mages," she explained matter-of-factly. There didn't seem to be anything arrogant in the way she said it, and Alex didn't think Helena had the slightest notion how different this school was from the school they had come from.

"Noble mages?" asked Ellabell, quirking a brow.

Helena nodded. "Oh, yes—you know, magical lords, ladies, dukes, duchesses, barons, baronets, those sorts of people?"

Ellabell gave a slight shrug of understanding. "I suppose."

"Well, they send their children here at a young age, to be trained up as the finest mages possible. It is very beautiful here, I know, but the work is hard and we put in so many hours. It is tireless, but it has to be this way in order to bring pride to our families. That is why we are sent here."

That explained the beautiful architecture, the lush landscape, the advanced lessons, the happiness and laughter he had overheard—every difference between this place and Spellshadow. These people, these nobles, were born to be mages. It was instilled in them, no doubt, from an early age that they were special. They were born understanding their powers, wanting to be mages, instead of being dragged unwillingly from their homes and families and forced into it. Knowing that, he felt a twinge of bitterness. It was so much easier for them. He wondered if they even knew there were others out there, less fortunate, less willing.

"What about security? Doesn't anyone ever try to leave?" he asked, wondering if there had ever been outcasts within the villa walls who did not want to abide by the status quo.

A look of curiosity passed across her striking eyes. "There are guards but not much else. Nobody wants to leave, and hardly anybody ever just turns up, so they don't bother with much in the way of security. Plus, most of us are very strong. If somebody got in who wasn't welcome or invited, they would undoubtedly be dealt with," she replied, not realizing how chilling her answer sounded to the group of trespassers.

"Has anyone ever tried to leave?" pressed Alex, his interest piqued.

Helena shrugged. "It is a great honor to be here. We are blessed to be here. Why would we leave?" she said, but somehow, she didn't sound entirely convinced. There was a monotone to her words that reminded Alex of his first days at Spellshadow, when Jari and Aamir had repeated phrases to him that sounded oddly rehearsed. A robotic, drilled characteristic.

"It's very beautiful," Alex acquiesced, though he was left with more questions than he had started with.

"I must be getting back now. I will bring you more sustenance tomorrow," she announced, rising. "And please, sleep well knowing I will keep your secret." She smiled her pleasant smile as she bade her farewell.

Seeing her leave, Alex was hit with a wave of inspiration. Getting up quickly, he ran after her, much to the confusion of the others. Helena was already some way down the shoreline when Alex caught up with her. There was something he hoped she could help him with, though he knew it was something of a bold move, in terms of trust.

"Is everything okay?" she asked, looking at him in surprise.

"Not really," he replied, catching his breath. "The thing is, we have a friend with us who is very sick. You didn't see him because he's inside the cottage, but he's getting worse every day and nothing we do seems to help. We're all worried about him. I saw you out there on the training ground—you're strong, and I was wondering if you might be able to help."

She frowned. "What is wrong with him?"

"There's a curse upon him. A really bad one. Now, I'm betting you have a pretty good library in that school of yours, and I was wondering if you could get us a spell-book that has instructions on how to break curses. Or, if you know of any way to remove it—perhaps you have something that would help in your medical center—we would be extremely grateful."

As much as he had tried to suppress it, Alex couldn't shift the weight of responsibility he felt for what was happening to Aamir. If he hadn't cut that band, perhaps Aamir would be okay. Or maybe he'd still be the Head's zombie. They'd never know. Whatever the case, they needed to fix him.

"I'll work on a solution," she said, flashing him a reassuring grin. "And thank you for trusting me. I know you didn't have to."

The words rang in his ears as he watched her hurry away into the night and scale the villa wall with the ease of a ninja. She was right. He didn't have to trust her.

He just hoped he had been right to try.

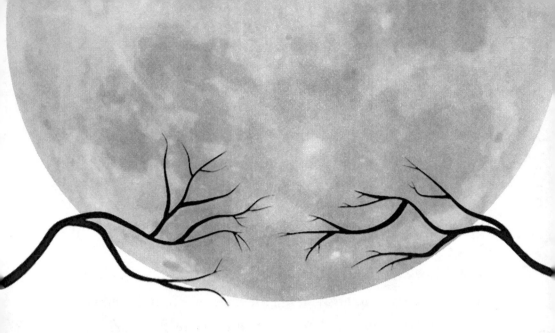

CHAPTER 8

TRUE TO HER WORD, HELENA RETURNED THE NEXT DAY with more supplies. She appeared from the dim glow of the sunset, managing once again to creep up on Alex and his friends unawares as she approached with her basket.

Alex was glad to see she hadn't forgotten to bring drinks, and he reached instinctively for the bottle after she'd entered the cottage. So far, he hadn't been able to find a spring or a stream in the narrow strip of forest that ran along the shoreline, and his throat was parched.

"Thank you for bringing this, Helena," said Alex, remembering his manners.

"No problem," she said, flashing her perfect white teeth.

"We really are *so* grateful," added Jari, apparently trying to one-up the disinterested Alex in the gallantry stakes.

"You know," murmured Helena, looking thoughtful, "if you were to move inside the walls of Stillwater House, I'd be able to get to you much easier, bringing you whatever you needed. It would be so much simpler for me to help if you were within the grounds."

Alex cast her a look of suspicion.

"I just think it might be easier, especially with your friend requiring some help," she added hastily, with a note of earnestness in her voice.

Alex had told the others why he had run off after Helena the previous evening, and although there had been a momentary grumble of displeasure at the idea, they had come around to it once they realized Alex was right. Helena had clear access to many areas of Stillwater House that they did not, and she knew her way around.

"We'll discuss the option," said Alex. If there truly was somewhere within the walls of Stillwater House where they could be safe and remain unseen, he knew it might be better to be hidden in plain sight than warily out in the open, as they were.

This news seemed to please Helena. For a while, an easy silence settled over the group as they ate. Jari shuffled over to where Helena was sitting beside Natalie, taking up the space between them as he offered the silvery haired girl a cake. She took it, nibbling daintily as Jari stared adoringly at her. Helena didn't seem to mind. Alex wondered if this was just a normal occurrence for her, having boys moon over her. He imagined it was, though his gaze rested elsewhere.

"Oh, we've been on the run for a fair few days now." Jari shrugged casually, responding to something Helena had asked.

Alex's ears pricked up.

"What is it you plan to do?" she asked.

"We just want to get back to where we're from," explained Jari with a dramatic sigh.

Helena frowned. "Where you ran away from?"

Jari shook his head. "No, no—we came from a school, but it's nothing like this. The school we came from is an *awful* place."

This seemed to shock Helena, and Alex eavesdropped with interest. He wasn't sure he liked Jari giving away their information, but it was intriguing to see her responses to it.

"Awful?" she gasped.

Jari nodded. "It's big and gray and depressing, and there are barriers on everything. It's as far from this place as you could get—there is no beauty, only ugliness and cruelty. There are curfews, and the teachers are mostly vindictive, punishing us for the *smallest* thing. Even the nice ones are there against their will, so it's pretty sad too."

Alex watched as tears began to glitter in Helena's eyes. Either she was a very good actress or Jari's story was seriously tugging at her heartstrings. He couldn't be sure. Jari himself, however, was giving it the full theatrical treatment, sighing heavily in all the right places, making sure he won Helena over with his tales of Spellshadow and how oppressed they had been.

"How horrible," she whispered.

"The Head, too—he's the worst of them all. He's this strange, evil creature who hides beneath a hood so nobody can really see his face. He has fingers that are so thin they almost look like a skeleton's hands, and he rules with an iron fist," said Jari, his voice low, as if he were telling a scary story... which, Alex supposed, he was. "He's probably after us right now. We caused a few issues for him, you see, when we escaped. But we couldn't stay there any longer. We were tormented and miserable, missing our homes and our families. Running away was the only option—if we ever want to see them again."

Alex noted a confused expression had crossed Helena's face as she absorbed what Jari was saying.

"I don't understand—why haven't you seen your families?" Helena asked, concern furrowing her smooth brow.

"Students where we ran from are stolen from their homes," said Jari.

"No!" gasped Helena, glancing for confirmation from the other members of the group.

Alex sighed. "Yeah… It's true. There was another Head, not the skeletal one, who came out of the school into the non-magical world and snatched anyone who had magical potential, hypnotizing them and taking them back to the school against their will. Nobody was allowed to leave, once they had been taken inside—it was more of a prison than a school, really," he explained grimly.

"Our families still don't know where we are. As far as they know, we disappeared one day and never came back." Alex was surprised as Ellabell spoke up, her voice thick with emotion. To hear his echoed thoughts coming from her lips made his heart twinge. It wasn't something any of them spoke about much—their families waiting for children who never came home—but they all had them.

This news seemed to shock Helena to the core, her strange, pale gold eyes wide in horror. "How could they do that to you?

It's terrible! Nothing like that happens here. I can't believe you have suffered these things—I am so sorry," she whispered, her voice laced with empathy. It was the most genuine Alex believed they had seen her.

"So, that's why we ran. We're just trying to get home," Jari concluded.

"You are lucky, to learn magic here," Natalie remarked after a pause. "What is it like?"

"It is a great honor to be sent here to study. Though we are away from our families, we get to see them a few times a year when they visit," she said shyly, clearly not wanting to rub salt into the wound. "Are you sure you want me to talk about Stillwater, after what you have just told me?"

"It'd be a nice distraction," muttered Alex.

"Well… we are sent here at around nine or ten to begin our studies. There is a junior wing and a senior wing, and this is where we learn the ways of the Mage, beginning with the basics and working our way up to the more complex stuff. There are no barriers on the walls and no restrictions—we are free to walk the grounds and the nearby hills, if we so please. The teachers here are strict but fair, and treat us with a mutual respect, which is nice. They were students like us once, so they know what it is like. Our Headmistress rules over the school, but she is as strict and fair as the rest of the teachers. There are school rules she makes us abide by, like at any school, but they are not unreasonable. They are simply there so we get the most out of our education, and to keep us safe. There is free time too, to use how we please, and we are never forced to do anything." She paused thoughtfully. "We are here, for the most part, of our own free will. Stillwater House is a necessary part of our transition into adulthood."

Alex heard that curious robotic note in her voice again as she said the last couple of sentences; he could not get out of his mind how rehearsed they sounded.

"What if you don't want to stay and study at Stillwater?" asked Alex.

Helena frowned. "Everybody here wants to stay and study."

"You're telling me nobody has ever tried to run away, or *not* wanted to stay?" pressed Alex.

There was a flash of confusion in Helena's strange eyes. The question seemed to throw her for a moment, as if she had never fully contemplated it before. "I suppose there have been deserters," she said finally, after a few moments of uncertain silence. Her choice of word concerned Alex. After all, it essentially described the five of them.

"What happens to the ones who try to run?" Alex ventured.

"They go somewhere else," she said simply.

"Where?" Alex wasn't dropping the bone; it was as he had suspected, and he was too intrigued to let it go.

Helena shrugged. "They go somewhere more suited to their needs, where they can get the help they require."

It perplexed Alex that people who didn't toe the line were always being sent 'somewhere else,' but nobody ever knew what or where that 'somewhere else' was. The memory of Blaine Stalwart rushed into his mind—that young man had been 'sent' to Stillwater, or so the Head had claimed. After discovering the manacles, with Blaine's name written on the clipboard beside them, Alex had thought Blaine's being sent to Stillwater House was merely a ruse. But now he was wondering if some part of Blaine *had* been sent here after all. It was a real place, but Alex couldn't quite put his finger on how it related to Blaine's disappearance. Alex had strongly suspected Blaine had been dealt with at Spellshadow itself—the slick, metallic-scented substance on the grim floor being a potent clue—but now, he couldn't help thinking the result of Blaine's demise might have been sent here for some reason. The thought chilled and confused him.

"I should be going," said Helena.

"Are you sure? Stay as long as you like," Jari chimed in, flashing a look of blame at Alex. Jari clearly did not want the beautiful girl to leave, especially after Alex had so monopolized her time with his line of questions. Alex had to wonder if he had, in fact, frightened Helena away.

She shook her head lightly, tossing her silvery blond hair. "Thank you, but I ought to be getting back. It's getting late."

"Will you come again tomorrow?" Jari asked hopefully.

"Yes, though do think on moving within the walls of Stillwater. It would be much easier," she said. "I could even introduce you to the Headmistress if you would like. She is a wonderful, fair, intelligent woman. I'm sure if she knew what you just told me, she would welcome you all with open arms," she added unexpectedly.

Alex frowned, and looks of concern passed between the four of them. Given their track record with Heads, Alex could see nobody thought that was a particularly good idea.

"It's a kind offer, but we are a little bit cautious about Heads," said Natalie with a friendly smile.

Helena seemed crestfallen. "I can understand that. She is

honestly very nice, but I can see how it might be tricky for you to trust her… I don't think the Headmistress would mind your arrival at all. In fact, I believe she *might* already know you are somewhere nearby, just not the exact location."

Alex thought about the scouts again. "How *might* she know?"

"Oh, well, there was a disturbance or something that set off an alarm, so I think she knows something is up. She sent some people to see what it was, but they came back empty-handed. That's how the gossip spread about intruders, but, obviously, I'm the only one who knows where you are." Helena grinned, her smile fading as she saw the suspicious faces looking at her. "I won't tell anyone where you are—I promise," she insisted.

Again, there was that honesty about her face that made Alex want to believe her.

"Why will it really be safer within the walls?" asked Natalie.

Helena glanced around warily, lowering her voice. "We don't often get outsiders around here, and there are others within the school who might not be so understanding. If they were to find you out here, there could be trouble." An expression of genuine alarm passed across her face.

"Then why are you so intent on helping us?" asked Alex, trying to keep the cold edge from his voice. "What's in it for you?"

She blushed, speaking softly. "I mean what I say when I tell you I want to keep you all safe from harm—after hearing your story—and that it's a tradition of my people to take in those who are in need… But there might also be something you can help me with later. Nothing big, I promise; I would never ask for something major. Just a small favor I may need. A little exchange."

Alex was wary of favors, but he could see a fragile, honest sort of hope in her striking pale gold eyes that he didn't feel he could sputter out. Glancing around the rest of the group, he could see their mistrust had also been muted by the genuine note of faith in the beautiful young woman's words. It was not a threat or an ultimatum, merely an optimistic request.

"Okay…" Alex murmured uncertainly.

"I have a suggestion to make," she continued, her voice timid. "As a gesture of goodwill, I would like to try to remove the curse that is on your friend. If you decide to move within the walls of Stillwater, I can do that more easily, and it will be much better for your friend if he is somewhere where assistance is close at hand, should he worsen. We can move in under the cover of darkness, and I will put you somewhere safe."

Alex exhaled. At this point, he wasn't sure what other option they had.

"Will you give us a few minutes to take a vote?" asked Alex.

Helena nodded, standing quickly and moving down to the shoreline, where she sent a few pebbles skittering across the beach with the toe of her boot.

"So, what do we think?" he asked, turning back to his friends.

"I say yes," declared Jari immediately.

Natalie nodded too. "If it will help Aamir, I think it is a good idea. It is what we wanted anyway, yes? To explore Stillwater and see if we can find someone or something that will further our mission to get home?"

"I don't know if we can trust her, but it seems to be our only valid option right now," said Ellabell quietly.

"What do you say, Alex?" Natalie turned to him, a glimmer of concern in her dark brown eyes.

"I say we go with her too," he concluded, hoping this was the right decision.

They called Helena back over, and she returned with an anxious look on her face. "Well?" she asked.

Jari grinned. "We have decided to say yes to your kind offer!"

"That is great news! I will keep you safe and do my very best for your friend," she affirmed, smiling brightly.

"We look forward to it!" Jari gushed.

"I will come back for you at the same time tomorrow. Be ready," she said. "I will not let you down."

A nervous energy plagued Alex as he lay awake that night within the confined space of the cottage. All around him, his friends fidgeted in their sleep. Ellabell called out something incoherent, making Alex sit up to make sure she was okay, but she was fast asleep beneath her blanket. It had only been a nightmare. Settling back down, he guessed he wasn't the only one who was worried about the agreement they had just made and what the next day would bring.

CHAPTER 9

ALL DAY THE GROUP WAS ON EDGE, WAITING FOR nightfall. At every moment, Alex expected to see a team of guards marching from the rising wall, ready to arrest them. The only one who seemed relaxed about the whole thing was Jari, who had wandered about the place in a daydream for most of the day, asking dumb questions every now and again about the beautiful Helena, like "How often do you think she brushes her hair?" and "If Helena were a sea creature, what kind of sea creature do you think she'd be?" It should have been a welcome distraction, but it only served to fray the nerves of everyone else.

It was only the knowledge of Aamir's illness that kept the rest of the anxious group from up and leaving. Aamir's condition was still bad, but it was no worse than it had been. Every hour, somebody changed the cold compress on his forehead and trickled water into his mouth. With the food Helena had brought, they found whatever was soft enough and mashed it up, feeding it him carefully so he didn't choke, in an attempt to restore some of his strength. If it had, nobody could tell.

Natalie had even offered to try to break the curse, after a particularly nervous episode during lunchtime when they had been convinced there was a boat on the lake, coming closer. It had turned out to be a floating log, and Alex had persuaded her not to attempt any curse-breaking. She was mostly back to herself and still drinking the lake water regularly, but there was a tremor in her hands whenever she lifted them to try out a spell. She could perform intermediate magic like solid-bowl-forging, but anything greater quickly drained the returned color from her cheeks. Alex could tell she was definitely getting better, but she needed a little more time before she would be back to her usual, formidable self. She was frustrated by her unfamiliar weakness, but he warned her not to push herself, in case it set her back even further.

As the others busied themselves in anticipation of Helena's arrival, there was little else for Alex to do except think. Sitting at the edge of the tree line, he gazed out at the glittering lake as it danced beneath the warm, glowing sunlight.

Spellshadow Manor seemed as if it belonged to another world entirely. In some ways, he supposed, it did.

Not wanting to dwell on the manor and the people they'd had no choice but to abandon there, he turned his mind to the people inside Stillwater House. 'Magical nobles' Helena had called them, but Alex still wasn't sure where they came from.

Where did these magical nobles live, and where did they send their children from? Did they live out in the real, non-magical world, just like Alex had, or was there a whole sphere of existence out there that he had no comprehension of? Were there worlds like this one, where the air crackled and buzzed with magical energy, just waiting to be discovered beyond the fabric of what Alex had always considered reality? It was a humbling thought, and Alex wasn't sure he could deal with it on top of the fractious anxiety that coursed through his body. Just accepting magic was real had been a tough enough wake-up call, but it seemed the magical world wasn't done surprising him.

He stayed, staring out at the lake for what seemed like hours, undisturbed by the others who were in equally solitude-seeking moods, with the thoughts of a million possibilities charging through his mind.

It was almost a relief when the sun finally went down, and they didn't have to find things to distract themselves anymore. They had already packed up what meager belongings they had, leaving them with very little else to keep them busy. They just had to wait a short while longer for Helena to arrive, which was arguably worse than the stretching hours of the day. It meant the uncertainty of their move into the villa was near and they couldn't run away anymore. Sitting together, they consumed what was left of Helena's gifted food and drink in nervous silence.

They didn't have to wait long, however, as Helena appeared just after the sun had sputtered out its last beam of light. They saw her this time as she approached, emerging ethereally from the shadows, her silver hair glinting.

"Shall we go?" she said cheerfully.

Taking her cue to leave, Alex and Jari ducked into the darkness of the cottage and picked up Aamir. He was awkward to carry, but they managed to run stealthily across the ground toward the wall with him, stopping only once to readjust their grip on his legs and armpits. Alex was almost glad Aamir was still unconscious, knowing the older boy would have hated the indignity. The girls were already standing beside the wall, waiting for the stragglers, when a sudden concern hit Alex. He looked up at the sizeable wall, then looked back down at Aamir.

"How are we supposed to get Aamir over *that*?" whispered Alex.

Helena smiled as a stream of liquid gold shot effortlessly from beneath her palms, snaking through the air toward Aamir, where it gathered beneath him. As she gracefully twisted her fingers, the golden energy puffed outward into a pulsing cushion of glowing light that held the weight of Aamir's body with ease.

"Won't someone see that?" Alex asked.

He thought he saw Helena roll her eyes at the insult of his question, before she twisted her right hand ninety degrees counter-clockwise, causing the bright glow of the cushion to dim down to an almost indiscernible mist of gold. It didn't look as if there was anything beneath Aamir at all, once Helena was finished, which was both impressive and unsettling. It was obvious she was far more advanced than any of them, even Natalie, who was looking enviously at the spell and the powerful mage wielding it.

Helena carefully lifted Aamir's body upward, clearing the wall with ease as she maneuvered him down onto the broad width of the battlement above. Alex had to admit it was a re-markable sight to behold. Once Aamir was safely above, Helena set to climbing the ragged stonework, reaching the top quick-ly as the others scurried after her, copying her choice to climb instead of fly—Helena's decision not to do so had made them cautious.

As they reached the top of the battlements, Helena led them all stealthily through a silent, sleeping Stillwater House. The darkened courtyards were empty of students, though Alex could hear the echo of cheerful voices coming from within the torch-lit hallways and the beautiful piazzas above them as the group slipped from shadow to shadow.

It seemed Helena was guiding them around the outskirts at the very back of the school, toward the farthest corner on the opposite side, where a stunning white bell tower spiraled up-ward from the darkness of a disused, abandoned courtyard that was scattered with the broken debris of old equipment and small piles of dumped rubble. No torches were lit, and the place was veiled in gloom as they dropped down onto the cracked tiles below.

"You'll be safe here. Nobody comes to this part of the House anymore," explained Helena as she led them toward the front door of the bell tower. Pulling a sizable bronze key from the front pocket of her black pants, she slid it into the lock.

"Where did you get that from?" asked Alex curiously.

Helena seemed insulted by the question as she turned to glance at him. "You ask far too many questions. You can trust me, you know—you'll see," she chastised, frowning.

It silenced Alex, but he had yet to feel fully comfortable in the young woman's presence. She turned the key, opening the door wide as she ushered them all inside. With a glance over her shoulder, she closed the door after them.

"Head upstairs," she said.

They climbed up the staircase until they reached a wide, airy, circular room close to the top. Alex was surprised to see a pile of blankets and pillows stacked against the wall, alongside boxes of food, huge glass bottles of water, and other supplies, like bowls and plates and cutlery. There were clothes too, for them to change into, to get out of their dusty, dirty Spellshadow clothes.

"You did all this?" Natalie asked with a note of awe.

Helena grinned. "I want you to be comfortable."

"Thank you," breathed Natalie, giving the silver-haired girl an unexpected hug. "This is wonderful."

"I'm glad you like it," said Helena bashfully.

"Thank you, Helena." Ellabell smiled.

"Yeah—this is amazing!" chimed Jari, though he didn't quite brave a hug.

"It's nothing." Helen shrugged, brushing it off. "You will have to be as quiet as mice during the daytime, in case anybody hears you, but you can stay here for as long as you wish until you've figured out your next course of action—please don't run off without telling me." There was a note of sadness in her voice.

"This is extremely kind, Helena. We promise we won't leave without telling you first," whispered Alex, his caution softening toward her. The tower was more than he could have imagined.

Helena smiled, holding up her hands. "Well then, I must fulfill the other part of the bargain," she said brightly.

Helena moved over to the window, which looked down onto the courtyard below. Pressing her palms against either side of the frame, a golden glow swelled beneath her hands. With a twitch of each middle finger, she morphed the golden magic into a deep navy blue color that spread out from beneath her skin and skirted out across the window, creating a dark shield that blocked any light coming from within the tower. The shield stayed put as she knelt beside Aamir on the flagstones.

Carefully, Helena placed her hands flat against Aamir's chest and closed her eyes, letting the glow of her magic run from her fingertips into his body. Alex knew she was searching for the gripping snake of the curse within him, as he had done.

She whistled quietly. "It's a strong one."

"Can you still remove it?" Jari asked hopefully. Alex supposed it must be a dream come true—the prospect of Jari's new crush being able to save the life of his best friend.

Helena nodded. "I think so, though it might take a lot out of your friend."

"Aamir. His name is Aamir," whispered Jari.

"It might take a lot out of Aamir," Helena repeated, smiling kindly at the blond-haired boy. "It's up to you what you want me to do." She glanced around the room, waiting for a reply.

The consensus was clear.

"Go for it," encouraged Alex.

At their agreement, Helena placed her hands on Aamir's chest once more and began to weave intricate strands of strong, crackling magic through his body. The fierce glow of it rose up through his skin, making each vein and artery gleam with a white-gold light that was both unnerving and beautiful. He tossed and turned, rejecting her magic. Alex watched as a fresh strand of luminescence snaked from beneath her left hand and shivered toward Aamir's mouth, covering it quickly with a magical gag to keep him quiet as she worked. His body contorted beneath her palms, his eyes snapping suddenly open as his lips opened in a silent scream. Although the gag muted the sound, the impression was clear—Aamir was in agonizing pain.

Alex was as much in awe of Helena's skill as he was worried for Aamir's state. It was impressive to see her conjuring and managing three complex spells at once. He wasn't sure he had seen anyone do that before and keep each one as consistently powerful as the next.

It wasn't long, however, before the pressure of removing the curse inside Aamir began to show on Helena's face as her breathing became labored. Even though she was a powerful mage, the curse seemed to put a strain on her as it fought back. She gritted her perfect teeth in determination, her eyes squeezed tightly shut as she layered magic upon magic beneath her hands, weaving further strands into the sweating, twisting body of Aamir. His mouth gaped like a fish, his eyes wild, but it did nothing to stop her as she persevered. The glow of his veins burned brighter, until Alex was certain he could see the shape of Aamir's bones beneath the blaze.

The group watched as the minutes wore on with torturous slowness. Helena's breath grew more and more labored as the first beads of sweat appeared on her brow, but still she did not stop. There was an admirable, fierce determination in her as she battled to dismantle the curse until, finally, after a long while and a great deal of exertion on her part, there was a quiet, eerie ripping sound. From the glowing center of Aamir, she seemed to physically tear the phantom entity of the curse and hold it tightly in her fist. The spirit creature writhed and wriggled in defiance, trying to escape Helena's grasp, but she quickly placed her other hand against it and sent a ripple of something dark and inky into the burning phantasm, dispersing it particle by particle. It burst outward in an explosion of harmless golden dust.

Helena sat back, breathing heavily as sweat glistened on her pale skin. A broad grin stretched across her flushed face. Hastily, Jari ran toward her, brandishing a cup of water. She drank deeply.

"Thank you." She beamed. It was Jari's turn to flush a light shade of pink.

Aamir lay still on the flagstones, but Alex could make out the steady rise and fall of his chest, letting them all know their friend was still alive.

"I should warn you," said Helena, drinking another large sip of water, "he will need time to recover, and he may not seem like himself for a long while after. He has been sapped of strength, but he will get better."

"How strong was it?" asked Alex.

"It was one of the strongest I have ever seen," Helena replied, the exhaustion of removing the curse evident on her face.

"And he will definitely get better?" Natalie asked.

Helena nodded. "He will, with time."

Alex smiled at Helena, feeling gratitude swell in his heart. The knowledge that Aamir would soon be getting better was all the group had wanted to hear, for such a long time. With her help, it was now a reality—she had kept her end of the bargain, and although Alex still wasn't sure how far he could trust her, he couldn't deny the good deed she had done.

"I'll take my leave of you now. I'm pretty tired." Helena got shakily to her feet, brushing the dust from the back of her pants.

"Do you need help?" Jari offered.

She shook her head. "I'll be fine. Here, you should have this," she said shyly, handing the tower key to Alex. "I wouldn't advise you to leave the tower, but I don't want you to feel like I'm locking you in."

It was a friendly gesture and one Alex appreciated. As he and the rest of the group followed her down the stairs to say farewell, key in hand, he noticed a tremble in her fingers and an unsteadiness in her gait as she clutched the banister tightly, her knuckles whitening.

"Are you *sure* you don't need a hand?" he asked as they reached the ground floor.

"I just need a minute," she assured him. As she waited for the wave of tremors to pass, she turned back to rest of the group. "I have to say, I'm glad you arrived when you did. You've come at a very exciting time."

Alex frowned. "What do you mean?"

"You'll see tomorrow," she whispered cryptically. "Sleep well." She flashed a grin at them before moving out into the dark courtyard and disappearing from sight.

CHAPTER 10

BEING SO CLOSE TO THE HOUSE NOW, ALEX FELT JUMPY throughout the night. No matter what he did to try to distract himself, he found he couldn't rest. He chatted with the others and flipped through a few of the novels Helena had left for them to read, but nothing seemed to work. Not having slept, with a thousand thoughts thundering through his brain all night, he was snappy and irritable, overreacting to the slightest thing.

Jari sat against the wall, munching on a gift-bag of crispy cookies Helena had brought—ones that were oddly lavender-flavored—and the sound of each crunch sent Alex's nerves on edge.

"Will you stop it?" Alex snapped suddenly. The others glanced up at him with startled looks.

"Dude, I'm almost done with them," Jari said defensively. "Do you want one?"

"No, I don't want any of your stupid snacks. I'd rather hear nails on a chalkboard," Alex replied.

Jari tossed the bag of cookies across the room. "Fine, I'll stop eating them, you grump. Sheesh."

"Why don't you stretch your legs for a bit, Alex?" Ellabell suggested softly. "Walking up and down the stairs did wonders for me. It's easy to get a little stir-crazy in all these small spaces."

"Yeah, that's a good idea," Alex sighed, running a hand through his hair. He felt embarrassed by his outburst; he needed to distance himself from the others before he said something truly hurtful.

"Does that mean I can keep eating my cookies?" Jari grinned, and Alex rolled his eyes.

He decided to explore the tower as best as he could, but there were only four floors to investigate. It was like the lighthouse all over again, only there was no secret domed paradise at the top. Instead, there was a small room with a wooden scaffold in the middle, where the bell, presumably, had once hung. It wasn't nearly as exciting as the lamp room, but it was far enough away from the others to give him a moment of the peace and solitude his tired, cranky self craved.

He sat in there, using the spare time to pull the slim notebook of Leander Wyvern from the back pocket of his new, clean black jeans. It had been a while since he'd had the opportunity and energy to look over it, but just holding it brought him a strange feeling of comfort. Contentedly, he opened up a thin panel of anti-magic between his hands as he went over the old ground written within the notebook, to see if there was anything he had missed. He knew there wasn't, but the book soothed him. They still had a few of the books they had stolen from the Head's office, shrewdly pilfered by Natalie, who had placed the books about her person as she had jumped from the office window, but none of them had proved useful so far. For starters, half of them were written in languages even Natalie couldn't read. He wondered with amusement whether they had gotten it all wrong and those books weren't magical at all—they were just cookbooks or self-help manuals, to keep the Head busy when he was in his office. The thought made him smile.

After an hour or so, Alex felt the need to stretch his legs. Standing up, he walked over to the window of the top floor and gazed at the view beyond. It looked out onto a wide stretch of field within a vast clearing in the shadows of the hills, which guarded behind in a long-reaching wall of lush greenery that ended in the rise of a low mountain. Within the field was an amphitheater of sorts, built from a pale sandstone, curving in a semi-circle on the side closest to the mountain. Raked seating ascended upward, and there was a large circular pitch painted in white on the neatly kept grass before the spectators' stand. Four silver posts stood up tall at each quarter of the circle, with a golden statue of a bird of prey perched at the top of each one, their savage beaks facing downwards at the pitch below.

The peculiar setup made Alex curious and eager to be back out in the open, but he knew he couldn't leave the tower. He wouldn't put any of his friends at risk just to make himself feel more comfortable. Instead, he moved back over to where he had left the notebook, folded open on the flagstones, and let his eyes run over the familiar terrain once more.

Later on, as twilight arrived, so did Helena.

Alex's mood had greatly improved after a late-afternoon nap at the top of the tower, and a jovial feeling had settled over the group.

"I swear you're a vampire," joked Alex as Helena entered the room. It was true—she did only seem to appear at night.

She laughed heartily. "Don't be silly. Vampires died out centuries ago!"

Alex frowned at her, not sure whether she was serious or pulling his leg. But if mages and Spellbreakers were real, why not vampires?

"It'd be funny if I was, though, wouldn't it?" She winked, leaving him uncertain.

Jari had been pouring water, but it was spilling out over the edges of the glass as his attention snapped to Helena, his eyes bugging out. She chuckled as Ellabell quickly tipped the bottle upright, bringing Jari back into the room. Alex could understand what had caught the blond-haired boy's eye so intently. Helena was dressed in a beautiful bluish-silver gown that seemed to be made of liquid rather than fabric as it rippled gracefully around her with each movement. Her gleaming blond hair had been braided in sections and intricately twisted up onto her head in an elegant style. A thin silver band wove within the strands of hair before meeting across the smooth skin of her forehead. On her wrists, simple silver bracelets jangled.

"You look beautiful," said Ellabell, speaking the words the boys couldn't.

"Thank you."

"How come you're so dressed up?" asked Alex.

"Questions again?" she teased. "I told you—you have arrived at a very exciting time at Stillwater House!"

"What's going on?"

"Tonight is the Ascension Ceremony," she announced.

A chill ran down Alex's spine. It didn't sound particularly exciting to him at all. In fact, it sounded an awful lot like 'graduation.'

"What's the Ascension Ceremony?" he asked, dreading the answer, though he tried to keep his voice calm.

With a gleeful smile, Helena gestured for them to follow her up to a higher floor. She held the front of her dress so as to not trip as she skipped up the staircase. Gracefully, she moved across to the far side of the third floor, to the window set within the masonry. With an elegant hand, she gestured out toward the amphitheater Alex had seen earlier. Except now, instead of being empty, it was beginning to fill with row upon row of people. Huge fires raged in broad, basin-like torches at various intervals around the amphitheater and up the raked seating, lighting the place with a warm, enticing glow.

For the first time, Alex noticed a large, elaborate chair in the very center of the amphitheater's seating, almost throne-like. He wondered who had the honor of sitting there.

"The ceremony is when the final-year students at Stillwater

House get to test their mettle against one another—a competition of sorts," Helena elaborated, gazing out upon the scene. "The Headmistress chooses the students at random from a scroll of names she has. She sits there." Helena motioned toward the throne Alex had noticed, answering his silent question.

"Who are they?" Natalie asked, pointing at the people filling the seats of the amphitheater.

Helena grinned. "They are the families of the students. They all sit in the audience and watch, hoping their child will be Ascended," she said wistfully.

"Ascended?" prompted Alex.

"Oh, yes—sorry, I was getting distracted." She chuckled lightly. "The students fight, and the victor is congratulated with the title of 'Ascended.' It is the highest honor that can be bestowed on a student. If a student wins, they get to go home with their families and take their rightful place among the magical elite, moving back into society to find a partner and a role among their people in order to prolong the magical lineages."

Alex sighed, feeling unsettled. "And the loser?"

"The loser is taken away to perform the Gifting Ceremony," she replied simply.

Horror gripped him. "What's that?"

"It is where the student's life essence is extracted and used for the benefit of their magical betters—a gift from the loser to those they have disappointed by failing their final test," she explained, so matter-of-factly that Alex worried she didn't even realize what she was saying.

The others stared at her in utter shock, as understanding dawned. Even Jari's admiration had morphed into an expression of abject horror.

It *was* graduation, though there was one subtle difference—these students *knew* what they were getting into, and, bizarrely, they didn't seem to mind. In fact, they seemed thrilled at the prospect of such a great 'honor'.

He wanted to shake Helena and make her understand what she was really saying.

"Are the students scared?" he asked instead, hoping to spark some human emotion in her.

Helena pondered the question. "I suppose they are," she muttered with a shrug. "But they know they have to bring their best on the day of the ceremony. You have to understand, we train for this day for years. If we don't bring our absolute best to our last match, the consequences are what they are. It is drilled into us from an early age: we must honor our families and win, or pay the price for our failure."

To Alex's disbelief, a smooth mask of calm still lay across her face. She could not hear the chilling message in the words she spoke—he was certain of it.

"Doesn't anyone try and escape the Gifting Ceremony?" he pressed, hating the term. It wasn't a gift. Gifts were things that were willingly given, and Alex was pretty sure life essence didn't fall under that category.

She nodded. "Some have. There is sometimes one in a class who will try and run."

"What happens to them?" Ellabell spoke up fearfully.

"They are sent somewhere else, to receive the help they need," Helena replied with a sad smile. "I know how it must sound to you, but the Gifting is seen as an honor here. It is the price for losing, and we all understand it."

Silence fell. Nobody could quite believe it.

"It doesn't always end in Gifting, though. Sometimes, a pair can tie, and then both get the title of Ascended," she added, filling the deathly silence.

Suddenly, music started up across the field as drums began to pound in a rhythmic, tribal beat. Helena smiled, clapping her hands in delight. Alex's stomach sank.

"Okay, I've got to go or else I'll be late, but enjoy the show—you have a great view from here. My friends and I used to sneak out and watch it from this window when we were first-years," she said. "It's always an amazing spectacle. I promise you won't be disappointed!"

With that, she disappeared in a whirlwind of shimmering gray and sweet perfume.

Despite the horror of the show that was about to take place in the arena, the compulsion to go to the window was like the urge to watch a car crash. It was impossible not to look. There was a morbid curiosity that the whole group seemed to share as Alex and Ellabell went upstairs to the bell tower itself, while Natalie and Jari stayed put at the window Helena had brought them to.

Aamir had missed all of the drama of the evening and was still sleeping off the effects of his broken curse. Although he had yet to fully awaken, his fever had subsided and he slept more peacefully, without twisting and turning beneath the agonizing pain of the curse. With it gone, it was simply a matter of recovery.

As Alex and Ellabell gazed out toward the arena, the music

thudded loudly in their ears, the bass shaking the very foundations of the tower. The sight before them was undeniably beautiful, in the most picturesque setting. It looked like something
pulled straight from the legends of ancient Rome. So much so,
Alex half-expected a chariot to appear and go tearing around
the pitch. The stars glittered overhead as fireworks rocketed upward from behind the amphitheater itself, lighting up the night
sky in a sparkling array of rainbow colors. A collective "ooh"
went up from the amassing crowd, as a particularly bright spray
of vivid red pinwheels exploded brightly in the darkness.

"Beautiful!" exclaimed Ellabell as the fireworks reflected in
her eyes.

Alex wanted to make a smooth comment, but he held his
tongue. It was too cringe-worthy. "I love fireworks," he said finally, smiling as she stood closer to him for a better view.

Watching the mages continue to arrive and take their seats,
Alex wondered where they had come from and how they had
arrived at Stillwater House. Their presence made him ponder
the strange mechanics of portals.

*Are there portals in the House, or do they just get conjured for
special occasions, like this?*

As the latecomers filed in, Alex thought he saw Helena slip
among the crowd and up into the seats, taking her place near the
top-center with a large group of similarly clad, similarly beautiful individuals. Beside them, to the right, sat another group all
dressed in golden clothes. To the left, they were all dressed in
bronze. Alex guessed they must be students from the older end
of the school, sitting in their year-groups.

Just then, trumpets pierced the air in a brash heralding. An exquisite creature had appeared on the field. A wispy dress of fine, gauzy gold flowed from her body as diamond-encrusted vines twisted among the curling tresses of her beautiful, almost white hair. She seemed to float across the grass, moving with an unearthly grace and elegance. Her face was striking and had an ethereal, otherworldly quality, yet it was familiar somehow, stirring something up in the back of Alex's memory. The image of the young woman in the portrait in the abandoned ballroom at Spellshadow came rushing back to him, only the woman before him was slightly older than she had been when it was painted.

An announcer stood up, and his voice echoed across the arena.

"Please rise for the Crown Princess Alypia!" the man demanded.

The congregation stood immediately in the presence of the hypnotic, golden woman, as she made her way toward them, heading for the throne-like seat in the center of the amphitheater. Gracefully, she stood in front of the throne, gesturing for everyone around her to be seated. They obeyed without a word.

She must be the Headmistress of this place, Alex realized, noting how the students watched her with bated breath.

"It is my great pleasure to welcome you all to the annual Ascension Ceremony," she spoke, her mesmerizing voice both booming and delicate in some defiance of vocal physics. "Without further ado, as I know we are all eager to begin, I declare the ceremony OPEN!"

In her hands, she unfurled a long scroll that Alex guessed bore a list of the students who would be undertaking the ceremony that year.

"Orpheus Llangollen and Mirabelle Scavo!" she bellowed.

Music erupted as two students sprinted out from twin tunnels set in the base of the amphitheater. A girl and a boy, each around eighteen, ran into the painted circle of the pitch and turned to face Princess Alypia. They were both clad in tunics of pure white silk, with thin plates of painted leather armor on top, one set colored red for the boy, the other set colored blue for the girl. They bowed toward their princess, waiting for her signal. As she raised her palms upward, the two students ran to opposite ends of the pitch.

Twisting her hands, Alypia raised a glimmering golden shield between the four posts with their bird of prey statues on top, creating a barrier around the battle arena. Alex guessed it was to protect the spectators from anything the students might do, as well as keep the duelers from escaping.

For a moment, nothing happened as the two students faced off. Seconds later, a fiery flare erupted from Alypia's hand, prompting the two to begin the duel. Instantly, streams of magic, color-changed red and blue by the battling students, twisted and turned in the air. Wave after wave of sharp-edged weapons were thrown on both sides as they ducked and dived, weaving in and out of complex spells sent in their direction.

Most of the magic, Alex had never seen before—the duelers were using spells he had only dreamed of. The boy sent a shiver of magic down into the ground, only to have it split the earth and shoot up close to his opponent's legs, trying to drag her down into the ground. In retaliation, the girl sent two crackling balls of energy after her combatant, which chased him around the pitch, firing arrows at him in rapid succession until he was forced to hide in the very crevasse he had made in the ground.

They were both skillful and agile, and seemed evenly matched. Alex watched the faces in the crowd, trying to make out which ones might be the parents of these two. There were too many worried faces to mark any of them as family, but there were eager faces too, spurring on the warriors.

The duel raged on, with spell after spell shivering through the air, until both combatants seemed exhausted. The arena glittered with spent magic. For a second, the boy seemed to pause, giving the girl the opportunity she needed. Swiftly, she sent an attack toward the boy that hurled him back against the golden barrier, his body crumpling against it. He slid down the shield and collapsed in a heap on the grass, unmoving.

The suspense was terrible.

Ellabell gripped Alex's arm as they waited for the boy to move.

Eventually, he stirred and looked up toward Alypia as he dragged himself up onto his knees, bowing his head and placing his palm flat on his heart in a motion of surrender.

"Mirabelle Scavo is the victor of the first battle!" she announced, firing a blue flare into the air as a cheer went up from the crowd.

Although she looked exhausted, the girl was grinning with pleasure as she punched the air and set off across the grass toward the raked seating. She sprinted up into the audience to find her family, who waved eagerly to her from their seats. They embraced her warmly, but Alex's attention was distracted by the scene below, on the field, as two assistants ran on to pull the boy away. He watched as they dragged Orpheus Llangollen back through the tunnel on the right. Looking back up into the audience, Alex examined two adults as they stood up from their seats and made their way slowly down the stone steps, their shoulders hunched, their faces hidden, before disappearing into the same tunnel the boy had been taken into. Sorrow twisted in Alex's heart as he heard the names of the next two duelers being called. After tonight, those parents would never see their son again.

He could not understand, for the life of him, why they allowed it. Why anyone here allowed it.

He and Ellabell continued to watch the events for as long as they could stomach it. It was difficult to stop watching, as sick as it made them feel. Alex felt as if he almost owed it to them, to watch, though he couldn't rationalize it.

Pair after pair ran onto the battlefield, brimming with enthusiasm, until there were no pairs left. The crowd had thinned after each pair had fought, with parents of the losers disappearing into the tunnel.

He and Ellabell had watched the death matches of fifteen pairs. Sixteen had survived after one tie, with fourteen hauled away to their Gifting Ceremony. All that work, all that strain, all that suffering, rounded off with the agony of having their life essence torn away from them. He wondered, with horror, if the parents stayed to watch. It was a no-win situation, and Alex wasn't sure which scenario was better—for them to stay and watch and have to see that, or for them to leave their child to suffer it alone.

Music pulsed through the night sky as the after-ceremony celebrations began, toasting the victors of the evening. Alex didn't need or want to see any more.

"I'm done," he whispered, turning away from the window.

Ellabell nodded, leaning into him. "Me too."

He glanced down at her, seeing the unexpected shimmer of tears in her sparkling blue eyes. She quickly brushed them away.

"Let's see what the others are up to," she suggested, her voice thick.

Alex wanted to stop her, but she was already at the top of the staircase leading down to the lower floor. He followed close behind, wandering back down to the other room.

Below, Jari was sitting beside Aamir, whose eyes were open, talking to him softly as he trickled water into his friend's mouth. Natalie was still by the window, entranced by the view. She turned as they entered, her eyes aglow with awe and envy at the power she had just witnessed. The sight disturbed Alex, knowing what that look usually meant, but then everything he'd seen tonight had disturbed him.

It was all horrifying, filled with nasty surprises, to the point where Alex began to wonder if this place actually *was* any better than Spellshadow Manor, or if it was merely dressed up in pret-

tier packaging.

CHAPTER 11

H ELENA DIDN'T RETURN TO THE TOWER AFTER THE
festivities that evening or appear the next day, though
when Alex wandered down to the bottom floor he
found a box of food waiting by the front door with a note on it:

My sincerest apologies for being absent, but my training schedule has notched up a gear today and is likely to remain that way for a while. It is always the same after an Ascension Ceremony—we have all learned new things and want to test them out! I will visit as soon as I am able. In the meantime, even if I can't hang around to chat properly, I will leave food and supplies. I hope you enjoyed the spectacle last night! See you soon. H.

Carrying the box of food back up to the main room, Alex could feel the tension in the air. After the events of the previous night, a feeling of awkward anxiety had spread through the group. Nobody could quite believe what they had witnessed, or that they had actually stayed to watch it. It seemed as if nobody knew how to put into words what they had seen.

The only person who appeared slightly more understanding about the whole thing was Jari, who shrugged off the horror of the ceremony as best he could. "I don't know why you're all so bothered about it—at least they *know* what they're in for. It's not like it's this big shock at the end of four years, like at Spellshadow. If it doesn't faze them, why should it faze us?"

His logic was sound, and yet Alex couldn't bring himself to agree.

"People died, Jari. Even if they knew what they were getting into, they're still dead. I think that's something to be bothered about, regardless of how—I mean, they just walked to their deaths like it was nothing! Don't you think that's a little weird?"

"If it's not weird to them, why should it be to us?" Jari replied.

"You don't feel anything toward those poor souls?" asked Alex sternly.

Jari sighed. "It's bad, of course it's bad, but what are we supposed to do about it? There's no use moping over it. It happened, it was very sad, but there is nothing we can do to change it."

Alex didn't say another word as he mulled over Jari's point of view. Whether the blond-haired boy was right or not, Alex wasn't ready to accept that verdict. People had died, and that always mattered.

Natalie was strangely silent on the subject, standing by the window looking out at the field beyond.

"I wonder how long they study for the ceremony," she said quietly, her eyes transfixed on the painted pitch.

"Eight or nine years," replied Alex, remembering what Helena had told them about students arriving at nine or ten. The students last night had looked to be about eighteen.

Natalie didn't respond, making Alex wonder if she had even meant to say the question aloud, as she retreated back into her daydream. There was still a glitter in her dark brown eyes that he didn't like. It made him think of the pink-tinged magic that had surged from his friend's hands as she had stolen away the portal, and the price she had paid for it. He was certain she imagined herself invincible, though there was no such thing.

Still oblivious to most of the things going on, though the tense atmosphere was hard to miss, Aamir had become more alert since Helena's treatment of his curse. Slowly, he had begun to talk again, involving himself in the group as best as he could, though he still looked weary and broken, sagging under the weight of untold exhaustion. Alex couldn't even begin to imagine what it was like to have something forcibly torn from within, especially something that had clung for so long to the inner being of a person. On occasion, Alex would catch Aamir gazing into nothingness, and the expression on the older boy's face was chilling—as if he were permanently staring, shell-shocked, at a ghost in the distance that nobody else could see.

Ellabell was more vocal about the night before; she was still in a state of shock, evidently struggling to absorb the truth of what she had seen. She couldn't seem to sit still, always busying herself with something to try to take her mind off it.

"I don't know if I'm happy about staying here anymore," she said suddenly. "After what we just saw, I'm not sure we can."

Everyone turned to look at her.

"We can't leave just yet, Ellabell," Alex stated calmly.

Her eyes narrowed. "Why not?"

"There are things we need."

"Like what? What's the plan, Alex?" she snapped, her manner agitated. "As far as I can tell, we don't have one."

Slowly, all eyes turned toward him instead.

The semi-spoken goal among the group was that they wanted to reach the real, non-magical world again. They wanted to get back to their families and friends. The only problem was, he could tell the idea weighed heavy on a few of them. He knew it did for him. It was a goal interwoven with guilt for those they had left behind at Spellshadow Manor. Alex could not get them out of his head, and so his plan had evolved slightly over the time they had been running, in an attempt to kill two birds with one stone.

He had wanted to move closer to Stillwater House and get inside the grounds, to try to find something they might use that could help them not only reach the real world, but gain the upper hand against those in charge in order to free the others who remained. What that entailed, he still wasn't sure, but he knew it would need potent magic. For the moment, it was a pipedream, and one of unknown feasibility. But he had made the first step in the right direction. They were in the grounds, after all.

As for the rest of his plan, he had a suspicion their hopes might lie with the black bottles and the glowing red embers he assumed must be inside.

"The plan is to get home, maybe saving the others if we can," he said quietly.

"Nice and vague," muttered Ellabell.

"To get back to the normal world, I think we're going to need to figure out how to create a portal," Alex continued. "Now, I'm guessing that is going to require a whole load of magic and a complex spell we don't yet know. I'm guessing it'll be in there somewhere." He pointed toward the school. "If we want to try and help the others, we need to gain an advantage over the Head."

"And how might we do that?"

"I think it might have something to do with the life essence that's being collected from students. The people in charge are harvesting it—here and at Spellshadow. So there *has* to be a use for it. There has to be a reason they need it, and that might be a weakness we can utilize," he explained.

Glancing around the room, he could see the others were creeped out by the mention of it. Even after seeing the losers being dragged off last night, Alex wasn't sure it had fully sunk in for his friends, what was actually happening to those who didn't win. It wasn't an easy pill to swallow.

"What are they using it for?" asked Ellabell, her former bitterness replaced with anxiety.

Alex shrugged. "That's something we're going to have to find out. If we know that, we can use it against them."

His eyes trailed toward Aamir, who was staring absently into space. If Aamir was listening to the conversation, he was showing no signs of it. Still, it made Alex curious; if anyone knew anything about the reasons life essence was being harvested from students, it was the former teacher.

CHAPTER 12

ALEX KNEW QUESTIONING AAMIR WOULDN'T GO DOWN
well with Jari, but they were wasting time not using
their biggest asset, who was sitting right there, his
brain full of secrets. Without the golden band on his wrist to
prevent him from speaking the truth, Alex was certain he would
be able to garner some useful information from Aamir, even
though he still wasn't certain which side the older boy was on.
If he was friend or foe, only time would tell. It was like Helena
had warned—the band and subsequent curse had gripped him
for a long time, keeping him under the influence of the Head's
manipulation. It might take more time than they had for his
loyalties to change.

But as Alex approached Aamir to question him, he began
to have second thoughts. Their friend looked like the husk of

his former self, fatigue and despair etched on his weary face as he slowly ate a croissant Jari had placed into his hand. The older boy's hands shook weakly. Alex hated that he had to interrogate Aamir now, but he felt the pressure of the task ahead upon him.

Deliberately, Alex settled down on the floor in front of Aamir, making his intentions clear. Jari bristled, frowning at Alex, as a look of understanding passed between the two older boys. It looked as if Aamir had been wondering when this moment would come.

Preparing to ask his questions, Alex opened his mouth to speak, but before he could say a word, Aamir raised his voice so the room could hear.

"Please, may you leave the room so I can speak with Alex alone," he requested, his voice croaky.

Jari shook his head vehemently. "No way."

Aamir smiled. "Please, Jari—I want to speak to Alex alone."

Jari glared at Alex, seemingly suspicious about what he intended to do with his Spellbreaker powers. The boy would not budge from his place beside Aamir, the reluctance apparent on his determined face. Surprisingly, it was Natalie who came to the rescue.

"Jari, you must come with us now. These two have things they need to talk out," she explained. "It is their opportunity to bury the hatchet. You have had yours—now it is Alex's turn."

The blond-haired boy flashed a look of displeasure at Alex, but he went nonetheless, ushered by Natalie's stern hand upstairs to the rooms above, with Ellabell following close behind.

"Why didn't you want them to hear?" asked Alex curiously, once he was certain they were alone.

Aamir sighed. "I think you know why."

The memory of the offer Aamir had made to only him surged into his mind, transporting him back to the ballroom of Spellshadow Manor for a moment, and the trepidation he had felt there. Knowing that Aamir had been the Head's puppet all along, he couldn't help but doubt the sincerity of that agreement. There were other things too—inklings Alex had had, once given time to think about Aamir's state. There were many unanswered questions Alex had for Aamir, and he wondered silently if his former friend was merely trying to lessen the collateral of his honesty. Jari, especially, took a rose-tinted view of their friend. Perhaps Aamir had chosen him for the truth, Alex thought, because he might be able to take the reality of it in a way the others could not.

"What things did the Head tell you when you became a teacher?" Alex began.

Aamir glanced around the room. "Where are we?" he asked, seeming disoriented.

"We are at Stillwater House," replied Alex, trying not to let his frustration show.

Aamir frowned. "Stillwater House?"

"Have you been here before?" Alex asked.

"I don't think so."

"You don't think so?"

"No… I remember now. I am certain I have not. What a funny place. How did we come to be here?" There was a glazed look in Aamir's eyes as exhaustion began to creep through the older boy's bones. Alex hoped he'd get to ask a few questions before Aamir became too weary to answer. Now, if only he could get him to focus.

"We escaped, remember?"

Aamir shook his head. "Everything is so hazy… Did you have a question?"

Alex sighed, trying again. "What things did the Head tell you when you became a teacher?"

"There were many things—there are many things that need to be explained when you become a teacher." He shrugged wearily, his shoulders sagging.

"Such as?"

"What would you like to know?" Aamir asked.

It was hard to know where to begin. As much as he wanted to ask the personal, selfish question of why Aamir offered to let him leave, he knew he would have to leave it until last. There were more pressing concerns upon him for now.

"Why did the Head leave the manor?"

"You know why," Aamir said simply.

"Does he leave the manor a lot?" Alex pressed.

"I'm not certain," replied Aamir.

"You're not certain?" Alex frowned, unconvinced.

"There are gaps in my memory—there are certain things I can't recall," he explained, prickling Alex's suspicions. It seemed a little too coincidental that Aamir might have selective amnesia on certain topics. Alex changed tactic, going for the jugular.

"Why are they collecting the life essence from student mages?" he whispered. "What is it being used for?"

Tension rippled in the air between them as defiance flashed in Aamir's tired eyes. For a good few minutes, Alex wasn't sure the older boy was going to answer.

"A great plague will sweep the land if it is not," he murmured, repeating the eerie warning he had cried out at the height of his cursed delirium.

"Oh, come on. You can do better than that," challenged Alex.

"There is a Great Evil that must be kept at bay," he replied, just as cryptically as before. It was not the first time Alex had heard a 'great evil' mentioned, but he was starting to get a little sick of not being told more on the subject.

"What does that mean?" he questioned sharply.

"It is why the essence is collected—that is all I know." Aamir shrugged.

"You're lying," growled Alex.

Aamir smiled. "I am not. They were passages read to me by the Head from a dusty old book at the back of his office. I think you are familiar with the bookcase?" There was a taunting note in Aamir's voice.

"Tell me the truth," breathed Alex, trying not to lose his temper.

"I am, Alex. I know only what the Head read to me," Aamir replied.

It didn't add up, but he sensed he wasn't about to get any more from Aamir on the subject. The hint of a jeer in the older boy's voice had made Alex unsure of how much of the Head's hold was still in play, controlling Aamir even after the curse had been lifted.

"What about graduation?" asked Alex, moving on out of sheer frustration.

Aamir frowned. "What about it?"

"What is it?" Alex pressed, wanting his suspicions to be confirmed.

"You know what it is."

"I want you to spell it out for me," insisted Alex.

Aamir looked sad for a moment. "Graduation is what comes, inevitably, at the end of studying. At home, it would mean graduation caps and a diploma. For the magically gifted, it means having your life essence removed—it has to be this way to keep the Great Evil at bay," he explained, pausing briefly to catch his breath. "Spellshadow does it a little differently than here, I'll admit, but it's the same thing. For most, it means death. I suppose there is hope here that doesn't exist at the manor. And it is something of a spectacle."

Alex frowned, not quite understanding how Aamir knew about the Ascension Ceremony when he had slept through it. Musing upon it, he guessed somebody must have filled Aamir in on what had gone on—Jari perhaps.

"But why is it done?"

It was Aamir's turn to sigh. "I will not say it again. It is to keep the—"

"Yes, I know that part," Alex interrupted curtly, not sure he could hear the words 'Great Evil' again without losing his cool. "I mean, why does the Head send people like Finder out to snatch students, taking them by force from their homes, and put in all that effort, just to kill them once they've been trained for a few years?"

"I will try and explain it to you as best as I can," Aamir began quietly. "Mages must be trained to ensure that their life essence has matured enough to meet the needs of its use—the better the wizard, the more potent the essence. It has to be aged like wine."

"Has graduation always ended in death?" Alex wondered.

"I can only speak of what I know, and I am afraid I do not know that. I can't remember what I was told," said Aamir. Alex wasn't remotely convinced. "It does not always have to end in death now, however," Aamir added.

"How do you mean?" Alex's interest was piqued.

"Well, there is always the very slim possibility that a mage—a very strong mage—will survive 'graduation.' It has never happened, as far as I know, but there is a myth of it happening," he elaborated, lowering his voice. "If it should ever come to pass, this person would prove to be a useful adversary against the Great Evil. The idea is, if the mage was strong enough to survive the removal of life essence, they would be strong enough to overcome the Great Evil and fight it. An even match, so to speak."

Although it was the most Aamir had said, Alex couldn't help but feel even more exasperated by the tale. To his ears, it sounded like fiction—nothing more than the regurgitation of a story he had been told before.

"That doesn't sound possible," he stated.

Aamir shrugged. "Well, it's all I know about it."

That can't be all, thought Alex irritably.

"But *why* do they do it? Why do these people think they can just take the lives of young mages, no matter which way they wrap it up?" he probed angrily. They had no right, and yet nobody was stopping them. Alex hoped Aamir would give him more than just the robotic recitation of the rhetoric he'd been told.

"It is for the greater good of the magical community." There was a haunted expression within Aamir's eyes that sent a shiver up Alex's spine. Aamir opened his mouth again, whispering softly. "It is your fault."

"What?" gasped Alex.

"We are forced to do this to keep the world safe from the Great Evil that was released by your kind, years ago," he hissed.

Alex flinched. "Released by *my* kind? A void was left behind because *your* kind wiped mine out! Don't you dare, Aamir—don't you dare," seethed Alex, his anger flaring.

A stillness spread out across Aamir's face, as the haunted, eerie stare disappeared, replaced with a sad, troubled expression. "Forgive me, Alex—I should not have spoken so," he said miserably.

It wasn't enough to calm Alex. "You say it is for the greater magical community, but who are these people? Who are these sacrifices protecting? If they're so interested, why don't they use their own essence?" he snapped.

"I don't think I can give you an answer that will satisfy you, Alex." Aamir turned his face away.

"Try," he pleaded.

"As far as I know… all this is done to protect the magical community and those in the world beyond it. The bottled magic taken from the linked havens holds the Great Evil at bay. There is an enormous force of power in this life essence—it is used to keep the havens hidden from this evil, whether by way of moving buildings and their inhabitants daily or shielding them in a realm of magical existence, like here. *This* is why the essence is taken—for all these purposes." He exhaled slowly. "The collected life essence is shared among the havens, so each one has a balanced quantity of magic to protect themselves and keep the chain linked, holding off the evil that would consume us all."

Alex listened intently, though it was as confusing as it was intriguing. Slowly, true understanding began to dawn. The shifting windows, the moving horizons, the crackling magic in the air all around them, in this peculiar world. It was all run on the stolen life essence. The knowledge made Alex feel sick.

"So why isn't Spellshadow more like this place?" Alex asked. He despised the beauty of Stillwater now that he knew the price of it, but he questioned why the Head hadn't tried to create a paradise to entice students to stay of their own free will. One caught more flies with honey than vinegar, after all.

Aamir smiled. "Even if Spellshadow were heaven, would you have really wanted to stay, knowing that some form of graduation was inevitable? The students here are all the sons and daughters of noble mages from the magical elite. Sacrifice is expected of them. They do not need to be forced to comply."

"How do you know that? About the students here being nobility?" Alex asked.

"I overheard that girl," he replied quickly—almost too quickly.

Suspicion plagued Alex as he leveled his gaze at Aamir, wondering if he had caught the man out in a lie. He could not shake the feeling that there were still residual threads tying Aamir to the Head and a continued loyalty to Spellshadow. It was clear to Alex that Aamir knew more than he was letting on, but the older boy was clever and knew how to evade the questions he didn't want to answer. Alex wondered if a day would come when he'd be able to get the whole truth. Unfortunately, today wasn't that day.

"Please, may we stop? I am tired," announced Aamir. "We can continue another time, when I am feeling stronger."

"We *will* continue this," Alex assured him.

Leaving Aamir alone, Alex headed up toward the top room of the tower with his head swimming. There was certainly plenty to think about. As he walked over to the open window to feel the cool rush of a breeze on his face, Alex's eyes rested upon the arena. Fear and horror twisted in his heart as he thought about all the ways in which the magical elite were taking the lives of so many young mages. Not just noble ones who expected it, but ones who never asked for it. The ones who were taken against their will. As the dread seeped into his bones, he found himself thinking about the other two havens that were out there somewhere, Kingstone Keep and Falleaf House. Were they being used for the same purpose?

As he gazed out at the empty arena, he realized the stakes had been raised, whether he liked it or not. His future, and that of his friends, had become about more than simply getting home—he owed the other young mages, at Spellshadow and Stillwater, and beyond, the same hope.

CHAPTER 13

I
T WAS EARLY EVENING, AND THE OTHERS HAD TURNED IN
for an early night. The events of the previous days had taken
their toll, and nobody seemed to feel much like socializing.

Alex had retreated upstairs to the bell tower and was watching the stars beginning to shine overhead when the sound of
strange, whispered voices floated up through the window on
the opposite side of the tower, distracting Alex. He rushed over
to the slim sill and peered cautiously down into the courtyard
below, trying to make out where the voices were coming from.
It was dark in the abandoned section of the villa, keeping the
speakers shrouded.

Only when a figure emerged from the shadows at the far
side of the courtyard did he see that it was the beautiful woman
from the night at the arena, though she was not quite as elegantly

dressed now as she had been then. She still wore a gown of sorts, in white and gold silk, but it was more modest than the gauzy, dazzling dress she had worn for the Ascension Ceremony. Her white hair, too, was held back simply with a plain silver band.

Her voice was stern and irritated as she became more visible in the dim evening light. She kept glancing furtively over her shoulder, as f to make sure she was alone. Alex's chest clenched in alarm as he saw her gaze turn briefly to the tower behind her. He hoped the others were being quiet in the rooms below, though he stopped short of calling out to them in case it drew any further attention from the glowering eyes of Princess Alypia. After a moment, she turned back around.

Alex's heart thundered as another figure stepped out into the courtyard—the speaker Alypia seemed to be snarling irritably at. Shrouded in dark robes that swamped the spindly body beneath, the long, skeletal fingers of the figure reached out toward her from the ends of wide sleeves, gesturing wildly. The hood of the robe was pushed backward to reveal a sunken, otherworldly face and lank, white hair that ran down the back of the speaker's skull in thinning strands. The new arrival was as familiar to Alex as his own reflection.

The Head had finally caught up.

Alex marveled silently at Natalie's skill in moving the portal; it had clearly taken the Head some time to physically reconnect with Stillwater, but he had done it—as Alex had known he eventually would.

It was strange to see the Head without the hood obscuring his face. He was a thin, skeletal creature with a vulture-like neck and a gleaming skull. A vision of the younger Head, given to him when he touched Finder's rotting skull, rushed into Alex's mind. The Head had looked younger then, standing in the sunlight with a yet-to-be ghostly Malachi Grey, his white hair thicker, his eyes a stormy blue instead of the eerie, dull hollows they were now. Alex wondered how the years could have wreaked such havoc on the man. Despite what had gone on between them, Alex couldn't help but think the Head looked almost pitiable.

The feeling only intensified as he watched the peculiarity in the Head's actions—the figure was talking in a soft voice, and the long, skeletal hands were held up in a gesture of surrender. The Head seemed almost cowed by the chastisement of the beautiful woman before him, and he shuffled uncomfortably beneath the stern gaze of her glittering eyes, which shifted from stunning to ice-cold in an instant. Alex didn't think he'd like to be on the receiving end of her displeasure either.

Listening more closely, he could make out some of what they were discussing, even though their voices were kept low. As far as he could tell, they were talking about the fight at Spellshadow and what had happened there. Alypia did not seem pleased by the outcome.

"Are you telling me you allowed your school to be overrun by a bunch of students?" she scoffed. "How could you let that happen? It's ridiculous—I could put my florist in charge of your school, and she'd run it better than you ever could. Every time I think you are about to prove yourself worthy, you go and do something stupid like this!" she barked as the Head shifted awkwardly. "I thought your little peculiarities were supposed to make you stronger, not weaker."

"It was out of my control, Alypia. I didn't have a choice after they managed to get their hands on Malachi. So I hardly think that is fair!" remarked the Head angrily, though Alypia didn't seem bothered by his sudden rage.

She brushed him off like an annoying bee. "You were an idiot to put your faith in that suck-up. He would have betrayed you the first chance he got, had he not been all see-through—don't think he wouldn't! You don't know the Greys like I know them. They're all snakes," she declared. "You're just going to have to find a suitable replacement. Pick someone and do to them what you did to Malachi Grey. That's if you can still remember how to do necromancy?" She raised her eyebrow, mocking him.

"And what if they can't do the job?" asked the Head sullenly. "I tried that with the new teacher—the one who escaped—but he couldn't do it; he couldn't seek out new recruits in the same way Malachi could. That's how this all happened! Professor Nagi couldn't manage it, so I had to go out there and find students myself. None of this would have been able to happen if I had been at the manor, but I wasn't—it really was out of my control," he insisted.

Alypia seemed bored. "And how is this any of my business? If you can't run your school, that has nothing to do with me."

"You know very well why it is your business, Alypia, so don't try and play the fool," he growled, his voice turning menacing. "Everyone knows that magic is dwindling in the nobles—without me and my school, you would soon struggle."

What did that mean? Alex wondered. Whatever it was, it had gotten Alypia's attention. Suddenly, she seemed more interested in what the Head had to say.

"Be that as it may, I still don't see why you have come to

me. I told you, I don't know where your escapees are. Until today, all I knew was there had been a disturbance at the portal. How was I to know you were in the throes of an uprising?" She shrugged. "Besides, my scouts didn't find anything when they went to check the portal, so who knows where they are by now."

Alex tensed at the mention of escapees, though he could feel the corners of his lips curving into a wry smile at the irony of it. If only the Head knew just how close he was.

"I didn't come to ask about the escapees—well, not entirely," the Head said. "I was wondering if I might borrow a student to turn into the new Finder instead."

Alypia looked horrified. "No—absolutely not! I won't spare another drop of noble blood on necromancy. It has to be one of yours."

The Head sighed. "Might I borrow some of the essence from the ceremony then, at the very least?"

"I'm afraid not, little brother. You said so yourself: with things the way they are, we at Stillwater need to hold onto what we have, while we have it. If you're short, you will have to start using your reserves—I know you have plenty," she stated. "In the meantime, I will ask the others if they have any they can spare, though I'm sure you're likely to get the same answer from them."

The conversation seemed to concern Alypia, especially the part about the dwindling magic, but something else entirely concerned Alex. He wasn't sure if he had misheard, but he was certain Alypia had just called the Head "little brother."

"Thank you," the Head muttered.

"Honestly, what would you do without your big sister?" Alypia smirked.

Alex definitely hadn't misheard that time. His stomach sank.

The resemblance was more believable, seeing them side by side, though time and looks had been far kinder to the beautiful Princess Alypia.

'Princess' Alypia? Alex paused in horrified thought. What did that mean about the Head? Was he magical royalty too? How could he be related to Alypia? Alex couldn't quite get his head around it. True, she had called him "little brother," but it didn't add up. The wrench in the works was Alex's strong, almost certain understanding that the Head was half-mage, half-Spellbreaker, an improbable hybrid of the two, so how could he be related to the pure mage royalty of Princess Alypia? Was the Head a mutant, Alex wondered, remembering when he had thought himself to be one. Or was it simpler than that—was the Head the result of a forbidden affair between a mage and a Spellbreaker, making him a half-sibling, perhaps, of Alypia? There were so many possibilities.

It made Alex think back to the portraits hanging on the walls in the Spellshadow ballroom, but there hadn't been one of the Head alongside them. Slowly, he counted them in his mind. There had been eight portraits on the wall, but there were supposed to be nine havens—or had been, once upon a time. Did that mean Spellshadow was the ninth haven and the Head the ninth royal, whose portrait should have been up there? It made a lot of sense to Alex that a hybrid would end up the black sheep of the family, especially a royal one. The figures in the portraits had all seemed fairly regal, with their crowns and tiaras twisting through the same white hair the two siblings shared. If the havens were manned by magical royals, Alex mused, it would explain why their portraits had been up in the school ballroom in the first place.

Somehow, in the confusing web of family ties, the Head was related to this stunning woman and seemed to be intimidated by her, which was something Alex had been sure he'd never see. The skeletal figure's fear of her was almost weirder than them being related. It made Alex fearful too. If someone as strong and powerful as the Head was scared of her, then there was definitely something to be scared of.

"I think we should go inside and discuss this further," Alypia announced. "These are things that should not be spoken of out in the open." Her eyes glanced uncertainly around, including up toward the tower, and Alex ducked down below the sill.

Peering tentatively back over the ledge, he watched as the duo quickly moved away, heading through one of the archways that led from the abandoned courtyard into the villa itself. Desperate for more information and seeing a prime opportunity before him, Alex tiptoed as silently as he could down the staircase, past the sleepers on each floor below. Turning the key in the lock and letting himself out, he knew what he had to do. He was going after them.

CHAPTER 14

A LEX SLIPPED OUT OF THE TOWER AND RAN ACROSS THE courtyard, following the path the two white-haired figures had just taken beneath the archway at the far end, into the school. The entrance wasn't lit from the outside, and he almost stumbled headfirst into the corridor as his foot connected with a narrow step that led up into the villa. Pain shot through his leg, but he quickly covered his mouth with his hand so as to muffle his groan. Once the ache had subsided a little, he carried on through the dim light, hoping there would be a torch at some point along the way. His toe throbbed dully as he crept through the shadows.

He knew it was an incredibly risky move, following the Head and the Headmistress. Glancing into the darkness behind him, he wondered what the others would say if they knew what he was up to. Undoubtedly, they'd want to know what the hell he thought he was doing. Doubt niggled in the back of his mind; it wasn't just himself he was putting in the firing line by going after the two figures. If the leaders of Spellshadow and Stillwater discovered him, he and his friends would be in a whole world of trouble.

For a moment, he thought about turning back, but the curiosity was simply too great. Alex was almost certain he would never get another opportunity like this, to observe the secret behaviors of the Head and Headmistress.

As he made his way farther into the villa, torches began to appear on the walls, lighting the way. *Good to see by, but also good for being seen,* Alex thought wryly. Hanging back slightly at each corner, he watched the duo as they continued to walk through a series of winding corridors, each one looking the same as the last. It worried Alex slightly, as he tried to memorize the route for the return trip; if he took one wrong turn, he knew he could find himself lost in the labyrinth of the place. The Headmistress, however, knew exactly where she was going as she marched elegantly ahead of her strange little brother, who hurried to keep up. Alypia had the limbs of a gazelle and took one stride for every two of the Head's.

Waiting tentatively at the corner of a shorter corridor, Alex ducked behind the wall as Alypia came to a halt in front of a door in the wall. He held his breath, wanting to peer around but not daring to. Instead, he listened for the sound of a key grating in the lock and the scuffle of footsteps on the stone as they entered the room beyond.

Once he was sure they had gone inside, Alex glanced down

the corridor, checking the coast was clear before he moved stealthily over to the door and crouched down beside it. As his head came level with the door's lock, his heart skipped a beat as the shrill, scraping sound of the key being turned on the other side rattled through his ear. They were separated only by the width of the wood the door was hewn from. He only hoped they would continue to be oblivious to his presence.

Hunkering down against the wall, Alex scanned the corridor leading away from left to right. The shadows made him nervous. Sitting in the very center of the hallway, he was extremely aware of how exposed he was. If somebody appeared at either end, they would see him silhouetted in the torchlight that beamed down from the two brackets outside the room he was keeping vigil over—and he couldn't use his anti-magic to try to conceal himself because Alypia and the Head were likely close enough to sense it.

Yet, to him, the risk still seemed worth the reward.

Turning toward the small keyhole, he pressed his eye up against it just in time to see Alypia walking away from the door, clutching a jangling set of keys on a large golden ring. Beyond the limited view of the spyhole, Alex could make out a fairly modest, windowless room—a study of some sort, he guessed, as he noted a series of well-stocked bookshelves along each wall and a broad, imposing marble desk which Alypia had just sat behind. On it were stacks of paper and an enormous yellow, blue, and green feather in a glass case, the brightly colored fronds curving over at the top toward a disc of gold plumage, like a peacock's feather, but much more exotic. There was a brown armchair to one side, in front of the desk, into which the

Head slowly sank down.

Within a few moments, Alex could hear the murmur of speech filling the air between them, but he couldn't make out what they were saying. With his senses on high alert, he scanned the corridor once again, praying that nobody would creep up on him from behind as he turned and pressed his ear to the keyhole instead of his eye, so as to eavesdrop better on their conversation.

"And what state is it in now?" he heard Alypia ask.

"It is still in utter disarray," the Head sighed. "There were some very powerful teachers at Spellshadow, as you well know, and they were not easy to overcome when they chose to move against me. I am still trying to fix what they have done. One decided to scramble the corridors to hide the students, and each time I am almost at them, she moves them again. I know she's getting weaker—she has to be. That amount of magic is enough to drain anyone of strength, but she's proving more difficult to wrangle than I ever imagined she would be. A tough old bird, that one."

Gaze, Alex thought sadly.

"You sound almost fond of her," scoffed Alypia.

"It is familiarity, not fondness, sister. Do not get them confused." There was a warning in the Head's voice, though Alex could not see his expression to confirm it. They had raised their voices slightly compared to the beginning of the conversation, and Alex turned to look back through, curiosity getting the better of him. From the keyhole, Alex could only make out the side of the Head's sunken face.

"Did you manage to instill loyalty in *any* of them?" she taunted.

The Head's long fingers picked agitatedly at the armrests. "Two. One is dead, and the other has caused me no end of trouble."

"In what respect?" asked Alypia, frowning.

A low, reluctant sigh rattled from the back of the Head's throat. "Professor Renmark made the reckless decision to kill a lot of the students, rather than round them up."

"How many?" Alypia growled. There was a twinge of annoyance in the curve of her delicate lips.

"Almost half, if I am not mistaken." The Head sagged in his chair.

"So much wasted essence! How could he be so foolish? How could *you* be so foolish?" she hissed. "Tell me you have at least punished the man?"

The Head shook his head. "Renmark is my only ally, sister."

"You are weak! You should never have been placed in charge!" she roared. "I told them so, but would they listen? I hope they're turning in their graves now!"

Goosebumps ran along Alex's skin as he beheld the fury of Alypia. He could feel it surging palpably from her, her eyes burning with rage. As much as the Head deserved everything he got, Alex did not envy him.

"I have made my mistakes, sister. I understand that, and I know I should have taken more care. But I am coming to you because I know when I need help. I *need* your assistance to restore the balance of the school so we can move on from this—so I can continue with my work to recruit students and replenish what Renmark destroyed. We need new students now more than ever," the Head pleaded, any trace of pride gone.

Behind the door, Alex seethed with anger. Those students who died in the library, at Renmark's hands, were more than an amenity in need of restocking. It wasn't like running out of salt at the grocery store. Yet that was how Alypia and the Head were discussing the young lives they wanted to snuff out for their own benefit. They were far more than 'wasted essence'—they were wasted lives, and it enraged Alex that they didn't care.

Alypia seemed to muse upon the Head's words for several moments, keeping her brother in suspense. Irritation still flashed in her eyes, but there was concern too.

Concern for their dwindling livestock, Alex thought bitterly.

"Very well. I shall select a team of guards and send them to you within the next few days, to help clean up the royal mess you have made. I trust you've managed to return the portal to its rightful place?" she said sourly.

"I wouldn't be here if I hadn't," the Head snapped.

Alypia glowered. "Do not get smart with me, little brother."

"Yes, the portal is back in place," he replied through gritted teeth. "Thank you for your kind gesture."

Alypia grinned smugly. "It's my pleasure. Hopefully we can get this whole disaster sorted out before anyone hears about it."

Alex listened in confusion as a stillness blanketed the room beyond. There was tension, as if one were waiting for the other to speak. The Head's nails scraped and tapped against the armchair's upholstery—a nervous tic, perhaps. Alex wasn't even in the room and Alypia was making him nervous.

"What is it? Do spit it out!" Alypia barked.

Alex was convinced he heard the sound of a gulp in the Head's thin neck.

"You have already done so much, but... there is the matter of my escaped students."

Alex watched as the Headmistress's face morphed into an expression of abject contempt. It was the kind of disdainful look that had to be practiced over a number of years, and she certainly seemed adept at it.

"Are you *entirely* incompetent?" she spat.

"I did mention that they had escaped."

"Oh, and that means I have to seek out these runaways for you?"

"I thought you might have seen them after the portal disappeared," the Head said quietly.

Alypia's expression was beyond contemptuous now. "And I said to you, I sent scouts out after detecting a disturbance near the portal. They came back with nothing. They saw no one. They had nothing to tell me of any intruders. All they said was that the portal was missing. I suspected something had happened to it, but I figured you'd come and find me if it were a problem—and here you are, with simply *awful* tales of missing teenagers."

"They are no ordinary teenagers, sister," replied the Head quickly.

Just then, the sound of feet pounding the flagstones sent a surge of panic through the crouched figure of Alex. His head snapped in the direction of the sound, and he waited for a figure to emerge from the shadows, but whoever they were, they didn't come up the corridor. Instead, Alex caught sight of the back of their head as they disappeared down another intersection, where they were swallowed up by the shadows.

Heart hammering, Alex turned back to the keyhole to see

what the Head had to say about him and his friends.

"That's ludicrous!" he heard Alypia cry, though he had missed the subject of her disbelief.

"I assure you, it is not—they are all very talented. Some of the finest students I have seen," remarked the Head. "They have Aamir with them too."

Alex froze.

"Who?" Alypia's eyes narrowed in curiosity.

"Professor Nagi."

Turning to see the Headmistress's reaction, Alex watched as her eyes began to glitter with something like surprise. Her mouth moved as she uttered something softly in the Head's direction, but Alex couldn't make it out. Hurriedly, he pressed his ear to the keyhole, but he was too late to hear what she had said. Still, her curious expression held some wonder in it that refreshed Alex's suspicions about his former friend. Had there been familiarity in her eyes, or had he imagined it?

"I'm afraid I have neither seen nor heard anything of these students. On that count, I can't help you—though I will be certain to return them, should they show up." Alypia smiled with a cold beauty. "Let's hope they haven't snuck back through to Spellshadow and taken over the place while you have been wasting time with me."

Alex cursed silently, realizing that might have been a good idea. Glancing back at the hallway, he wondered if there was any way that might still be possible, only to be called back to the keyhole by two words that made his blood run cold. His name.

"I don't think you understand the urgency, sister," insisted the Head. "We need to find Alex Webber."

"He can't be *that* talented. You should adjust your focus toward new students—these ones will find their way back once they're sick of running. Hunger is very persuasive, you know." She grinned icily.

Her brother shook his head. "You don't understand… Alex is not like the others. There is something special about him— something which might bring an end to all of our troubles, sister."

Alypia lifted her chin haughtily. "What do you mean?"

"I didn't realize at first, but there is something different about him. I think we can use it—if we could just find him, I'm sure we could," he stated firmly.

Alex wasn't sure whether Alypia was irked or intrigued, as a confusion of thought passed across her stunningly beautiful face. She seemed to want to make another comment about her brother's ineptitude, as the same cold, derisive look flashed for a moment in her eyes, but she held her tongue, clearly thinking better of it. There was more to it than the Head was letting on, and Alex could tell Alypia knew that. For some reason, the Head was only drip-feeding her information. Alex guessed it might be so the Head could have some credit for once: if he could do something tremendous, Alypia wouldn't be able to scorn him anymore.

As much as Alex found it hard to wrap his head around the idea that the two were siblings, they certainly acted like siblings. The power plays, the dirty looks, the taunting, the jeering—it reeked of familial ties.

Watching intently, he could see Alypia's mind working quickly as she assessed what her brother was telling her and what he was keeping from her. At no point did Alex hear the word 'Spellbreaker,' but that didn't mean the Headmistress hadn't guessed. There was a curiosity in her eyes at the mention of this new, special boy, but Alex clung to the reference of him ending all their troubles. It wasn't the first time he had heard himself pointed out as 'different' from the others, but he still wasn't sure why, specifically, they needed him and his alternative powers. The only thing he knew for certain was that it couldn't be for anything good. Nothing between Spellbreakers and mages ever was, based on the history books he had read.

"As I said, I will return them if I find them. Rest assured, I will keep an eye out, though with this much time gone by, I imagine they will be deep in a forest somewhere, scavenging. They will come out when they are hungry enough and tired enough—rats always do," Alypia purred with a glinting smile.

"You're certain they're not here?" asked the Head, gesturing around at the general expanse of Stillwater House.

Alypia's eyes narrowed. "*Nobody* could have gotten within the walls of this school without me knowing."

Alex felt uneasy as he heard the words fall from Alypia's lips. If that was the case, then how had they managed it? He didn't have much time to dwell on it as he saw Alypia rise from her seat.

"You're sure?" pressed the Head.

"You may go, little brother," she whispered, a threat lingering beneath the command. "Don't worry, I will send the promised guards to help you. Let us both hope you can keep things in better order once they have dealt with your mess."

She stalked toward the door, casting a shadow over the keyhole.

Alex ducked away and ran to the end of the corridor, slipping behind the wall just in time to hear the clunk of a heavy key unlocking the door. He didn't wait to watch them leave as he took off through the labyrinth of hallways, hoping he was going the right way.

As he reached the courtyard, he paused to catch his breath, praying he hadn't been seen by anyone on the journey back. It gave him time to wonder whether Alypia had been bluffing, or whether she genuinely wasn't aware of their presence inside Stillwater. She had seemed pretty sure they weren't there, but Alex didn't know how much could be trusted from her hypnotically beautiful face. Still, he hoped she had been telling the truth. The thought that Alypia *didn't* know bolstered his trust in Helena. Nobody had come after them yet, after all.

As he opened the tower door and headed up to the first floor, he was met by the soft sounds of sleeping people. Not wanting to wake them with his news, he made a promise to tell them what he had discovered as soon as he awoke the next day. As he climbed up to the bell tower, however, he saw a figure waiting on the steps.

"Where the hell have you been?" hissed the speaker.

Alex squinted into the dark. "Ellabell? Why aren't you asleep?"

She frowned. "I could say the same of you."

"Fair point."

She waited. "So—?"

"The Head was here—"

"What?!" she gasped, panic flashing in her sparkling blue eyes. "We have to get out of here!"

"Calm down," Alex shushed, slowly sitting down beside her on the stairs. "You'll wake the others."

"They need waking if the Head is here!" she hissed.

Boldly, Alex took her hand in his and squeezed it tightly. "There's nothing to worry about," he promised.

"What do you mean?" she breathed, her voice tight with anxiety.

"He was only here to talk—neither of them know anything," he assured. "I saw him talking in the courtyard with Princess Alypia, and I followed them. I listened for a while, and learned that the Headmistress doesn't know we're here yet. Helena, I think, has done as she promised. We're not in any immediate danger. If we were, do you think I wouldn't be down there like a shot, waking everyone up and getting them out of here?"

She frowned. "I suppose not."

"I wouldn't put you," he paused, his voice thick, "or anyone else in danger."

"Shouldn't you wake them up anyway—tell them what you've just told me?" she asked quietly, turning her face from his.

He shook his head. "It can wait until morning."

"I should get some sleep," she said, standing.

He nodded. "Me too."

"Sleep well, Alex," she sighed, dropping his hand as she walked toward the staircase leading down.

"Sweet dreams, Ellabell."

CHAPTER 15

H IS OWN DREAMS, HOWEVER, WERE NOT SWEET.
It was still dark when he awoke to the sound
of something moving across the other side of the
room—a soft, whispering sound like fabric brushing against the
stones beneath. Fear shot through his nerves as he peered into
the darkness, trying to see what was making the eerie noise. It
was such a quiet sound, like curtains flapping, but there were
no curtains on the windows. With a thundering pulse, he let his
eyes grow accustomed to the light.

Appearing in the dim glow of the room was a twisting mist
of shadow, outlined hazily by the sliver of moonlight glancing
in.

For a moment, a strange sense of hope gripped Alex's heart.
"Elias?" he whispered. Though a minute or two passed, Elias

did not appear. "Elias, is that you?" he tried again. Still, Elias did not show.

Alex frowned as the peculiar, smoke-like mist coiled and curled, flitting to and from the window and the staircase in a repetitive pattern. It paused longer on the top of the stairs, unfurling the edges of its inky mist toward the steps themselves, as if beckoning for Alex to follow.

"Elias?"

If it was the shadow-man, he was being particularly elusive in his game-playing. After coming through the portal, Alex wasn't even sure it could be Elias—could shadow-people move between portals like mortal beings? Remembering the dull red glow within the bottle the Head had held captive from Elias, Alex wondered if that might have given his shadow-guide freer rein of movement. With it no longer in the Head's possession, perhaps Elias could move away from the confines of Spellshadow Manor, if that had been what held him to the grounds. Or maybe that was the strange creature's fate, to live out his bizarre half-life in the shadows of that place. Alex wasn't sure, but this misty being definitely didn't look like Elias.

The flowing, dark gray vapor seemed more insistent, moving more quickly between the window and the staircase.

Brimming with curiosity, Alex got to his feet, wondering wryly if he would ever get a good night's sleep in this magical place. The twisting ball of energy seemed to perk up at Alex's sudden movement, and it shifted a short way down the stairs. Alex followed, keeping up with it as it swooped and swayed all the way down to the ground floor, past his sleeping friends, and out into the courtyard. He glanced at Ellabell as he passed her, hoping she wouldn't wake again and reprimand his recklessness. This one would be harder to explain than his excursion in pursuit of the Head and Headmistress.

Following the vapor across the courtyard and up into the school, Alex was forced to break into a tiptoed run as it darted with ease through the hallways and corridors, zipping this way and that, apparently knowing exactly where it wanted to go.

Although he was fearful of being caught, it was nice to be able to explore the school during the quietude of the night, when there was hardly anybody about. He was getting to see parts of the villa he had not yet encountered, though he quickly learned there were corridors upon corridors running beneath the beautiful veneer of the school—almost too many to put to memory. At night, though most of the hallways were deserted, some were patrolled by the odd guard, doing the rounds of their section of the school.

As he was about to move around the corner of one hallway, the dark, twisting mist of shadow flew at his face, pressing him back against the wall with icy tendrils that stole his breath away. It kept him pressed there, shrouded in shadow, until a beautiful guard with long auburn hair and bright green eyes passed by, oblivious to his presence in the corridor. It was a strange sort of magic—the kind within the wispy coils of the shadowy mist—making him feel cold and warm all at once, like being out in the snow too long. Each time it flung him against a wall, the bitter fronds took away his breath, winding him. It took some getting used to, but it kept him safe within the walls of the villa; not a soul saw him from within the camouflaged vapors of the shadow being.

Finally, after a seemingly endless array of hallways, it led him toward a large set of imposing, white double doors before disappearing behind them. It took some strength to push the doors open wide enough to get his body through, but eventually Alex stumbled in after the hazy entity.

He gaped when he saw the room beyond, though 'room' was something of an understatement. It was a library, far larger and far grander than any he had ever seen before, including the one at Spellshadow with its lofty towers. It was more beautiful, too, than a library had any right to be. The ceiling was painted in the most astonishing fresco, with billowing clouds and angelic cherubs flying on tiny wings, between the coiled, scaled bodies of dragons and the vibrant, exotic plumage of Thunderbirds. There were tasteful nudes, dancing in a circle, as golden magic spiraled upward from the center of their linked hands, and casually reclined figures watched from shimmering pools and flower-woven swings. Everything seemed peaceful and beautiful, and Alex couldn't take his eyes off it. There was something surprising in every corner, and that was only the roof of the library.

The rest was just as exquisite, with carved statues of ancient gods and goddesses, elegantly shaped, placed among the luxurious seating and in the stacks themselves, protecting the front rows with their sculpted arms extended. The floor was white marble, flecked with gold. The walls were hung with fine masterpieces in vast golden picture frames almost as intricately carved as the statues.

Glancing around, Alex was certain he could hear the sound of running water, and sure enough, there were four water features—one in the center of each wall. Crystal liquid flowed from the screaming mouths of sculpted marble birds, down to a foundation of rocks, where it trickled over the jagged edges and surged toward the center of the room, then connected with the other canals before disappearing into the floor to start the whole process again.

As jaw-dropping as the library was, it was the books that drew Alex's eye most keenly. He couldn't help but grin as he saw the endless stacks, filled with row upon row of tomes. The stacks rose up in broad towers on every wall, with smaller bookshelves scattered throughout the grand hall, and he could already tell there were more books here than there had been back at the manor.

He didn't have much more time to investigate, as the vaporous being seemed intent on taking him over to the farthest stack. Alex followed tentatively, climbing up a precarious set of ladders as the shadowy mist shot up toward the very top of the stack. Looking down, Alex felt queasy as the ground plummeted away beneath him, and he suddenly doubted the security of his footing on the slippery wooden rungs. It was a nervy climb, his palms sweaty as he reached the second highest landing of the far stack.

Here, the misty creature bobbed along, waiting for him. Alex trailed after the being, wondering why he had put his trust in a wispy bit of fog. Making a silent promise to be less impulsive in the future, he walked along the platform, not daring to glance over the balcony, until he reached a small clearing in the stacks, where a few comfortable-looking armchairs were scattered around a sleek reading table. Suddenly, the shadowy wisp disappeared in a puff of inky smoke, leaving Alex alone.

Anxiety rippled through Alex as he scanned the area, wondering why the creature had brought him here, only to evaporate. Perhaps it had simply wanted to show him the library, he thought, though he knew that was a little naïve. When would he learn that magical things couldn't always be trusted?

Alex waited for a while, expecting somebody to pounce at him from the shadows. When nobody did, he turned his mind to the exciting books all around him, reaching toward a few of the closest tomes and thumbing the spines with quiet admiration. As he read the titles of a few, he found himself squinting every so often into the darkness of the room to make sure there really was nobody watching him.

Panic shot through him once more as he realized there *was* something hiding in the darkness. It was in the corner of the reading cubby, appearing slowly. Alex peered closer, watching as a bundle of dark energy amassed—shapeless at first, but gaining definition as the moments passed. Alex stayed frozen to the spot, not sure whether to run and hide or stay and find out what it would become.

It didn't take long for Alex to realize that the being was undeniably Elias, though he wasn't as well-formed as he had been back at Spellshadow. There was a fractured quality to this iteration of Elias, as if he was physically trying to hold his various shadowy pieces together in one whole, and was struggling hopelessly. Alex wasn't sure if his shadow-guide might be stretching himself too far from where he was supposed to be, leading to this strange fragmentation.

"How do I look?" the shadowy figure quipped.

"Not your best," replied Alex.

"Charming! I drag myself all this way and *that* is the best you can do? At least lie to me—tell me you can see the stars in my eyes or something." He grinned, his galactic eyes twinkling. Alex could see that, although Elias was struggling to hold his physical self together, he had lost none of his usual, sarcastic humor. "I'd have thought you'd be better at compliments by now, what with that pretty little troublemaker of yours," he added, with a sour note.

Seeing Elias again, Alex couldn't decide how he felt. On the one hand, Elias had done them all a great service in their last battle against the Head, but on the other hand, he had to think about what Ellabell had told him, about believing Elias to be the shadow who attacked her. Regardless, he couldn't bear to hear the mention of Ellabell coming from Elias's mouth, not after what he might have done to her.

Alex's eyes hardened as he surveyed his shadowy acquaintance. There was an extra twinge of bitterness toward Elias that he hadn't felt before. There was distrust, too—more than he had ever felt toward the shadow being.

"And here I was, thinking you'd be happy to see me," teased Elias with a flash of inky teeth. "What's with the pouty face?"

Alex glared. "I didn't ask you to come."

Elias smiled. "Always so ungrateful!"

"I'm not ungrateful, I just—you keep putting me in harm's way," said Alex quietly.

A flash of amusement sparked across Elias's shifting features. "You're the one who followed a weird, wispy bit of smoke through a strange school, in the middle of the night, without second-guessing it," he purred. "I think it's because you missed me—you secretly hoped it was me, so off you ran, into the night, desperate to see your shadowy friend." An unnatural grin spread out across Elias's shadowy lips. "You didn't even wake up your little girlfriend to tell her you were off. I can't imagine she'd be pleased about that."

Alex's cheeks burned in anger. "Don't you dare," he seethed.

Elias's face morphed into something akin to a frown. "Temper, temper—where's all this hostility coming from? I put up a decent fight back there so you had time to get free, and here is my thanks," he sighed, a hint of annoyance creeping into his strangely distant voice.

"You did it all for yourself!" snapped Alex.

Menace glittered in Elias's endlessly dark eyes. "What?" he whispered.

"You did it all for yourself," repeated Alex, more quietly.

Elias gave a bitter laugh. "None of this is for me," he said simply.

"Liar," Alex muttered.

"If you would begrudge me my own life essence, perhaps you are not the man I thought you were," said Elias sadly. "But that was not why—call it an unexpected surprise. I want you to succeed, Alex. That is all I have wanted and continue to want."

"Then why hurt those I... care for?" demanded Alex, choosing his words carefully. Without Elias, Alex knew he'd be at square one; the shadow being had aided in helping him learn of his heritage, in helping challenge the Head, in so many things, but Alex was struggling to forget what Ellabell had said.

Elias's eyes glittered with curiosity. "I don't follow?"

151

"Why did you attack Ellabell the way you did?" he ventured solemnly.

For a moment, silence stretched between the shadow-man and his acolyte. Alex could see the thought gathering beneath the shifting, starry contours of Elias's face, now even harder to pin down with his fragmenting form. As the silence continued, Alex convinced himself Elias was going to deny it. It was the shadow-man's way.

"I was going to lie," admitted Elias, "but I know you wouldn't believe me."

"So you did it?" Alex gasped. The truth was harder than the lie.

Elias moved his head in what Alex supposed to be a nod. "I did, but I have my reasons."

"What possible reason could you have had?" spat Alex.

"Well, if you'd let me finish, you'd know," quipped Elias, growing irritated. The shadow-man waited, the impossible oblivion of his eyes surveying Alex haughtily, like a teacher waiting for a class to quiet down.

"Go on," said Alex reluctantly.

Elias smiled, flashing his inky teeth, though Alex wasn't sure it was appropriate. "I did it because that curly-haired nuisance was reaching for a very dangerous book on dark magic."

Alex raised an eyebrow, unimpressed.

"You're telling me books can't be dangerous? You've seen the damage those sorts of books can do," he whispered with a sly grin.

Alex frowned. "What do you mean?"

Elias sighed. "You're not very sharp today, Webber—this

place has made you so slow," he remarked, pulling a rude face. "That other one of yours. The French one."

"She's not my 'other one,'" muttered Alex defensively.

Elias grinned with amusement. "I meant your other *friend*— I've no idea what you're referring to," he mocked playfully, apparently delighting in Alex's discomfort.

"What about her?"

"She has been sick, right?"

Alex nodded slowly.

"You're not stupid, Alex. Well, not all the time," goaded Elias. "You've been told about magic that moves things. Now piece it together. I will *not* be getting my silver platter out today!"

Alex frowned as fear gripped him. He looked to Elias for further confirmation of the suspicions he'd had about Natalie, but the shifting, shadowy features gave nothing away. He loathed how vague Elias could be.

"It takes a lot of magic?" ventured Alex.

Elias moved the misty fronds of what should have been hands together in a silent, mocking clap. Seemingly, Elias's favorite gesture. It irked Alex every time, which he guessed was the point.

"She used life magic?" he asked, wanting his thoughts confirmed once and for all.

"Ding, ding, ding! Give the boy a prize—how about the giant hippo for the lucky lady?" Elias smirked, his shadowy mouth curving up into an eerie smile.

"But she got better."

Elias rolled his mysterious eyes in exasperation. "So, as long as it doesn't kill you, that means it's okay? I think I'm some sort of proof that's not true." A flash of something strange moved across his face, as if he had said something he hadn't intended to, but the expression disappeared as quickly as it had appeared. "Anyway, that's not the point. I'm just saying, books can be dangerous. Your power-hungry pal read that spell in a book and made herself ill because of it. Mind you, she was doing it to save you all, so maybe we shouldn't be too hard on her," he retorted. "And hey, she's okay now, so that spell wasn't any of the really, really bad stuff—but this stuff, in that book, is stuff you don't want anyone you care about touching."

"How do you know what's in it?" asked Alex.

Elias paused. "I just know," he breathed, his voice suddenly drenched in a sadness so heartrending, Alex wasn't sure he could take it. From within the starry, shadowy form of Elias, a thousand echoed sorrows seemed to surge forward, whispering all around Alex's head, creeping through him with shivering tendrils, until they had seeped into every cell within his body. "I know, firsthand, what that book can do, and I didn't want her to have it."

Elias made me, and I am Elias, the universe within the shadow-man whispered.

Alex wasn't sure if Elias meant he was trying to stop Ellabell from reaching for a book on strong, terrible magic in order to protect her from it, or because he simply didn't want anyone to know about such dark magic. As much as his suspicions told him it was the latter, there was an internal battle that Alex couldn't balance. It was the sadness in Elias's voice that made him think twice about the shadow-man's intentions with the book—the sound haunted him. Yet, he could neither forget nor forgive what Elias had done to Ellabell. No matter what the reason, there was no excuse for the bruising and trauma that girl had suffered. Anger flared inside him once more.

"You can't win me over with your sob stories, Elias. What you did to Ellabell was unforgivable. There were ways you could have done it that didn't involve attacking her, but you chose violence and fear. You use them as weapons, to control people—it's cruel and twisted, like you!" he shot back.

Elias's eyes flashed with anger. "After all I have done? I expected better from you, Spellbreaker. Everyone turns their back on Elias, blinded by the tattle-tales of others," he seethed, his supernatural voice making Alex's bones tremble.

"You hurt her, for no reason but to keep her from saying something to me," Alex hissed, his heart pounding. He thought of how Ellabell had avoided him all those weeks after the attack, of the bruises on her face, and he wanted to tear Elias to pieces. The shadowy figure wasn't nearly so fearsome when he was struggling to hold himself together. Alex's anger seemed to break him apart much faster, somehow. Rippling fronds snaked away from Elias's body, fragmenting it sliver by sliver.

"I protect you, Alex—I help and I serve and I get stabbed in the back, every time," breathed Elias, his voice somehow omnipresent. The black pools of his eyes glimmered with starry grief and sparking rage. "I didn't mean to hurt her; I just wanted to stop her. It may have escaped your notice, but my motor skills aren't exactly on point." He flapped his shadowy arms almost comically, though Alex was in no mood for amusement. "What I'm saying is, I can't always control what I do or how I do it—touch isn't always easy, and sometimes I can overdo it, by accident. I know you won't believe me, but I do not lie. If you knew what that book did, you would not be so quick to speak this way to me—you ungrateful little boy." He paused, his inky teeth curled up in a grimace. "Well, when you're no longer blinded by love, you'll realize the mistake you have made. You'll see—you will need me, Alex. You *will* need me."

As Elias said the last four words, his figure became whole for just a moment, more human than Alex had ever seen the shadow-man's form, before he disappeared in a snap of swirling black mist.

As Alex watched the space where Elias had been, he wondered where the shadow-man had gone. Had he gone back to Spellshadow, or was he still within the walls of Stillwater? Alex wasn't sure if he'd ever find out, after that terse, cold ending.

Though he hated to admit it, Alex had a feeling Elias was right. It wasn't a case of 'will need'—Alex *did* need Elias. After all, without access to the Head or Elias's books, Alex was back to square one as far as his heritage, his abilities, and his next move were concerned. Elias knew things. Elias had nudged Alex in the right direction, at every turn. Then there was Alex's plan to see what he could do with the black bottles, and how to get the others home—the only one with access to that sort of information was Elias. The whys and hows of the schools and the magical world were all within Elias's grasp; of that Alex was certain. They were not, however, within Alex's grasp.

"I *do* need you... I hate that I do," whispered Alex, feeling entirely alone in the empty, still library.

CHAPTER 16

D EVOID OF PEOPLE, THE LIBRARY SEEMED MORE CREEPY
than beautiful. Part of Alex wanted the shadowy shape
of Elias to return, if only for some company. The route
back toward the bell tower was foggy in his mind, and though
the security of it tempted him, he knew he couldn't simply run
from the opportunity he had been given. All around him, row
upon row of untapped knowledge met his eyes. Bitterly, he knew
he had Elias to thank for this, yet again. Even if the shadow-man
had ulterior motives, he still managed to put Alex on the right
track.

The library was brimming with new information—knowledge that might not have been available at Spellshadow. Perhaps,
Alex thought, noble mages were given more exciting things to
learn. It would certainly account for their superior ability.

Staring down the walkway to make sure he truly was alone, Alex was surprised to see an enormous book at the end of the platform, opened atop a wooden lectern. He walked toward it, feeling a sense of familiarity as he realized what it was. From the size and well-thumbed pages, it could be none other than Stillwater House's version of the Index, containing all the authors and titles of the books that filled the vast room.

Intrigued by the prospect of what lay within, his mind wondering about havens and Spellbreakers, much like the last time he stood in front of one of these, he decided to see if the Stillwater Index would be more forthcoming with information. Maybe it wasn't just spells and advanced magic that the noble students had better access to, but history as well.

Heaving the pages to 'H' and 'S' respectively, Alex was pleasantly surprised to see there wasn't just one or two, but many books on both subjects. Too many to read in just one evening, he thought wryly, wondering if he'd have another opportunity to come and absorb the library's riches. No matter what happened, he knew he'd have to try. This place was a goldmine.

A curious thought came to him as he was tracing a finger down the dusty page, searching the list on Spellbreakers. Carefully, he lifted the Index pages until he reached the end of the 'W' section, hoping nobody heard the hefty slam as the weightier side fell back toward the plinth. His eyes ran down the browned page, until he saw the words he had been hoping to see: *Leander Wyvern*. He couldn't believe it.

Is this why Elias led me here? he wondered.

Even when he wasn't physically present, the shadow-guide was somehow helping. Hastily, Alex flipped back through the

Index and tried to memorize as many of the numbers as he could, in order to check the stacks for the corresponding books. Fortunately, the system was much the same as in any library. Even in the magical world, books and libraries didn't change.

Darting along the walkway and up to the top floor, he followed a short passageway down to the very back shelves and shuffled along a narrow set of bookcases before he found the number he was looking for. Half-expecting it to be gone, like the censored sections at Spellshadow, he couldn't contain his excitement as his hand closed around the leather-bound spine. It was there. Bringing it down, cradling it in his hands, he brushed off a thick layer of dust as he read the title: *Leander Wyvern, a Biography*. A whole book dedicated to the man whose notebook Alex possessed. It was almost too good to be true. Alex flicked through the first few pages, making sure it wasn't a hoax. To his delight, every page was filled with text. So far, so good.

Tucking it under his arm, he ran along walkways and climbed up and down ladders, in search of more. Adding to his collection, he picked up a book on havens entitled, rather helpfully, *A Comprehensive Guide to the Havens*, which seemed promising, followed by an entry entitled *Spellbreaker Spells and How to Defend Against Them*. Suddenly, the fact that the books were even here made more sense. If the students at Stillwater were to truly be the best, they had to know the ins and outs of their sworn enemies, even if they had died out decades ago. Strangely, it reminded Alex of a faded motivational poster stuck up on a wall at his old high school: "Fail to Prepare, Prepare to Fail." He supposed that was why they read these books—to prepare, on the off-chance they should ever come up against a Spellbreaker.

Little did they know, the book could also be useful *for* a Spellbreaker, should he get his hands on it. Alex grinned, running his thumb over the embossed words, hoping it might give him some ideas for advanced spells he might use to fight mages. It was about time he came up with some new material.

Along another set of shelves, he came across a bright green tome called *Spellbreaker Lineages* and beside it, to his sardonic amusement, a book entitled *The Royal Households*. It hadn't been on his list of titles to pick up, but in flicking through the contents page, it looked as if it might be useful. As far as Alex could tell, it was a detailed history of the royal mages. Intrigued, he added it to his growing stack, figuring it might give him some insight into the beautiful, white-haired woman and the mysterious hybrid of the Head, who was somehow related to that exquisite creature. He wondered hopefully if there might be a passage inside the book that explained how that had come to be.

With a decent haul in his hands, Alex moved back toward one of the small reading areas and set the books out on the sleek, circular table in front of him. Conscious of how exposed he was, out in the open of the empty library, he decided he ought to set up a perimeter around himself, to hide his work from prying eyes. Slowly, he let the twisting tendrils of silver and black coil around his fingers, before sending them out to form a thin, crackling sheet of anti-magic around him. It thrummed quietly in the air as he constructed a rudimentary shield around himself, making sure it wasn't detectable as he dimmed its glow to an almost imperceptible sheen. It worked like a two-way mirror; he could see out, but nobody could see in—or so he hoped. If anyone came too close to the barrier, he knew they'd be able to sense it, but he hoped he'd be able to dart into the stacks and hide before that happened.

Once he was sure he wasn't visible to anyone who might catch sight of him on the walkway, he reached out and picked up the biography of Leander Wyvern, desperate to start with the history of the Spellbreaker he felt he almost knew, from reading the words of his final days and learning of his fate. It wasn't a huge book, but Alex could not quell the excitement he felt for what might be inside. Taking a deep breath, he opened it.

It began with Leander's heritage and made mention of the six Great Houses of the Spellbreakers, one of which was the House of Wyvern. Reading the other, familiar names, Alex couldn't help thinking about his own, unknown father, and hoping that somehow he had belonged to one of those Great Houses. Of course, there were hundreds of other Spellbreaker lines, but Alex wanted, secretly, for his father to have been from one of the Great ones, if only to make his own lineage more exciting.

He read through a bit more of Leander's heritage, but it was information Alex had already learned. As he flipped through page after page, a sinking feeling began to creep through him, that there wasn't much in the biography he didn't already know. That was the problem with one-sided history—there was only ever one account, repeated over and over again.

For a moment, Alex thought about giving up and reading something else, but he persevered, scanning each chapter for something new. It was only as he came to the back few pages of the book that the read started to bear fruit, growing a little more colorful as it delved into the personal life of Leander Wyvern. Alex raised an eyebrow as he scanned over a section that remarked upon Leander's penchant for non-magical women. Apparently, he was known to have a strong affection for these ordinary women, despite it being frowned upon to fraternize with people of non-magical origins.

Alex wasn't exactly surprised by this bigoted mindset, though it made him think of Helena's warning comments about others in the villa not being so welcoming of outsiders—perhaps some noble mages still upheld the values of the past, he thought, as the biography said.

It made him smile to think of the heroic Spellbreaker as something of a Casanova, wooing whomever he pleased, regardless of what they were. Intrigued by this new facet to Leander's character, Alex read on:

Though he never married, it is thought Leander Wyvern had a favored mistress from the non-magical world; however, the rumors have never been confirmed and the woman has never been identified. Whether it was a tale spread simply to mar the man's reputation, or it was the very real truth of a notorious Lothario, we will never know. What we do know is, he was an eligible Spellbreaker in his time: a man of considerable fortune, a heroic warrior with great skill on the battlefield, the heir to the House of Wyvern, and a tall, powerful, genetically blessed individual. He certainly made the ladies swoon wherever he went, yet remained a bachelor until his death upon the Fields of Sorrow in 1908. No woman ever garnered a proposal from the legendary Spellbreaker—at least not as far as history is concerned. If there was a woman out there who captured the heart of Leander Wyvern, her name died with him.

Alex frowned, re-reading the part about Leander's love of non-magical women. It brought to mind unspoken thoughts about Alex's heritage and the anomaly of his own bloodline. He had the power of a Spellbreaker, there was physical evidence of that, but, as far as he knew, his mother wasn't one and nor were his grandparents. That meant the Spellbreaker abilities *had* to have come from his father's side, but Alex didn't know what had gone on with his father. He knew his father wasn't around anymore, but what had actually happened to him was something his mother had never mentioned, because as soon as Alex had begun to ask, she had broken down in tears, silencing the subject from Alex's lips. At least from that, Alex could guess it hadn't been something good, though he was still in the dark about the specifics.

Confusion itched at the back of Alex's mind as he dwelt upon his father and the root cause of his powers. With it, memories of the *Fields of Sorrow* came rushing back, only adding to the mystery. In the accounts of the *Fields of Sorrow* he had read and heard, it was assured that every single Spellbreaker in existence had been wiped from the face of the earth. It was written in black and white. *Every* Spellbreaker. The extinction of a race. Yet he was alive and he was a Spellbreaker; he had the anti-magic to prove it.

Curiously, he wondered if it might be that his father, and his father before him, and his father before him, all the way back to 1908, were the product of a union between a Spellbreaker and a non-magical person? Perhaps that was the loophole to his continued existence; if an ordinary woman had been pregnant with a Spellbreaker child at the time of the final battle, then truly, every *living* Spellbreaker would have been wiped out on that day of absolute elimination. But there would have been a child, with

Spellbreaker potential, yet to be born.

It was food for thought, and the idea made Alex tremble with giddy anticipation, though there was disappointment in the knowledge he could never really have it confirmed. All those who might have been able to corroborate it were dead.

Suddenly, Alex became aware of soft footfalls creeping below. He had been so absorbed in the book that he hadn't heard them advancing, until now. Crawling cautiously over to the very edge of the walkway, he saw shadowy figures moving across the marble floor of the library, stealthily heading for the stacks. For him, no doubt.

Panic shot through Alex's body as he stepped back and looked at the books spread out across the table. If he left the books, the creeping guards beneath would undoubtedly suspect a trespasser in their midst. Hurriedly, Alex shoved the tomes back among the shelves, though he made sure to grab the one text he really wanted to keep—the Wyvern biography. But when he looked down at the book beneath his arm, he realized he had made a mistake. He had grabbed *The Royal Households* instead.

The footsteps below quickened, and Alex cursed under his breath. It was too late to switch out the books. He turned and struggled to climb up to the top of the closest stack, only to feel Leander Wyvern's notebook slip out of its familiar spot in his back pocket and land with a smack on the marble floor.

Everything went still.

Fraught with dread, Alex sent out a snaking tendril of anti-magic, copying the floating spell he had seen Helena do with Aamir, as he maneuvered the book into his outstretched hand. Pushing it firmly back into his pocket, he scrambled up the rest of the stack, before rolling along the top surface into a crevice in the wall behind it. Swiftly, he sent up another camouflage barrier around himself, just in case any of the assailants decided to peep over the very top shelf. He had just managed to dim the shield to a barely discernible sheet of anti-magic when he heard the creak of the ladder, leading up to the platform he was on. Alex's heart was pounding, but it was his labored, panicked breathing he was worried about. He was convinced they would be able to hear it, as he sensed the approach of figures below.

They were whispering in low, refined voices, and Alex could hear the scrape and thud of moving furniture as they pushed the table and armchairs to one side, searching for any sign of recent occupation. Alex had pushed his reading selections far back into the stacks, but he couldn't help but feel a shiver of fear that the lurkers would somehow find the books and, in seeing titles about havens and Spellbreakers, would presume the reader to be an intruder.

The Royal Households book dug into Alex's side as he waited and tried to hold his breath, his cheeks reddening and his eyes bulging.

The investigators seemed to take forever, rustling pages and shifting objects, making Alex's pulse race even faster every time they came too close, but eventually he heard the subtle sound of them disbanding. The ladder creaked, signaling their departure, but even after they had gone, he didn't dare to move; he stayed there, staring up at the ceiling of the library, for what seemed like hours.

Only when enough time had passed did he chance a peek at the walkway below. Scanning the area briefly for any changes, he caught sight of several small objects flashing at the corners of the platform, that had not been there before. Squinting for a better look, he couldn't work out what they were, but he knew the searchers had placed them there for a reason. A recollection flashed in his mind; they looked a lot like the clockwork traps he had read about in a book Ellabell had recommended to him once. If that's what they were, thought Alex, he'd be caught the moment he set foot on the ground.

Rolling back into the crevice, he waited, trying to come up with a solution from his hiding place. Suddenly, he remembered the clockwork mouse, still buried in the papery depths of his pockets. He had transferred it from his Spellshadow pants into his Stillwater ones, almost without thinking; he had grown so used to the weight and feel of it that he had almost forgotten it was there.

Retrieving it, he held the delicate, metal creature in his hand, knowing the message he needed it to carry. Without paper, it was going to be difficult, but he was hopeful the mouse would let the others know what to do.

Cupping his hands around the intricate, detailed clockwork, he let his anti-magic flow into the tiny being, feeling the cogs begin to whirr and the metal eyes light up with a silvery glow, as he willed it to find Helena and bring her back to where he was hiding. As he set it down on the wooden shelf-top, he wasn't sure if it would work, but within seconds the mouse had scurried off. Staring back up at the ceiling, he hoped it would. Otherwise, he would never be leaving this library prison.

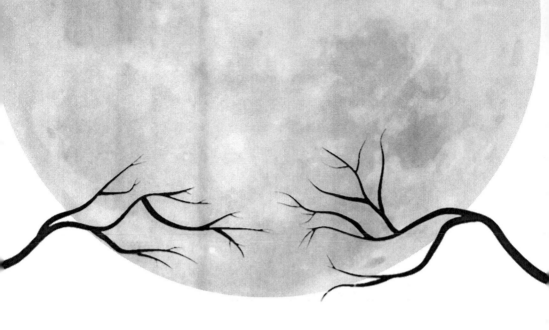

CHAPTER 17

AS THE SUN CAME UP, GLOWING WITH HAZY WARMTH
through the huge library windows, the world around
Alex fizzed with chaos. It seemed the news had
traveled fast, and Stillwater had gone on high alert following the
suspicion that there was an intruder among their ranks. With
dwindling optimism, Alex awaited Helena's assistance, though
he was beginning to wonder if it was ever coming.

From his perch in the library, he listened to the hushed,
worried whispers of students talking about the intruder, all of
them oblivious to his presence. Each time someone passed close
to where he lay, his ears pricked up with curiosity. There was a
childish glee in eavesdropping unseen, Alex thought, although
the stakes of him being discovered were somewhat higher than
when he was a kid.

"Aurelia told me the guards were sent out last night to investigate some kind of disturbance," a pretty female voice said.

"Did they find anything?" replied a rich baritone that made Alex immediately picture a musclehead with a chiseled jaw and perfect teeth.

"Not really," the girl sighed. "But I think there *is* someone on the loose, although heaven knows where they've come from or what they're doing here in the first place. Everyone is talking about it!"

"Well, what if there's more than one? There could be a handful of intruders lurking around, for all we know. A whole flock of them."

"Don't joke about that, Lars! It's scary."

Many students had colorful guesses about the intruder's motives, and Alex smiled as he listened to the long list of what he might be. Some said the intruder was an escaped prisoner from a neighboring community; others said it was the crazed remnant of a student who had survived their Gifting Ceremony or a spurned ex-lover of the beautiful Princess Alypia who had come in search of revenge for a broken heart. Alex sensed this last speaker had read one too many romance novels, but it amused him nonetheless. Another said it was probably just Siren Mave, messing around, setting off alarms by accident as she wandered the school in the middle of the night. This last one caught Alex's attention, making him wonder how they knew who she was. Surely, it had to be the same toady woman as the one from Spellshadow—there couldn't be too many women with a name like that.

The day stretched on. Alex's muscles ached, and his eyes

itched. He didn't dare fall asleep in case he rolled off the bookshelf, so he stayed awake, his body cramped into the shallow recess of the wall. Eventually, every appendage felt numb. From his dim hiding spot, he watched as the bright sunlight moved across the sky, deepening to a burnished orange glow as the day began the slow move toward sunset.

Around early evening, when all of the other students had abandoned their studies in pursuit of more pleasurable activities, Alex heard a creak on the ladders.

"Alex?" whispered Helena.

Alex breathed a heavy sigh of relief as he rolled across to the edge of the stack and gazed down. "Up here!"

His muscles had seized after so long spent in one position, and the sudden movement of his roll along the bookshelf sent jolts of dull pain ricocheting through his nervous system. Seeing Helena looking up at him, he was more than pleased to see her; he was hungry and thirsty, and she had come to get him out of there. Scanning the walkway, Alex noticed that the clockwork traps were no longer there—Helena must have disabled them, he presumed, as he shuffled his body toward the edge.

He clambered awkwardly back down, before trying to jiggle some life back into his muscles as he stretched and flexed, steadily regaining the feeling in his toes and fingers.

Helena held up the glinting mechanical mouse. "I believe this is yours?"

Alex grinned. "I'm just glad it worked," he said, taking it from her.

"It was Ellabell who told me about it, actually," she explained, as she waited for Alex to stop his latest stretch.

Alex frowned. "Ellabell?"

She nodded. "Yeah, it went to her, and she figured you'd sent it because you were in trouble—trouble seems to follow you, doesn't it?" she mused, though there didn't seem to be any malice in her words. It was merely a truthful observation; trouble *did* seem to follow him. Or maybe he just followed trouble.

Alex smiled with a touch of embarrassment, realizing it must have been Ellabell he was thinking of when he sent the message, instead of Helena. Still, he was glad Ellabell had managed to decipher his message and pass it on to Helena, though he knew he'd definitely be in for a reprimand when he got back to the tower. Not that he'd be able to blame Ellabell; he'd put them all at risk.

"I suppose." Alex shrugged. "Thanks for coming to get me—I don't know how long I could've lasted up there."

"You should thank the mouse," she quipped. "That's quite the little piece of clockwork. Did you make it?"

Alex shook his head, lifting the mouse to his eye-line. "Sadly not. The magic is mine, though."

"I meant to ask you about that. How come it has that strange color running through it?" Helena asked, trying to get a closer look at the inner workings of the creature.

Alex shoved the mouse swiftly into his pocket, keeping his hand over it as he sucked the anti-magic out. "I changed it to that color so it would blend into the clockwork better."

Helena frowned, and Alex could tell she wasn't entirely convinced.

"Well, whoever made it must have been very skilled," she said finally, the frown lifting. "We'd better go," she announced as she led the way toward the banister of the walkway and rested her palms on it, readying herself to jump over the edge. She paused as she saw Alex's hesitation.

"I'll take the ladder," he insisted.

She flashed him a puzzled expression. "Why?" she said flatly.

He shrugged. "It's embarrassing."

"What do you mean?"

He shook his head. "I can't say—it's stupid."

"What's the matter, Alex? We don't have time for this," she muttered, looking displeased.

"I'm afraid of heights," he fibbed, hoping she'd believe him.

Amusement glittered in her striking gold eyes. "You're afraid of heights?"

"It's not funny."

She grinned. "Fine. You take the ladder, and I'll see you at the bottom."

He watched as she soared over the banister and landed gracefully on the floor below. It was something Alex wasn't sure he'd ever be ready to try, anti-magically speaking.

Trying not to look past his feet, he climbed back down from the lofty heights of the second highest platform, and didn't exhale until he reached the ground, where Helena was waiting for him, her foot tapping impatiently on the gold-flecked marble.

They hurried across the library toward the door, where Helena held her palm up in a gesture that made Alex stop. He did so, and she peered out into the corridor beyond, ensuring that the coast was clear. Then she slipped out. Alex followed, not wanting her to get too far ahead as she raced through the hallways, probably knowing the layout of the place like the back of her hand.

"Excuse me, Helena!" a gruff voice called out.

Helena skidded to a stop and shoved Alex into a doorway with a frantic look. Alex pressed himself flat against the doorframe, hoping it would keep him hidden from view. He'd have thrown up a shield to hide himself better, but he knew he didn't have time to dim it down to the level he needed. The shadows would have to do. He heard the jingle of keys as the man approached—a guard, most likely. Alex swallowed hard.

"Where are you headed?" the guard asked Helena.

"Oh, I'm just heading out to the lake. It's such a beautiful night," she replied casually, and Alex was sure she was wearing that persuasively cheerful grin of hers.

"It is indeed!" the guard replied. "Well, be safe. There's an intruder on the loose, you know. Wouldn't want your—"

"I'll be sure to keep an eye out. I appreciate your kind thoughts," Helena interrupted.

"Of course. Good night to you then, my lady," the guard said congenially.

"Good night!"

Everything about these people is elegant, he mused, as he hid in a doorway with his imperceptible camouflaging shield around him. Helena appeared in front of him again, her smile both relieved and giddy.

"Let's go!" she whispered.

Eventually, after what seemed like a much longer journey than the one he had taken with Elias's misty messenger, they reached the familiar gloom of the courtyard, and the tower spiraling up in the corner. Walking through the front door, Alex was anxious about the reaction he was likely to get. He had been reckless, he knew he had, but for a good cause.

He needn't have worried. As soon as he was over the threshold, he felt Ellabell's arms around him as she rushed to hug him. She held his face as she looked him over, her expression showing she was just glad to see he was okay.

"Don't you *ever* worry us like that again!" she chastised.

Glancing around at the others, he saw similar expressions on their faces. Worry, mainly, mixed with a relief to see him returned to them in one piece.

"You really had us going there, man," said Jari with a nervous smile. "When we woke up and you weren't in the tower, we knew something was up, but we couldn't just go out looking in the daylight for you—we'd have been caught like *that*." He snapped his fingers loudly. "We thought we'd lost you, dude."

Natalie nodded. "Yes—we thought somebody had, perhaps, taken you in the night. We were so worried, Alex," she whispered, her brow creased.

Alex felt a twist of guilt for putting them through that. Natalie wasn't exactly wrong, either. Somebody *had* come for him in the night, just not who they might have expected. He thought about telling them about the shadow-man, but he felt the prickle of Elias's displeasure shivering up his spine as he came to say the name aloud.

I thought we were over this, Alex grimaced to himself, but he held his tongue.

"Yeah—but then when that mouse appeared, I knew it had to be a sign from you, that you needed help. It kept butting against the front door, like it wanted me to follow, but I knew

I couldn't," explained Ellabell, diverting Alex's attention away from thoughts of Elias. "So when Helena came with food, I told her about the mouse and how you were missing, and suggested she follow it."

"Quick thinking on her part," Helena nodded as she stepped into the room. "You could see the mouse wanted to go somewhere, so I followed it as far as the library. I could never have gotten you out in broad daylight, so I had to wait until evening, when it was quiet. Sorry about that." She grinned.

"I'm just glad you found me," Alex said.

"It's not me you should be thanking," reminded Helena pointedly.

Alex nodded. "Of course—sorry. Thank you, Ellabell." He gazed at her with slightly bashful gratitude.

She shrugged it off. "I say the mouse is the hero here," she beamed, though her freckled cheeks had flushed ever so slightly, and her blue eyes had an added sparkle to them.

There was an overall sense of relief in the tower, to have Alex back in the fold. Even Aamir seemed happy to see him. In fact, the older boy seemed much happier in general, as if he had regained some of his former energy in Alex's absence. The lines of exhaustion that had been etched onto his face were softening, with more of the familiar Aamir returning to the surface. Life had begun to shine again in formerly vacant eyes, and it was having much the same effect on Jari, who seemed to be brimming with energy. The younger boy stood grinning beside Aamir, nudging him in the arm as he whispered something into the older boy's ear.

"People in glass houses, Jari Petra," teased Aamir, a jovial smile curving at his lips.

Jari scowled playfully. "Why does everyone keep saying that?"

"Because it's true—the amount of damage control I have had to do for you. You have no idea how much magic it took to make a thousand roses disappear." He chuckled softly.

Alex smiled as he watched the two young men bantering like they used to, even if he had been the butt of the whispered joke. It didn't matter; they were laughing in the corner over a shared jest, and it was the closest to normality Alex had seen from them in a long while. It was truly a happy sight to behold. In his heart, he felt the threads that had come loose beginning to be tied together again, bringing the friends closer once more.

Helena's mood, however, was not so merry. There was a deep concern in her eyes that worried Alex, as he noticed her glancing warily toward the front door of the tower.

"What's the matter?" Alex asked, sensing Helena's agitation.

"I'm sorry to do this to you," she began, giving Alex palpitations that someone was going to barge through the door and arrest them that very moment, "but I am going to have to move you once everyone in the House is asleep."

It was not quite as worrying as Alex had imagined, but there was still fear to be taken from the girl's words.

"Why?" asked Jari, looking crestfallen.

"I don't think it's safe for you here, in the tower, anymore," she explained. "It was fine when nobody suspected anything, but the school has tightened security after Alex's nighttime excursion, and I'm just not sure this is the right place to keep you hidden anymore."

Alex felt discomfited by the blame, but he knew it truly did fall on him.

"I think you're right," he said sheepishly. "I'm sorry to put you all through this again."

Around the room, the others passed him expressions of sympathy, but there was no anger in the faces he saw. They didn't seem to bear a grudge, and Alex was grateful for that.

"When must we leave?" asked Natalie.

"We should set off in a couple of hours," suggested Helena. "Let's eat something now, pack all your things up, and then get ready to go."

The group nodded, and Jari handed out food. An anxious silence sat heavily in the air, peppered only by the sound of nervous chewing and the glug of water being drunk. With the knowledge of Helena's fears, a couple of hours seemed like a long time.

With everything packed up, they stole out of the tower and followed Helena across to the thicket of trees, where they had hidden the boat. They heaved the vessel out from the densely packed branches and pushed it across the shore and into the water as swiftly as possible.

Alex felt the shiver of the lake running icily up his legs as he waded through the shallows. He tried to ignore the feeling as he hopped up into the boat and shuffled over to the middle bench where he took up an oar. Once everyone was aboard, they rowed swiftly over to the island with the lighthouse, where Helena assured them they would be safe. She promised to continue bringing supplies, though they would not be as frequent—every other day, rather than every day. It seemed to surprise her to hear they had already been on the island, but she said little more about it as they made their way over.

Rowing deftly into the narrow inlet, the group watched anxiously as Helena moved onto the central bench and took up the oars. She was taking away their only means of escape, and Alex wasn't sure how happy he was with that fact. He thought about saying something, but the others were already positioned to wave her off, cheerful smiles on their faces. It didn't seem to bother them at all that she was going to row away with the boat, leaving them alone on a very small island with no way off it, except to swim. Alex didn't want to say it smelled like a trap, but he felt a sense of uncertainty regardless.

As she disappeared into the darkness, the quintet made their way into the familiar lighthouse. It was deathly quiet as they marched up the winding staircase, into the rooms above, and laid out their beds.

A short while after everyone had settled, Alex could hear the soft sound of oars, slicing through the water, rising up through one of the windows. Presuming it to be Helena, he moved to the ledge to peer out, only to see a very different sight before him on the black water of the lake.

A boatful of figures, dressed in glinting armor, rowed across the lake toward the opposite shore. Alex ducked back from the window's edge, guessing they must be the guards Alypia had promised to send to Spellshadow, to regain control at the request of the Head.

"What is it?" hissed Jari, seeing Alex crouched beneath the sill.

Jari's voice drew Natalie and Ellabell, though Aamir remained below.

"Peer out as carefully as you can," said Alex.

They did as he asked, their faces pale with terror as they drew back from the opening.

"Are they coming for us?" asked Jari.

Alex shook his head. "They're headed for Spellshadow."

"How do you know this?" Natalie asked skeptically.

Alex sighed. "I meant to tell you this morning, but, obviously, I got held up," he began. "I saw the Head the other night—"

A collective gasp cut him off.

He glanced at Ellabell, realizing she hadn't told them what he'd seen. Flashing a look at her, she shrugged in response—it was apparent she'd had other things on her mind, and her bashful expression kept him silent on the subject of her not telling the others.

"Where?" whispered Natalie.

"I saw them from the tower—the Head and Alypia. They were out in the courtyard for a while, then they moved inside. I followed them and overheard some things," he continued.

"They were outside?" hissed Jari, his eyes wide with shock.

Alex nodded. "They were, but they didn't see us. As far as either of them knew, we were still nowhere to be found." He grimaced, knowing he might have thrown a wrench in the works with his library visit. "Anyway, they got to talking about

Spellshadow, and how the Head had lost control—she promised to send a team to help him. I presume *that* is the team." He pointed toward the window, the sound of oars fading.

"What can we do?" asked Natalie.

"There is nothing we can do for them," he breathed.

The words hung in the air. It had remained unspoken for so long, but the realization was no less crushing. The people of Stillwater were far stronger. Even if they wanted to fight back, what hope did they have? Listening to the last whispers of the boat moving across the lake, toward their old school and the unsuspecting classmates within, Alex could not help feeling the vile hands of sorrow and grief clawing at his insides. He could only imagine what was about to happen to their former classmates and teacher, as he prayed their punishment would not be too severe.

It was an optimism he clung to, remaining quietly confident that, at the very least, their former classmates would not be killed. Alypia had said as much. Those students would be needed when they were stronger, for the harvesting of their essence. It was a very poor consolation, but enough to give Alex some hope of still being able to rescue them at some point in the future, once he had discovered a way out of this whole mess. He was more certain now than ever that the stolen essence could play a major role in the mission ahead, if only he could get ahold of it. Not only could he use it as a bargaining chip—one bottle in return for something he wanted—but it would also be a way to exact revenge on the people who had done this to his friends, and to those innocents in Spellshadow and on the field of the arena at Stillwater, and those who were still to be stolen from the outside world.

Alex desperately wanted to find those bottles and either confiscate or destroy them all, leaving those who had created these prisons with nothing. They couldn't very well use the essence of under-matured students; it would be as fruitless as having no essence at all.

If you want to keep the evil at bay, he thought coldly, *you'll have to resort to your own ranks.*

If he had his way, there would be no more innocent blood spilled. Not as long as he still drew breath.

CHAPTER 18

AWAY FROM THE GLEAMING WHITE WALLS OF Stillwater House, the atmosphere was much calmer. Although it frustrated Alex that they were isolated, with no immediate way to move forward with their mission, he comforted himself that this was just a temporary measure, and they'd figure something else out soon enough, once things had died down a bit on the mainland. In the meantime, they could work on honing their magic and anti-magic—never a wasted endeavor.

They were freer in the lighthouse, without as much worry of being spotted by a passing student or guard. Natalie had learned from Helena how to shield the windows from outside eyes, and slowly, they grew in boldness. It was like stretching after sitting for a long period of time, and it felt good.

Ellabell was still a little wary of Alex's abilities; they weren't natural, as far as she had been taught, and it had taken some getting used to, seeing the glimmer of black and silver instead of gold and white, but Alex could tell she was coming around to the idea.

A few times, he had seen her watching as he and Natalie sparred, in their strange peripheral way, with Alex aiming for marks dotted on the floor instead of his actual opponent. It was almost as if the bespectacled girl was studying his style and movement, making him feel scrutinized as he fired thin bolts of twisting black toward the wall behind Natalie, though she attempted to snatch them from the air. It was strange; the anti-magic seemed almost slippery to the touch of a magical being, running through their fingers if they tried to grasp it, as well as burning them if they made contact with it. Still, once or twice, Natalie almost managed to pull the anti-magic from the air between them, wincing as the icy-cold energy bit the edge of her skin, forcing her to let go.

By the end of their sessions, both of them were grinning, sweat glistening in a sheen on their foreheads. Ellabell grinned too, a peculiar expression of interest on her face. She would put in her two cents as they debriefed the fight, giving pointers on where she thought they needed to improve, as seen from her ringside seat. It was nice to have an outside opinion, refereeing their strengths and weaknesses. Alex knew it certainly helped him to hear where she thought he needed to focus. On occasion, some of his rapid streams of anti-magic lacked solidity and impact, his conjurations less robust if he had to make them quickly. He knew it was simply a matter of practice, and he needed to make sure his spells were consistently strong, whether he had ten minutes to prepare or a fraction of a second.

Natalie had improved in leaps and bounds too, ever since her steady recovery from the dark magic she had used to relocate the portal. Her hands no longer shook, and it took a fair amount of time before she started to tire. It was a good sign, and one Alex was glad to see. Since his visit with Elias, he had been reluctant to ask her again what had happened that day, but with the shadow-man's insight, he knew he had to keep an eye on his friend's advancements. Yes, she was almost entirely healthy again, but he couldn't help worrying that it might lead to her further pursuit of 'strong' magic. He couldn't forget the gleam he'd seen in her eyes as she had watched the Stillwater students compete. In addition, she had been spending an awful lot of time huddled in corners with Helena, chatting in low voices away from the rest of the group.

The silvery-haired young woman kept her promise to visit every other day, bringing bigger boxes of supplies to tide them over, and each visit led to these secret, hushed talks—Natalie monopolizing the girl's time, much to Jari's annoyance. He had grand plans of flirtation and courtship, and had been unable to carry any of them out during Helena's brief stopovers.

Each time Alex and Natalie sparred, he would see a spell he didn't recognize, twisting toward him from her palms. Sometimes they were surprisingly potent ones which sent him sprawling backward in a dense mist of snow and ice, leaving him wondering what the spell would have done if he had been an ordinary wizard. It was almost as if he had become Natalie's guinea pig, a means for her to semi-harmlessly try out her new tricks. It was clear Helena was teaching her these things, innocently enough, and he just hoped they were within the natural sphere of magic, and nothing from the dark, unnatural realms beyond.

"Why don't we pair up today?" Ellabell suggested one morning.

Alex frowned. "It won't be the same as sparring with the others, you know."

"I know. I've been watching, remember?"

"You think you're ready to take me on?" he grinned, flirting a little.

"I know I am," she purred.

Bristling with excitement, they moved to either side of the main room and faced each other. Ellabell drew crosses on the floor with the edge of her magic, burning the symbols temporarily into the stonework.

"Ready?" Alex smiled.

Ellabell nodded. "When you are."

Alex sent out the first attack, ducking to his knees as he pressed his palms against the stonework, sending a ripple of anti-magic through the floor of the room. It was a trick he had tailored from the one he'd seen in the arena, and it worked like a charm. Spirals of anti-magic shot up through the masonry all around Ellabell's feet, surprising her, though he had made sure they wouldn't touch her.

"Nice trick!" she gasped, slightly startled.

"Thanks," he replied brightly, as he waited for her move.

Holding her palms up, she built a golden ball in the air before her, twisting her hand sharply until the ball began to spin, faster and faster, sparks careening off it as it hurtled around. Lifting it up, she pulled her left hand inward, causing smaller globes of glittering gold energy to be flung from the center of the larger orb, where they tore through the room toward Alex's head, missing him by a hair. The globes were relentless, however, as they proceeded to surge from the larger orb, whizzing past him at all angles as he tried his best to duck and weave away from them. A few hit him in the shoulder and hip with a hefty punch, but they turned swiftly into flurries of cold snow, leaving him with little more than a light bruising.

"I think you got me!" he said as the balls continued to spin through the air. He lifted his hands in surrender.

With a turn of her wrist, the larger, spinning ball disappeared in a glimmer of gold dust. "Did I hit you?" she asked, a look of worry on her face.

He smiled. "A few times—I'm okay, though."

"Are you sure?"

He nodded. "Of course. I can take more than that."

"Well, if you insist." She conjured several bolts in both palms and sent them speeding toward Alex.

"No, I didn't mean—" he stuttered, not able to get all his words out as the hurled missiles forced him to bob and weave, cutting his sentence short.

Quickly, he sent up a glinting shield around himself, blocking the thin bolts as they soared in his direction. They slammed harmlessly against the barrier, much to Alex's relief, giving him a chance to catch his breath.

They spent a good hour testing each other's skills, with Alex trying out some of the spells he had picked up from the students

in the arena, though inverted to his own anti-magical purposes. Some were more successful than others—the burning figure of an eagle was one he would have to work on, as a paltry
conjuration of loose, glittering mist was all he could manage,
making Ellabell chuckle. It was strange; some spells seemed to
invert easily, whereas others seemed to be solely for the use of
mages. There was no anti-magical translation, or not one Alex
could figure out, anyway. The conjuration of creatures and birds
was proving particularly difficult. Ellabell could almost manage
a sleek, golden bird of prey, but he just couldn't get one to stick.

They stopped when Jari and Aamir appeared in the doorway.

"You mind if we cut in?" Jari asked with a cheerful grin.

It was an expression that had been on the blond-haired boy's
face a lot since Aamir's apparent return to normality. And it was
so close to the memory of how his friend had been, that Alex
could just about pretend to believe Aamir was entirely Aamir
again, despite their encounter the other night.

Aamir definitely seemed more buoyed up; that was undeniable, with some energy and color restored to his demeanor—
enough for him to want to indulge in a bit of playful sparring
with his old friend, anyway. Jari looked thrilled that he was
about to spar with Aamir again, like old times.

Alex and Ellabell sat to the side, sipping from brightly
colored bottles of fizzy juice that Helena had brought, as they
watched the two old friends. They went at an easy pace, the exertion of more than the basics making Aamir tire quickly, but
it was a pleasant match to watch. It seemed to be more of an
excuse for Jari to talk about Helena, who had gone back to the
school, rather than a chance to actually improve his magic skills.

"Don't you think she's the most beautiful woman in the entire world?" he asked, as he sent a twisting spiral of golden energy in Aamir's direction.

"I think she is very beautiful," the older boy admitted, "but I have not seen every woman in the entire world, so it would be unfair of me to give her that title." He grinned playfully.

"Very funny. I *know* she is the most beautiful. She is more beautiful than any supermodel—you can keep your Kate Mosses and your Naomi Campbells, I'd rather have Helena," he replied wistfully. "*And*, she's super smart and really powerful. You should see her; she'd put the Head to shame, she's that strong," he gushed.

"So, what is it *you* would bring to the relationship?" teased Aamir.

Jari pouted. "Humor, good looks, charm, adoration… The list goes on."

"I think you've definitely got 'adoration' down—you might have to work on the others," laughed Aamir, the sound rippling pleasantly across the room.

They sparred a while longer, sharing their lighthearted ribbing of one another, until Aamir visibly began to tire. Stopping, the group decided to head up to the room above, to eat some lunch and see what Natalie was up to.

As they climbed the stairs and entered the next room, Alex saw that Natalie was tucked away quite happily in the corner with her blanket wrapped around herself, engrossed in a red, canvas-covered book that Helena had brought for her, entitled *The Juggling Act of Multi-Magic* by Salome Rothschild. He presumed it was an education in how to operate a number of consistently strong spells all at once, just as Helena had done, most impressively, when she had removed Aamir's curse.

It seemed a safe enough avenue of learning, and it made Alex happy to see his friend back to her usual self, her nose buried in a book, studying intently. In fact, everybody seemed to be happy, and it was a nice feeling to know they were safer now than they would have been back at Spellshadow. Here, they were doing things on their own terms, with good food, clean water, warmth, and company, giving them the chance to learn and grow and mend, without death looming over them in an unspoken whisper of dread. Companionship and camaraderie had returned to the group, however fragile they might be.

Sitting down beneath the sill of one of the windows, Alex pulled out his pilfered book on *The Royal Households* and began to read. Ellabell sat down beside him, peering over his shoulder, her eyes flickering over the sentences.

"Why are you reading that?" she asked quietly, her eyes still following the words on the page.

He shrugged. "I picked it up the other night—figured it might tell me a bit more about who the magical royals are and what they do within the magical world," he explained, letting on a little more than he usually would have.

"Who they are?" questioned Ellabell curiously.

Alex nodded. "The Princess Alypia—that beautiful, terrifying woman from the arena—is the Headmistress here at Stillwater, and I was just wondering whether all royals were at the helms of these magical schools," he ventured, keeping Alypia's utterance of the words "little brother" to himself, until he could be more certain of the relation between Alypia and the Head.

A look of contemplation passed across Ellabell's face. "There were some books back at Spellshadow," she mused. "They had information about the royals in them."

"What kind of information?" asked Alex.

"Well, you remember that battle I was telling you about, when you came to see me in my dorm?"

Alex flushed slightly. "Yeah."

"Well, it's interesting—the royals, after the battle came to an end, had to make a decision. So many mages had died during that final war between..." She trailed off, looking him guiltily in the eye.

"It's okay, you can talk about it. It was a long time ago," he said. To him, it was still a fresh wound, but she didn't need to know that.

She sighed softly, pushing her spectacles nervously back up the bridge of her nose. "Well—many mages had died during that war between the mages and the Spellbreakers, and they had this 'Great Evil' to contend with too—the one released on that last day. So, naturally, somebody had to take charge and try to protect those who were left. That job, as you would imagine, fell to the royals—the rulers of the magical world," she began, her eyes glittering with intellect as she spoke. "Now, it has never been confirmed in any of the books I managed to get my hands on—I mean, there weren't all that many to steal at Spellshadow—but there was a rumor that, in order to protect the rest of the magical community, the royals took charge of magical institutions after the battle, as a means of... Well, I don't know why they did it, and I've never found any other information on it. It was just one page in one book, saying that is what they did, but it didn't really go into much more detail. Curious though, right?"

Aware of other eyes watching them, Alex turned to see Aamir staring at them intently. The older boy shifted his gaze away with awkward swiftness as soon as he realized he'd been seen, but Alex had caught the expression.

Alex turned back to Ellabell, nodding slowly. It certainly was curious.

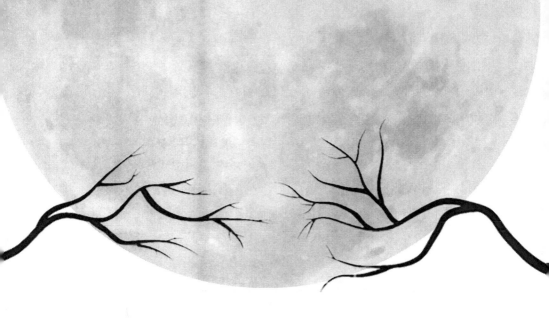

CHAPTER 19

FOUR DAYS PASSED, AND ALEX'S NEWFOUND OPTIMISM quickly turned to dread as Helena did not return to the lighthouse. Nor did she send a note, to placate his fear. The others did not seem to think much of it, but Alex was beginning to panic.

"Something's wrong," he said, pushing away his uneaten breakfast. They still had food left from Helena's last visit, since she had brought a particularly large box, but he knew that didn't mean anything. "She should have been back by now."

"There is nothing to worry about, Alex—Helena *is* coming back," Natalie replied calmly. "Maybe you should rest today. You seem a little tense, and perhaps it is making you react in a way you would not, if you were not already so on edge."

Alex shook his head. "I'm not on edge. I just feel there's

something wrong."

"You've taken on too much, and it's messing with your head," Jari chimed in, smiling warmly. "You've gone to such huge trouble to keep us safe, and so many terrible things have happened that it must be really hard to get out of that mindset—but we *are* safe. Just relax."

"Helena is busy with duels and trials and studies. She said herself that things ramp up in their final year here, and she wants to be ready. That is all," assured Natalie.

Alex had trouble accepting that as a viable excuse for Helena's no-show. He couldn't help getting up every hour to check the windows, making sure there was nobody sinister rowing across the water toward them. Each time, he was relieved to see nobody was.

As night drew in, Alex moved up to the smallest room, just beneath the lamp-room, and pulled up a chair so he could sit by the windowsill, peering out toward where he knew the school to be in the distance, though the torches had been extinguished as the hour grew late. He couldn't help but wonder at the peacefulness of the place, despite its grim purpose. It was certainly the most beautiful slaughterhouse he'd ever seen.

Alex looked up as he heard the sound of footsteps on the staircase. It was only Natalie, creeping up from the floor below, concern etched on her forehead.

"I thought you'd still be up," she said softly, as she sat down on the floor beside him.

He nodded. "I can't sleep."

"Mind racing?"

"About a hundred miles a minute," he admitted wryly.

"I thought so." She smiled. "I just wanted to come and check on you."

"I'm fine—just struggling to relax is all," he explained. "After everything that's happened, I'm just not sure I can quite accept the luxury of safety."

She nodded. "I do not blame you. We have all been through so much. But honestly, I believe us to be safe now. Helena will come back—you will see."

"Even so, I'm just going to stay up a while longer," he murmured.

She smiled sadly. "Very well... Just please get some rest, Alex. Promise me you will sleep?"

"I'll try."

"You will break if you continue this way. We must all try and put what has happened behind us and look forward, to our path home," she said, turning back to him with a sorrowful expression on her face. "Goodnight, Alex."

"Goodnight, Natalie," he replied. He watched her wander back down to the room below.

He heard her shuffling about for a while, before everything went quiet. The others had gone to bed some time ago, Ellabell in the same room as Natalie, with Jari and Aamir in the one below. Gazing back out toward the lake, Alex was drawn to the mesmerizing sight of the water rippling beneath the moonlight. His thoughts sank below the dark liquid, focusing in on something entirely less pleasant—the bodies trapped underneath. The ones he had seen on their exodus over the lake. Looking down, he swore he could see ghosts floating, just beneath the surface, though it was likely just the shift of the water being whipped up by the evening breeze. Still, he could not shake the image of their pale, haunted faces.

He considered, not for the first time, that he didn't belong. Mages had wiped out an entire race. His race. He only existed because of some loophole.

Alex's brow furrowed as he pondered the meaning behind his life more deeply, looking at it from an angle he hadn't noticed before—did that mean *he* was a descendant of Leander Wyvern? The grandchild or great-grandchild to the progeny of the legendary Spellbreaker and some non-magical woman?

Unless there were other Spellbreakers who indulged in non-magical affairs, he thought grimly. Just because it fit, didn't mean it was true, and unless Alex could be certain that Leander Wyvern was the only Spellbreaker to create a child with a non-magical woman, he was no closer to being certain of his heritage.

Dejectedly, Alex stared into the water and wondered if Leander was beneath the glittering surface of the lake too, forgotten by everyone except him and a few dusty history books.

CHAPTER 20

I N THE MIDDLE OF A RESTLESS SLEEP, ALEX BECAME AWARE of a strange sound filtering up the narrow staircase from the floor below. His eyes snapped open; it was a familiar, eerie sound. Glancing around, he realized he must have fallen asleep beside the window—he could see the stars twinkling beyond the sill, but he couldn't figure out where the sound was coming from. As he stood and walked quietly toward the top of the staircase, the whispering noise grew louder.

For a moment, he thought it might be another of Elias's shadowy beacons, intended to lead him to some new, enticing information, but the sound was decidedly more human than that. Peering into the darkness at the bottom of the stairs, he saw subtle movements, as if there were something shifting in the shadows below. Tentatively, he placed his hand on the banister, not knowing whether to step into the unknown or stay at the top of the stairs, until his eyes had at least grown accustomed to the dimness beneath.

The sound of Ellabell's scream made the decision for him. It pierced the air, and Alex flew instinctively down the stairs, knocking shoulders with something solid in the darkness as he raced toward the spot in the corner where she usually slept, his anti-magic jumping into defensive action as he tried to make out her figure in the blackness. Desperately, his eyes scoured the room, until they rested on two shapes tussling in the center. One of the figures had her, though Ellabell was fighting to get free.

"There's another one!" an alien voice cried.

Alex wasted no time as he began to work silvery threads of anti-magic between his fingers, building a burning ball between his hands as the shadows swarmed, moving toward him as if drawn to the light. He fired the first barrage of anti-magical artillery at the would-be ambushers, the silver light illuminating their faces for the briefest of seconds as they tried to get closer to him, only to be thrown back by the crackling surge of his energy. They had the beautiful faces of Stillwater residents, all chiseled cheekbones and perfect symmetry, but right now, to Alex, they were as far from beautiful as it was possible to be.

Another blast from his palms sent them flying backward, but it knocked down Ellabell too, who was caught up in the fray. Alex wanted to rush to her, but she was already scrambling to her feet, snatching her hand away from the guard who held her and darting quickly between the invaders, to stand by Alex's side. She forged golden magic between her own palms as the guards closed in around them.

From the next floor below, Alex heard the thud of magic against the thick stone walls and felt tremors shiver through his body as Natalie cried out. Panic rippled through him as he looked around the room, only just realizing that Natalie wasn't in her usual place, close to where Ellabell slept. She was below, perhaps already being taken away by the guards.

"What happened to Natalie?" asked Alex, glancing at Ellabell.

"They dragged her down the stairs," she replied, her voice strained with fear.

It spurred Alex on, and, together, he and Ellabell managed to hold the guards back. Flakes and flurries of snow and ice filled the air as Alex sent barrage after barrage toward the approaching strangers, knocking them back time and time again, but it quickly became apparent that their opponents were extremely strong—just as Alex had known the Stillwater folk to be. Each time he knocked them back, they got up and kept coming, shrugging off the deep chill of his anti-magic. The barrages were one of the only spells he knew that he could use against multiple people, and it did not seem to be strong enough to keep them away indefinitely. He knew his anti-magic weapons might have been stronger, or the underground spirals, but throwing individual weapons would have left them vulnerable to the other attackers, and he was still coming to grips with the latter spell. All he could do was keep sending out the icy barrages, in hopes that the aggressors would eventually stay down.

It was an optimistic hope.

There was something else, too, that alarmed Alex. Squinting into the dark, he was surprised to see something strange happening each time the silvery light of his anti-magic lit up their attackers' faces, just prior to impact. It was like a mirage, distorting the faces of the guards, making them seem twisted and odd for a moment. He wasn't sure if it was a figment of his imagination, but he couldn't stop looking at those faces as each icy wave hit them with full force.

Finally, Alex saw an opportunity—a gap opening up between several guards, who seemed to be flagging slightly as he sent yet another pulse of fierce anti-magic. Taking Ellabell's hand, though the burning gold of her palm sent a shiver up his arm, he ran with her toward the stairs and sprinted down to the lower floor, where Jari was putting up the best fight he could alongside Natalie, who had apparently battled herself free of the guards.

It was easy to forget how skillful Jari was, but his talent was undeniable as the spells twisted and turned from the delicate movements of his hands, his body turned sideways to reduce the target as his eyes tried to read the actions of his attackers. Regardless of their strength, they were not evenly matched with the beautiful aggressors, and there seemed to be more of them pouring in from all angles.

Aamir, in his weakened state, was being hauled away at the edge of the room, unable to put up much resistance, though Jari was trying to make a path toward him through the guards. Seeing his friends' struggle, Alex sent a flurry of gleaming silver attacks at the guards, stopping them in their tracks as they tried to retaliate, only to find themselves face to face with another wave of pulsing anti-magic.

Using the brief intermission in return attacks, Jari and

Natalie ducked forward and grasped Aamir away from the arms of the two guards who had been holding him captive. From below, the staircase was filling with more guards, and the ones from the floors above were streaming into the room. It was clear to Alex that they were cornered. Any and all exits were hidden behind an army of Stillwater mages.

A last-ditch battle ensued as magical shrapnel filled the room in a glittering miasma, exploding from the close-quarter combat and rising up from the blizzards of snowflakes created by Alex's defenses. Natalie sent shivering snakes of liquid gold toward the attackers, putting to use some of the most recent additions to her magical arsenal, as each of the five friends struggled in vain to hold off their opponents. They were strong, but the Stillwater residents were stronger. The ambushers pressed inward, concentrating their superior power on the small group until their five victims were too drained to fight anymore. Alex was still managing to cause a bit of trouble, though, as the attackers labored to fend him off; they were not practiced with his particular brand of power.

Alex was in the process of snatching magic out of the air and redirecting it toward the other guards, when four of the assailants launched a singular attack on him. It came out of nowhere, catching him in the knees, sending him crashing with a painful crunch to the floor. It was the opportunity the Stillwater mages had been waiting for, as the rest surged in around him, physically knocking his friends out of the way as they rushed to restrain Alex. One particularly tall, handsome-looking guard held a pair of horribly familiar manacles in his hands as he loomed over Alex, yanking at the young man's arms as he held them upward and locked the manacles around Alex's wrists.

Things with locks hadn't proved much of a nuisance to Alex, but, to his horror, he saw that the manacles were entwined with twisting vines of the dull, gray ivy that littered the walls of Spellshadow. Moments later, he felt the icy creep of its draining energy working its way through his arms. Another guard skirted behind him, wielding something heavy. The unseen object hit Alex in the back of the skull with such force, he thought it had taken his head clean off. It was the last thing he remembered fully as the world went black.

With barely a sliver of consciousness left, Alex was aware of chains scraping and indecipherable noises clanging in an echo around him. He could make out the defiant sound of Ellabell's voice, followed by Natalie's, but it was Jari's voice that soared above the rest in a loud, angry snarl as he sniped something nasty at somebody, though Alex couldn't see any of them. His eyesight was fuzzy and his head pounded, and he tasted dirt in his mouth as he felt the cold, hard texture of the stone beneath his cheek.

Moments later, he felt the thud of something being shoved to the ground nearby—his friends, he presumed grimly, as he heard agonized groans. Though he couldn't see or move, it did not stop the feeling of rage that burned in his chest. Several times, he tried to break free of the manacles, though he wasn't sure how intently his limbs were listening to what his brain wanted, and the ivy continued to keep the anti-magic at bay.

Shortly afterward, Alex became aware of the sensation of being carried, followed by the hefty thump of his shoulder hitting something wooden. For a while, nothing happened in his blind confusion, until the soft sound of oars slicing through the water rushed through his ears, letting him know they were on the lake. He had already guessed the destination, though they seemed to travel for a much longer time than he remembered the trip taking, from the lighthouse to Stillwater.

He was forced to put his trust in the competence of his hearing as he listened to the boat run aground on a distant shore. Hands grasped him and hauled him along for a long while, it seemed, before his body was unceremoniously thrown down onto more hard, cold flagstones, though these had a certain dank dampness to them that felt unpleasant against his cheek. The place smelled musty and sour, making his nose wrinkle as he struggled to sit up. His head snapped toward the sound of a key turning in a lock, as an image pieced itself together in his mind. He was in a cell of some sort, he guessed, as the sounds and scents and sensations made things a little clearer.

It wasn't long before his eyesight returned, confirming his suspicions. Glancing around, pain pulsing behind his eyeballs, he saw that he was in a dark and damp cell. The walls were slick and dripping with some unknown substance, and a metallic undertone soured the fusty tang of the room. It was a smell he recognized, and, as he brushed a cautious finger along one of the wall stones, the sticky substance that came away shone with a red tinge that made him shudder. Two torches dimly lit the room, but Alex wasn't sure whether the low visibility was a blessing or a curse. There was no telling what horrors lurked in the shadowed corners.

As soon as he became more familiar with his surroundings and his sight had returned fully, his thoughts turned immediately to the welfare of his friends. Moving toward the thick wooden door, his head still thumping with dull pain, he tried to peer out of the grate, but could see only the wall beyond.

"Guys?" he shouted, squeezing as much of his face through the narrow bars as possible. "Guys, can you hear me?"

"Alex, is that you?" Natalie replied.

"It's me—are the others with you?"

"I'm here!" called Jari.

"And me," said Aamir.

"Me too!" Ellabell responded, from farther down the corridor.

None of them sounded too worse for wear, though perhaps a little groggy. He wasn't surprised. If they felt anything like he did, they were bound to sound shaky.

"Are you all okay?" he yelled.

"My head is a little sore," said Natalie.

"Yeah—mine feels like there's a herd of elephants doing the conga!" shouted Jari, making Alex smile.

"My brain feels like it's about to explode," sighed Ellabell wearily.

"I'm pretty sure I've lost all my memories before my tenth birthday," grunted Aamir. "How are you?"

"Same." Alex grimaced, rubbing his thumbs against his temples in a vain attempt to get them to stop hurting.

There was a welt at the back of his head, the swelling coming up beneath the skin like an egg as he rubbed the tender spot. Although he hurt and they were all suffering somewhat, it was nice to hear the others. It calmed him a little, as he sat up against the door—it was by far the driest spot in the cell.

Nobody talked much as they sat in isolation, seeing to their wounds. Alex had a few mystery bruises and scratches, brought on by their brutish transportation. There was one just above his right eyebrow that stung every time a bead of sweat ran into it, like squeezing lemon juice on a cut. All in all, though, he seemed to be in one piece.

An hour later, the sound of scraping metal and jangling keys alerted Alex to one of the doors being opened, farther up the corridor. Standing quickly, despite the dizziness that followed, he tried to peer out of the grate to see who was being taken away, but couldn't crane his head far enough around.

"Who is it?" he yelled. He heard the sound of scuffling feet on the flagstones and the muffled fear of someone struggling, silenced by a hand over the mouth. "Who is it?" he repeated desperately.

"Alex!" Ellabell called out for him, and the sound nearly broke his heart. There was abject terror in her voice.

"Ellabell—be brave! You'll be okay!" he called, though he still couldn't see her. He could only hope she believed him.

He listened as her footsteps faded away to nothing, his voice no longer echoing after her down the hallway. There was nothing left to do but pace while he waited for them to bring her back. Frustration twisted inside his stomach as he walked up and down the cell, hoping she was safe, wherever they had taken her. He couldn't bear to think of them hurting her in any way.

A while later, he heard the scrape and jangle once more, only Ellabell didn't seem to be with the jailer. Instead, they had come for someone else.

Alex listened hopelessly as Natalie cried out, just before she was dragged to wherever they had taken Ellabell.

Jari was next, assuring Alex and Aamir he would be fine.

"I won't say a word to those—" Whichever expletive Jari had been about to use, it was cut off by the hand of someone smothering the blond-haired boy's mouth.

Aamir went after, shouting to Alex.

"Be strong, Alex!" he called as the sound of jangling keys disappeared into nothingness.

Left alone in the prison, with nobody neighboring him to keep him from going mad, Alex paced his cell like a caged beast, his mind racing with worry and concern for the other four who had gone before him. He knew it probably wouldn't be long until they came for him, and, as much as he would have liked to fight back, he was no longer sure of the point.

There was one thing he was sure about, though—he was next on the chopping block.

CHAPTER 21

THE FAMILIAR SOUND OF A KEY TURNING IN THE LOCK made Alex's tired eyes snap toward the door of the grim cell. He had moved back to its center, to give himself more distance if he found himself with the opportunity to bum-rush whoever was on the other side, but the thought stopped dead in its tracks as he saw the figure standing beyond the door. It was not someone he had been expecting.

Siren Mave stood in the hallway, holding a weighty bunch of keys, peering at him over her horn-rimmed spectacles.

"If you'd like to follow me, Mr. Webber," she instructed. "Peacefully, if at all possible. I've had enough of strugglers for one evening." She flashed Alex a warning look, puckering her overly painted lips in displeasure.

Alex nodded, cautiously following the plump little woman

who had waddled on ahead. "What are you doing here?" he asked, still in shock.

"Oh, you know, keeping things interesting. Sometimes I'm here, sometimes I'm there—I go where I am needed," she replied cheerfully. "Though *you* have significantly reduced my enrollment duties at Spellshadow Manor. Quite the little scallywag you turned out to be, hm? I knew you were different when you arrived. There was something about you—the rest are always plain as punch, but in you came, and I just knew I'd be seeing you again." She smiled strangely, readjusting her spectacles as they turned a corner.

"I wouldn't say I—" Alex began, but Siren Mave cut him off curtly.

"No use denying it, Webber—quite the state you left that place in. I wasn't sure whether to be impressed or appalled," she cried. "Mind you, I suppose I *do* have you to thank for being more part-time now. More time for myself, you know? I always meant to do it, but you've done it for me," she mumbled as they walked through a few more corridors.

Alex had been so surprised to see her that he found he no longer felt the previous trepidation coursing through his body.

As they passed through another set of hallways, he felt a spike of curiosity; it struck him as odd that, along the way, there were so few guards. What was there to stop him from running away? He couldn't see any walls or barriers either.

"Don't even contemplate it, Mr. Webber—don't even begin to think about contemplating it. I may be small, but I can take you down without moving more than my pinky finger," she warned, somehow preempting his train of thought.

Glancing at her, with her dumpy frame and elaborate spectacles, and her cheeks glowing from too much blush, Alex thought she didn't look like a typical magical ninja, but there was a confidence in her voice that alarmed him, making him reluctant to test her. A flash in her eyes told him not to dare, and for once he felt he ought to listen.

"Where are the others?" he asked, once all thoughts of escape had ebbed away.

She waved her hand, which twinkled with hefty jeweled rings that seemed much too tight for her chubby fingers. "They are safe, although they weren't nearly as accommodating as you," she replied. Alex couldn't tell if she was mocking him, or if that was just her voice; there always seemed to be a hint of some private joke on the tip of her tongue.

"Yes, but where are they?" he repeated, with growing frustration.

She turned, meeting him with a stern glare. "They are safe. That is all you need know."

Turning back around, she strode off down a side corridor until they reached an unassuming wooden door at the very end. Twisting the handle, Siren Mave pushed it open and stepped into an empty room. It was a plain, square chamber with high stone walls and a bare stone ceiling, with no furniture except for a bench that ran along one side. There didn't seem to be another exit, or any windows either, but Siren Mave seemed to be searching for something against the far wall. Alex frowned, wondering if this was a holding room of some sort.

It quickly became apparent that this was merely a brief stop-off, as Siren Mave held a black doorknob to a section of wall and twisted, revealing another doorway behind it. It reminded him of his first day at Spellshadow, when he had met Elias for the first time, only this seemed less strange to him now. It was almost par for the wizarding course, to see doors and entrances where they shouldn't be. As she opened the door, she wasted no time in ushering Alex through it, forcing him past the threshold with a firm shove in the back.

The door opened out onto an antechamber, with a set of large, white double doors ahead. They were tall and imposing, and Alex wondered if, somewhere along the line, he had actually died and this was his arrival at the pearly gates. It would make a lot of sense, he mused wryly as he followed Siren Mave, pondering with amusement whether that made her a squat archangel of some kind. A sudden glare from her alarmed him, leaving him wondering if she could hear his thoughts. However, he didn't have time to think about the strange little woman rooting through his brain, as she knocked on one of the vast doors and shoved him through, before disappearing behind him with a twist of her magical door handle.

The whole journey had left him truly disoriented, and it was only made worse as he stepped into the most beautiful office, which looked more like a greenhouse than a place of work. Above his head, there was a glass ceiling that let in the hazy glow of the daylight, bathing everything in golden sunshine. Exotic, fruit-bearing trees and plants were growing healthily all around the room, which was especially warm, encouraging the lemons and limes and oranges to swell to a tantalizing plumpness. There were olives too, and some fruits Alex didn't recognize, though everything looked ripe and inviting. The whole office, in and among the foliage, was tastefully decorated in white and chrome, the lines crisp and clean, and there was an impressive white marble desk at the very head of the room, set in front of a large window that looked out upon the lake.

The sight of it made Alex bubble with rage, to note that the Headmistress's window, too, looked out onto the lake filled with the buried remains of his people. He wondered bitterly what their obsession was with such a gruesome trophy.

Does it make you feel almighty? he thought sourly as he watched the water shimmer beneath the sunlight.

Alypia was sitting behind the desk, her white hair almost glowing in the warm sunlight, like a halo around her beautiful face. With a slender, graceful arm, she gestured for Alex to come and sit too. He walked forward, his hands still manacled, and sat in a large, high-backed chair that was covered in pure white fur from an animal Alex couldn't identify. *In keeping with her murderous theme*, he thought as he plonked himself down on the soft upholstery.

Smiling kindly, she held out her hands for his manacled wrists. He obliged, allowing her to take them off with a small key she wore around her neck. The cold, sapping energy of the ivy drained from his body, giving it life again as he rubbed the chafed skin of his wrists.

Looking up, he became speechless for a moment. He had known Alypia to be a truly beautiful woman, but in close quarters she was utterly mesmerizing, stealing the very breath from his lungs. There was an intelligence and grace about her that Alex found hypnotic, and, as much as he wanted to despise her, he found that he couldn't. One look into her strange eyes and he was rendered awestruck again.

"I am the Crown Princess Alypia, but you may refer to me as Headmistress," she stated, her voice clear and regal.

"What have you done with my friends?" he asked, regaining his voice. "Are they okay? Tell me where they are!"

She smiled. "May I offer you something to drink, before we get into the nitty-gritty of negotiations?" she suggested, her voice showing light amusement.

Alex frowned, wondering what she meant by "negotiations", but his thirst got the better of him. "A drink would be great," he replied evenly, feeling the dryness of his tongue and the rasp of his parched throat.

Nodding primly, Alypia turned to the table beside her and lifted two crystal glasses onto the desk. Slowly, she poured a pale, sparkling liquid from an ornate glass jug, the handle shaped like an ancient Roman goddess, into the two crystal chalices, and pushed one across the marble surface toward him.

Suddenly, he wasn't so sure he wanted a drink anymore. Watching the bubbles rise, he couldn't help but feel wary; he knew Alypia was not to be trusted. She could have slipped poison into it or something, without him knowing.

As if sensing his mistrust, Alypia picked up the glass she had poured for herself, from the same jug, and sipped the contents, assuring him of its purity. Tentatively, he lifted his own glass to his lips and drank deep of the sweet liquid. It tasted a bit like the sparkling juice he and his mom always had on New Year's Eve. Whatever it was, it quenched his thirst in an instant, leaving him free to ask his questions again.

"What have you done with my friends?" he pressed, draining

the glass dry.

Her strange eyes glittered. "They are all well. They have all been treated as you have," she explained, apparently unwilling to elaborate.

"How is Ellabell? What have you done with her? And Natalie? Are they okay?"

Alypia grinned, flashing Alex a knowing look as he spoke of Ellabell. The expression made Alex worry, hoping he had not given her a weapon she might use against him—an exploitation of something she might see as a weakness. He waited for an axe to fall, but it did not; if she had plans to utilize his affections for Ellabell, she wasn't ready to put them into action just yet.

"The two girls are well," assured Alypia.

"And the two boys—Aamir and Jari?"

Alypia smirked. "Jari has been… something of a handful, shall we say. But dear Aamir has been more than compliant. He is recuperating well in the infirmary after his… recent illness," she said softly, offering glimmers of awareness as she spoke. There was a knowledge in her words that made Alex suspicious, and he wondered why she was referring to the older boy as 'dear' Aamir. There was familiarity in the way she spoke his name.

For a moment, Alex thought about mentioning Helena, but a desire to protect her held his tongue—he wasn't convinced she had been involved in their capture at all. No matter which way he looked at it, it didn't make sense that Helena had dragged them all the way out to the lighthouse to be captured, when she could just as easily have sounded the alarm when they were in the bell tower, or even when they were just outside the villa walls. If she hadn't been responsible in any way, Alex didn't want to get her into trouble. Besides, if she *had* been the cause of their capture, he was fairly certain it wouldn't have been on purpose. Perhaps somebody had seen her rowing to the island, or caught wind of what she was up to. Until he saw Helena again, he couldn't be sure of what had actually led the guards to the lighthouse.

"You intrigue me, Alex. You and your friends," Alypia purred. "You are all very talented individuals. Even the weakest among you is still stronger than most, especially the caliber one expects among that motley crew at Spellshadow. I can see the frustration in some of your friends, Alex—the desire to be taught properly, which is something I know you weren't experiencing at Spellshadow Manor. It isn't seen as all that important to teach well over there, and goodness knows the place has been run into the ground. Always the bare minimum, copying lines out of textbooks and learning rudimentary magic. It's not exactly thrilling stuff, that's for sure, and it leads to sedentary, bored minds. Not the kind of minds required of superior mages. For you and your friends, that kind of teaching and learning is simply not good enough." She smiled, flashing pearly white teeth, but it didn't quite reach her eyes. There was a twist of displeasure in her voice, leaving Alex to guess whether it was the reminder of her brother that had brought on such annoyance.

"My friends should never have been brought to Spellshadow in the first place—it's sick and it's wrong," Alex remarked.

She nodded thoughtfully. "A barbaric necessity, truly, but a necessity nonetheless. We can debate the morality of such things another day, but for now, we must make the most of where we are. See it as an opportunity and not a curse. I know certain friends of yours see it that way. They understand that there are things to be learned here—interesting, wonderful things, that nowhere else can offer," she murmured, her voice like honey. "But Alex, you are a different notion entirely. I can see a talent in you that was not fully nurtured at a place like Spellshadow Manor. And it could not have been fully nurtured; they simply don't have the skills or resources necessary to teach somebody like you. Someone with such rare promise," she whispered, her eyes gleaming with excitement.

Alex froze, remaining silent. He did not know how much Alypia knew of his special circumstances; he guessed she was suspicious, at the very least, about his Spellbreaker abilities, thanks to the Head's vague statements about the importance of him being found, though he was fairly certain she already knew precisely what he was. Alypia was not a stupid woman, by any stretch of the imagination. That was why she had referred to him as 'special'—he had come to realize 'special' actually meant 'Spellbreaker'.

"You must miss your mother terribly," she said evenly, switching the subject as she looked him straight in the eyes. "It must be hard for you. I can see why you were so desperate to escape. I don't blame you, in fact. If it were my mother and she were sick, perhaps dying, I know I would do the same. Quite honorable, really. It's not the same for the others, is it? At least their families all have each other, but your mother has no one, does she? All she had was you, and then you followed our little French girl through the gates and that was that—she lost you. Tragic, really, as you would never have entered that place otherwise. You were not on any radar, nor did we think we wanted you—but along you came anyway," she whispered. Alex wasn't sure if she was taunting him, but the mention of his mother made his throat clamp up.

"Don't talk about her," he snapped. It was clear, as she spoke, that she knew things she shouldn't know, making Alex aware that she and the Head had spoken further of him and his home life. Knowledge was power, and she held the ace. But there was no toying involved in the way she spoke of what she knew; it was not an attempt to tug on his heartstrings, as Aamir had done with his offer. Alypia was much more matter-of-fact about it, stating what she knew and what could be done.

"I speak only of her to give you hope, Alex. I don't mean pie-in-the-sky, fairy-dust hope—I mean real, solid potential. Your mother is still ailing, and yes, she is alone, but her treatment is working and she will be well for a good while longer. She is naturally heartbroken that you are gone, but it's almost as if the hope of your return is keeping her going—she will not give up until you are home, and I don't think we should let her down, do you?" she continued. Despite Alex's feelings toward Alypia, he could not deny that her words gave him courage.

It was all he wanted, to see his mother again. To hear from Alypia's lips that she was alive was the greatest gift anyone had ever given him, and he had to thank the Headmistress for that. Night after night, he would dream of his mother and the loss he felt. Sometimes, they would be nightmares, in which he would run down the street and knock on the door, only to find that hundreds of years had passed and his mother was long dead. Others were less farfetched, as when he dreamed he had made it home, only to discover he was a few days too late, and she had died of a broken heart. There were happy ones too, in which they were joyfully reunited, but mostly they were dark, twisted, terrible visions that haunted him long after he awoke.

"I don't understand why you're telling me all this," said Alex quietly.

"I have an offer to make you, Alex," she explained. "I wish to teach you at this school, which is a little non-traditional for us, but I can see great talent in you and your friends that requires the proper tutelage, not some place where you will waste away, your skills never fully realized. You will study here for five years, and at the end of those years, you will undergo the Ascension Ceremony with the rest of your class. If you win, you walk free, back to your mother and the non-magical world if you so choose. If you lose, you will be subjected to the Gifting Ceremony."

It was not nearly as generous as the offer Aamir had made to him, under the duress of the golden band, but it sounded like a more honest one. In fact, it sounded so genuine that it made Alex wonder about the offer Aamir had made him, and whether or not it had truly been a real one.

"You have a stronger chance of survival here, with me, than with any other offer you are likely to receive," she added, with a slight wink to her words that only made Alex more suspicious of Aamir's previous offer.

Alex shrugged. "I don't know what those ceremonies are. How can I say yes to something when I don't know what I'm getting into?" he said, playing dumb.

Alypia's eyes narrowed, flashing with underlying threat. She was onto him. "Don't play the fool, Alex—you know very well what they are."

"Very well," he murmured. "What happens to the essences you collect from the Gifting Ceremony?" He figured it was as good a time as any to ask the woman in the know.

"They are stored for further use," she replied, the harsh edge of her voice softening.

The response made Alex think about the row upon row of black bottles and one name in particular.

"Did Blaine Stalwart come here?" he asked. The question seemed to confuse the Headmistress for a moment as she mulled over the name. "An older boy, tall, very skillful, though he wasn't ready to graduate yet—he got in trouble for breaking one of the golden lines at Spellshadow and was taken away. We never heard from him again, except the Head said he had been sent to Stillwater House," Alex elaborated.

She smiled coldly. "I remember the boy."

"He did come here?"

She nodded. "He was permitted to fight for his survival at a special event, but he could not defeat the skill of the Stillwater student he was pitted against, and so he was returned to Spellshadow Manor to undergo his own Gifting Ceremony—or 'graduation,' I believe you call it?" She waved her graceful hand. "His essence is in storage somewhere—though much good it was. He wasn't strong enough, so the essence was a pitiful one."

It came rushing back to Alex—'Not matured enough.' Blaine Stalwart hadn't been strong enough to compete against a Stillwater student and had lost his life, as well as having his essence torn away much too prematurely, all for one twisted rule. A pointless, useless, wasteful exercise. Alex felt the familiar prickle of resentment rising through him.

"How could you?" he spat.

"The boy was given a fair chance. He had more hope in my arena than he did in the dusty halls of Spellshadow, believe me," she remarked calmly.

He could not deny her logic, and yet he couldn't shake his anger. Fury burned bright within him, at all of them—all the cruel, uncaring, magical beings.

"Now, I need an answer," she pressed, ignoring his distress. "My way or the hard way?"

Through the red mist of anger, he thought about her offer. It was certainly tempting. "Repeat the terms to me again."

"You will study here, with your friends alongside you, for five years. I will teach you and make sure I can find somebody who can assist with your particular skillset—I will build you all up, until you are ready to compete in the Ascension Ceremony, at the end of your five years. In that time, you will have free rein of the place, and be treated as any other Stillwater student. At the end of the ceremony, if you win, you walk. If you lose, you will undergo the Gifting Ceremony."

"No hidden surprises?" he asked, raising an eyebrow.

Alypia shook her head. "I ask only that the bargain be upheld. There are no hidden surprises, but if, at any stage, you or I should break the terms of agreement, then the offer will change." She smiled icily.

"How will it change?"

"If I break my side of the treaty, I will let you and your friends go home, no further strings attached. If you break your side of the treaty, your essence will be immediately forfeit," she declared, her cold tone making Alex shiver.

Unbelievably, Alex thought it seemed fair. Plus, it meant he had more time, in a safer environment, to come up with a plan for how to get his friends safely home. Within this magical world, he still wasn't sure how to get back to the real world, but he knew he could research portals and travel techniques with the great library at his disposal. Knowledge wasn't only a weapon Alypia could use—he could use it too. As much as he hated to admit it, the more he thought about it, Stillwater House seemed to be a far better prison than Spellshadow Manor.

Slowly, hardly believing the words coming out of his mouth, Alex made his decision. "I agree to your terms."

Smiling, she pulled a scroll from the top drawer of her desk and pushed it across the marble toward Alex. It had the terms of the offer already written upon it in an elegant, italic hand, which made it seem all too real. Frowning suspiciously, he suspected the scroll to be magical in some way, to ensure the agreement was carried out, but, as he pressed his hands to the words, he felt that it was nothing but paper.

The contract was between them alone, and neither was sure of the other keeping their side of it.

CHAPTER 22

AFTER SIGNING THE CONTRACT, ALEX WAS SWIFTLY dismissed from the Headmistress's office. Princess Alypia watched him as he was led away, toward a different wing of the villa. Through the windows, he could see that it was late morning, with the sun not quite at its highest point in the sky, and though he and his friends had only been captured less than half a day before, he felt as if he had been awake for weeks.

The walk was long but scenic, as Alex took in the intricate tapestries that draped the walls of several hallways, showing ancient scenes of battle and beautiful maidens bathing in lustrous forests, being watched by sprites and mythical beasts. It reminded him of a gallery trip he had been on during high school, where they had been asked to pick a painting and sit in front of it with a sketchbook and pencil, to try to emulate the far superior work on the wall. The images on the tapestries and in the large murals that adorned the villa were of the same exceptional artistry, and though he was tired, he marveled at the beauty of the place. Everything was thought out, to the smallest detail. Hanging baskets full of fragrant, vivid flowers showered the neutral masonry with much-needed color, filling the air with a heady, sweet scent. Fountains babbled pleasantly in the piazzas as he stepped across the sun-dappled tiles, listening to the running water that flowed from the tilted urn of a perfectly sculpted statue.

Although it couldn't yet be midday, the sun was warm on Alex's face as he followed his guard out into the courtyards and semi-open walkways, emerging from beneath archways only to duck back into the cool shade of other cloisters and down endless corridors of the same beautiful, pale stone. Wherever he was being led, it was a long way from the Headmistress's office.

After heading up some stairs into a well-lit, glass-fronted hallway that looked out over a small square, filled with a few benches and slender trees that shaded any sitters from the hot sun, the guard paused beside a door marked with a golden "43."

"This is your room," stated the guard, a six-foot Adonis with wolf-like gray eyes.

"Thank you," mumbled Alex. He pushed open the door.

He was expecting a dormitory, much like the one he had shared with Jari and Aamir back at Spellshadow, but was surprised to find it was a single room—small but comfortable, with a bed against one wall and a desk that sat beneath a large, shuttered window. There was another door at the far end of the room that led to a private bathroom, complete with a tub. Everything was simple, clean, and elegant, much like the rest of Stillwater House.

When Alex turned around, he saw that the guard had gone, leaving him to get acquainted with his new living space. The bathtub called to him; he could feel the layers of grime crawling along the surface of his skin, begging to be sloughed off in a deep pool of hot, soothing water.

He was about to turn the faucets on when a light knock came at the door.

"Come in," called Alex cautiously.

Aamir poked his head into the room, a broad grin on his face. "I'm just next door—thought I'd come and see how you were doing," he explained.

Alex frowned. "I thought you were in the infirmary?"

"I was. They ran a few spells through me and released me with the prescription of 'bed-rest,'" he replied. "I do feel pretty worn out… It has been a trying few weeks," he added with a sheepish expression.

It was the understatement of the century, but Alex was warmed by the awareness within Aamir's eyes; it was as if his former friend were coming back to him, piece by piece, the real Aamir gathering strength every day.

"What happened to you back there?" asked Alex, plopping onto the soft sheets of his new bed.

"With the Headmistress?" Aamir replied.

Alex nodded, realizing he could have meant any number of things when it came to Aamir. "Yeah. Did she make you an offer you couldn't refuse?" he joked, doing his best *Godfather* impression.

Aamir chuckled. "She did. I never expected to be making another deal with the devil, but, honestly, this one seemed almost... reasonable. Five years and a fifty-fifty chance of survival. Is that weird?"

"Not at all. It's one of the most reasonable offers I've heard." Alex shook his head, glancing at Aamir with curiosity. The older boy was struggling to look Alex in the eye, and Alex thought he knew why. Seizing the opportunity, Alex dove in. "Speaking of offers... did you mean the one you offered me, back in the ballroom at Spellshadow, when you were still Professor Escher?"

It was a question that had been bugging Alex for some time, especially as it kept coming up. Even Alypia had seemed amused by the notion of Aamir's offer, when she alluded to it in her office. But, more than that, Alex couldn't get out of his mind how strange it was that the golden band on Aamir's wrist hadn't buzzed or crackled or made Aamir wince, when he had made the offer, which it surely would have done if he had been doing something he wasn't supposed to be doing. Which begged the question: had Aamir been acting on his own impulses, or had he been instructed by the Head to make the offer, never meaning the words he had spoken? It hadn't occurred to Alex at the time, that the band hadn't made a peep when Aamir offered freedom, but the longer he had thought about it, the more it bothered him.

Aamir shifted uncomfortably, a plea in his eyes to not be made to answer.

"Tell me the truth, Aamir. You owe me that much," pressed Alex, trying not to let frustration taint his words.

Aamir shook his head miserably. "The truth is, Alex... I

don't know. I don't know if it came from me or if it came from the Head and I was merely his pawn—for what awful purpose, I cannot tell you. The lines were blurred back then; my mind was as much his as it was my own. It was like he was in there, moving things around without my say-so. I was a puppet, being forced to say and do things I would never have done, had I been in control of my own mind. But I was not in control, Alex. You have to believe me when I say that." Aamir looked at Alex with wide-eyed desperation. "When the curse was broken, it jumbled everything—I couldn't tell you which thoughts belonged to me and which to the Head. And though I know you don't believe me, there are many memories that are shut off to me now… It's like the curse being broken locked pieces of my mind away that were not intended for my own eyes. Everything was all mixed in together and so hazy I couldn't think straight. I am *still* trying to fix it all back together. Do you understand?"

"So you don't know anything. Is that what you're saying?" asked Alex, somewhat dejected.

"The golden line on my wrist had such a strong hold over me—I can't be sure if my offer was genuine or not, and for that I am eternally sorry," murmured Aamir wretchedly. "But please believe that I would never have done anything to hurt you. I would like to hope it was the real me coming through, trying to set you free before anyone powerful found out what you are, but I can't promise it was. The memory of it is like a fuzzy, warped picture in my mind, and though I wish I had a better answer for you—I am afraid I do not."

Alex wanted to be angry with the older boy, but the note of genuine sorrow in Aamir's voice forced Alex's irritation to subside. Warmth and life were returning to Aamir, and Alex could see that it was true: Aamir *was* becoming more like his old self with each day. Perhaps one day, he would have a more complete answer to give Alex. For now, Alex guessed that was the best he was going to get.

"Thank you for being honest," Alex said with a resigned nod, although another question rested on his tongue. "Aamir— have you been to Stillwater House before?"

Aamir was about to answer when another knock sounded at the door. Without waiting for a welcome, Natalie and Ellabell burst into the room, their faces cheerful. They seemed to have changed clothes and washed too, much to Alex's envy.

"You're here!" Natalie smiled. "We are just down the corridor."

"So the Headmistress made you an offer too?" asked Ellabell.

"Yeah," Alex replied, "we both received offers. Five years of study, followed by the usual gambit of the Ascension Ceremony and a fifty-fifty chance of surviving this place. What was yours?"

"I received the same offer, though Alypia said I might join the magical elite if I want to, should I survive my Ascension Ceremony," said Natalie quietly.

"Would you want to?" asked Alex.

She shrugged. "I have five years to think about it."

"Mine was the same as you two," replied Ellabell quickly, seeming slightly flustered as it came to her turn. It made Alex curious, though he didn't press her. They had all been under a lot of strain lately—perhaps it was simply that.

"This is all just a ruse, though, right?" ventured Alex, know-ing he had no intention of staying at Stillwater House a moment longer than he had to. He didn't trust Alypia's word, but nor did she trust his. If the agreement was a pretense for something else, as it was with his promise, the real motive behind her offer was yet to appear to him. He could sense it had something to do with his being 'special,' like it always seemed to. When nobody appeared to be forthcoming with a response, Alex elaborated. "We're still getting out of here, right?"

Silence and shifty stares followed.

"You're joking," he muttered in disbelief. "Well, *my* goal here is to find another portal, or *make* one if I have to, and get the hell out of this place. I want to get home—I thought that's what we all wanted? Did I miss something? Did she offer you something else, that she didn't offer me? Because otherwise this is ridiculous."

Ellabell nodded. "Absolutely, we're leaving. That's the plan and we're sticking to it. I know I'd like to see home again," she agreed.

Aamir and Natalie didn't seem entirely convinced. Alex caught a look passing between them, though they made noises of agreement toward their waiting friends.

"You shouldn't even have to think about it, guys! Both of you have friends and family out there who are worried sick at home, thinking you're dead or worse. I mean, Natalie—your family sent you off to a foreign country and you *never came back*! Aren't you upset? Don't you feel like you should get home to them, so they can stop worrying about the girl who just vanished off the face of the earth?" Alex struggled to keep himself from yelling. He wanted to shake them into seeing sense. "And though I bare-ly know anything about your family, Aamir, I imagine they feel the same. I bet they're home right now, wishing you would just walk back through the door. Is the power of magic really more important than them?"

The tirade seemed to cow them, forcing them to sheepishly come around to the idea Alex was talking about—as if his words and the memory of their families had removed them momentarily from a slight trance. Their state of mind worried Alex; he did not like to see that they were losing sight of what was important: home.

"Has anyone seen Jari?" asked Alex, realizing their friend was missing.

Aamir shook his head. "Not since the cells."

"Yeah, not since he got taken away," agreed Ellabell, pushing her spectacles anxiously back up the bridge of her nose.

"I have not seen him either," Natalie frowned.

Concern fell over the group as Alex felt a twist of guilt in the pit of his stomach, realizing with some certainty that Jari must have been the only one among them to deny the offer Alypia made. It was the only explanation for his absence.

"Do you think he—" began Alex, only to be interrupted by another knock at the door.

It was Helena, whose face was pale and fearful as she peered around the door, as if she already expected the suspicion they must feel about her. Hurrying in, she closed the door behind her and jumped straight to defending herself.

"I had nothing to do with it!" she yelped. "I didn't tell anyone, I swear—somebody must have seen me rowing over to deliver supplies and sounded the alarm. I didn't say a word about you. You have to believe me!" There was honesty in her plea, but

Alex and the others still maintained a level of caution.

"I thought that might be the case," said Alex, trying to calm the girl.

She nodded. "As soon as I knew they had taken you, I tried to get the guards to let me down to the cells, but they wouldn't, no matter how much I begged. They've never said no to me before, but this time they wouldn't do as I said, and then someone came for me too—I was taken away and punished for hiding you," she explained woefully.

On her pale, porcelain skin, just below the sleeves of her t-shirt, she bore the livid, deep purple bruises of whatever that punishment had entailed. It looked painful, though she didn't show it on her face. As soon as he saw the bruises, Alex felt guilty for what she had suffered, musing grimly how guilty he felt about everything these days.

"Do you know where Jari is?" pressed Alex.

She nodded quickly, lowering her voice. "I know where they're keeping Jari, but I won't be able to get to him to set him free—not today, anyway. He is under heavy guard. I'll need a couple of days to come up with something, but in the meantime, I need you to keep your heads down and do as you're told. It'll give him a better chance."

It was a warning as much as a suggestion, and sounded kindly meant. She seemed genuinely sad about Jari, and Alex could see she shared their concern for him.

"For now, you should rest, clean up, and come down to the refectory for something to eat if you're feeling hungry," she encouraged brightly. "You won't be put onto the schedule for a few days, while you get settled in and recover fully, but you might find you have a guard or two show up if you wander too far into the school," she told them apologetically. "The key places are easy enough to find though—the refectory is down the stairs, through the square, into the building opposite and down the corridor. You can't miss it. Everything you'll need is pretty much signposted, and if you get lost, just ask somebody. I'll meet you at the refectory in a few hours, if you'd like?"

"Thank you, Helena." Alex smiled kindly.

They watched her leave.

When she was gone, the foursome sat around Alex's room, saying very little, though their faces spoke volumes. It was clear they were all thinking about Jari, feeling guilty about their decision to take Alypia's offer.

CHAPTER 23

AFTER A LONG BATH, UNABLE TO RELAX MUCH THANKS to the worry he felt for their still-absent friend, Alex slept for a while, waking as the afternoon was at its peak. It seemed the others had the same idea, as he found them coming toward his room just as he was leaving it to search for them. Though they were all still anxious for Jari, they had little to do with their schedules empty and their bodies rested, and so they decided to explore the school a bit.

As they walked the hallways and sauntered across the piazzas, trying to get to grips with the gigantic villa, Alex noticed that the beautiful students of Stillwater eyed them with a certain wary curiosity, as if they had not seen strangers in a long time. It made Alex think back to Helena's comment about other Stillwater students not being as welcoming as her, but he shrugged it off as they came to a beautiful water garden at the far end of the school.

The air was heavily scented with floral perfume, and vibrant butterflies flitted from flower to flower under the steady hum of unseen bees. A large pond glistened in the center of the garden, koi fish twisting and weaving beneath the water's surface, darting away from streams poured by the hands of expertly sculpted statues into the pool below.

The four of them sat for a while on stone benches, in the shade of a delicate willow, though Natalie stretched out on the slate tiles by the pond like a cat, bathing peacefully in the sunshine as she trailed her hand in the water for the fish to nibble at. Not long after, a Stillwater student came running up with a tray of cakes and drinks. Alex figured this wasn't normal behavior, but he was hungry, and the snacks looked so tempting. They tasted as delicious as they looked. The cakes, moist and light and flavored with lemon, washed down easily with a cup of some exotic red juice that tasted somewhere between cherry and strawberry.

Outside, the architecture could be truly appreciated. All along the archways and levels of the villa, Alex saw tiny details that could only be noticed if you were really looking, like the ornate carvings above the windows, and the clusters of stone grapes, complete with vines, twisting around the eaves of the domes and spiraling towers. Everything at Stillwater House was exquisitely crafted, taking from contemporary and Renaissance influences. Alex knew the villa had to be ancient, yet it didn't look dated—it was fresh and bright, gleaming in the dazzling, hypnotic sunlight.

As the heat became too intense, making the perfume of the flowers seem almost suffocating, the quartet moved back inside to explore the interior some more. They passed several classrooms and saw glimpses of the lessons going on within, led by teachers of beauty equal to that of the stunning students, and who seemed to encourage the talent of their pupils. It was curious to watch the teachers shout out the sections of each spell, assisting students with a firm but friendly hand, so that nobody got left behind. They seemed to genuinely want their students to do well, which surprised Alex. He guessed it must have been because their jobs weren't on the line, as they were at Spellshadow; the teachers in that grim place lived in constant fear of being usurped and having their essence torn away from them. Here, he supposed, if they Ascended and chose to become teachers, their survival and position were surely guaranteed.

Moving down some stairs into a section of subterranean corridors, Alex was pleased to see a mechanics' lab, with a lesson on clockwork taking place within. It meant the students here had a much more varied education than the one at Spellshadow, if clockwork was an actual fixture on the class schedule, as it appeared to be. The sight of it made Alex smile with the bittersweet memory of Professor Lintz, tinkering away at the delicate husk of a clockwork owl, though that thought led his mind back to the students of Spellshadow, and how they were faring. The boatful of guards hadn't returned, as far as Alex knew, but he wasn't sure whether that was a good sign or a bad one; it simply meant the matter hadn't been resolved, one way or the other. He only hoped they were okay, whichever way things were going.

On their second day as actual residents of Stillwater House, a message came for Alex, instructing him to attend an introductory lesson in the Queen's Courtyard at ten a.m. As he washed and dressed and stepped out into the corridor, he saw that the others had received the same message. They walked toward him with anxious looks on their faces.

"Introductory lesson?" he asked.

They nodded.

"Breakfast first?" he suggested.

Another nod, and they all went down to the refectory together, filled with first-day-at-school nerves. Helena appeared at the bottom of the stairs, waving excitedly to them as she led them the rest of the way to the refectory. Having been spoiled the day before with tray service, they had not met with Helena, as they had promised to do, but had gone back to their rooms instead, with stomachs full of cake and chocolates and delicate finger sandwiches. It seemed she didn't hold a grudge, as she dragged them over to introduce them to a group of her friends, who did not seem nearly as impressed as she was.

They ate a simple, clean breakfast of fruit salad and yogurt, sitting in awkward silence as Helena tried, and failed, to stir up conversation between the two different groups. Once they were finished, they all walked together toward the Queen's Courtyard, Helena leading the way, still chirruping enthusiastically as the rest of them followed sullenly, not sharing her delight.

Stepping out into the same courtyard where Alex and Jari had first seen Helena, the quartet were a little intimidated as they saw the rest of the students gathered around them. Some of them, particularly the ones clustered toward the far side of the courtyard, looked much younger than Alex and his friends. All eyes were on them as they waited anxiously for instruction. It came sooner than anticipated, and they were split into pairs with the younger group of the gathered Stillwater students, and set to the task of dueling. The older class, including Helena, paired off on the other side of the courtyard, apparently serving to inspire the younger students.

Alex already knew it would be a wreck for him. He stared hopelessly toward the place where his partner had moved off to. It puzzled him, that he should have been asked to come to this lesson with the others, making him wonder if Alypia knew as much about him as much as she had pretended to.

"Do not worry—I will make you look good," whispered Natalie with a wide smile, as she walked behind him toward her partner.

Alex hoped she could as he stood face to face with his opponent—a tall, waif-like creature a few years younger than him, with long hazelnut hair and striking violet eyes. On her beautiful, perfect face, she wore a grimace of displeasure that made Alex feel about two feet tall.

"Shall we begin?" asked the waif in a clipped, upper-class kind of voice.

"I suppose we should get this over with," he joked, though he wasn't sure her unamused face was capable of laughter.

As they set about fighting, Natalie was more than true to

her word, making Alex an almost even match for his violet-eyed opponent, much to the girl's apparent annoyance. Feeling somewhat smug, he watched as golden vines and shimmering streams surged from his palms, whizzing toward his rival with a speed and vehemence that almost took the girl by surprise. For his own part, he managed to avoid taking any shots to the body, ducking and weaving skillfully to avoid the girl's expert strikes, except for one surprise bolt that hit him straight in the chest. He covered the area quickly with his hand, rushing to stem the flurry of erupting snow. Nobody seemed to see it, though it left a peculiar wet patch that he hoped he could pass off as sweat.

Along the line of paired duelers, Alex noticed that Aamir seemed to be doing well with his young partner, though he was still prone to tiring quickly, and Ellabell was out-and-out excelling against hers. It made Alex smile, to see the determination on the bespectacled girl's face as she sent wave after wave of twisting, coiling magic toward her opponent, peering behind a strong force-field that was proving a tough object for the young man she was pitted against to get through. Natalie was winning her battle too, even with her attentions diverted by Alex's need for help. The extra practice they'd had in the lighthouse and whatever tricks Natalie had learned from Helena during their stay there seemed to be paying off, as Alex watched the French girl send her opponent crashing to the floor in an ungainly mess. Even though their adversaries were younger, there was still a sense of pride at winning; these were not ordinary twelve- and thirteen-year-olds, after all.

Pretty soon, the stern, disapproving looks of the other Stillwater students had turned to smiles and whoops of encouragement, as a good-natured vibe settled across the court-yard. In a way, they had proven themselves worthy to be around the Stillwater elite, and it felt nice to be welcomed into the fold, even if Alex knew his own 'skills' were thanks to Natalie.

Even the teacher, Master Montego, seemed pleased. He was a six-foot-six god of a man with a friendly voice, and his face seemed to be hewn from rock rather than flesh, with a shock of long blond hair and piercing gray eyes that apparently made Natalie go weak at the knees, much to Alex's amusement. Whenever Master Montego passed her, he would remark upon her skill and talent, leaving her tongue-tied and glittery-eyed.

Alex wondered what compliments Natalie would get if the teacher knew she was doing the work of two people and *still* winning.

It was funny to watch her awkwardness around the beautiful young teacher as he distracted her, causing her to fire a bolt directly into a statue's head, blowing it off entirely. She blushed furiously as Master Montego turned to see what the crashing sound was. Alex nudged her lightly in the arm as the teacher walked off again, leaving Natalie to her embarrassment.

"You're almost worse than Jari," he whispered.

Natalie snorted. "At least he never executed an innocent statue."

"That he did not—you're still a long way from kittens, though." He smiled, watching as Natalie returned her focus to the task at hand, a foolish grin on her face.

Alex thought it was strange how easy it was to talk of Jari without the thought continuing to bother him, but there was something intoxicating about the atmosphere of the courtyard;

there was a buzz that would not allow sad thoughts, so Alex didn't allow himself to think any.

As the lesson came to a close, the initial hostilities between the students had become fledgling friendships. The class headed to the refectory together for lunch, the quartet of friends included in the group. The food at Stillwater House was another improvement on Spellshadow, with everything smelling and tasting delicious. Picking up a plate of delicious pasta with fresh tomatoes and artichokes, Alex followed the others and sat down at the table they had chosen, which looked out onto the lake. The sight of it turned Alex's stomach, making his food seem less appealing as he pushed it around his plate. All around him, laughter and a feeling of general contentment warmed the room, though Alex's happiness was peppered with feelings of guilt surrounding Jari. He knew they shouldn't be having a good time while their friend was locked up under heavy guard, but something about the villa seemed to sap away any negativity, replacing it with an inescapable feeling of enthusiasm and positive energy.

It made Alex curious, wondering if there was something in the air that made it so.

By the end of the meal, having brought himself to eat the delicious pasta and a large bowl of raspberry ice cream, Alex found himself musing upon whether five years in this place would be so bad after all. The people were friendly, the food was good, the rooms were comfortable, the teachers were encouraging, the grounds were beautiful, and he had his friends with him.

Maybe this will be a good thing, he thought.

It was at this point that Alex knew there was *definitely*

something wrong with the air, or something in the air at least. There had to be, for him to be thinking that way, in a place he clearly didn't belong, among people who would most likely want him dead if they knew what he was. No, there was definitely something amiss; he could feel it in the crackle of the magic all around him.

Something was manipulating the way they felt.

CHAPTER 24

EVERYONE'S CHEER CONTINUED INTO THE NEXT DAY, though Alex struggled to watch the happiness of the others, who seemed to have easily forgotten the absence of their much-loved friend. He knew they didn't mean to forget him, but it was difficult to see their joy while Jari was suffering, somewhere within these walls. Whatever it was that lingered in the air, it didn't seem to affect Alex as much as his friends, making him wonder if it was because of what he was. Much like with the barriers at Spellshadow, the anti-magic in him seemed to dampen the effects of this magical manipulator.

As they sat down to a wonderful lunch, an announcement interrupted them.

"Students of Stillwater House," began a tall gentleman with curly brown hair. "A special celebration is to be held this evening, to honor our new guests—the first outside students to be enrolled in our fair school in many decades. A truly special occasion deserves truly special festivities, and you are invited to join us by the lake at seven p.m. Everyone's attendance is required, to help welcome our new friends into the fold."

The news seemed to excite Helena, who sat opposite Alex. "This *never* happens!" she squealed, grinning. "There is hardly ever a spontaneous event in the academic year—there was one perhaps a year ago, but that feels like ages ago now. This is so exciting!"

Alex frowned, wondering if she was talking about Blaine Stalwart's ill-fated battle in the arena. "What kind of event was it?" he asked.

She shrugged. "A fight of some sort. Most unusual, but I can't really remember it now. It was so long ago! This really is very exciting—it's always nice to celebrate!"

She didn't seem to recall it very clearly, making Alex wonder if it was due to whatever was in the air, molding and melding the thoughts and memories of the students within Stillwater, so as to keep up the pretense of everything being wonderful, with no negativity of any sort.

Helena's excitement was infectious, her excitement spreading to the others—even carrying Alex along slightly, despite himself. Ellabell appeared especially encouraging toward Alex's dour state, trying to get him in the party spirit.

"It'll be good to let our hair down!" she insisted. "Things have been so bad for so long. We deserve to have a little fun."

Around the table, the others chattered excitedly about the evening, asking Helena questions about what they might expect, though they were particularly curious about the music, the food, and the dancing. Alex watched them fondly as they talked, wishing he could feel so carefree.

He just couldn't stop thinking about Jari. As Helena was about to leave the refectory for her afternoon lessons, Alex caught her by the arm and pulled her to one side, waiting until everyone had gone so that he might speak with her in private.

"How is Jari?" he asked.

A regretful look passed across Helena's golden eyes. "I'm still working on the plan to break him out, but I have it on good authority that he's okay—they are treating him well and they aren't hurting him or anything. They're simply figuring out what to do with him, I believe." She sounded genuinely sorrowful as she relayed the news to Alex.

He frowned. "What did he do to get locked up in the first place?" he asked, though he was already fairly sure he knew the answer.

"I think it was because he wouldn't do what the Headmistress wanted him to do… She can be like that," replied Helena sadly. "She won't hurt him, though. He's no use to her dead."

Alex tried not to grimace as she stated the obvious. He could be sure of that much—the people in power in these places were not in the habit of wasting the life essence of mages. Leveling his gaze at Helena, he wondered how much she knew about the offers the Headmistress had made to them, but she wasn't being forthcoming with that information, if she did know it. Not once in her mention of Jari's imprisonment had she said a word about any offers.

"Thank you for caring," said Alex softly.

"Of course. I care deeply about what happens to all of you," she replied with sincerity. She walked with Alex out of the refectory and through the halls to her next class. He accompanied her most of the way, wanting to seize the opportunity to talk more openly with her, one-on-one.

"We might need your help again, in the near future, if you can give it," he said, keeping his voice low.

Helena nodded. "Have you thought any more on what your next move is going to be?"

"I want to find or make a portal to the outside world," he answered as vaguely as he could, careful to avoid any mention of his desire to steal or destroy the bottles of essence, which he was certain were hiding somewhere in the school.

Her golden eyes went wide with excitement. "The outside world? You mean the non-magical one?"

He smiled. "Yes—home is out there. That's where we want to be."

"Tell me about it," she pleaded, suddenly melancholic.

"What do you want to know?"

"Tell me of somewhere beautiful." Her expression was almost wistful.

"Okay… If you walk to the edge of my town, there's a patch of woodland that you can walk through, and sometimes you'll see a deer or a squirrel or a raccoon. The cars honk at you as you cross the road to get to it because there's no sidewalk running next to it, but once you get into the forest, it's silent—you can't hear the cars on the road or the people." He paused, seeing that Helena had closed her eyes. He wasn't sure if she even knew what cars were, but he continued, "Then, you walk through the woods and come out the other side, where there are train tracks running from one side of a ravine to the other. The river isn't much to look at, but it's down there. Sometimes, in the spring, it fills with rushing water from the ice melting in the mountains miles and miles away. When I was younger, I used to walk to the edge of the ravine and climb under the railway sleepers—my mom would have gone mad if she knew, but it's what all the kids did. I'd climb along the frame underneath the railway line until I reached a place where two wooden beams connected in a cross, a short way below the actual tracks. I'd lie there for hours, staring up at the sun beaming down between the slats, just waiting for a train to clatter across the top. It only did it a handful of times when I was there, but the noise was something else—the rattle of it in your ears, leaving them ringing for days afterward. It was scary and terrifying and wonderful, but somehow beautiful, with the river and the ravine walls and the trees and the silence."

Stopping, he saw a tear running down Helena's perfect cheek. It surprised him—these Stillwater folk looked too faultless to show such raw emotion, but, nevertheless, she was crying. She even did that beautifully.

"Are you okay?" he asked quietly, reluctant to disturb her reverie.

She nodded. "It has been so long that I can't remember what the non-magical world looks like. I was a small child the last time I saw it, before I came here. What a beautiful place it must be. Thank you for telling me that story. I shall treasure it," she said shyly, brushing the tears away from her face.

"You've been out there?"

"Once upon a time." She smiled wanly.

"Do you think you can help us get back out there?" he pressed, pleased to see her taking an interest in it.

Glancing around furtively, she leaned closer to Alex. "I believe I can," she whispered. "I may even wish to come with you, if you would allow me."

This revelation surprised Alex, and he glanced curiously in her direction. He had presumed she was happy here at Stillwater, but he could now see that a seam of anxiety had run in the background of every thought and action she had made, up to that point. Where others happily obeyed every rule, she had dared to go against them. Where others smiled, she had cried. Where others would have handed them in, she had defied the Headmistress to keep them hidden. Where others would have seen him on the wall and raised the alarm, she had smiled and let her curiosity lead her to them. It was as if she were not quite as affected by the magic in the air as he had thought; she was not as hypnotized as the rest of them, and he wondered silently if this anxious, rebellious streak of hers had something to do with it.

However, before he could give an answer to her request to come with them, she stopped him by placing her fingers gently on his mouth, shocking him into sudden silence. It was as if she already knew he wanted to say "I'm not sure about that" to what she asked.

"Don't answer now—I implore you to think on it. Please, Alex—I am begging you to just think about it," she said, before turning and disappearing down the hallway, leaving Alex to his shock.

His mouth tingled strangely where she had rested her fingers, and he felt the burn of her magic on his lips for a long while afterward as he returned to his room in a confused daze.

Opening the door, he was in for his second surprise of the day, as he noticed the suit that had been lain out on the bedcover. Reaching out to touch it, he could feel that it was made of some exquisite, silken fabric. He held it up to get a better view, and saw that it was a suit cut in a more Indian style of dress—a long coat-style jacket with a high collar and intricate embroidery, to be fastened up the front with shining buttons. There were brushed silk trousers of the same dark gray color that he hoped would suit him. With the magic of Stillwater, he was almost certain it would—they didn't allow anything short of perfection, after all.

It was beautiful to behold, though Alex had never owned a suit in his life, and there was an envelope on the bed beside it. He picked it up and slid out the card; it was a formal invitation to the evening's proceedings, the text written in an elegant hand on the cream vellum of the card.

Dear Mr. Alex Webber,

You are cordially invited to celebrations in your honor at Stillwater House. Please meet at the dining area beside the lake at seven p.m. sharp. You are expected to dress formally for the occasion, and shall sit at the high table with the rest of our honored guests.

We look forward to your presence.

Warmest Regards,

The Crown Princess Alypia.

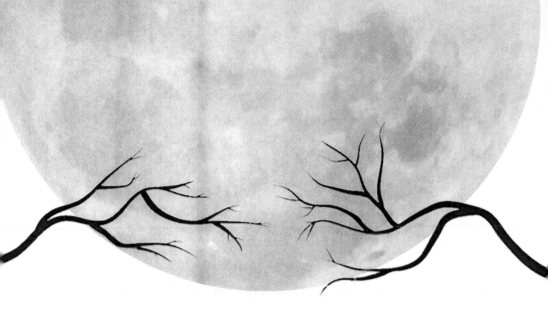

CHAPTER 25

A S AFTERNOON TURNED INTO EVENING, ALEX TOOK A
bath and put on the suit, hoping it was the right
size. Buttoning up the last fastening, he needn't
have worried—it fit him like a dream, making him look more
handsome than he had ever looked. He didn't know if it was
some trickery or glamor within the suit that made him look that
way, but he couldn't deny it made him feel good. Standing in
front of the small square mirror that hung on the wall in the
bathroom, he brushed his hair neatly, as his mother would have
reminded him to do, and looked at himself properly for the first
time in ages.

After so long looking rough and exhausted, with all manner
of muck and grime on his face, it was nice to see the shadow of
his former self—that the boy who had anxiously accompanied

Natalie to a high school party, like any normal teenager, hadn't disappeared for good. He had just been buried under layers of dirt and misery and struggle.

As he stepped back into the main section of his bedroom, there was a light knock at the door.

"Come in," called Alex brightly, and Aamir appeared.

Alex smiled. Aamir looked great, the style and dark, cobalt blue of the outfit suiting the older boy perfectly. He was grinning from ear to ear, and the sight warmed Alex's heart. It seemed like it wasn't just Alex who was feeling more like his former self.

"You ready to go?" asked Aamir.

"You bet," replied Alex, patting his friend on the back.

They walked down to meet the girls, chatting amicably, but their words came to an abrupt halt as they caught sight of Natalie, Ellabell, and Helena. The boys' jaws dropped. All three young women were dressed in stunning gowns that fit to perfection, made in the perfect color for each one. Helena's silvery gown was similar to the one she had worn on the evening of the Ascension Ceremony, but Ellabell and Natalie's were in colors Alex wasn't even sure he knew the names of. Natalie's gown was a deep, gun-metal gray that complemented her tan complexion, whereas Ellabell's was a pale turquoise shade that matched her eyes. In their intricately styled hair, jewels glittered alongside interweaving bands of precious metals, catching the light whichever way they turned.

Alex couldn't take his eyes off Ellabell, and she seemed equally smitten by the sight of Alex in his suit.

Speechless, the two young men walked toward the ladies. Aamir took Natalie's arm and Alex took Ellabell's, before following the beautiful Helena out of the villa toward the lakeshore, where tables had been set up all along the sunset-drenched banks, draped in pale cream and gold cloths that billowed gently in the light, warm breeze that blew across the lake. As they arrived, a banquet fit for a king was being laid out, the smells making Alex's mouth water as he passed. Helena led them to the head table, where they were to sit as guests of honor, facing the other tables. The four friends glanced at each other, quietly stunned, as they took their seats and waited for the other students to arrive. They didn't have long to wait, as the other tables quickly filled with the rest of Stillwater, in all their finery.

Alex caught Natalie blushing as Master Montego strode up to the high table and personally welcomed the new recruits, planting a suave kiss on the hands of Ellabell and Natalie, though it was only Natalie that the action flustered. It was hard not to smile, even while Alex kept trying to focus on Jari and the need to find information about creating portals. He feared that if he lost sight of his goals for long enough, he would never be able to recall them. However, each time he managed to distract his mind, his attention was snatched up again by Ellabell laughing or asking him something, drawing him in with her sparkling blue eyes and her easy humor. Other times, his attention waned thanks to the taste of something delicious on his plate, or the sweet tang of the drinks being poured. He doubted they were alcoholic, but the sweet, sparkling liquid made him feel unexpectedly giddy and suddenly more affable, making it harder and harder to focus on the desire to leave this place.

After the banquet was over and they were all stuffed to bursting, the Headmistress stood.

"In honor of our guests, I have arranged for celebratory games to take place in the arena this evening!" she announced, and a cry of joy went up from the students. "If you could make your way over, we shall begin the next part of our festivities, welcoming our new students!"

Full and satisfied, everyone rose and walked slowly from the lakeshore toward the arena, the dinner making them sluggish as they chattered excitedly about the rest of the evening's festivities. Already, the great torches had been lit, illuminating the raked seating and the circular pitch that had been freshly repainted on the grass. Alex could feel the warmth of the flames on his face as he followed Helena to the top of the amphitheater, where they were shown to their seats.

For once, Alex permitted himself to feel happy—he even whooped along with the others as the first duel began on the field below. It was a friendly match between two Stillwater students, with no dire consequences for either of them; it was simply a display of Stillwater strength. Somehow, it seemed almost enjoyable to watch a duel, when Alex knew nobody was going to die at the end of it.

It was fascinating to watch the twist and turn of golden magic as it surged from the palms of the duelers, controlling when and how their opponent moved. The duel was as much about defense as offense, and Alex couldn't stop following the rapid movements of their hands as they conjured spell after spell, trying to outdo each other. Most matches were evenly balanced, with some opponents being masters of shield magic, while others were experts at building magical weaponry. In one pairing, a young woman seemed faultless at swiping magic from the air and turning it back on her opponent, much to their annoyance as they had to duck and run from their own magic. It was a trick Alex wanted to master himself, and he made a silent promise to practice it, the next opportunity he got.

They watched a few more duels as the hour grew later. Each one was more thrilling and powerful than the last, making Alex wide-eyed in anticipation of what would be next.

When Helena stepped up to the pitch, it was clear that she was, indeed, more ferocious and intimidating than any of them had thought possible. Twisting her hands so fast they weren't even visible, Helena made quick work of her opponent, grinning a touch manically all the while, as she sent waves of fierce, crackling, deep bronze magic at him. Everything she did seemed easy, though the spells were powerful. She tore his magic from his hands before he even had chance to use it and stretched it into a shield that wrapped itself around him, constricting him each time he tried to fight back. Alongside it, she conjured shivering snakes of golden light that rippled toward him, making his body seize and shake as they hit him. At one point, she seemed to be conjuring four things at once, to Alex's awe and admiration. Aside from the crackle of her magic, it was silent enough to hear a pin drop as everyone watched, enraptured.

She won with ease, reminding Alex of the terrifying female warriors from the *Battles* book Elias had given him—the Gilded Vipers.

As the field cleared, Alypia stood up from her throne at the center of the amphitheater, opening her arms wide as she made her announcement. The rest of the students fell silent, going still with anticipation as they watched one of their own run out from the tunnel beneath them. He waved at the crowd, garnering an enthusiastic cheer.

"And now, I give you the main event!" Alypia bellowed.

All eyes turned to the arena floor. A slow-moving figure walked out from the other tunnel, his head bowed.

Nobody cheered.

Horror flooded Alex's senses as he saw who it was. There was a golden glitter rippling down the stooped back of the figure, forcing him to walk forward, even though Alex could see that he was trying to fight it with all of his might, twisting against the magic that pushed him on.

Alex turned to the others. They were staring at the arena too—an echoed expression of horror on their faces.

Jari had entered the arena.

CHAPTER 26

THEY HAD BEEN ENJOYING THEMSELVES, AND, ALL THE while, Jari had been beneath the stands, tormented and tortured into walking onto the arena floor, for the amusement of the Headmistress and her merry band of zombie students.

Once inside the circular lines of the arena, the thrum of the barrier went up, trapping Jari inside with the Stillwater student. From where he was sitting, Alex could see that Jari was already on the brink of exhaustion, his stance sloping, his knees shaking, his face drawn and his blond hair lank.

Alex's gaze flitted anxiously across the amphitheater, trying to seek out Helena, to ask her what the hell was going on, but she hadn't yet returned from her stint on the battlefield. Suspicion prickled up Alex's spine—Helena had promised him that Jari hadn't been hurt, but he looked pretty hurt from where Alex was sitting.

Alex watched in horror as the Headmistress gestured for them to begin. With terror distorting his face, Jari backed desperately up against the barrier, trying to claw his way out, only to be hurled forward by a blast of energy from the barrier itself, forcing him into the fray. He crumpled to the ground, lying still for a moment as Alex willed him to stand up again. Slowly, the blond-haired boy managed to pick himself back up, dragging himself to his feet as the Stillwater student sent strands of glimmering, vicious magic in Jari's direction. As one sailed straight for Jari's head, the younger boy succeeded in snatching it from the air and sending it hurtling harmlessly toward the barrier instead.

More magic rushed toward him, in wave after wave of golden artillery, but Jari swiped the blows away, managing to duck whatever he couldn't disperse. For the first ten minutes or so, Jari put up a good fight, not allowing anything to hit him, but Alex could see that he was faltering. With each swipe of his hand, Jari faded. Watching the vile scene unfold, Alex felt the familiar sensation of fury building inside him, burning brighter at the sight of his friend in trouble.

He stood sharply, but Natalie grabbed his arm.

"There is nothing you can do," she hissed, trying to get him to take his seat again. "There are too many, Alex—you cannot help him. Think of what might happen if you were to reveal your powers in front of so many mages. Think of what they will do to you." Her dark eyes begged him to sit down.

Alex paused, sinking slowly back down to his seat in utter

disbelief. Glancing toward Aamir for support, he saw that the older boy had turned his face away. Beside him, Ellabell was staring blankly down into her lap, not wanting to acknowledge what was going on below.

Alex could not believe Aamir's response to what was happening, after the lengths Jari had gone to when Aamir had needed help. Jari had always been there for his friend, and now his friend was turning his face away.

"How can you let this happen, Aamir, after everything Jari did for you when you needed him?" snapped Alex. "How can you just sit there?"

Aamir would not look him in the eyes.

On the field, Jari was close to collapse, his knees buckling and his eyes rolling back into his head. Rage coursed through Alex—he knew his friend didn't have long.

It was the spur to action that Alex needed. He rose from his seat once more, anger seething through every cell in his body, strengthening his powers. A surge of pent-up angst and rage flowed inside him, coiling through his body like a viper ready to strike.

As he blinked toward the arena, his eyes felt strange and hot, as his anti-magic swelled. Lifting his hands, he sent a bolt of pure, electric energy crackling through the air toward the barrier. The noise of it was like thunder overhead, booming through sky, shaking the ground beneath them. Natalie tried to reach up and stop him, but she couldn't get near without hurting herself. A shield had appeared around him, swirling in the air in ripples of black and silver, bristling and thrumming with energy, keeping anyone who tried to stop him at bay.

Ellabell called to him, begging him to stop, but he was deaf to her voice, focusing only on the arena and the crumpled figure of Jari, who had fallen to the ground and did not seem to be getting up.

The face of every Stillwater student turned and watched him with dread, but Alex didn't care. He barely saw them as he fired another pulse of pure silver energy toward the barrier, watching with satisfaction as the shield shattered around Jari and his opponent in a great blizzard of snow and ice. Jari's adversary was still firing magic, though Jari was unable to fight back, his body bending and contorting with each blow. Enraged, Alex let his anti-magic flow toward Jari, wrapping the younger boy in a shield that protected him from his adversary's golden blasts.

By this point, the student fighting Jari had stopped what he was doing to look in fear at the air pulsating around him, black and silver, and the flurries of snow that rebounded from the shielded Jari. Frowning, Alex noticed that the opponent no longer looked as perfect as he had previously. Somehow, the shimmering heat of his anti-magic had distorted the face of the Stillwater student.

Alex walked down the stairwell, his body pulsing with energy, his eyes still burning with a hot fury. His hands crackled with pure anti-magical force, and the students in his way moved swiftly from the terrifying power that gravitated around him. Alex saw that they, too, seemed to have lost their sheen of beauty, as he viewed them from behind the lens of his anti-magical shield. Which version was the truth? Alex was no longer sure.

Knowing he didn't have time to mull it over just now, he strode down the rest of the stairs and out across the field. As he moved toward Jari, he caught sight of the Stillwater student, attempting to fire a spear of golden energy at him, but Alex was too fast. He turned swiftly and swiped the weapon away, managing to send it back toward the student. Ducking just in time, the returned magic skimmed past the student's ear. A look of sheer terror passed across the young man's face.

Alex walked over to where Jari lay and knelt on the ground beside his friend, reaching out for Jari's hand. The anti-magic that flowed from his hand parted around Jari's skin, so no fleck of anti-magical energy wounded him. Alex wasn't sure how he had managed it, but he wasn't about to complain, when it meant he could comfort his friend.

"I'm here, Jari. You're safe now," he whispered.

Jari wept softly into the grass, his weary shoulders shaking. When he looked up at Alex, a strange expression crossed his face—fear. Alex was taken aback, but he didn't remove his hand. *Fear of what?* Alex thought. *Of me?*

As the flurries settled and melted from the shattered barrier, Alex glanced back at the crowd and caught sight of the Headmistress in her throne, smiling smugly, as if Alex had just confirmed what she already knew. He found that, in that instant, he didn't care. Jari was safe, and if his own secret was the price for that safety, then so be it.

He frowned, however, when he saw the shrouded figure standing beside her. The figure moved as if to step into the light, but the Headmistress lifted her hand quickly, holding her arm out to prevent the shadowed being from doing so. The hood was familiar. Alex knew exactly who it was—the Head come to gloat, no doubt. Seething, Alex flashed a glare of hatred toward them both, casting it across the other students as well. Their altered faces and terrified eyes stared back.

It was only as the tremor of his anti-magic began to subside that their faces returned to normal, the sheen of beauty restored, though the fear in their eyes did not go away. They had seen something in Alex that had scared them, but he had the feeling there was more to it than just his Spellbreaker heritage. The burning sensation in his eyes and the pulse in his veins alarmed even him, not quite knowing where they came from. It wasn't like any anti-magic he'd ever felt before.

"This is over!" he roared.

Lifting Jari to his feet, Alex carried the boy away toward the tunnels, knocking into Helena as they ducked into the entrance of the one on the left. She looked up in surprise and alarm as she registered the savage expression on Alex's face.

"Where is the infirmary?" demanded Alex, the rage still thick in his voice.

It appeared that Helena had missed the whole debacle, as she glanced from Alex to Jari, her golden eyes going wide in surprise as she saw the state the latter was in. He was barely able to hold himself up, his body broken.

"I didn't know, Alex—oh my goodness, I didn't know!" she cried as she rushed to assist, looping Jari's arm around her neck.

As they made their way back toward the villa, Alex refused to look back. If he did, he knew he would not be able to control the hatred he felt. If he kept his eyes forward, there was hope. Hope for Jari, hope for all of those who had watched and done nothing.

CHAPTER 27

ALEX SAT BESIDE JARI IN THE INFIRMARY, TRYING TO stay awake as he watched over his friend.

Jari was asleep but alive, though the wizard on duty explained to Alex, with somber warning, that it had been a close call. He was recovering, but it was likely to take a while—the boy had taken a beating, and not just on the battlefield. From the bruises and welts all across Jari's skin, Alex could tell that he had been suffering long before he ever made it to the arena floor. Whoever had done this to him had wanted to make sure he was weak enough to fail quickly. Jari was a fearsome mage, and even though he had been pitted against a Stillwater student of superior ability, he would never have simply given up as swiftly as he had, without being broken to within an inch of his life. He would have kept fighting, kept taking the hits, until he had nothing left, but Alex knew Jari had walked onto that field already beaten.

Alex had expected the Headmistress to come straight for him, but she did not. If she meant to torture him by stringing out the suspense, Alex no longer cared.

On the other side of the bed, Helena sat in an identical chair to the one Alex sat in, trying equally hard to stay awake. She hadn't left Jari's side for a moment, her hands clutching his as he slept.

"I feel so responsible—I should have known this would happen. I should have known they were lying," she said quietly, brushing tears from her eyes.

Alex turned to her. "What happened? You told me he was fine. You *promised* me he was fine."

"I thought he was. It's what they told me. They said he was fine," she replied miserably, shaking her head.

"Who are 'they?'" he asked, frowning.

Suddenly cagey, Helena turned her face away. "Just somebody I know in the villa, who was supposed to be taking care of him," she explained vaguely.

Alex didn't get to ask any more questions, as Jari stirred beneath the covers, interrupting their conversation. He awoke slowly, his manner groggy and his eyes swollen. He glanced around in confusion.

"Where—?" he rasped.

"You're in the infirmary. You're safe," said Alex.

"Alex! Thank you," whispered Jari in a dopey voice. "Hey— your eyes were silver! I've never seen you do that before," he mused deliriously as a grin spread across his face.

Alex looked at his friend with confusion, putting the strange comment down to Jari being tired and disoriented after the suffering he had undergone. The exhaustion was still apparent on his face, but the boy seemed intent on fighting sleep as he gazed around the room, his eyes coming to rest adoringly on the face of Helena.

"Are you an angel?" he asked slowly.

She giggled. "No, Jari—it's just me, Helena."

"So, you *are* an angel." He grinned like an idiot, lifting his hands with slow surprise as he saw her clutching them. "Well, if I'd known *this* was how you got the girl, I'd have done it ages ago!" He chuckled to himself, hopped up on whatever spell the medical mage had run through him.

Alex smiled, happy to see his friend hadn't lost his sense of priorities.

"Jari?" he said, waiting for the boy to make the laborious turn back toward him.

"Alex, my man!" Jari giggled.

"What happened to you?" Alex asked, trying to keep the smirk from his face. As much as he wanted to have a serious conversation with Jari, the boy was being amusing.

"What happened to me? I'll tell you what happened to me. That *woman*, you know, the big, tall, pretty one with the evil stare," he began dramatically. "Well, she made me this offer, and I was like 'Dude, I'm not taking that—no way, Jose.' And she got real mad. It was like five years and then a fight to the death or some nonsense—I guess it was more like five minutes and a fight to the death, eh?" he cackled, clearly pleased with himself. "Thank you, by the way, for coming in guns blazing with your weird little eyes!"

Alex smiled. "It was no problem, Jari. Did she say anything else to you?"

Jari paused thoughtfully. "Yeah. She wanted me to spy on you and report back, like some dastardly supervillain. I was like, who do you think I am? The name's Bond, James Bond." He grinned, making finger guns as he dove headfirst into a poor Sean Connery impression. "Not sure why—something to do with powers and stuff. She was all like 'I'll kill Alex if you don't do what I say,' and I was like 'Yeah, good one.' I didn't believe her because you're too mega special to kill. Everyone's always like 'Alex is so special,' 'look at his special glowing powers,' 'super special Alex.' Everybody wants you alive, man. I knew she was bluffing—can't get nothing past me!" He grinned, trying and failing to wink as he turned back toward Helena, who was chuckling away in her chair.

Alex laughed softly, though he felt responsibility weighing heavily on him once more. Because of him and what he was, a friend had almost died.

"Hey, Mopey McMope!" yelped Jari, as if he'd read Alex's mind. "None of this is your fault, man. I know you'll think it is because you're you and that's what you do, but it's not—you brought us the closest to freedom we have been. I could almost taste that sweet, sweet freedom, and we'll still taste it, my man. You'll see. Hope is not lost," he assured Alex with another failed attempt at a wink, before turning back to Helena with adoring, dopey eyes.

"And I can still help with the portals. I'm much closer to finding the book I need," Helena chimed in quietly, much to

Jari's confusion.

"Portals? Are we going back to Spellshadow? Why are we going back?" He flashed Alex a look of concern, though his eyes were somewhat crossed.

"No, not Spellshadow. Helena has agreed to help find information on portals so we might find one or make one that can get us back to the outside world… to home," explained Alex.

The idea seemed to perk up an already perky Jari. "Can you really do it?" he asked.

"It can be done. It will take a lot of energy and a lot of magic, but there are books on the subject, and I am trying to find them," she assured Jari, squeezing his hand.

"How about the library?" suggested Jari, suddenly speaking in a farcical British accent that made Alex and Helena laugh out loud.

"Some books are kept away from students, you see," began Helena, wiping the merry tears from her eyes, "so I can't merely try the library."

Just like at Spellshadow. "Any way you could get a hold of those books?" asked Alex.

She shrugged. "I can get into the private areas—they're only really meant for teachers and the Headmistress, but I've learned how to sneak in without anyone knowing," she murmured, looking as if she regretted imparting this information to them.

"How?" pressed Alex.

Helena looked as if she *really* regretted it now. She fidgeted. "I just know a way—it's complicated," she answered finally with a grimace, as if she knew it was a weak excuse.

Alex wondered what Helena wasn't telling them. She

certainly seemed to have secrets of her own. He had wanted to come clean with her about *his* secret, but her caginess kept him from bringing it up. Besides, he was certain she'd find out what he was soon enough. Right now, Helena was probably the only mage in Stillwater House who *didn't* know what he was.

"Hey, how come you guys didn't get all beat up like me? Did you have to fight too?" asked Jari, distracting Alex from his train of thought.

Alex felt a twist of shame as he heard the hope in Jari's voice. The boy, Alex understood, had yet to realize that he had been the only one to reject Alypia's offer. The rest of them had been cowardly.

Alex shook his head. "We took the offers, Jari. Ours were slightly different from yours, I think. She didn't ask me to spy or anything," he admitted sheepishly.

"What?" breathed Jari, his forehead furrowed in confusion.

"I had no intention of staying, though. It was just an excuse to buy more time. I figured we'd be better off at Stillwater, coming up with a plan, what with the library and everything… but we were never going to stay. Don't worry," he assured Jari.

This news seemed to cheer Jari up. "How about the others—were they in on it too? Where are they?" he asked, glancing around for them.

Alex didn't feel he had the stomach to tell Jari that the others—particularly Natalie and Aamir—seemed to like Stillwater House, and had been less than forthcoming with their continued desire to leave Stillwater. He didn't think he could deal with the disappointment he knew he'd see in Jari's eyes, once the blond-haired boy learned of it, so he didn't say a word on the matter.

"The arena was pretty crowded. I'm sure they'll be along soon," he replied instead, hopeful that they would show up, despite the creeping sense of dread he felt at their absence. He guessed the Headmistress would be angry about what had happened at the arena; he just hoped his friends would not be punished for his actions, especially when they had tried to stop him.

Jari nodded. "Cool. I might take a little nap. You wake me when they get here," he muttered, his eyelids sliding shut. Within a minute, he was snoring softly. Alex wasn't surprised. The evening had sucked out about as much energy from Jari as was possible. He hadn't even expected the blond-haired boy to wake up for a long while, but Jari had never been one to disappoint an attentive audience.

"Do you mind if I stay?" enquired Helena uncertainly.

Alex nodded, smiling at her. "You *should* stay—he'd want you here."

They both sat back in their chairs, watching Jari as he slept soundly beneath the covers, resting away the exhaustion and pain of the last few days. It was a relatively new sensation, but Alex couldn't help feeling a profound sense of protectiveness over his friend, and though he knew he, himself, needed some rest, he kept his eyes open, determined to stand sentinel over his ward.

"What happened out there?" asked Helena.

"In the arena?"

She nodded. "Jari said something about blazing guns and silver eyes."

"I have a secret." He sighed, realizing he was going to have to tell her after all.

"What kind of secret?"

"I've not been entirely honest with you—about what I am," he explained.

She tilted her head. "I don't follow."

"See, the thing is," he began, finding his throat dry, "I'm not a mage… I'm a Spellbreaker."

Her golden eyes flashed with astonishment. "What?" she gasped.

"I would say don't tell anyone, but I think everyone saw." He shrugged dejectedly. The admission made it seem real, all of a sudden, and he wasn't sure how comfortable his new position felt.

"Do the others know?"

He nodded. "They do."

She looked at him strangely, as though she were trying to figure out whether to despise him or be in awe of him. Her expression settled on a mixture of the two. "I can't believe you're a—"

She was cut off by a knock at the door, which stirred Alex from his thoughts. The other three entered the room, looking decidedly sheepish. As annoyed as Alex was with their tardiness, he was pleased to have the distraction; he wasn't sure how much more he wanted to say about his heritage to Helena. He just hoped she didn't loathe him for it. It wasn't exactly his choice, after all.

Alex glared. "Where have you been?" he asked quietly, not wanting to wake the sleeping Jari.

"We were detained—the Headmistress wanted to speak with us, but we came as quickly as we could," replied Aamir, his eyes flitting toward the curled-up figure on the bed.

Alex walked across to Ellabell, pulling her to one side as Aamir and Natalie pushed past him toward Jari.

"What happened?" asked Alex, concern flashing in his eyes as he saw Ellabell's worried expression.

"The Headmistress had us taken away. She questioned us," she explained rapidly, her voice shaking. "She wanted to know how long we had known about your powers."

"Did she hurt you?" he murmured, checking her arms for any bruises.

She shook her head. "No. She didn't seem mad or annoyed or anything. It was odd."

Alex frowned. "So what *did* she say?"

"She just told us we could stay, as planned, despite what had gone on," said Ellabell, holding onto Alex's hands tightly. Her own hands were shaking as she relayed the information to him, her blue eyes wide with stress.

"And me?"

She nodded. "You too."

Alex sighed loudly. None of this added up. He knew Alypia was not a benevolent creature; she would come for him in due course. Until then, it seemed, she had chosen to hide behind a masquerade of goodwill and kind intentions. It did not sit well with Alex. It was like spotting a lion in the bushes and simply waiting for it to pounce.

Turning back toward the bed, Alex saw that Aamir was by Jari's side, apologizing profusely. Jari was awake again, though he looked a little groggy.

"Forgive me, Jari. I have been an idiot. I should have stood up and done something, but I was scared and stupid. I'm so sorry, Jari—please forgive me," he begged.

On the other side, Natalie was holding Jari's hand, having taken the place of Helena, who stood to one side, allowing the old friends their moment. It was a sweet image, and Alex didn't want to disturb it with his frustrations and the residual anger he felt toward his friends for standing by as Jari was almost killed. He guessed it had something to do with the magic that crackled and buzzed in the air, so quietly they had almost forgotten about it, but he knew he needed to clear his head before he did or said anything he would regret.

"I'm just going to step out for a moment," he announced, before turning on his heel and leaving the infirmary.

As he stepped out into the hallway, he realized his error. Within the infirmary, he had been in a bubble of friends, but out here he had to face the music. The corridors were still full of Stillwater students, filtering in from the festivities. He could not turn a corner without bumping into one, and each time, he was met with the same frosty reception and fearful scrutiny. They observed him with cold stares, low voices, and whispered threats as he passed by. Where once there might have been fledgling friendships, now there was wariness, as they peered at him in fear.

"You're not welcome," whispered one.

"You know what we do to your kind," hissed another.

"Let's see if you sink with the rest of them," growled a third.

They knew what he was, but they had never seen one before—he may as well have been an alien to them. He was an unknown entity, and they feared the unknown. Helena had said so.

They didn't like outsiders, much less ones with powers they had never seen, only heard about in ancient tales.

Oddly, there was awe too. In some faces, he saw a flash of it. It had been the same with Helena—that blend of disgust and wonder. Not having seen it for himself, Alex wondered what it was he had done that had caused so much fear and amazement, in almost equal measure. As he felt the burn of eyes staring him down, he wasn't sure whether he was cast in the part of hero or villain. Shrugging them off, he realized he didn't care which role they wanted to pigeon-hole him into. Standing up to the Headmistress had made him lose that desire to belong. In that moment, with Jari's life on the line, he hadn't cared whether he belonged. It had been his difference that had saved Jari's life.

Swiftly, he made his way across the Queen's Courtyard and scrambled up the outer wall, following the familiar route as he dropped down onto the field beyond, his eyes seeking out the crumbling white cottage, hidden away in the tree-line. He headed toward where he remembered it being, longing for the privacy and freedom they'd had back then, in their first days on the shores of Stillwater.

It had been a mistake, going into the school. He sensed that now.

In this world, they were no longer safe. None of them were… if they ever had been.

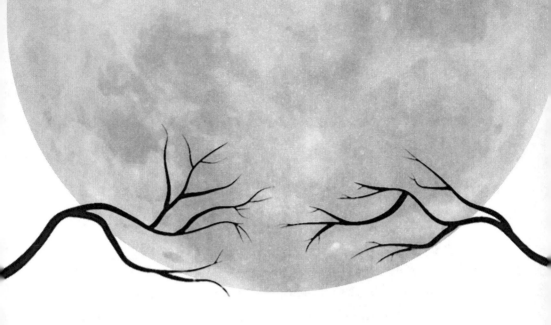

CHAPTER 28

D ARKNESS FELL WITH ALEX STILL OUTSIDE THE SCHOOL
walls. He couldn't face any of them—not his friends,
not the other Stillwater students, none of them. So he
stayed hidden, taking a moment for himself. He figured they
would come looking for him if he was needed, and so he sat
within the small cottage, gazing out toward the sparkling lake,
allowing his mind to wander.

It seemed impossible that more than a year had passed since
he had made the doomed journey to Spellshadow Manor, following Natalie through the gate. Sighing, he wondered if he would
ever get to see his mother again. He missed her so much it hurt
to think about her. Each memory physically stung, scraping at
his insides, gripping his heart. Helena's optimistic thoughts on
portals had made him slightly more positive, but he couldn't be

certain the girl would come through; there was still too much he didn't know about her, and he didn't feel comfortable with the gaps in his knowledge.

Closing his eyes, he let the magical world fall away, thinking instead about what life might have been like if he and Natalie hadn't left the real, non-magical world. If he had somehow managed to prevent her from following Finder, or if neither of them had been supernaturally gifted in any way, where might they be now? With a wistful smile, he thought about a world without magic, where nobody came for Natalie and nobody bothered them. Where he was still a regular teenager, staying up all hours to get through a stack of programming, showing the new French exchange student around town. They would have eaten pancakes with strawberries every morning, and his mother would be singing in the kitchen, pleased to see her hermit of a son socializing with such a nice, intelligent girl. He imagined the college applications, the final exams, the school interviews and the anxious wait for letters to fall onto the mat in the hall, offering him a place somewhere. Maybe he wouldn't have gone to college at all; perhaps his business would've taken off and he would be doing that full-time, saving up enough money to pay his mother's medical bills and buy a bigger place for them, where she could be comfortable.

There might even have been enough money left over for plane tickets to Europe. A visit to see Natalie, maybe, if his initial crush hadn't faded to simple friendship. If they had never come to Spellshadow, who knew what might have happened? He doubted she would be his girlfriend, what with the distance, but she might have been a summer romance, had they had the luxury of time. It felt strange to think of his friend like that, especially now he found himself drawn to Ellabell; she was one of the few bright lights in the darkness of walking through those Spellshadow gates, and if he had never followed Natalie that day, it was certain he would never have met the pretty, bespectacled girl with her freckled nose and sparkling blue eyes.

He knew his mother would adore Ellabell. More than pretty, she was intelligent and kind and funny too.

His reverie was disturbed by a scuffling sound within the cottage. Alex's eyes snapped in its direction. Trying to see through the darkness, he wasn't sure if it was friend or foe within the building, and, as Elias appeared near the entrance, he still wasn't sure.

The crackling magic of the world around them still seemed to be playing havoc with Elias's form, as he struggled to gather all of his pieces together. Most of him was still fragmented, and his shifting body was strangely translucent, like peering through a thin, black cloth, though he was more whole than he had been on his previous visit. Alex sighed dismissively, his head already so full of other things that he wasn't sure he even wanted to see his shadowy acquaintance, who would no doubt fill his brain with frustrating thoughts and vague suggestions that would plague him for days. There was already too much going on; he didn't need Elias adding to it.

"What do you want?" he said sullenly, turning his gaze back toward the lake.

"You're a fool, Alex Webber," snapped Elias. It seemed to Alex that his shadow-guide was on an accusatory objective, and it was not one he much cared for.

"What have I done this time?" he remarked sourly.

"I should never have trusted you to get on with things on your own. You seem to have a habit of making a royal mess of things. Not much else, but *that* you are an expert at!" Elias rolled his starry eyes.

Alex glared. "I seem to be doing just fine, thank you. My friends are safe—they know what I am, and I'm still not dead. I'd say that was pretty close to success."

Elias sniggered. "That little display you put on has landed you in more danger than you know, Alex. Before you rose up, glowing like a Christmas tree, they were only curious about you—now they fear you. Fear is treacherous. Fear makes people lash out. Fear makes people feel out of control," he warned, his teeth flashing in a stern grimace that was halfway between scowl and smile.

"Why would they fear me?"

Elias sighed, the sound like a million distant whispers. "You are different. They can't control 'different.' It is unpredictable, and it threatens their existence—you are the fox in the henhouse, and they want you dead. Whether or not you believe otherwise is your prerogative. I am only here to make suggestions," he purred, his shadowy mouth curving upward in a definite grin.

"They can't do anything to me," said Alex uncertainly, feeling dread claw at his stomach.

"You know that's not true." Elias smiled. "Just because you're 'special' doesn't mean they won't use you—they already have plans for you. By showing your hand, you have become a pawn between the power-plays of the magical elite."

"Are we playing cards or chess here?" muttered Alex.

Elias chuckled in the back of his wispy throat. "Don't get smart with me, Alex. They are both games of patience, and they can be very patient if they need to be, but do not mistake their tolerance for acceptance. They will put their plans into action, the moment opportunity presents itself."

"Who?" Alex frowned.

"Please tell me you're joking," said Elias, gesturing in exasperation with his floating limbs as he lounged against the wall. "I thought you'd picked up that book?"

"The royals?"

"All is not lost—there is hope yet!" he mocked, grinning.

Alex sighed. "I've been learning a bit about them, but I've not exactly had much time."

"You know enough though, yes?" prompted Elias, his galactic eyes peering curiously at Alex.

He shrugged. "I know the Head and Alypia are royals."

Elias whooped unexpectedly, startling Alex. "Perhaps you have not been entirely remiss while I've been away."

"I'm not stupid, Elias. I overheard them talking, and Alypia called him 'little brother.' It wasn't hard to put the pieces together," he remarked, pausing as a thought entered his mind. "What actually is he—the Head, I mean?" asked Alex, certain Elias would know.

The shadow-man lifted his weightless shoulders in an attempted shrug. "He is an abomination, but one of royal blood, nevertheless," he replied, in his usual, frustratingly cryptic way.

Alex clenched his teeth in annoyance. "What's that supposed to mean?"

"Surely, the question is, 'Why is that important?' After all, you are as much a pawn in his game as you are in Alypia's," taunted Elias.

"How am I a pawn?" snapped Alex, his eyes narrowing.

"Think about it—what are you?" encouraged Elias with a twist of his shadowy wrist as he languished on the floor, contorting his fluid body to look up at the ceiling.

"A Spellbreaker."

"Good. And your heritage? I know you've been thinking about it." Elias smirked, tilting his head back at an unnatural angle so he could stare into Alex's eyes.

Alex shrugged. "So what if I have?" he muttered, remembering his thoughts on Leander Wyvern and a mysterious, non-magical partner. The loophole that had, perhaps, given him life. "It makes no difference. I can never get a proper answer, so why bother thinking about it? They're all dead."

For once, Elias didn't throw a sarcastic remark back at Alex, but looked at him with something akin to kindness. It was almost as frightening to behold as his usual disdain. Nothing on Elias's face did what it was supposed to, with everything shifting and moving of its own volition.

"You have a truly powerful heritage, Alex—and they will fear you more, once they know." An expression of remorse twisted Elias's face. "They have been looking for you. They have been searching for such a long time. They never thought you could exist, yet here you are. Nothing can ever be the same now."

Alex frowned, not knowing what to make of Elias's mysterious words. "You're like a sphinx or something, always talking in riddles—why do you always have to be so vague? If there are things you want me to know, why don't you just spell them out for me? It'd be a lot more help than this rigmarole." He gestured between them, a look of sheer frustration on his face. "Do you know how annoying you are?"

Elias grinned. "Do I vex you, Alex?" he purred. "There'd be no fun in simply *giving* you the answers." There was a strange flash of something in his galactic eyes that Alex couldn't put his finger on, as if there was something more to it than Elias was letting on.

"I swear you just show up to irritate the living hell out of me!" snarled Alex, his temper flaring. "Maybe you just shouldn't bother anymore."

Elias twisted back up to a standing position, most of his lower half trying to float away from him. "Well, then maybe I shouldn't bother with *this*," he said, pulling a book from the cavern of his starry ribcage. The bizarre, nauseating act didn't seem as simple as it normally did—retrieving the book from his chest seemed to cause Elias a great deal of strain, a few minutes passing before he finally managed to maneuver it out into the open. Sections of his shadowy figure had disappeared, dissipating into the atmosphere.

"Are you okay?" asked Alex, suddenly concerned by the pieces of Elias that had simply vanished.

Elias tilted his shifting features in a nod. "I will be."

Taking the proffered book, Alex looked up at Elias's starry eyes with a frown. "How are they going to use me? These royal mages?" he asked.

"It's funny," mused Elias, "that you come to me with all these questions, when a source of great knowledge is in your midst every day. I must say, he's doing a rather good job of keeping his mouth shut. I suppose he wouldn't want to spoil things, now that he's one of you again." Elias grinned sharply, his black eyes teetering on the edge of menacing.

"You mean Aamir?" whispered Alex, as the seeds of distrust started to sprout again. They had never truly gone away, but he had hoped he had learned all he could from his friend—he had just begun to trust Aamir again. Glancing at Elias, he wasn't sure whom to believe, though Elias seemed to be on a roll of generously giving information. Surely, the shadow-man had no reason to lie? Alex was about to ask another question when the wispy figure of Elias simply disappeared into the shadows, with a whorl of his transient body.

The last thing Alex heard as the shadow-man evaporated was a whisper on the wind, murmuring. "You think Aamir hasn't been here before? You're smarter than that, Alex. Not much, but definitely smarter than that."

Left alone with his thoughts, his mind full to the brim with yet more mystery, Alex looked down at the book he had been given. It had a plain, brown cover and did not seem to have a title on the front or the spine. Flipping through the first couple of pages, Alex saw that they were blank, though he could tell there was definitely text later on in the book. Just as he was about to turn to the page he hoped the title might be on, he found himself distracted by the sound of more scuffling around the side of the cottage. It sounded oddly like somebody trying to creep away. Knowing it couldn't be Elias, Alex moved around to the other edge of the cottage, in time to see the familiar figure of Ellabell trying to leave as stealthily as she could. It was almost comical, her movements exaggerated, like she was a cartoon character trying to slink away.

"Ellabell?" he called.

She froze, then turned slowly, a look of concern in her eyes. Alex walked toward her.

"What's wrong?" he asked.

"I didn't want to interrupt," she said quietly, bashfully lifting her gaze. "I shouldn't have spied on you, but I saw Elias, and—he worries me, Alex. I don't believe he is a friend to you. He's capable of dark deeds, and I just don't want you getting caught up in them. I'm sorry… but I just can't believe his intentions are good."

Alex felt the urge to defend himself, to convince Ellabell that he wouldn't willingly associate with her attacker. "I know Elias is a tricky creature, but I don't have any say in when he visits me. This wasn't planned—he comes to me when he feels like it, and I take the information he gives with a pinch of salt. Most of the time, it's all just riddles anyway," he assured her, resting his hand on her arm. She seemed a little shaky at the sight of the shadow-man, and Alex couldn't blame her, after what Elias had done, but she was putting on her bravest face.

"What is that?" she asked, pointing at the book in his hand.

"A book Elias gave me," he replied.

She sighed sadly. "You shouldn't trust him, Alex. I know he's useful, but you can't trust a word he says or a gift he gives—promise me you'll be wary of him?"

Alex nodded with vigor. "I don't trust him either! I just have to hope there's some good in him somewhere, that's driving these visits and all the information he gives me." Swiftly, he tucked the book into the waist of his pants.

Ellabell shook her head. "I don't think that's why he does

it. Anyway, we should be getting back. The others were missing you." A worried look passed across her face, quickly hidden behind a half-smile, and she took his hand in hers.

As they wandered back toward the villa, Ellabell's words left Alex a little uncertain. He knew she was right, but he also knew how much better he seemed to feel after many of Elias's visits. They were his only window into the unknown, and, as much as Alex hated to admit it, he looked forward to them. Although it made him feel somewhat ashamed, part of him was glad Elias was still around.

As they grew closer to the villa, however, he began to feel a strange sensation prickling at his skin, raising the fine hairs on his arms. It was an uncomfortable feeling, as if there were eyes on him, peering through the darkness in his direction. Shrugging it off as Elias, he tried to ignore the sensation.

On his way over the wall, with Ellabell already over and down the other side, out of sight, Alex paused for a moment and darted across to one of the statues that lined the battlements. Glancing around, he no longer sensed eyes on him. *Elias must have gone back to whatever it is Elias does*, he thought. Reaching up, he tucked the book into the folded stone arms of the chosen statue, pushing it right back into a natural well that dipped at the back, perfect for the safe-keeping of Elias's gift. Alex still wasn't sure how scrutinized they would be within the villa walls, but he figured the Headmistress and her cronies were less likely to find the book here than if he stashed it away in his room somewhere, where they'd have easy access to it.

He'd return for it when he had a better idea of how safe they were.

CHAPTER 29

ELIAS'S WORDS PLAGUED ALEX, AS THEY HAD A NASTY habit of doing. Lying back on his bed, staring at the ceiling, his mind was drawn to the faint movements of the older boy in the room next door. It pained him to think it, but he knew he had to confront Aamir on what Elias had alluded to; with everything going on, if there was *anything* Aamir wasn't saying that could be helpful, Alex needed to know.

Dragging his feet, he moved out into the hallway and paused in front of Aamir's door, his knuckles poised above the wood. Softly, he knocked.

"Come in," called Aamir.

Alex stepped inside, his reluctance made all the more difficult by the grin that lit up Aamir's face. He didn't want to have to question Aamir again, but the pull of what Elias had said was too strong.

Closing the door gently behind him, Alex wandered over to the desk and sat in the chair opposite to where Aamir was sitting, at the edge of his bed. Instantly, Aamir's face fell, seeing Alex's grim look. It was no doubt a look he had seen before, so he knew what it meant.

"There are some questions I need answered, Aamir. I hate to do this to you, but I can't leave this room without asking them," muttered Alex.

Aamir rolled his eyes as if to say "not again," but Alex wasn't going to let it go this time. Elias's words had given him a re-newed desire to dig into the wells of Aamir's untapped, hidden knowledge. But that made Alex wonder at Elias's motivations for telling him about Aamir in the first place. Had he even been telling the truth? Ellabell's warning flashed in his mind: *"You shouldn't trust him."* Alex knew he was about to see how far Elias could be trusted.

"When were you taken to Spellshadow Manor?" he asked, not wanting to jump in with the big queries. There was still a lot he didn't know about Aamir, he realized, glancing at the older boy with his copper skin and dark hair.

Aamir seemed surprised. "What?"

"When were you taken to Spellshadow Manor?" he repeated.

Aamir frowned. "I must have been fifteen, maybe," he re-plied after a long, thoughtful silence. "It seems so long ago, now."

"Do you remember it?"

Aamir smiled sadly. "Some of it. I remember being out in the garden. It was hot, and the sprinklers were on. I'd been read-ing, I think, and I heard something. There was a fence behind the trees, where the garden backed onto a field. Perhaps it was a whisper—I can't remember, I just know something distracted me and I put down my book and went to investigate. I remember my grandmother calling to me from the veranda, but I was already in the shade of the trees, trying to find whatever it was… That was the last thing I remember before the manor. My grandmother's voice calling me and the sound of sprinklers. Funny, the things you remember."

"Do you miss it?" Alex wondered, trying to picture Aamir's world before Spellshadow.

"Of course I do," he breathed, as if there were a great weight upon him. "I miss it every day, but if you think about it all the time, it will drive you mad. I tried that once—it was more painful to remember than to forget."

"I hear that," agreed Alex grimly. "Who's waiting for you, back home?"

"My grandparents, my parents, my little sister," he replied.

"You have a sister?" Alex hadn't known about a sister. It reminded him of the promise he'd made to Natalie's little sister, to get her back safely. He was still determined to make good on that promise, no matter how long it took.

Aamir smiled. "Samaira. She was only five when I disappeared. I doubt she even remembers me."

"I'm sure she remembers you, Aamir. She'd definitely want you back home, where you belong," Alex encouraged.

"You really believe we're going to get out, don't you?" he remarked kindly, though there was uncertainty in his eyes.

"I have to. Don't you want to get back to them?" Alex asked, wanting to gauge Aamir's reaction. When Aamir said nothing,

Alex pressed him. "The thing is, I need to know who I'm taking with me, *when* I figure out a way back. I need to know if that includes you."

Aamir sighed heavily. "I'm up for leaving… Of course I'm up for leaving this place. Home is all I have ever wanted, though it has long seemed impossible," he replied quietly, with such emotion in his words that Alex half-believed him.

Talk of family seemed to have relaxed Aamir somewhat, though he kept glancing anxiously around, speaking only in a hushed, whisper-like voice, as if they might be overheard. Seeing this shift in Aamir's manner, Alex seized his opportunity, though he almost regretted having to; he was enjoying hearing about Aamir's past and the people from Aamir's reality, outside in the non-magical world.

"What did they do to you, back at Spellshadow? When you became a teacher, what happened?" ventured Alex.

"It's like I said, there are gaps in my memory, and there are things I was never told. The teachers certainly know more than the students, but they are still not told everything. Some things are reserved solely for those in charge," he explained, no longer seeming disdainful of Alex's line of questioning. He almost appeared eager to answer him. "What I do know is, the Head wanted me to be the new Finder—he wanted to turn me into some magic-seeking specter, but it turned out I didn't have the natural knack he needed, for seeking out magical talent in the outside world." He smiled bleakly.

The idea still horrified Alex, making him wonder how things might have turned out, if they had not reached Aamir in time. Perhaps the Head would have tried anyway, doing to

Aamir what he had done to Malachi Grey, all those years ago, in the garden of Spellshadow Manor. He shivered at the thought of that day in the tombs when he had touched Finder's gaping skull.

"Is that why you came back?" asked Alex, recalling the night in the manor when the dark-cloaked figure of Aamir, then Professor Escher, had chased them. "Why you were in the manor that night, when you came after us?"

"I had been sent back, that much is true, but I chased you because I caught Jari searching for a book on necromancy—a very dangerous, awful book. I wanted to stop him, so I pretended to be someone I wasn't and ran after him, forcing him to abandon his search," he explained.

Alex frowned. The tale was deeply reminiscent of Elias's, in which he had tried to prevent Ellabell from reaching out for a particular book, hidden away in the depths of the Head's library. He wondered if the incidents were somehow related, but shrugged it off for the moment as he turned back to what Aamir was saying.

"I realized then that you had come on with your powers. You gave me quite the shock with your snowy barricade," he chuckled softly.

Alex smiled. "Sorry about that."

"No apology necessary. I threatened you; no doubt I deserved it."

"What were you doing at the manor? I mean, nobody knew you were there—we all thought you'd gone with the Head," said Alex, remembering the terror he had felt when he heard the heavy footsteps on the flagstones, running after them.

Aamir nodded. "The Head had sent me back to guard the school in his absence, after realizing I was truly useless at magic-finding, but I wasn't supposed to make myself known to anyone. I think he hoped the students would believe he was still in the manor, somehow—an omnipresent being, that could be both away and there, at the same time. He's not, if you were curious. He can appear quickly, if he wants to, but he can't be in two places at once," he assured Alex with a wry smile.

"So, was there ever a time he didn't have eyes on the place?" Alex asked curiously.

"Yeah. I was sent back shortly after the new rules were put in place, so there were, maybe, two weeks when he didn't have anyone watching over the manor. Except Siren Mave, who checked in from time to time, I believe. She's always flitting about, though, by all accounts. He could never get hold of her when he needed her. So I suppose he relied on your fear—the students' fear—and it failed him." He shrugged.

Not for the first time, Alex pondered the curious entity that was Siren Mave. This strange being that seemed to be everywhere, able to move easily from place to place, not really belonging to the faculty but not belonging to any one school either. She seemed to be a law unto herself, and it made Alex endlessly curious to know more—though, if what Aamir was saying was true, he wasn't sure how he'd be able to pin her down to ask. Like Elias, she never appeared when you wanted to see her; she simply showed up when *she* felt like it.

"What about once we discovered you? Did that get you in trouble?" mused Alex, feeling slightly sorry for the extra drama they had put Aamir through.

He nodded. "As soon as you realized somebody was in the manor, watching over things, I had to travel back to the Head and explain what had happened. I didn't want to. I'd have been quite happy for you to discover me, but the combination of the golden band on my wrist and the mask on my face drove me to do it. Besides, thanks to the mask, he already knew I'd been detected."

"What do you mean?" Alex frowned, puzzled. He had thought the mask was there simply to cover Aamir's true identity, but it appeared there was more to it than he had first thought.

"The band and the mask were both used to control me, meaning I pretty much always had to tell the Head what I had seen or done. But through the mask's eyes, he could see everything I did—like a camera, almost. When it broke on the ground, it severed the connection, I suppose; he couldn't see anything anymore," Aamir elaborated.

That made sense to Alex; it would explain why the Head hadn't known there was an uprising going on until it was much too late. "Wait a minute. How did you travel to the Head, to tell him you'd been discovered? I mean, you showed up the next day—how did you get from the manor, to the Head, and back again so fast?"

"Magical travel. Once you're outside the manor walls, the magic barriers preventing it don't work anymore," he said, gesturing to the air above them. It made Alex thoughtful, wondering, as he had on the lakeshore, if the crackling magic in the air here had the same effect as those barriers.

"So, you flew off to see him?"

Aamir nodded. "Yes, I zipped off and explained what had

happened—he gave me that poor kid he'd found, told me to put a spell on him to make him compliant and take him back to the manor under the ruse that I was some new professor, here to take over Deputy Head duties, while the Head continued his search. He told me he'd be back in a week or so, once he'd tried to acquire some more magical recruits. I think your uprising put a wrench in the works there, though, seeing as he came back empty-handed." He grinned, his eyes glittering with merriment.

Alex almost didn't want to ruin it with his most pressing question—the one that still bugged him. "And the offer you made me?" he said, as lightly as he could.

A strained silence stretched between the two young men.

Eventually, Aamir sighed, breaking it. "I've had the chance to think long and hard about this… and I believe it was something the Head asked me to do, though I have no idea why. I can't come up with a reasonable explanation behind it, and I know for certain the Head would never have told me his reasoning for it. I only know that it *was* him who made me do it. I wouldn't have been able to, with the band on my wrist. I know that now, and I'm sorry for any pain it caused you. I can only imagine—being offered that freedom, only to have it snatched away." He gulped, trying to clear his throat.

It was exactly as Alex had imagined, and to finally hear it said brought him a strange sense of peace. At least this way, there had never been a hope of seeing his mother. It had been a cruel jest, or something more sinister, perhaps, but it had never been real.

"What about the notes? Was that you?" Alex ventured, recalling the clockwork mouse, still in his pocket, and the warning messages the little creature had delivered in the dead of night. He still had not found the culprit, and had long thought it to be Elias, but with Elias's admission to having little control over his faculties, Alex had begun to think otherwise. There was only one other culprit, as far as he was concerned.

"I thought you might have forgotten about those," said Aamir quietly.

"So, they were you?" Alex breathed.

"Those, I know for certain I was responsible for," he said sadly. "They were my way around the mask and the band."

"But why?" Alex's brow creased in disbelief. "Some of the things they said—why would you say that?"

Aamir ran an anxious hand through his hair. "Too many people were finding things out about you—you needed to be more careful, but you didn't seem worried. A secret is only a secret if one person knows it. After it spreads beyond one person, it becomes a liability, and that's what you were becoming." He coughed nervously, catching sight of Alex's disapproving glare. "Despite what you might think of me and what I did, I was only trying to protect you. I didn't want the Head finding out what you were, fully. I knew he'd try and use you for his own purposes, if he discovered the truth, and you were making it so difficult to keep your secret hidden." He looked down into his lap, his shoulders slumped in remorse.

This wasn't the first time Alex had heard such a phrase spoken, and he hoped his friend might be able to shed some more light on it, in a way nobody else seemed willing or able to.

"It has been said before, that others might try and use me—what do they mean?" he pressed. "Do you know what it means?"

Aamir lifted his gaze. "I'm not sure. All I know is there is a myth surrounding Spellbreakers and the Great Evil, but it was never elaborated upon. It was just that—a myth, the details forgotten." He shrugged apologetically.

While this frustrated Alex, he could see the honesty on Aamir's face. The older boy was telling him all he knew, at long last. But there was one question left, conjured by the last words from Elias as he had disappeared into the shadows.

"Aamir—have you been here before? To Stillwater House?"

A flash of panic glittered in Aamir's eyes. "I don't think so," he replied, a touch too quickly.

In that moment, Alex knew his friend was lying. After almost believing every word, he was back to square one again on the trust board, but he could not understand why Aamir was being so cagey about having visited Stillwater before. What wasn't Aamir telling him?

"I should be going," said Alex, standing swiftly. "I'll see you later."

"Yeah, see you later."

"And, Aamir?"

Aamir nodded.

"Thank you for being so honest," Alex spoke, keeping his voice as even as possible.

On the edge of the bed, Aamir's face crumpled. With that, Alex left the room and returned to his own.

Running a bath and sitting in the tub, Alex went over the things they had discussed. As they had been talking, Aamir's answers had seemed complete and honest, but thinking about them in retrospect, Alex could see the holes and gaps in the stories he'd been told—all of the "I'm not sures" and "I can't re-members" and the constant line of "there are gaps in my memo-ry, and there are things I was never told." He wondered gloomi-ly if he would ever be able to fill in the missing pieces.

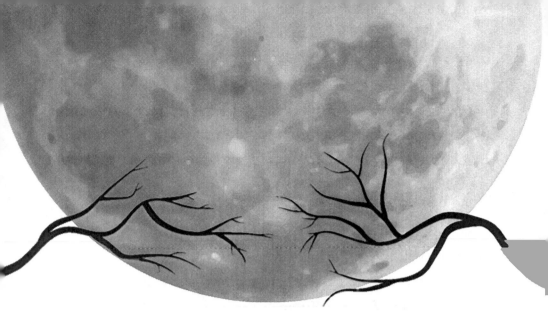

CHAPTER 30

AFTER SEVERAL FAILED ATTEMPTS TO GET HIS BOOK, finding himself perpetually halted in the corridor by the stern glare and probing questions of a uniformed guard, Alex drifted toward the infirmary, spending a short while with Jari and the others, until Jari grew too tired for company. He was recovering nicely, but still had a way to go. There was a greater sense of calm among the rest of his friends, after they had received the understanding that they would all be permitted to stay, without further consequences for what Alex had done. Alex himself still felt on edge, unable to trust a word of it, but Alypia had not come to tell him otherwise.

On his way back from the infirmary, he tried to slip out once more toward the villa wall, only to be stopped again by a curious guard who seemed to materialize out of nowhere, forcing him to retreat to his room, where he began trying to figure out the an-ti-magical equivalent of some of the spells he'd seen at the arena of late, hoping they might be useful in the future. It seemed a better use of his time than moping about, hoping the guards in the hallways would disappear.

A knock at the door disturbed Alex from his spell inver-sions. He opened it to find a slender young woman with fiery red hair standing in the hallway.

"The Headmistress wishes to see you," she commanded.

Fear gripped Alex's stomach as he slipped the sheets of pa-per he'd been working on into his pocket, hoping they'd be safe there. "Now?"

She nodded. "If you'd be so kind." There was a note of sar-casm in her voice that got Alex's guard back up as he followed her.

For a brief moment, he thought about defying the red-haired girl, refusing to go with her to see the Headmistress, but after the trouble he'd caused in the arena, and the already tenta-tive safety of his friends, he didn't feel like he had any choice but to go willingly. As much as he wanted to fight back, he wasn't stupid; he knew he was in a sticky spot, with his choices influ-encing what might happen to his friends. To be taken to Alypia's office by force, after causing more trouble—he had a feeling Alypia wouldn't take too kindly to that.

They moved quickly through the hallways and corridors, Alex noting the familiar route as he ran to keep up with the red-haired woman's swift stride. She didn't seem willing to talk as she led him toward the Headmistress's office, her eyes set dead ahead, her mouth unsmiling. It was another glorious day, the sun beating down warmly on his face as they crossed one of the piazzas, the scent of flowers hanging heavily in the air, emanating from the vivid roses that draped the pale stone walls. He drank in the sights and sounds and smells, wondering if it would be his last taste of sunshine and fresh air as they ducked back into the shadow of another walkway.

Arriving at the tall, white double doors, he thought his heart was about to explode, it was racing so fast. He hadn't seen Alypia since the arena, though he had expected her to summon him, but now that it was happening, he wanted to turn and run as far from that place as possible. Sensing his hesitation, the red-haired girl opened the door and pushed him inside with an unexpectedly brutal shove.

He staggered into the beautiful, glass-ceilinged office, struggling to regain his balance and stop himself from sprawling across the marble. It wasn't exactly the elegant, confident entrance he had hoped to make.

Sitting at her desk, Alypia beckoned him forward, the friendly smile on her face worrying Alex more than any dour expression might have done. "Fionnula can be a little forceful—my apologies," she purred, clearly amused.

Regaining his composure, he walked over to her desk and slowly sat down in the high-backed chair with the white fur covering, the fibers tickling his neck as he shuffled backward, trying to get comfortable. He figured he might as well, if she were about to sentence him to some unknown torture.

Looking up, he met her gaze as fearlessly as he was able. "You took your time," he remarked brazenly, trying to regain the upper hand.

She chuckled softly. "I thought I'd give you the chance to calm down first, before I called you here."

Her words made Alex feel like a child being scolded at elementary school, needing a timeout for losing his temper. "That was kind of you," was all he could muster, though he knew how paltry it sounded.

"I trust you are fully recovered after your outburst the other evening?"

"I am. My friend is still in the infirmary, however," he replied curtly.

Her eyes flashed. "An unfortunate incident," she said diplomatically. "I have ensured he is getting the best care, to aid in his recovery. The problem is now—what am I supposed to do with *you*?"

Alex frowned. "I don't follow."

"While I abhor disobedience, you certainly gave me food for thought with your show of power. I had my suspicions about you, Alex Webber, as I presume you well know?" She waited for him to respond.

He nodded. "I thought you might."

"My little brother suspected too, but you slipped out of his fingers before he could get you to break," Alypia explained. "Now, I knew you didn't need breaking in order to show yourself. I knew it would simply take something big to get the confirmation I needed, of how powerful you were. You would never have revealed your secret willingly, and so I had to… How shall I put it? *Encourage* you to show me. I had to see your strength with my own eyes."

Alex felt anger twist in his stomach. She had set him up. She had clearly longed to see the impressive extent of his power, and she had set a trap, to try to get Alex to show his hand. And he had, just as she'd hoped he would. He wasn't sure whether he was more annoyed with her for doing it, or himself for performing exactly the way she had wanted him to.

For the life of him, he couldn't understand the woman's motivations in arranging such an extreme ploy. Surely, there would have been an easier way to test whether he was a Spellbreaker? She could have fired a tiny morsel of magic at him, and she would have seen the truth. It seemed to Alex that Alypia was something of a dramatist, relishing the spectacle of things—it would explain why she had chosen to present the extraction of life essence in such a theatrical manner, making it a bold, exciting event instead of conducting it beneath the cover of secrecy. That flair for the theatrical, combined with her clear taste for sadism, created a worrying picture as to what lay behind her beautiful exterior. She had *wanted* him to suffer.

"How could you?" he hissed.

"Oh, quite easily. You see, I know a little of your kind already." She smirked.

"The Head?"

"So you *did* notice his little peculiarity?" she teased. "Quite sweet really, that you should find each other in this strange world of ours. Now, of course, he's not quite like you—he's what we call an abomination, whereas you are simply a surprise," she quipped, speaking coldly of her brother with apparent ease.

"I won't let you use me," Alex growled.

She smiled icily. "Who said anything about *using* you? I presume you've heard this nonsense from my dear brother," she sighed. "I don't wish to use you, Alex—I wish to improve you, nurture you, assist you in becoming a very powerful Spellbreaker."

The word sounded strange, coming from the lips of such a fearsome mage. "Why would you want to help me?" He glared.

She tutted with irritation, toying with a pen on the marble top of her desk. "This is what we do here. We create the world's finest mages. Why would we not want to do the same for you? It would be the highest honor to have the world's greatest Spellbreaker in our midst—admittedly the only one, as far as I know, but that doesn't mean you have to wallow in mediocrity. With me, here, you could be wonderful," she encouraged, her eyes gleaming with excitement. "If you were willing to stick to the terms we have already laid out, I would be willing to overlook your little transgression. I mean, you were only trying to protect one of your own, and I am not a monster: I see the nobility in that. It shows the strong bond you all share, and I could certainly forgive that, if you were to stay," she taunted. Alex realized she could very well use that "strong bond" against him, and no doubt would, given the opportunity. After all, she already had done so, to make him reveal what he was.

Silence gathered between them. She was waiting for an answer, and Alex knew she wasn't a patient woman.

"I have one condition," he said finally.

Her eyes narrowed. "I am not usually one for negotiations, Alex—but I will hear you out."

"I will remain a student here, and abide by your terms, if you permit Jari to stay. I realize he turned down your offer, but that is my condition. He stays, or I refuse," he demanded, knowing he had nothing to lose, but his friends had everything to lose if he couldn't get her to agree. Even though she hadn't come for Jari, and it was implied that he was allowed to stay, Alex wanted to hear the words directly from Alypia's mouth. As untrustworthy as she was, she seemed to put a lot of importance on the value of agreements.

Alypia tilted her head at him. "This is highly unorthodox, you realize?"

"I do."

She frowned, tapping her manicured fingers against her chin in thought. "Well, I suppose this way, we both get what we want," she sighed. "I will agree to this new term, if you will agree to remain within the walls of Stillwater until such a time as you are ready for Ascension."

He cleared his throat. "I agree."

She smirked. "Oh, I do wonder how that will play out. Perhaps it won't be fair to whomever you are pitted against, but it will certainly be a spectacle," she chuckled coldly, no doubt delighting in the fantasy of such a dramatic conclusion. "Well, then, it seems we have a deal, and I must say it is a most satisfactory one."

"Will I be studying with my friends?" he asked.

"Oh, goodness no, we couldn't have that—think of the distraction! No, I will teach you alongside another teacher who has some knowledge of the Spellbreaker histories, with more grasp than most mages of the theory behind anti-magic," she clarified.

"How do *you* plan to teach me?" he asked, intrigued despite himself.

"I've been thinking about that. I was going to enlist my

brother's help, but you seem to have kept him very busy of late, and I doubt relations would be particularly warm between the two of you." She smiled thinly, a touch of threat in her voice. "I'll figure something out, don't you worry. We'll see to it that you have an excellent education here."

"Is that everything?" Alex sighed, putting his hands on the armrests of the chair, as if to stand.

She raised a hand, demanding he sit back down. "We aren't finished, Alex. Now, I am a fair woman, but I have certain provisos also. As long as you and your friends toe the line, they can all stay. I do not accept any bending of the rules. There will be no misbehavior, no midnight jaunts outside the House's walls, no lateness, no defiance, no disobedience of any sort. Is that clear? I will hold you as responsible for the actions of your friends as if it were you, yourself, who had done the deed."

Alex swallowed hard. "I understand, Headmistress. May I go?"

"One more thing," she said sweetly. "I won't stand for anything like what you all did at Spellshadow Manor, so I suggest you quash any remaining feelings of rebellion you might have. I'm not stupid, like my dear brother—I can sense your desire for revenge. I can see it, bristling all around you, and I am warning you to cease and desist. There is no point. If you try it, I will crush you." Her eyes blazed with malice.

"I agree to all your terms, Headmistress. Consider my feelings quashed," he said drily. The agreement, though he didn't mean it any more than he had the last time, would still buy him more time to forge a plan, and, though there would be restrictions, he sensed it might give him and his friends a fragile cocoon of security to hide behind, while they figured out a way to leave.

Plus, despite everything, he could understand the value of Stillwater, and how much the others could learn from it, in a magical sense. It was a beneficial place, with people to challenge and educate them to the best of their abilities. At Spellshadow, they had been pushed to a point, but here, they might actually learn something they could use later on, when it was needed. He guessed there would be a time when they might need such experience, in the fights that were undoubtedly to come—when the moment came for them to battle their way back home, to the real world.

"I'm very much looking forward to having a Spellbreaker here at our fine school," she purred, something strange lurking behind her eyes.

"I look forward to learning here," he replied bitterly, trying to feign enthusiasm, though he knew neither of them was buying it.

"Our history and that of your kind are so closely linked, it makes perfect sense." She smiled, her delicate wrist gesturing out toward the glittering lake behind her.

Alex forced down the bile that threatened to rise up his throat as he watched the smug expression spread across her face. He didn't trust himself to speak, but that didn't mean Alypia wasn't going to. It was clear she had something she wished to get off her chest. A look of delight flashed in her peculiar eyes as she opened her mouth to speak.

"Let's not forget," she whispered menacingly, as she turned to glance out toward the gleaming water, "the very foundation of Stillwater House is built upon the backs of Spellbreakers."

CHAPTER 31

I T DIDN'T TAKE LONG FOR CLASS SCHEDULES TO ARRIVE, though Alex suspected Alypia's hand in the swiftness of their delivery; the sooner she could distract the five friends, the better. The others had all received theirs, but they were different from Alex's, as he had known they would be.

His sessions, as promised, were to be with the Headmistress and one other teacher, named Master Demeter, one-on-one. Alex wasn't sure how he felt about that, wondering if it was intentional to make him feel isolated from the others. At no point in the schedule did his educational path cross with those of his friends, not even for subjects such as Clockwork, which he didn't think he needed to be segregated for. It confirmed Alex's suspicions that he was being kept away from them as much as possible.

He wasn't the only one with a differing schedule, however. On closer inspection, it appeared that Aamir's was different too. Alex supposed it made sense, considering Aamir had been in his final year at Spellshadow. But the older boy's skillset was not up to the standard of final-year Stillwater students, so it was revealed that he was to have private, one-on-one sessions also, to build him up to the same levels that were expected of a final-year Stillwater student. The two of them shared a curious look as they went over their schedules. Alex could tell Aamir was wondering why he had been segregated too, when he could just as easily have joined a year-group of a similar skill level. Alypia, it seemed, was still playing games with them, although to what end, Alex couldn't be sure.

Natalie seemed excited about the prospect of learning again, especially from teachers who were so formidable and encouraging of their students. There was only so much that could be self-taught, as Alex knew too well, and all of them knew they were a touch rusty after so long without any real guidance.

"I wonder what we will learn?" Natalie squealed, a renewed vigor in her dark eyes as she looked over the lessons she would be attending. Alex peered over her shoulder at her schedule and spotted some unusual class titles, including Mechanoid Magic and Barrier Combat.

Ellabell seemed excited too, though she was less vocal about it. There was a nervous energy about her as her eyes scanned the schedule she had been given.

"Looks like we have most of our classes together!" she exclaimed to Natalie.

As the two girls went on speculating about what the classes

would be like, Alex felt somewhat envious. He wished he could have the comfort of being with his friends throughout the day—and have every class with Ellabell. Still, he was glad she wouldn't be on her own with a bunch of strangers who had still not made up their minds about the newcomers, thanks to Alex's behavior in the arena. The Stillwater students showed a general wariness toward the group of them, guilty as they were by association with Alex. But Alex could see that his friends were eager to start classes. It was a routine they had all been lacking, of late, and one they knew they could slot easily back into. No matter whether it was magical or non-magical, school was school.

The only one who had yet to receive a schedule was Jari, who was still safely tucked away in the infirmary, enjoying the daily attentions of Helena. The young woman still felt responsible for not knowing what was going to happen to Jari in the arena, and she seemed to be seeking his forgiveness by spending as much time with him as he wished. It had all worked out unexpectedly well for the boy, who had even whispered a "thank you" to Alex, the last time he had been there, when he had caught sight of Helena coming into the room with a plateful of cakes, cookies, and drinks. Jari was living a life of luxury, and it made Alex smile—at least someone was benefitting from the danger of this place.

"Well, we'd better be off," announced Ellabell, checking her schedule.

With that, the others departed to their various lessons. Aamir had a private tutorial at the same time, in the same wing, but Alex had a thirty-minute window before he was due at his first session with Master Demeter, on the other side of the villa. His lesson was to take place in a room just off the Queen's Courtyard, giving Alex an idea as he set off toward it; with thirty minutes to kill, he had more than enough time to fetch the book he had stowed away, and now he had an excuse if anyone were to stop him.

Alex walked toward the wall, striding quickly across the empty courtyard, which wasn't being used that morning. Reaching toward the stonework, he was just about to begin his upward climb when a trumpet blared loudly above his head, from somewhere farther up the battlements. Intrigue pulled Alex's attention from his hidden book as he quickly scaled the wall and ducked down, sprinting as fast as he could in the direction of the sound, careful to skirt past the guard-posts as he did so, to avoid detection. Technically, he wasn't going against the terms he had agreed to; he wasn't outside the walls, he was merely on them. Still, he knew Alypia wasn't a shades-of-gray kind of person. She was entirely black and white, and he didn't want to test her patience so soon after their last meeting.

In the near distance, he saw people moving toward the villa.

Alex knew the gargantuan doors to the villa rested a short way from where he crouched, and he guessed that must be where the special visitors were headed. Looking ahead, he saw the spire of one of the corner towers and rushed toward it, clambering up through one of the windows into the room beyond. To his relief, it was empty—little more than a storage room, filled to the brim with clutter and broken furniture. However, the window looked out onto the stretching fields below, giving Alex the perfect vantage point from which to watch the arrivals.

As they neared the main entrance, Alex could see the small band of individuals was made up, mainly, of guards. The same ones, he supposed, as the ones he had watched rowing away, from the lighthouse. Two of the guards carried a shrunken figure awkwardly between them, shrouded in a heavy woolen blanket, though the being beneath seemed to be putting up something of a decent fight despite its diminished size. Once or twice, the two Amazonian guards almost lost their grasp on the blanketed figure, though they always managed to regain control of the prisoner.

Much to his displeasure, Alex saw that the Head was with them too. Alex marveled at this yo-yoing of the Head's, consistently showing up at Stillwater to beg assistance from his sister, but there seemed to be a more relaxed quality to the Head this time as Alex watched the hooded figure embrace Alypia, who had emerged from the doors beneath to greet the arriving party.

"Has it all been dealt with?" she asked insistently, holding her brother at arm's length.

"Thanks to you, everything is back in order," replied the Head with a strained smile, the expression looking deeply unnatural on his drawn, skeletal face.

It was then that Alex noticed the additional figure, trailing behind the rest of the group. It was a face and form Alex had not expected to see.

Behind the guards and the prisoner, a graying, spectral figure moved slowly, as if through molasses. He was dressed in threadbare clothes, the edges of his robe frayed and torn, though not quite as ragged as Alex remembered. Catching sight of this awful being, Alex found himself combatting horrifying flashbacks of the last time he had seen Finder, in the tombs at Spellshadow, wondering if Finder had come back from his second death, somehow, and was hell-bent on haunting him. But, on second viewing, Alex realized this figure was not quite the same. He was wearing robes of some sort, but they were more modern than Malachi Grey's had been, and his face was altogether less ancient, though it bore the same vacant, disturbing stare.

Understanding dawned—the Head had done as his sister had asked and found a replacement for Malachi Grey.

It was Renmark.

Renmark was the new Finder, a mass of floating, ragtag gray, with one sole purpose. The Head had done to him what he had done to Malachi Grey, all those years ago, reducing him from mortal being to phantom helper with a wave of his hybrid hands. As much as he hated Renmark, he couldn't help feeling a pang of remorse for what the teacher had become, wondering if he would end up feeling the same way about it as Malachi had, in the end, resenting the Head and everything his half-life had become.

Suddenly, Renmark's gaze lifted toward where Alex was watching from. Instinctively, Alex ducked back behind the wall of the tower, even though Renmark shouldn't be able to see him, just like Malachi couldn't. Still, the last thing he wanted to do was run into a phantom Renmark, which was possibly the only thing worse than running into a living Renmark.

His previous pang of remorse turned to a feeling of grim irony.

You finally got the high-powered position you wanted so desperately, Renmark, he thought to himself. After all, being the new Finder technically made Renmark the second Head; a position of authority high enough to satisfy Renmark's hunger for power, surely? Alex wasn't certain it was quite what the ex-teacher had had in mind.

Alex didn't dare peer back out, though he strained to hear what was being said as voices filtered up from below. Annoyed that he couldn't make out what they were saying, he braved a glance out the window, just in time to see the Headmistress walking toward the prisoner, who struggled vehemently between the strong arms of the guards. Alex willed Alypia to remove the blanket from the prisoner's face, so that he might see who was beneath it. But she did not, leaving his questions unsatisfied. Instead, Alypia simply turned and walked back toward her brother, apparently unimpressed by the blanketed gift he had brought for her.

As intensely as Alex scrutinized the shrouded prisoner, he couldn't work out who it could be. There was an androgyny to the shape, and he couldn't discern any defining features, aside from the size. But then, the guards standing next to the figure were of such a towering height that anyone would've looked small beside them.

He ducked back into the tower as he spotted Renmark raising his ghostly gray eyes once more toward where he stood. Unsettled, and frustrated at no longer being able to see what was going on, Alex shuffled as close to the edge of the window frame as he dared, straining to listen.

"And everything is back as it should be?" Alypia asked, her tone tinged with doubt.

Drily, Alex wondered what it must have been like for the Head, growing up with a sister like Alypia, but he found he could not easily picture them in the domestic setting of ordinary siblings. These two were as far from ordinary as it was possible to be, and who knew how many more royal siblings were out there who had been part of this dysfunctional family unit? It made him think back to the portraits on the walls of the ballroom at Spellshadow, pondering how many of those had been siblings and how many had been other relatives.

"The faculty has been restored, though rather more hastily than I would have liked, and I have managed to regain control of the school—all those who proved troublesome have been dealt with," insisted the Head, though Alex could garner little else from the conversation. Every time they began to speak of something interesting, the wind changed, carrying their voices away from him so he couldn't make out what it was they were saying anymore.

Still, what he had heard was enough to cause a wave of dread to pass through him, sinking to the pit of his stomach. If the Head had regained control and everyone had been dealt with, what did that mean for the students? He felt slightly more optimistic at the sight of only one prisoner, but it wasn't much of a consolation; he hadn't expected the guards to bring anyone back at all.

He listened as the group moved through the doors and into the villa itself. Only when he was sure they had moved far enough inside did he dare to look back out of the window. Glancing at the field below, he froze, his blood running cold. Staring straight back at him, meeting his gaze head-on, was the full, blazing stare of the ghostly Renmark.

This time, Alex knew he had been seen.

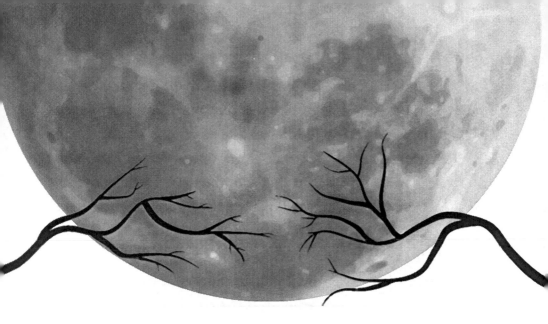

CHAPTER 32

A FTER HOLDING THE SPECTER'S GAZE FOR THE BRIEFEST of moments, Alex ducked back against the wall, his palms sweating and his heart racing. In the gloom, he listened for the sound of the villa doors closing with a heavy thud. Daring to peer back out, he saw that the field was empty. The strange group had gone inside the villa walls, following Alypia. The thought of Renmark being in the building did not sit well with Alex at all, especially now he'd learned that, somehow, this Finder could see him.

He wanted to go and find Helena to ask if she had any information on the person who had just been brought into the school, but he knew he didn't have time to find her *and* retrieve his book from the statue where he had hidden it. Knowing he'd have more chance of finding her later, when he wasn't so pressed for time, he decided to go and fetch his book instead. He had about fifteen minutes before he was due at his first session with Master Demeter, and he didn't feel like pushing his luck.

He climbed out of the tower window and darted back along the walls toward the statue that stood sentinel just above the Queen's Courtyard. Careful not to be seen, he reached up to the folded stone arms and then inside the natural recess behind them, half-expecting the book to be missing. It was still there, just where he had left it. Relieved, he plucked it from the hiding spot and tucked it awkwardly into the band of his black pants, pulling his t-shirt over the top and hoping nobody would notice the square shape at the base of his spine.

However, just as he was about to climb down, his eye was caught by the tree-line nearby, where he knew the cottage was. It was strange, but, peering toward it, Alex felt a peculiar sensation at the back of his mind, as if something wasn't quite right. Although he knew he was really pressed for time now, and Alypia would be straight after him if he was a no-show at his first lesson, compulsion forced him to clamber down the other side of the wall and walk toward the cottage.

As he neared it, he was glad he had listened to his gut instinct. Something *was* wrong. The place had been disturbed, the ground all churned up outside as if there had been a lot of people scouring the perimeter of the tiny cottage. The most obvious sign of disorder was at the entrance, where the earth was a muddy mess. Stepping cautiously into the interior of the cottage, he saw that the whole place had been ransacked. Everything had been turned over and shoved out of the way, as if somebody had been trying to find something within. Whatever furniture there had been was now a crumpled pile of debris, good for nothing but kindling, and the floorboards had all been torn up to search the foundations beneath.

Alex felt a tingle of trepidation. Somebody had been here, and it looked as if they had been searching for something. It seemed strange that this should have happened so soon after he and Elias had spoken there. It made Alex nervous, wondering if somebody had, perhaps, seen him speaking with his shadowy acquaintance.

Trying to focus on the memory of the night Elias had appeared to him, he recalled the sensation of eyes on him, the strange, unsettling feeling that came with being observed unawares. He had ignored the feeling at the time, but perhaps there had been someone else—someone who had watched Ellabell and followed her, leading them to see the exchange between himself and Elias, or at least Alex speaking into the shadowy darkness. That would have been a mysterious sight to an outside observer. Perhaps a guard had spotted him and passed on the information, thinking there might be something in the cottage worth investigating. It was the only reason Alex could think of.

Still confused, but having run out of time, he reluctantly returned to the school walls. As he walked, he became aware of eyes on him again, prickling the hairs on his arms until they stood on end. Glancing around, he couldn't see anyone watching him from the windows and spires in his line of sight, but no matter what he did, he could not shake the feeling of being watched.

Hoping it wasn't Alypia, he climbed the wall and dropped down the other side, moving quickly across the courtyard and under an archway that led toward the study room where he needed to be. He arrived outside it just as Master Demeter did, much to Alex's relief. The teacher was younger than Alex had expected, around late-twenties, with the same flawless features that were found on all the residents of Stillwater House. He had light brown eyes, curling bronze hair, and an olive complexion, the combination making his heritage difficult to place.

"Excellent—punctuality is next to godliness!" Demeter smiled, mixing up his proverbs in a way that Alex would come to realize was normal practice for this clever, if slightly eccentric, man. "Remember, Alex, a watched clock never boils, so I want no boredom from you—you'll find the time passes much more swiftly if we take no heed of it. So, let's hop in and begin," he encouraged as he unlocked the door to the small study room and ushered Alex inside.

They spent the whole morning in the stuffy study, though it wasn't exactly uninteresting. Master Demeter proved to be an enthusiastic, animated individual who possessed a wealth of knowledge on Spellbreakers. There was almost a streak of hero worship in the older man whenever he told a particularly good story he liked about a battle or a war in which the Spellbreakers had been fearsome foes. He spoke of Spellbreaker warriors like they were comic book superheroes, gesturing wildly as he informed Alex of their great deeds, sometimes acting out sections, to Alex's total bemusement. He had no idea what to make of this teacher, who seemed so oddly passionate about a subject Alex had thought to be taboo among mages.

He was also prone to poor dad jokes, though Alex had no idea whether to laugh or stare most of the time. Demeter's love of humor didn't seem to fit with the aesthetic of the rest of the school, but then neither did his subject matter. Aside from Demeter, Alex couldn't actually recall the last time he had heard somebody crack a joke in this place, and it was as refreshing as it was weird.

Most of the lesson covered historical education, and although Master Demeter didn't tell him anything he hadn't already heard, Alex didn't want to interrupt the flow of the man's stories by saying so. Alex simply sat back and let Demeter do the talking, answering only when absolutely necessary. It was an easy session, to say the least, with him nodding along with the teacher's madcap theatrics and enthusiastic tales, like when his high school teachers had put on movies before school vacations—informal but interesting. Alex wondered in disbelief if he might actually come to like his sessions with Master Demeter. His lessons with Alypia would be a different ball-game entirely, he guessed, but these ones he could definitely see himself enjoying, especially if they moved beyond things he already knew.

As the lesson came to an end, the clock on the wall showing it was almost lunchtime, Demeter turned sharply toward Alex, startling him with a clap of his hands. "Alas, we must end our session here for the day. That wasn't too bad, was it? I'd say that went pretty quickly, if you ask me?" he said, prompting Alex.

He shrugged. "Pretty fast."

"Remember, Alex," Demeter lowered his voice, as if about to share a great secret, "time flies like an arrow, but fruit flies like a banana!" He cackled, clearly pleased with himself and his joke. Alex found he couldn't help a smile from pulling at the corners of his mouth—Demeter's clownish humor was oddly infectious.

Still, he also couldn't deny he was glad the lesson was over; the book still tucked into his jeans had been digging a cleft into the flesh of his back, which had gone worryingly numb.

"Very good, sir," he encouraged, as he stood to leave.

"More of the same this afternoon?"

"If your joke book can take it," quipped Alex.

"Very good!" Demeter grinned. "You must be ready for some food by now?"

Alex nodded. "Yeah, I'm pretty hungry."

"Hi, Pretty Hungry, I'm Master Demeter!" he howled, thrilled that Alex had walked into his joke.

Alex tried hard not to roll his eyes. "Another zinger, sir. Can I go to lunch now?" he asked, half-expecting the man to do the usual teacherly jest of, 'I don't know, can you?', but he didn't. He simply waved Alex off with a nod, returning to a box of sandwiches he had already opened on top of his desk.

Alex didn't need telling twice. He ran off across the empty square and clambered up the wall, following it until he reached the abandoned courtyard at the far side of the school. Not knowing whether the door would be open or not, he snuck in through one of the windows instead, pleased with the quiet solitude he found within, as he landed on the familiar flagstones of the vacant bell tower. He glanced back at the window to check that nobody had followed him, before disappearing up to the very top floor and sitting back against the wall. Pulling the book, with great relief, from his waistband, he opened it in front of him, seeing that it was another history of Leander Wyvern, entitled *Leander Wyvern: The Last Spellbreaker*. Excitement coursed through him as he flipped to the first page, wishing he had retrieved the book sooner. It was a nice surprise, after so many bad ones, and he found that Master Demeter's lesson had put him in a history sort of mood.

He devoured the book as rapidly as he could, knowing he only had an hour for lunch before he would be expected back at the poky little study room. To his slight disappointment, the text went over a lot of the same ground as the other books he had read containing Leander, including the notebook still in his possession. It wasn't that he didn't find it interesting, it was just that he wanted to know more; he was fed up with the brick wall of information he kept crashing into.

Three-quarters of the way through the book, however, he chanced upon a bombshell. It was entitled *Fields of Sorrow*, and though Alex began the section expecting it to be more of what he already knew of that final battle, he realized quickly that he had entirely misjudged the chapter. Instead of explaining the details of what went on leading up to Leander's last stand, it skipped straight to the end, describing instead the Great Evil that was released in the last moments, on the final day of the battle:

Leander Wyvern, last of his kind, stood atop the scaffold as he was fettered in chains, his wrists shackled—roaring to the heavens, his eyes burned with a fearsome silver light; an unnatural, ungodly sight, terrifying to behold, though none could stop him crying out, nor the glow of his eyes.

A firing squad took position before him, though their hands trembled as they raised them to strike. They were more scared for their lives than Leander himself. Golden light filled the air as the assembled squadron fired wave upon wave of golden artillery toward the great Wyvern, but Leander had fallen silent, the magic barely seeming to worry him. His silence was more frightening than the blood-curdling war cries many heard in their last moments, face-to-face with him on the battlefield. A peace had fallen across his handsome face, his burning eyes still wide, though glassy with concentration.

With each blow of piercing golden magic, Leander's eyes burned brighter, the glare blinding all those who looked upon him, until his whole body seemed to burn with the same glowing, crackling silver. Beneath his feet, the very earth shifted as liquid silver rose up from the death-soaked battlefield. Like phantom dust, it gathered and soared across the broken ground, swarming in the air around him, swirling like a tempest overhead.

Desperate now, the congregated Mages let their magic surge toward him, but no matter what they did, they could not get him to stop. No spell could penetrate the light spinning around him.

It was they who stopped, as a great blast, so loud it could be heard for miles around, exploded from the very center of Leander Wyvern. A bolt of unholy silver lightning shot from the sky, shivering violently through his body, sent from the swirling clouds overhead, and burst into the ground in a pulsing beam of pure energy that seemed to go on for eternity, channeled through the burning figure of the last Spellbreaker. The earth trembled and the ground cracked, though none were looking to their feet; they saw only horror as the mist of anti-magic cleared. The Spellbreaker and the tempest above were nowhere to be seen—they were gone, obliterated by the force of the final spell Leander had used against those who had persecuted his people, down to the very last one.

How were they to know what he had done?

The earth shook as wisps of shadowy silver, shot through with black, snaked away from the spot where Leander had been, undulating through the air and the grass, toward the Mages who stood before Wyvern's place of death. As the silvery mist clawed at their flesh, biting through their skin and deep into their core, it began to dawn on them, what he had done. It moved like liquid, smothering the Mages in a poisonous mist as it snatched their essence from within, taking what it was owed.

What Leander had done was mythical, unheard-of anti-magic—a spell they could never have been prepared for. A Doomsday spell, conjured from the book of its namesake; the tome had always been the source of legends, mere fairytales told to children to scare them at night. Only the nightmare had been released, myth rushing toward the fabric of reality—a Great Evil, ravenous for the taste of life magic, sated only by magical sacrifice. If not given willingly, the Great Evil took forcefully instead.

They could not have known the price they would pay for taking Leander's life that day, but Leander Wyvern released the Great Evil upon the Mages, in vengeance for what they had done to his people. It is said that when a void appears, that void must be filled with something, and Leander Wyvern ensured that it was; he left nothing to chance. He wished for the punishment of those who had ended his race to live on, long after he was dead.

It was a wish that came true—the Great Evil prevails, and Mages know not how to rid themselves of it.

Alex sat back, breathless, as understanding began to shape itself in his mind. The specifics were still hazy, but he was starting to get a better grasp on things that had seemed perpetually closed-off to him before. It was eerily invigorating to learn of what his potential ancestor had done as a last-ditch move of revenge against the mages. As he absorbed it all, Elias's words came back to haunt him, though Alex knew they were as relevant to Spellbreakers as they were to mages.

Altering the phrase to suit his newly gained information, Alex thought about what Leander must have been going through, his heart bursting with pride and horror, in equal amounts, at what the last Wyvern had done. *Desperate people do desperate things, and people with nothing left to lose are the most dangerous of them all.*

Never had truer words been spoken.

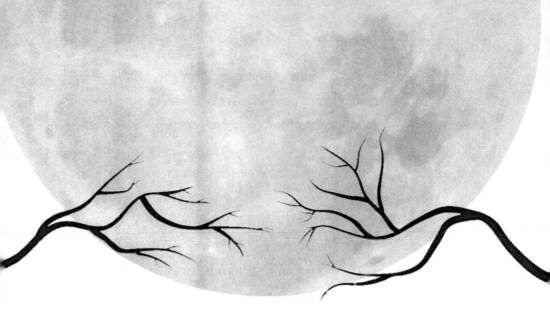

CHAPTER 33

AS THE DAY CAME TO A CLOSE AND EVENING FELL, ALEX decided to go and visit Jari in the infirmary. His afternoon with Master Demeter had been as strange as the morning, though he hadn't been able to focus on much after the revelations of his lunch break. They raced through his mind, refusing to be silenced. He figured a bit of time with friends might quiet it a little, enough to think straight at the very least.

Stepping into the room that had been designated to Jari, he saw that the boy was once again enjoying the attentions of Helena, though it wasn't just Helena by his bedside. To his surprise and delight, he saw the others were there too, clustered around Jari's narrow bed on various chairs they'd managed to pilfer. He couldn't put into words how pleased he was to see them, despite the weight of his new knowledge. It was a relief, knowing their presence would mean he wouldn't have to worry too much about the things he had been finding out; they were his distraction and his sanctuary, regardless of the seedlings of mistrust he still felt toward Aamir. He didn't want to think about that; he just wanted to be a teenager for a bit.

Besides, who was to say what he was feeling wasn't Elias's intention all along—to divide and conquer, siphoning him off from the herd, as it were? He almost hoped that was the case, because he wasn't sure he could take any more suspicion. It was eating away at him, driving him a little mad, wondering what was real, what was fake, who was trustworthy and who wasn't. Nor would he put it past Elias to think of something like that, assuming Alex wouldn't notice the game being played.

The others were mid-conversation as Alex approached, and they seemed just as relieved to see him.

"Where have you been?" asked Natalie sternly.

He frowned. "What do you mean?"

"We waited for you at lunch, but you didn't show," Ellabell chimed in, her brow furrowed.

He shrugged. "I didn't think we had the same lunch-breaks, so I just went off for an hour, did some reading." He flashed Ellabell a conspiratorial look, making her look of concern deepen.

Although he didn't want to keep what he had learned a secret, he also found he didn't have the energy to talk about what he had read in the book—right now, he just wanted to have a normal conversation and hear about their days.

"So, how have things been going?" he asked, smiling in readiness for the onslaught of their tales.

"We had several new lessons that we have never had before—they were good, but they were different. The work here is very hard!" Natalie beamed, clearly in her element. "The teachers are pleasant, and they are extremely encouraging, but it was difficult to keep up. Wasn't it, Ellabell?"

Ellabell nodded, though she appeared somewhat distracted. "It was pretty tricky. The students are younger than us too, and it was just nuts watching them do everything so easily. I think we did okay, though."

"Yes, we did fine. The teachers seemed pleased with us and said it will only be a short time until we are more advanced," agreed Natalie. "We learned so many new things!"

"Did you find out what Barrier Combat is?" asked Alex.

"It is a very strange thing—it is dueling within a chamber that is filled with magic, so your own magic is suppressed, and you have to figure out ways around it. I believe it is to test our skills in any situation," explained Natalie, still grinning. She had evidently had an interesting, eye-opening day.

"That sounds pretty cool," Alex remarked, meaning it. It made sense, to teach the students how to fight in any scenario; he just wished they had something like that for him, so he could practice how to fight in different settings and situations.

"It was," Ellabell smiled, sharing a slice of Natalie's enthusiasm.

"Everything is so different here! It is all new and exciting, and there is so much to learn. They have taught us, in one day, how to focus magic and go beyond the basics. It is truly wonderful to be learning so much. And they care about learning, and they want us to do well. It is most refreshing!" Natalie enthused.

The excitement they exuded made Alex feel a little disappointed with his own education. So far, Demeter had only told him stories and histories—nothing remotely useful in terms of practical applications. Still, he had to hope that would be coming and that today had been more of an orientation session. A getting-to-know-you kind of thing. He wasn't sure he could take history lessons indefinitely.

"How about you? How did you get on?" asked Aamir.

"My teacher is a little bit… kooky, shall we say," chuckled Alex. "Master Demeter? Any of you have him?"

The others shook their heads, which puzzled Alex, making him wonder where Alypia had dredged the peculiar Spellbreaker-loving man from.

"We just went over some histories and things. Nothing quite as interesting as what you guys are learning," he said a little bleakly.

"I'm sure it'll pick up, man," encouraged Jari. "It beats being cooped up in here with nothing to do!"

Alex smiled. "I guess it does."

"How're things with you?" Jari turned to Aamir.

He shrugged. "It's strange. A bit like with you, Alex, only more focused on the magical side rather than the anti-magical," he began. "My tutors, Master Garai and Mistress Winter—do you have them?"

Natalie and Ellabell nodded in concurrence.

"They have been going over school things, mostly." Aamir paused, as if wondering whether or not to elaborate. "Well, not even school things. They've mostly just focused on the Ascension Ceremony."

The room went still.

"What about it?" pressed Alex.

"Just how important it is to everything they do here," he murmured. "Don't worry, I've not been drinking the Kool-Aid," he assured them with a smile, seeing everyone's worried faces. "I think they just wanted me to understand, so I pretended I did. Then they went over the behaviors and spells from the winners and losers of the last few years—they have it all written out in these huge scrapbook-type things, with lists and lists of spells used and successes and things of that nature. It is very peculiar, but fairly interesting too. After a few hours of that, they took me on a tour through the tunnels beneath the arena. You know, the ones the combatants come out from and get taken back into... if they, you know, lose." He looked as baffled as the rest of them did, as he relayed the day he had had.

Alex, however, found himself intrigued by what Aamir said, as he remembered the night of the Ascension Ceremony and the strange, hypnotizing horror of it, to have what was essentially 'graduation' so openly cheered and celebrated. Even they hadn't been able to tear their eyes away from the scenes that had played out that night, as wrong as they knew the Ceremony to be. He thought of those poor, tortured mages, forcibly dragged away by guards to have their essences removed—from students to sacrificial prisoners in the space of one evening.

Somehow, his remembrance of those guards turned his thoughts to the prisoner he had seen from the tower, brought in with the guards who had come back from Spellshadow. With Helena there, he figured it was as good a time as any to ask.

"Helena, do you know anything about the prisoner who was

brought into Stillwater today?" he asked.

The others looked at him in surprise, clearly not having heard anything about a prisoner or anyone new arriving at Stillwater House that day. Neither had Helena, Alex thought, seeing the blank expression on her face.

She shook her head. "I don't know of any prisoner. Nobody told me," she replied, seemingly perplexed.

"When did you see them?" quizzed Ellabell.

"I went for a walk before my first lesson. There was this loud trumpet, and I just followed it and happened to see someone being brought in," he explained. "I think they came from Spellshadow."

Aamir frowned. "How do you know?"

"The Head was with them… and so was Professor Renmark, only not the one we knew," he sighed grimly.

"What do you mean?" Jari chimed in, eyes filled with macabre interest.

"Renmark is the new Finder."

Natalie gasped. "No—what do you mean, he is the new Finder?"

The faces staring back at him were pale with dread. It had not been an easy thing for him to absorb either, and he had seen it with his own eyes. He felt a pang of remorse for Natalie, whose face showed more horror than the rest; she had known Renmark better than any of them, taking private lessons from him in dark magic, and he knew she had learned a lot from the professor, which had built a certain mutual respect between them, despite the hatred Renmark had incited in the others.

"The Head needed a new Finder, so he chose Professor

Renmark," explained Alex. "I wouldn't have believed it if I hadn't seen him with my own eyes, all raggedy and gray—the same state Malachi Grey was in... Only, weirdly, it seemed like he could see me. He looked my way."

Alex's friends stared at him in confusion. "I have no idea why," Alex shrugged.

"So... does this mean Spellshadow is back in the Head's hands?" asked Jari.

Alex nodded. "I think it must—why would the guards have come back otherwise?"

"Do you think they're okay?" wondered Ellabell sadly.

It was a question Alex couldn't answer. He could only hope the students at Spellshadow were doing fine, or were in no worse state than they had been in before, though he imagined the Head must have implemented some new rules to try to prevent an uprising from happening again. What those new rules were, he shuddered to think.

"Whatever happens, we know they aren't dead, and as long as they're alive, there's hope," Alex stated, trying to give courage to the drained faces of his friends. "One person who isn't going to be okay, however, is that prisoner. Do you know where they might have taken them?" He turned to Helena, certain she could shed some light on the matter.

"I don't. I can find out, though." Helena tilted her head thoughtfully. "Just leave it to me."

The group looked up sharply as the door creaked, disturbing their hushed conversation. At the far end of the room, a stern-looking wizard had entered, his eyebrow raised as he saw the congregation gathered around Jari's bed. With slow deliberation, he looked from his watch to them and back again, tutting loudly.

"Isn't it time you were leaving? Visiting hours are long over," he declared.

"Just five more minutes," Jari pleaded, but the dour medical mage could not be swayed.

"Out—now!" he barked. The group said their swift farewells to Jari and scurried from the room with promises to come back tomorrow.

Though the others headed straight for their rooms, Alex waited until they weren't looking and slipped away from the group at one of the hallway junctions, with other ideas on his mind. Aamir's words about the tunnels had inspired him, bringing back memories of what the Gifting Ceremony entailed. With those recollections, a decision had come to him: he would use the cover of darkness to investigate the arena.

Alex had a sneaking suspicion that the black bottles, or whatever fancy glasswork the Stillwater folk used, might be stashed away beneath the amphitheater, at the end of the tunnel where the losers were hauled away. It made sense; Helena had told them that the Gifting Ceremony happened beneath the amphitheater, so Alex figured that had to be where they stored the stolen essence, in the same way that the antechamber attached to the room with manacles was where they stored the pulsing black bottles at Spellshadow.

The hallways mostly empty given the hour, he crept uninterrupted through the villa and out across the lakeshore, sticking as closely to the shadows as he could and making his way toward the vacant arena. As he walked along the eerie pearlescent shingle and up over the field toward the amphitheater, he felt a rush of dread. He became aware of the familiar sensation of eyes on him, making his skin feel hot and prickly. Someone was watching him.

Glancing back toward the villa, his eyes scanned the exterior, but he saw no one. Turning his head away, he instantly snapped it back, unsure whether he'd seen a flash of something in the top room of the abandoned tower at the far edge of the building, the exact place he had watched the Ascension Ceremony from. He squinted, trying to make out a shape in the window, but if there had been something there, it was gone now. Turning back, Alex tried to convince himself it was a figment of his imagination—he would have managed it, too, if he hadn't been able to sense the burning heat of eyes upon him still.

Reaching the amphitheater, he slipped around the back, hoping it would block him from the sight of whoever seemed to be watching. Sneaking along the rear wall, trying to remain unseen, he was hoping for a back way in. It appeared he was out of luck. Then he happened upon a narrow side door in the masonry. He skirted along the far edge of the curving structure. Opening it with some force, Alex moved swiftly into the belly of the amphitheater. Initially, in the dim light, it was a disorienting place to be, with all the walls and corridors looking identical. But as he moved along the tunnels, he saw two rectangles of light in the distance that he suspected were the tunnel entrances—the ones the combatants used to come in and out of.

It was dark beneath the arena, but, after stumbling about for several minutes, he came across a long hallway of doors. He cursed loudly, the expletive echoing—he knew it would take him ages to find the right one, if it was even there. Walking along slowly, he hoped the right door would jump out at him, but they all stared blankly back, each looking exactly the same as the next.

Through some of the grates in the doors, he could see manacles dangling over grills in the floor. The rancid scent of blood and fear rushed into his nostrils, but he couldn't see any doors hidden away in the walls beyond the grills. He searched the length of the corridor, but none of the rooms contained the bottles he was looking for. There were no antechambers in any of them, and certainly no stashed essence. Perhaps, he thought, the bottles were hidden in a secret cellar or behind a trick bookcase, which meant his search was an entirely pointless endeavor.

Frustrated, Alex moved away from the doors and chambers and headed back out into the balmy evening, wondering with irritation where the Headmistress was hiding her stolen treasure of life magic. A thought came to him, as he mused upon one place she might be keeping them: her office. It would be just like Alypia to keep them close at hand, where she could view them at her grim pleasure, delighting in so much suffering. If they *were* in Alypia's office, he realized, they may as well be on the moon—the Head's office had been hard enough to get into, but he imagined the Headmistress's would be a truly mighty feat. It didn't seem difficult to enter, but that was the beauty of Alypia's restrictions—nothing was ever supposed to *look* like a barrier. He wasn't even sure he could remember the way to her office, the directions fuzzy in his mind.

The idea of the bottles being in her office perplexed him even more, and he walked back quickly, creeping beside the lakeshore as he tried to skirt around the obvious routes back into the villa. Still, he could feel the unnerving sensation of eyes on him.

Peering up at the wall, he wondered if it was Elias, keeping an eye on him, though when he looked up into the shadows to search for any sign of the shadow-man, he could see none—only impenetrable, watching darkness.

As he stole back into the realm of Stillwater House, panic jolted through him. Somebody had grabbed his arm. Turning, he half-expected it to be a guard or someone who had seen him creeping around the arena, intent on punishing him for his flouting of the rules. Instead, with some relief, he saw that it was Helena, though she looked less than pleased to see him.

"What are you doing?" she hissed.

"I was just out for a walk." He shrugged, not wanting to give up too much information.

Helena didn't look convinced. "You shouldn't be out there at night," she warned.

"Why not?" he challenged, wondering if Helena knew more about Alypia's offers than she had been letting on.

"It's not safe. You never know what might be lurking out there," she replied, half-disappointing Alex. It seemed she didn't know about the additional provisos, after all.

"How come you're out here?" He smiled wryly.

She raised an eyebrow at him. "Well, if you must know," she said, lowering her voice to a whisper, "I've just come from where they took that prisoner."

Alex's eyes lit up. "You know where they are?"

She nodded. "I do."

"Will you take us there?" he pleaded.

Another nod. "I can get you all to the prisoner. If I come and get you in a few hours, will you be ready?" she asked.

"I'll go and let the others know."

"I'll see you then. Make sure you're ready to go," she insisted, leaving Alex alone in the villa.

He took off with a lightness in his step, excited to tell the others what he had learned, though he couldn't stop wondering who it was the guards had brought in. Whoever it was, they would find out soon enough. He just hoped the others were up for a midnight adventure.

CHAPTER 34

T RUE TO HER WORD, HELENA CAME TO GET THEM IN THE
middle of the night. They had all gathered in Alex's room,
though conversation was lacking thanks to the anxious
tension that had settled between them. It was quiet enough to
hear a pin drop, but they still didn't make out Helena's stealthy
approach. She was so silent, the knock on the door sent them
jumping out of their skins.

They recovered quickly as Helena beckoned for them to follow her. The girl led them through a bewildering labyrinth of
hallways and tunnels, stretching below an area of the villa Alex
wasn't at all familiar with, until they eventually ended up in a
prison of sorts. He knew it was a prison because he remembered
the slick, dripping walls and the stale stench of unclean bodies
and despair.

"Down there," whispered Helena, pointing to a door at the very end of a long, dripping corridor, the walls covered in a thick, moss-like substance. Alex was surprised to see that there were no guards patrolling the area. Helena, he presumed, had taken care of that detail for them.

Alex walked down the corridor, checking the door with a firm push of his shoulder. It was locked, as any good cell ought to be.

"Here, let me try," said Natalie, moving past him to slip her magic into the lock. Golden light surged for a moment, but the lock would not break. "There is something blocking it," she remarked, trying again. It was as if there were some sort of barrier, compressing any kind of magical energy used on the lock. Before Alex could offer up his services, Helena presented a key, sliding it into the lock and turning it smoothly. With a clunk, the door unlocked.

Alex shot Helena a look, but she swiftly gestured him inside, her eyes downcast. He pushed the door open. A collective gasp susurrated through the corridor as they saw the huddled figure on the dank, dirty floor of the prison cell.

Professor Gaze looked up at them with watery eyes, her knees tucked under her chin in a strangely girlish fashion. She looked exhausted and unbearably vulnerable, but she mustered a smile as she saw her visitors, though it was a weary smile that barely reached her usually mischievous eyes. Alex's heart clenched at the vision of her; she didn't look well at all.

Despite her weakened state, Alex managed to catch sight of Gaze's eyes narrowing as she saw Helena fidgeting uncomfortably in the background. He wondered what was causing such suspicion, but he didn't feel right asking, as everyone rushed toward Gaze in a flurry of affection.

"My dear students!" she cried cheerfully, embracing them all. "I had no idea I'd be seeing your glorious faces! Had I known, I'd have dressed up a little for you," she joked, tugging at the edges of her frayed, tattered robes.

"We had no idea, Professor!" exclaimed Natalie.

"Nor should you—those false little upstarts wanted to sneak me in without so much as a whisper of my being here, but they hadn't bargained on their prisoner being a bit of a firebrand." She grinned, though her cheer wavered as tears welled in her eyes. "I gave as good as I got. Goodness, am I glad to see you. I thought I'd be on my own at the end." Her voice cracked, breaking the hearts of those present.

"You're safe now, Professor. We'll get you out," promised Alex, though he had no idea if that was even possible. He just wanted to comfort the old woman, who had brought him tea every day to warm him. The woman who had thought of nothing but her students. It was because of them that she was here, suffering alone in a dark cell, with tears in her eyes and fear in her voice.

"Nonsense. This place is a tough nut to crack. I'm just happy you're all okay. You came just in time, I feel," she sighed, her hands trembling. "I don't have long, my little chickens." She patted Natalie's hand.

"You're going to be fine, Professor," insisted Ellabell.

"Sweet girl, you mustn't worry about me. Oh, I have lived a long old life, my lovely ones—this part of it is long overdue." She smiled bitter-sweetly, her eyes going somewhere far away. "I never thought my life would end up like this, you know. I had such dreams when I was a girl. I remember, it was just after the war, and I wanted to be a nurse so badly. My big sister had been a nurse, tending wounded soldiers and running around beneath a hail of bombs, sewing people up, real front-line business, then having all the handsome ones ask for her hand in marriage. It was sad too, no doubt, but I remember thinking she was so brave. She was my hero, and I wanted to be just like her," she chuckled wistfully. "I think she did end up marrying one of them—but that's by the by… I never saw her again, or any of my family, for that matter. I've often wondered what happened to them all. Most of them are dead now, I'd imagine. I've been around far longer than I ought to have been."

"And you'll be around longer still," said Alex, his throat thick with emotion.

Gaze simply shook her head. "I don't fear it—I welcome it. My old friend Death and me, at last, riding off into the sunset!" She laughed softly. "You mustn't do what I did. You mustn't allow yourselves to become part of this world. It's so easy to forget, when remembering is so painful, but you must use the pain and never settle here. Not if you want a life—your life, not one set out for you by others. Especially *this* place. Don't stay too long here if you can help it. I remember when I came here for my training, after I won my place as a teacher. It was funny, the air was like a drug; there was a magic in it that made you all happy and peaceful, even if you weren't. It made you forget—and you must never forget, little ones!"

Alex glanced accusingly at Aamir, who quickly looked away, his cheeks reddening.

"I'm sorry for not being able to keep everyone safe. I really tried my very best," she said sadly, reaching out for Ellabell's hand as well as Natalie's, squeezing both firmly. "I kept that scrawny little twerp on his toes for a good long while, you know, moving the corridors. I bet that really annoyed him! If he'd not gone running for help, I'm sure we'd have managed." She frowned thoughtfully.

"You did everything you could," assured Alex.

"I could have done more," she whispered.

"Why are they keeping you here?" asked Aamir, speaking for the first time, his face showing his shame at the lie he had told.

She smiled triumphantly. "Oh, those clueless drones keep coming for me to try to extract my life essence, but I'm a tough old cookie. So far, they haven't been able to get near, and I plan to keep it that way!" she cackled.

It made Alex boil with rage, that they could treat her that way, but he knew there was nothing he could do to help her. After everything she had done for them, there was nothing they could do for her. It didn't seem fair.

"What happened at Spellshadow?" he asked, trying to keep her talking. She was weak and only getting weaker; he could see it in her face.

"Well, that scrawny imp went off to fetch help, didn't he? Off he went, crying to that self-absorbed drama queen, and the next thing I know a load of guards have turned up." She paused sorrowfully. "Now, by this point, no tea in the world could give me enough energy to move the corridors again, so they got through. I did what I could, but they rounded everyone up like sheep and locked me away so I couldn't be a 'bad influence' on anyone. Me? A bad influence? Never." She smiled merrily. "With me out the way, they installed new faculty to replace us old fogies, though it was a bit of a rush job if you ask me—they picked four students and turned them into teachers. Most unorthodox. In the old days, they'd never have stood for it, but I suppose they were desperate? Who knows. I guess they had to be quick about it. I mean, usually, they'd have been brought here to have proper training with that white-haired hag—it's just how it's done, but I guess they had to get on with it." She shrugged.

This time, *everyone* looked at Aamir, though he stayed silent, lowering his gaze to the floor as his cheeks burned an even brighter shade of red. He had been found out, at last. Whether it was a relief to the older boy or not, to have the truth out in the open, Alex knew that conversation would have to wait until later.

"One positive thing I can tell you is nobody else died and everyone is as safe as they can be—it has just made any escape plans that little bit harder. It's like Alcatraz at Spellshadow now, but it was worth a shot." She beamed, encouraging them. "I mean it, though. You really shouldn't stay here too long. What sort of plan have you got in mind? You're good little schemers; I know you've got something good up your sleeves."

"We're planning to try and use a portal to get back out into the non-magical world," replied Alex quietly.

She nodded vigorously. "Tricky, but excellent! Yes, good, superb, definitely worthwhile if you can get one going."

For a moment, she fell silent, her head tilted in wonderment at the figure still hovering in the hallway, not wanting to come into the cell. Alex watched Gaze as her eyes flitted from the floor to Helena and back, mumbling incoherently to herself.

"What's wrong?" he pressed, kneeling beside her on the stones.

She stared at Helena. "What on earth are you doing fraternizing with a girl like that?" she whispered.

Alex frowned. "What do you mean?"

"Her—that silver-haired creature. She's one of them," explained Gaze, though their expressions remained blank. "She is royalty!"

"All the mages are nobles here," Alex said, somewhat confused.

"No, no, you don't understand," Gaze sighed. "That, if I'm not mistaken—and I don't think my eyes have managed to get *that* bad—is Princess Helena."

The group turned in alarm toward Helena, but she simply smiled and waved, not sure why they were all looking at her with such strange expressions on their faces, having been out of earshot of the conversation while standing guard.

"She's Alypia's daughter, and bound to be bad news if she's anything like her mother. I've never known anyone as vicious as that white-haired harpy," Gaze muttered.

Suddenly, things began to make sense to Alex. It explained Helena's ability to move in places she wasn't supposed to and her mysterious 'sources.' Alex had to wonder if one of those 'sources' was Alypia herself. The thought made him shudder with dread, not knowing how much Helena had told her mother, either on purpose or by accident. Alypia wasn't a stupid woman—maybe Helena had slipped up somewhere and given her mother information she needed.

Trying to stay hopeful, he clung to the knowledge that Helena kept them hidden and safe when she could simply have outed them to her mother. Then again, he wasn't sure if her kindness had only been a ruse to gain their trust. Like the beauty of Stillwater, perhaps Helena's beauty had blinded him to a darkness that lay beneath.

Gaze mumbled softly. Alex could tell she was fading fast, though she was struggling to hold on a while longer.

"Are you quite well?" she asked Natalie suddenly.

Natalie flushed. "I'm fine."

Gaze narrowed her eyes. "No, no, no—there's something… you are not entirely yourself. Typical, losing my skills just when they'd come in handy." She gestured toward the blushing girl. "I wish I had my tea chest. I'd have just the thing!" She stared at Natalie intently. "Aha! I feel it now—dear, foolish girl. Oh goodness, you risked a great deal, chicken, a very great deal. You must promise an old woman on her deathbed that you won't do such a thing again," she chastised quietly. "I have seen too many go to a dark place, unable to return. I would hate for you to venture there."

Natalie nodded, her eyes filling with tears. "I promise I will not. I would enjoy one of your teas right now," she chuckled, brushing away a droplet as it fell.

Alex looked at Natalie, piecing together Gaze's meaning. He thought back to the portal and how weak she was afterward, and felt horror as his suspicions were entirely confirmed. It was as Elias had implied, that night in the Stillwater library. Natalie had delved into life magic, in order to save them, and had lost a piece of her soul on the way. Gaze's senses had picked up that she was no longer entirely herself, but Alex realized that the ancient woman meant it literally. Natalie had paid for the portal with a piece of her soul—a piece she would never get back.

Natalie had a thoughtful look as she held Gaze's hand tightly. Watching her, it made Alex think about how deeply his friend was actually suffering. She had seemed fine on the outside, but it made him wonder if she was struggling on the inside. How many pieces of soul did it take to change a person entirely? Perhaps she had not used enough of it to cause any visible alteration in her manner or character. He vowed never to let her use any more precious pieces, and to try to pay closer attention in the future.

It made him think about the strange, crackling magic that seemed to suck away any negativity, and he wondered whether that had something to do with her happier state of mind— whether it could even manipulate the happiness in someone who was missing part of themselves.

"And you, our special one? How are you coping? Are you still cold? I knew I should have smuggled in some tea," Gaze murmured, turning her attention toward Alex. Her breath was becoming more labored, and Alex's concern for her grew.

"I've been surrounded by magic for so long, my body doesn't seem to notice it as much anymore," he replied.

"And your powers?" she asked. "Any progress? I always knew you were capable of great things."

He sighed. "It's been getting me into more trouble than good, lately," he admitted.

"Oh goodness, what on earth do you mean?"

"I had a bit of a mishap a short while ago," he said vaguely.

"Mishap?" She frowned. "Big or small?"

"Big." He grimaced.

"Go on," she encouraged, her eyes flashing with worry.

"I think Alypia set me up. She put Jari in a fight, but made it so he was so weak he needed my help, and I ended up showing off my Spellbreaker powers in front of everyone," he elaborated hesitantly, knowing how bad it sounded.

Gaze's alarm was instant. "Then you must hurry your plans along, my little chickens! Oh goodness, people will be after you now—you aren't safe anymore, Alex. There will be people seeking your power for their own uses, now that they know you exist. This is bad, very bad. Oh dear." She shook her head, descending into anxious mumbling.

From Gaze, Alex didn't mind hearing what he already knew.

Suddenly, her head snapped up, her eyes lucid. "And Elias? Did he make it out?" she asked. "He's helping you, yes?"

It lasted only a moment before delirium reclaimed her, and she fell back to her mumbling. She spoke in hushed tones, her words wistful, but Alex caught fragments of what she was saying in her weary, broken state.

"So handsome… talented… one of the greatest, maybe the… I adored him once." She smiled.

"Yes, I believe Elias escaped," he assured her, though he didn't know if she could hear him anymore.

Gaze's words made him curious about how she had come to know about Elias. Searching his mind for a link, he came upon a memory of the mysterious portrait on the wall, with the engraved name torn off, and the strange teacher who had been watching a young Lintz and Derhin in the hallway of the flash-back he'd seen, when he had plucked Derhin's black bottle from the storage shelf. Was that Elias? Alex was suddenly intrigued. Gaze had spoken of Elias as if she knew him. If he had been a teacher, she would have been on the faculty at the same time as him, what with her being so much older than Lintz or Derhin. He found he had so many fresh questions for Gaze, but he knew he'd never get the chance to ask them as he glanced at the crum-pled, huddled old woman. She was almost gone.

The memory of Lintz made Alex thoughtful. "Professor Gaze, what happened to Professor Lintz?" he asked.

She looked up at him, her eyes misty. "Oh, goodness… I don't think he… Did he?" she said dimly, trailing off, her voice weak. "No… I'm not sure he could have." Her answer was confused, her brow furrowed in uncertainty, though it soon smoothed out in an expression of quiet peace. She was close to the end now, Alex could tell; she had no more words to say.

Gathering around her world-weary frame, Alex let her rest her exhausted head on his shoulder as the two girls held her hands and Aamir sat on the floor in front of her. They stayed with her until the lights went out in her eyes. She fell asleep for the very last time with a smile upon her lips, and Alex felt a small, sad consolation that nobody would be able to tear her essence from her. It would go with her, sinking harmlessly into the earth where nobody could claim it as their own.

She could go peacefully to the place where there were eter-nal picnics on sun-soaked riverbanks, and all the handsome sol-diers asked for her hand.

CHAPTER 35

"WE HAVE TO GO," WHISPERED HELENA FROM THE hallway, glancing anxiously toward the far end.

Alex looked up, grief-stricken. It didn't feel right to leave Gaze all alone in the dank, dirty cell, resting up against the slick walls.

"We really have to go!" she insisted.

Forced to retreat, they stood and filed out of the prison cell, each bidding a murmured farewell to their former teacher, who had been strong until the bitter end. Alex felt an overwhelming swell of pride, interwoven with unbearable sadness, as he looked at her still form. A well-earned sleep, that was all; if he thought about it that way, it didn't feel so desperately sad. She and Lintz had done so much for them, in helping them escape Spellshadow, and they had both ended up dead.

Even though Gaze had put on a brave face, Alex wished it hadn't had to be that way. His mind rested briefly on the memory of Lintz too, feeling sorrow for the final sacrifice he had made against the Head, wielding his bombs and clockwork trickery. Although he hadn't seen the body of Lintz with his own eyes, he had heard Gaze's uncertainty as to the professor's fate and knew it was unlikely he had made it out of that fight alive. They were both heroes until their final moments.

Helena turned the key quickly in the lock as her golden eyes flitted toward the shadows at the end of the long corridor. Beyond the flickering torches and dripping walls, Alex thought he could hear the scuffle of unseen feet. Brushing a tear from his cheek, he rested his palm against the wooden door, wishing Gaze nothing but sweet dreams, before they left her for the very last time.

As they walked, Alex could feel the tension in the air. Everyone was wary of Helena.

Though she didn't seem to notice it for the first few minutes, Alex could see her slowly becoming aware of the strange atmosphere. There was no comfortable chatter, no easy humor, no jokes or divulged stories about the professor they had just seen; nobody was forthcoming with any kind of goodwill. Perhaps thinking it was because they were all feeling bereft, she continued to say nothing about it until they were almost at the door with the number forty-three written upon it.

"Have I done something?" she asked finally.

Alex held his tongue, not knowing if it was fair to tar Helena with the same brush as her mother. He needn't have bothered to try to spare her feelings, however, as Natalie stepped forward, her mouth set in a grim line. It made sense that Natalie should feel betrayed; she had grown close to the girl, closer than any of them, and still Helena had kept her secret.

"Why did you not tell us who you were?" Natalie demanded. "Why did you keep such a secret from us?"

Alex heard the subtext in Natalie's bitter words—*why did you keep such a secret from me?* He could see it in the glitter of her dark eyes, still rimmed with red from the tears she had shed over their beloved Gaze.

Helena looked crestfallen. "Believe me, I told no one about you. I haven't breathed a word—not to my mother, not to anyone. I know you must find it hard to trust me, after learning who I am, but trust that I have been looking out for you all—all this time. It's all I have wanted to do." She stared down at her feet, scuffing the toe of her boot against the flagstones. The earnest note in her voice had returned, and it was hard not to believe her. Still, Alex could not suppress his suspicions about why she didn't tell them who she was sooner, when she was someone of such importance. It seemed Natalie couldn't suppress her doubts either.

"But *why* did you not tell us? If you had wanted us to trust you, you would have told us who you were," she said, hurt bleeding into her words.

Helena looked up, her expression suddenly bold. "You honestly don't see why? Any of you? I didn't tell you because I wanted you to treat me like a normal, ordinary person. All my life people have tiptoed around me and wanted things from me. I just wanted you to know *me*—is that so hard to believe?" she said bitterly. "Besides, if I'd told you, you'd have run a mile! You'd never have spoken to me, let alone trusted me, if I'd told you the truth. I know you'd all like to believe you're better than that, but the truth is... you aren't. You know I'm right," she sighed.

Alex could see the honesty in that, and he wanted to believe in her, but he was no longer certain he could trust anyone or anything but himself. It brought to mind Aamir's words. *A secret is no longer a secret, once it is shared.* The only way to keep a plan private was to tell no one. It was a hard truth he was finally coming to terms with, for himself as much as for the others; the only way to keep everyone safe was to hide the truth from them.

One good thing to come out of so much negativity was the knowledge that the evening's events seemed to have snapped the others out of their happy-go-lucky trance. Alex could see that the dazed expressions and easy smiles had gone, replaced with a keen intent to break free once more, their focus restored by Gaze's death and the secrecy of their closest ally. Sabotage was the order of the day, and they were all ready to get going. He had waited days to have them all on board with as much enthusiasm as he had. He only wished they had come to it a different way, without anyone having to die.

"I suppose I'd better go," said Helena miserably. "I know you don't want to, after what has happened, but you should get back to your rooms before the guards do their rounds... Please don't think too badly of me. I'm still here to help you."

With that thought playing on their minds, Helena left, disappearing into the darkness. It was the opportunity Alex had been waiting for, as he gathered everyone together in a huddle. If what Gaze said was right, about his actions in the arena meaning they were in graver, more immediate danger then he had believed, then they were running out of time. They no longer had the luxury of ambling happily through life at Stillwater. If they ever wanted to get out, it had to be soon. Still, he wasn't sure tonight was the night to discuss a plan of action—his mind was foggy with grief, and he suspected the others would be in a similar state. They needed time to decompress and gather their thoughts, with Jari alongside them. He only hoped it could wait until tomorrow.

"We need to work quickly," whispered Alex. "We should meet tomorrow, once lessons are over, and come up with our plan of action."

"What about Helena?" asked Natalie. She was obviously still reluctant to leave out her friend, even after what she had admitted.

Alex shrugged. "We'll cross that bridge when we come to it. We may need her, but who knows how far we can trust her? Let's keep her at arm's length for now, and bring her in if and when we need to."

The group nodded, satisfied with the idea.

"Shall I tell Jari?" asked Aamir. "I spoke to the medical mage today, who said they were going to discharge him tomorrow morning anyway. He's supposed to be starting classes with you two." He nodded toward Ellabell and Natalie.

"Yeah, get him to come along," agreed Alex. "You should probably fill him in on what happened tonight," he added with a grimace, knowing Jari wouldn't take the news too well. At least the rest of them had had a chance to say goodbye.

Aamir sighed. "I'll tell him."

"Where should we meet? Is anywhere safe enough?" Ellabell asked.

"We should meet in the library. I've no idea if it's safe, but it has the books we might need. Plus, it's huge, so we can hopefully find somewhere away from prying eyes," he replied, though he wasn't sure such a place existed within the walls of Stillwater House. He'd started to feel the prickle of eyes upon him wherever he went these days.

Parting ways, Alex knew nobody would be sleeping well that night.

CHAPTER 36

THE NEXT DAY, THE QUINTET ASSEMBLED IN THE GRAND library, with its gold-flecked marble floors and trickling water features, pooling away, down the abyss in the center of the room. Other students eyed them cautiously, but most of the five were too distracted by the beauty of the place to notice. It was only Alex, who was already familiar with the alluring, airy space and its entire universe of books, who noticed the wary observation of those around.

It was nice to see Jari up and about, too, though there was a melancholy to his usually cheerful face that Alex found heart-rending. To hear of Gaze's passing and the truth of Helena was not exactly a pleasant way to start the day. Still, the distraction of finding a way out soon brought some life back to his eyes, as they made their way up to a large reading alcove, similar to the one Alex had almost been discovered in. It was high enough that Alex could keep an eye on anyone trying to approach them, but tucked away enough that it gave the illusion of privacy. Whether it would provide any such security, they had yet to find out.

They paused on the walkway, and Alex pulled out a list of research topics. As he read them aloud, the others put their hands up at the subjects they liked and took that as their responsibility, wandering over to the Index to check out any entries before braving the stacks.

The group went their separate ways among the many floors. Alex clambered up to the very top platform and rooted through several shelves until he found some books he thought might be useful. He had brought his *Royals* book and *Leander Wyvern* book along too, realizing it had been a while since he had delved within their pages. So much had happened, he had almost forgotten about the two books. As he returned to the reading area, he wondered if there'd be anything juicy inside the tomes that they could use.

Regrouping, he chuckled to see that both Natalie and Ellabell were teetering along with enormous stacks of books, while the two other boys only had a few in each hand. Nevertheless, the tables became a mess of literature as everyone spread their books out on the surface, picking up ones that caught their eyes, before they all settled back in their armchairs to read what lay within.

As they read, talk turned to what could be gained from the lessons they had been attending.

"We could see what Master Montego knows of cloaking spells," Natalie said, flipping through some pages of a book entitled *Cloaks and Their Many Uses*.

"I've just started learning explosion spells," Jari chimed in. "It'd be cool to blow stuff up. You know, if we need to create any diversions," he quipped, a glimmer of mischief in his eyes.

"What about your classes, Alex? Anything interesting we could use?" Ellabell asked, turning to him.

Alex pondered the question. Master Demeter's classes were mainly focused on the theoretical, which didn't seem very useful in this case. "I could see what I can find out about the history of Stillwater, I guess. He might know more about the portals between havens or something."

He wished he had more to offer from his classes. He had still only been taught by the clownish Master Demeter, even though he was supposed to be having lessons with Alypia. On the occasions she had been listed on his schedule, he had shown up at the correct room, only to find Master Demeter again, who would cry out, without fail, "Is this a devil I see before me?" with something held aloft in his hand, mixing his Shakespeares as badly as he mixed his proverbs.

"I wonder if Alypia is up to something," he said, after he had explained her continued absences to the others.

Natalie frowned. "The Headmistress is always up to something, as far as I can tell."

There was residual bitterness, in the wake of what had happened to Gaze. Alex could sense it in the air, mirroring the resentment he felt pulsing inside his own heart.

From the table, Alex picked up his research list and looked over it. Portals, Great Evils, uses for life essence, powerful spells, magical travel—the Stillwater library had a lot of books that skirted around many of these subjects, but none that explicitly detailed any of what they needed. It was frustrating to watch his friends discard book after book, finding nothing of much use at all.

"Any good?" asked Alex as Natalie threw down a large, yellow-covered book on *How to Get from Point A to B: A Mage's Journey* by Frederik Scott.

"No, it is some autobiography. Nothing is what it seems in this place!" she cried in exasperation. Alex knew exactly how she felt.

"We've got to remember what Helena said—there are books the students aren't allowed to see, even here," he explained. "So what we're looking for might not even be here."

This revelation put a damper on everyone's mood as they continued to sift through the stacks of books, hoping that one of them would have at least a glimmer of hope within.

Alex's mind, however, was distracted by a far bigger picture. He was trying to focus on his other idea, the one running alongside the plan to escape to the outside world. In his mind's eye, he pictured the black bottles with their pulsing red interiors, and felt the overwhelming desire for their destruction course through him, making his eyes burn. He had been thinking about it ever since his failed trip to the arena, though he still wasn't sure if he wanted to destroy them all or steal them all, in order to keep them out of the hands of the Head and Headmistress. They could also be a useful bargaining chip for the freedom of those at Spellshadow, perhaps, and for the five of them to be returned to the real world too, should they fail to find a way of their own. He knew it was pretty optimistic, but he also knew the value of that stuff, especially after hearing Alypia's fears about it running out. If he played his cards right, he could find himself in control.

The only problem was, he still didn't know where the bottles were hidden, and the only person he could ask wasn't with them, because they had chosen to push her away. He sighed, wondering if leaving Helena out was the right thing to do. She was still useful and willing to help, despite the white lie she had told. How many of *them* were guilty of similar lies?

Remembering Gaze's words, Alex turned to Aamir. "Do you think we've been too hard on Helena?" he asked, addressing the group, though his stare remained with Aamir.

"She lied," replied Natalie.

"Yeah, but haven't we all lied at some point? You can understand why she didn't tell us—we *would* have run a mile," Alex said thoughtfully. "What I can't understand is why *you* lied to us, Aamir." He waited for Aamir to reply, as the others turned their gaze toward him.

"I'm sorry," Aamir whispered. "I know it was a stupid thing to do. I should have just told you, but I was ashamed of the things I did when I was Professor Escher. When they brought me here, I was trained in so many foul things. I was taught how to keep students in line, how to manipulate them using mind techniques and magic that made them experience pain and suffering like you wouldn't believe. Those post-curfew punishments we were all so worried about? We had a right to be scared. They trained me in how to lash students, how to curse students, what to do if they broke the rules—it was a death sentence… and I was expected to dole it out." He drew in a breath, his throat tight as sorrow gleamed in his eyes. "So many awful things were expected of us. We were told to use whatever means necessary to hold our positions as teachers. They taught me so many vile spells, to hurt and punish and emotionally scar students. They taught me all of that here, and I didn't want to think about it—I didn't want you to think of me that way. I wanted to bury Escher for good, and I went about it in entirely the wrong way." His brow furrowed as he held his head in his hands.

This tale seemed to placate the others, who rushed to embrace the softly weeping Aamir, but Alex knew the tears were rooted in something deeper. The shame he believed, but the teachers had a choice; they had seen as much with the likes of Gaze and Lintz. Yes, there were bad eggs, but it didn't mean they didn't have a choice.

Alex had a feeling that it was this that lay at the root of Aamir's shame. Through fear or uncertainty or not knowing, Aamir had done the bidding of the Head, being too naïve or too frightened not to. It made sense—Gaze and Lintz were older, with less to lose. Aamir had gone along with it, perhaps because he had seen no other option. Alex could understand that; he just wished he could hear Aamir admit to it, just once. The raw, honest, vulnerable truth. He could have truly respected his friend for that, because it wasn't easy to say. Still, Alex believed the hurt in Aamir's words and the meaning behind them and knew it was enough. His friend had been through enough, and the trust between them had been restored, however tentatively. It wasn't an easy thing to admit, when a person was wrong, and so he looked to Aamir, realizing that, if this was all he was going to get by way of an apology, then that was fine by him. It was just nice to have the old Aamir back, or as near to him as it would ever be possible to get.

As Aamir regained his composure, Alex brought out the book Elias had given him and began to read. Ellabell shot him a curious look. She wandered over to where he was and sat on the armrest, peering down.

"What are you reading?" she asked.

"A Spellbreaker book," he replied.

The sight of it seemed to perk up her interest. "Any good?"

"I'm still finding out," he whispered. She smiled back at him, making him feel close to her as a warm, conspiratorial moment passed between them, reminding him of the last time they had bonded over stories from Spellbreaker history.

"It makes sense now, your sudden interest in battles." She grinned. "Did I help at all?"

He nodded. "You helped more than you know."

"I'm glad." She nudged him lightly, leaning close as she tried to read some pages over Alex's shoulder.

The moment was disturbed as Helena appeared, looking flustered.

"There you are!" she cried. "I've been trying to find you."

She froze, her pale eyes snapping toward the book in Alex's hands. Her expression morphed into one of shock as she read the title, *Leander Wyvern: The Last Spellbreaker,* and leveled her gaze at Alex.

"Where did you get that?" she breathed.

He shrugged. "It was just in the stacks."

"Don't play the fool, Alex! I know every book in this library, and *that* does not belong here," she hissed. "That is a very rare book—rarer than you know. It has always been kept in my mother's office, not here. You didn't simply find *that* in the stacks, so

I'll ask you again—where did you get it?" Her eyes burned with annoyance.

"Why does it matter?" remarked Alex, genuinely curious to know why it did.

His comment seemed to soften Helena's angry expression. "I suppose it doesn't," she said through gritted teeth, her words lacking conviction. "I was just surprised to see it in your hands, is all."

Alex frowned, his suspicions piqued that she was no longer on their side. Her startling reaction had been unexpected to say the least, and he wasn't quite sure what to make of it. Even as she got back to the reason she had been seeking them out, her eyes kept flitting to the cover of the book in Alex's hands, her expression anxious.

"I come bearing good news," she explained, a forced brightness in her voice.

"You do?" asked Natalie hopefully. "We have not been having much luck."

Helena nodded. "I couldn't find the book I wanted, with all the portal magic inside, but I did manage to find something else," she whispered, as the others leaned in to hear.

"What did you find?" Jari asked, instantly doe-eyed in her presence. No lie could suppress his adoration for the girl.

"I managed to find a portal to another haven," she said softly.

They looked at her in surprise. The only reason Alex had contemplated traveling to other havens was to seek out more bottles of essence, but the renewed idea was pleasing to Alex's ears. It could maybe lead them to an abandoned site where they might have a lot more time to think, unburdened by the pressure of being pursued or used for ulterior purposes. Besides, if the black bottles *were* in Alypia's office, he knew he might need to find essence elsewhere.

"Which haven is it?" Alex asked, remembering the note with the names of the remaining four havens upon it: *Falleaf House, Kingstone Keep, Spellshadow Manor, Stillwater House.*

Helena shook her head. "I don't know. I just know it's a portal to somewhere else."

"How do you know?" he pressed.

She sighed, narrowing her eyes at him. "You really do have endless questions, don't you? I know because there is a still, unmoving image through a door in one of the rooms in the deepest part of the school—it looks out onto a castle courtyard. Now, I don't know about you, but you don't tend to find many castles sticking out of subterranean rooms, do you? So I'm guessing it's a portal," she remarked, flashing a look at Alex. "Nobody goes down there. It's close to the derelict quarter, so people tend to keep away. There's nothing much to see there, and I saw in a book that portals can often be found in that kind of location—isolated, quiet, mostly empty places."

"Which book?" asked Alex.

"I don't remember—look, time is ticking. We need to get going, if we're going," Helena said. It didn't escape Alex's notice that she was pointedly ignoring his question. "The longer we stay, the less chance we have of being successful," she added.

"What do you think?" asked Alex, looking at the others. Helena had a very good point, echoing what Gaze had said about them needing to step their plans up if they were to have any hopes of leaving.

"I think it could be our best shot," Jari said eagerly, jiggling in his seat. It was definitely the most proactive plan anyone had come up with so far.

"I think we need to get as far away from the Headmistress and this weird magic air as soon as possible," Aamir agreed.

"There is something not right here—there is something that keeps distracting us." Natalie nodded, though there was a touch of reluctance in her voice, quickly masked with a smile.

"I think we should give it a try," Ellabell said.

Alex paused. "We should go sooner rather than later though, yeah?"

The group agreed wholeheartedly. There was no point in staying somewhere that had such bizarre control over them. Besides, who was to say the magic in the air wouldn't try to make them forget their plans, if they stayed a while longer? They had to believe Gaze; they had to get out as fast as they could, before anything could stop them.

"Then we're going," Alex said, pleased with the conclusion.

Helena cleared her throat. "May I come with you?" she asked.

"You can come, if you take us to see the room with the portal in it," he bargained.

Helena smirked. "I'm not an idiot, Alex. After all your talk of distrust, I don't think I'll be taking you there unless you truly promise to bring me with you."

She had a point. Alex wasn't happy with the idea of letting Alypia's daughter follow along. It made him feel guilty, to be called out like that—to have his honor called into question. And yet she had been right to do it. His need to protect lay only with those who had come with him from Spellshadow; it did not fully extend to the silver-haired girl, but she couldn't help her heritage.

"Then you'll have to take us, and come with us," he said quickly, before he could change his mind.

She grinned excitedly. "I'll come and fetch you all at midnight, and lead you to the portal! You won't regret this, I promise," she whispered. "I'm sorry for not telling you about my mother, but I swear upon everything I hold dear that you can trust me." A glimmer of emotion flashed in her gold eyes, letting Alex know he had done the right thing.

"Why do want you to leave?" said Jari suddenly.

She sighed. "It's complicated… I don't want to be a royal. I never wanted to be a royal. I want more from life than what I can expect if I stay—there are duties and expectations, and I don't want any of them. I never asked for them, and I want the same choices and opportunities that I've heard people can have out in the real world," she explained sadly. "That is what I long for—to be normal. No magic, no royalty, no title, no pressures. Just me."

It was the most genuine Alex had ever seen her, with her soul bared and her expression vulnerable. There was a lifetime of hurt and remorse in her voice, but there was hope too—they were the hope. They had turned up at just the right moment for Helena to hold onto her dream. Without them, he wondered what her plan might have been.

Whatever it was, he began to understand that they had more in common than he had realized.

He, too, just wanted to be normal again.

CHAPTER 37

A LEX SAT IN HIS ROOM, ANXIOUSLY WAITING FOR NIGHT to come. The others had gone down for something to eat, but he knew he couldn't stomach a mouthful. Excitement and nerves made it as impossible as sitting still.

Gazing out the window at the rolling, emerald fields that shone dimly beneath the evening sky, he knew he couldn't just sit there anymore, twiddling his thumbs. His muscles were tense and in need of stretching; he needed to not be surrounded by the echoing voices of students and people, clamoring through the corridors outside, which were only serving to increase his anxiety. He needed peace, to get the plan clear in his mind, like preparation before a big game. He needed room to go over some spells, to calm his nerves. It made him think about what Helena had said about the abandoned quarter of the school and nobody ever going there—he knew firsthand how quiet it could be out there. It was the perfect spot to get his head clear. Plus, if they made it out, he knew this would be his last chance to explore that part of the school, and he liked the idea of saying a fond farewell to the bell tower that had kept them safe in those early days.

Slipping out of his room, he headed cautiously through the hallways and corridors of the school, moving toward the abandoned courtyard with the bell tower in the corner. From there, he would spread out and explore the derelict section of the villa, going over a few defensive spells as he walked through the halls.

Nobody bothered him as he slunk from shadow to shadow, putting up a shield whenever somebody came too close, the crackle of it prickling the hairs on the back of their neck if they got too near, like an unseen breath in the darkness. Spooked, the intruders quickly moved away, leaving him to advance onward.

Stepping out into the familiar courtyard, piled with rubble and dust and forgotten debris, Alex spun on his heel and turned to face the shaded façade of the villa's exterior. Ahead of him lay the corridor that the Head and Headmistress had vanished into, that night he had listened to them talking in a windowless study, thinking themselves alone. Seeing it, an impulse tugged at his mind, making Alex want to head toward it. He could see the bookshelves in his mind's eye, and they made him curious— perhaps there was something in them that might prove a useful addition to his collection.

He gave in to the impulse, following the half-remembered route through the dim hallways, the torches sputtered out and gathering cobwebs in their brackets. Turning this way and that, he hoped he was going the right direction; otherwise, he knew he'd never find his way back out. It was like an old Greek story he'd loved as a kid—Theseus and the Minotaur. He was Theseus, holding one end of an imaginary ball of golden twine as he wandered through the labyrinth in search of a mysterious creature that could well kill him. A real ball of twine would have been nice.

Alex turned down a short corridor that seemed gloriously familiar. It was the same one he had followed Alypia and her brother to, that night—he was almost certain of it, though most of the hallways in this place looked alike. Checking both shadowy ends of the hallway for anyone who might sneak up on him, he stopped in front of the door he had once crouched beside. Drawn by curiosity, he ducked down and peered through the keyhole, seeing the same windowless study beyond. It brought back troublesome memories, but it was definitely the same spot where he had seen Alypia and her brother talk. Wanting to get a closer look, feeling convinced that those bookshelves on the back wall contained something of use, he placed his palm on the lock and let the silvery black of his anti-magic flow through, building a spell around it, trying to break it with force. Nothing happened.

Frustrated, Alex poured layer after layer of strong energy into the mechanism instead, closing his eyes to try to visualize the system within, using it like clockwork to lift and move the bolts with his anti-magic. It was a tough job, taking all his concentration, but the bars slid backward. With a satisfying click, the door unlocked. Alex had never felt such relief, not knowing how much longer he could stay out in the hallway, exposed like that.

Ducking quickly into the room, he did the same trick to lock the door behind him. A broken lock, he knew, was always a telltale sign of trespassers.

Glancing around, letting his heartrate return to normal, he saw the study looked exactly the same. The sleek wooden desk and the high-backed chair. The promising bookshelves running along each wall. One thing that was definitely different, however, was the sight of another door, tucked into the wall at the far right side of the room. It was too far away to have been visible from the keyhole, which would explain why he hadn't been able to see it until now.

Fear and anticipation gripped his heart in a vice, quickening his heartbeat once more, until he thought it might jump from his ribcage as he approached the narrow wooden door. This had *not* been what he was expecting. It didn't seem possible that it had been within his grasp, all this time. It looked much like the one in the chamber at Spellshadow, only not so unpleasant. Here, it was far away from the terror and viscous byproducts of the actual extraction.

Holding the black iron ring that hung to one side, he twisted it and felt his stomach sink as it gave, the door pushing open with relative ease. Beyond it, in the dim glow of torchlight, he saw shelves upon shelves, stacked with smoky black bottles no bigger than pepper shakers, glowing with the familiar red pulse of somebody's life essence. Acrid bile rose up his throat.

Suddenly, he heard the mutter of voices and the sound of a key turning in the lock, not far from where he stood. His heart was in his mouth, fear freezing him to the spot for a moment before action kicked in. Quickly, he pushed the door shut behind him as he ducked and rolled beneath the wooden shelving units, dust getting in his mouth and nostrils, scratching at his throat. He hoped the glowing life magic of many hundreds of mages would hide the strange, angered crackle of his own anti-magic.

Every flurry of dust made him want to sneeze, and he imagined all kinds of creatures crawling over him, in the grimy darkness beneath the shelves. It took everything he had not to reach up and rub the dust from his nose, instead staying perfectly still as he listened for the new arrivals. The muttered voices had definitely entered the study, but they did not come toward the antechamber where Alex lay. Straining to hear, he could make out the clear, crisp sound of the Headmistress's voice, but he couldn't determine the intonation of the other voice with her. He didn't think it was the Head, but he couldn't be sure. The voice was too distorted, too fuzzy.

After what seemed like an age of listening to the two speakers drone on in a hardly coherent buzz, his chest burning as he struggled to take small breaths, the sound of the lock turning again granted him a desperate reprieve. Still not daring to inhale deeply and clear the muck from his airways, he rolled out from under the shelving and crawled toward the door. Opening it a crack, he peered tentatively out into the study, but there was nobody in the room beyond. Whatever they had come to discuss, they had done it and left. Only then, stepping away from the antechamber, did he gasp for air, filling his lungs as he coughed the debris out of his croaky throat.

Moving toward the door, he unlocked it and let himself

out into the corridor, running as quickly as he dared back to his bedroom. The sands of time were against him, but he wasn't about to give up when he had come so close to the prize. He refused to be foiled by something as insignificant as lacking a bag.

Reaching his room, he dove toward the wardrobe and pulled out boxes and drawers he had barely opened, seeking out a bag of some sort—something suitable he could use to carry as many of the bottles as possible. He didn't need to take all of them, but a hefty sum would be good. Raking through the piles of clean clothes, and shoes he'd never worn, his hands clasped around a black satchel. It was perfect for what he needed.

Checking the clock on the wall, he saw with astonishment that it was almost ten. By the time he had returned and found the satchel, he had left himself barely any wiggle room if anything went wrong—it was down to the wire now, with two hours to get in and get out with as many bottles as he could lay his hands on before they left with Helena through the portal.

Not wanting to waste any more time, he sprinted from the room with the satchel bouncing against his hip. He ducked into doorways and crouched in the shadows whenever somebody passed, feeling as if he were on a gameshow of some sort, until he reached the doorway, his pulse racing with nervous excitement. Reaching out for the lock, he stopped the threads of his anti-magic just in time, as he heard the rise of voices coming from within the room beyond.

Squatting, he peered through the keyhole to see whom he had almost revealed himself to. The Headmistress was standing behind the desk, speaking animatedly with the auburn-haired Master Demeter. Whatever they were discussing, Alypia wasn't happy with Demeter. She was gesturing wildly, her peculiar eyes glowering at the cowed figure of Alex's tutor. Their conversation had something to do with information that Master Demeter had failed to provide, but that wasn't what drew Alex's attention.

Standing to the side of the two heated speakers, Alex was shocked to see the ghostly, raggedy specter of Renmark, watching the Headmistress and the teacher intently, a strange expression on his ghoulish, foul face. Glancing back at Alypia and Demeter, Alex wondered if they even knew the phantom figure was there. Were they like him, able to see Finder-like beings, or were they like the others, blissfully unaware of their ghastly, gray presence?

He didn't want to stay around to find out, nor did he want to get caught and blow his chance for the others to escape. He returned the way he had come, slipping unseen back into the bright lights of his bedroom. As he sank down on the edge of the bed, reality dawned. He had missed his chance. He had lost the opportunity to take some bottles and destroy the rest.

Pacing the room, he had nothing to do but wait for Helena to arrive, to take them to the portal and far away from here. As he moved, the empty satchel still slung across his body taunted him, devoid of the promised bottles. The frustration he felt at their loss crawled beneath his skin, tugging at his nerves, making him feel twisted up inside. But there was nothing he could do about it now.

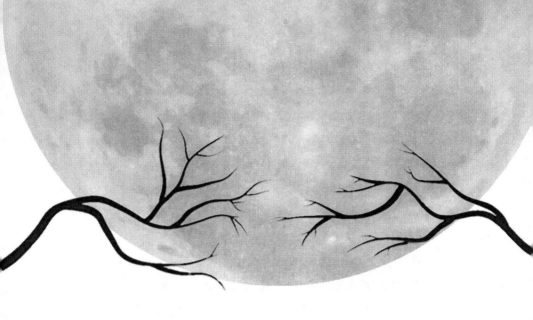

CHAPTER 38

H ELENA APPEARED, AS PROMISED, AT THE STROKE OF
midnight.

The others had gathered in Alex's room, awaiting
her arrival, though nobody felt much like talking. Alex was still
in a sour mood, and it seemed to have spread among the congregated individuals, though he didn't feel like telling his friends
why he felt so low. It physically pained him, to realize how close
he had come to achieving the other part of his plan, only to have
it fall away at the very last moment.

They looked up as knuckles rapped against the door.

"Is everyone ready?" asked Helena, popping her head
around.

Alex nodded. "Ready as we're ever likely to be," he replied
glibly as he stood to follow the others out, bringing up the rear.

The school was eerily still as they moved in single file through the hallways, catching glimpses of the glittering stars outside the windows. The torches flickered in their brackets, casting frightening shadows against the walls—wispy creatures that seemed to creep after the would-be escapees, playing out a frieze against the pale stone. More than once, Alex heard one of the others gasp in fright, mistaking a shadowy shape for a real person as they turned a corner or tripped over a band of darkness, splayed out on the flagstones at their feet.

Alex took in as much of the view as he could, knowing they might never return to this place. Regardless of the magic that hung in the air, he couldn't deny that Stillwater House was a thing of dark beauty. It looked like something torn from the pages of a luxury vacation brochure, where elegant, fashionable ladies in oversized sunglasses sipped espresso and talked rapidly in a foreign language he couldn't understand.

Even at night, the villa was beautiful. Lamps and delicate strings of hanging lights lit up the courtyards, mirroring the stunning glitter of the cosmos above and shedding a soft glow upon the flowers and statues, giving them an otherworldly aura in the twilight hours. At some point, he figured, somebody must go around turning them all off, because he hadn't been able to see the lights from the lighthouse—he wondered whose job that was, conjuring up the image of the toady Siren Mave. She seemed to do anything and everything and yet was never anywhere at all. He settled on believing it was her task to put out the lights, as they continued on through the lengthy labyrinth of corridors.

They passed doors and empty hallways, always listening

for the sound of footsteps. The only sound Alex could hear was the anxious whisper of their collective breath as they followed Helena, who led the way. In the dim light, her hair seemed to glow ethereally, creating a halo around her head as it swung side to side with the rhythm of her movements. Perhaps it wouldn't be so bad to have her around, he thought. Everyone seemed to like her, including him, and it would definitely improve Jari's mood, he mused. Plus, she was incredibly strong, which was definitely an asset for whatever hardship might lie ahead.

If only I could get rid of this doubt, he thought to himself, watching Helena more closely than he realized. It was only when he caught sight of Ellabell watching him that he quickly dropped his gaze, which had been lingering a moment too long, perhaps. Sneaking a glance at Ellabell, he saw a subtle look of dismay on her face, which he desperately wanted to wipe away. He hadn't been looking at Helena because he was attracted to her, although she was undeniably beautiful, and now he was worried Ellabell might have gotten the wrong impression. Indecision plagued him—if he tried to reassure her he wasn't looking at Helena, it would no doubt confirm her suspicions. If he left it unmentioned, she'd probably think that anyway.

When he turned to speak to her, deciding to go with reassurance, she had already moved on ahead, whispering companionably with Natalie, who was leaning in to hear better. He wished he could hear what they were saying, as he heard the tinkle of a hushed giggle, echoing through the air toward him.

With his mind so distracted by the whisperings of the two girls, Alex didn't realize they had entered one of the many parts of the villa he had never seen before. They were in a narrow corridor, leading down beneath the earth. They treaded carefully on the stone steps as they descended, coming out into a long, rubble-strewn corridor, with peeling doors tucked away all along the length of it.

Helena paused, her mouth moving silently as she counted the doors, pointing toward one midway down the hall. She stopped beside it, gesturing for the others to do the same. Alex felt nerves clawing at his insides as he watched the girl reach out for the handle and pull it open with startling force. She stepped over the threshold, and the others moved to go in after her, following suit, but the blood-curdling scream that erupted from the girl's lungs stopped them dead in their tracks.

Beyond the door, Alypia was waiting with a menacing grin and a team of armed guards.

Helena turned, her golden eyes wide in desperation. "Run!" she cried.

In a mess of confusion, Alex tried to urge his friends toward an exit, only to find that they had all been blocked. Guards had appeared along the length of the corridor, standing ominously in front of the entrances to every hallway. There was no way out.

They had been betrayed.

Alex's eyes snapped toward Helena, but she looked just as horrified as he was. She ran toward a row of guards, trying to force her way past them. Golden, fierce energy crackled from her palms, but they were ready for her, as several guards at a time sent up shields of superior strength to block her magic. Helena roared, sending spears that thrummed with life directly at their heads, only for the missiles to shatter into a thousand glittering pieces, falling harmlessly to the floor.

367

The guards moved inward with their gleaming shields, forcing Alex and his friends into the center, where they could not break free. Although they all tried to use their magic, there wasn't enough room to forge anything potent, the bolts and streams of gold and silvery black getting lost in a mist of confused energies, until nobody could tell what belonged to whom. In the fracas, Alex couldn't think straight, struggling to get his mind to focus clearly enough to conjure something useful. The surprise had robbed him of his skill, and the guards edged ever closer.

Once they had been pushed back in front of the door, the guards shoved them roughly into the chamber beyond it, pinning their arms behind their backs.

"I didn't do this!" Helena cried to the others, her eyes glimmering with furious tears as she looked upon her mother with such palpable hatred that the guards standing beside Alypia had to lower their gazes, uncomfortable beneath the ferocity of it. "Please believe me—I didn't do this!"

Alypia smiled, her voice cold and calculating. "Of course this wasn't my daughter, though I can see why you might have mistrusted her. You don't seem to like me very much, so it only seems natural you'd find her deplorable by association." Her mouth curved into a vicious grin. "No, no. You have been betrayed by someone much closer to home."

Alex struggled against the guard holding him, and the sight made Alypia chuckle icily, her eyes glittering with malice.

"Oh, you're going to find this one *very* hard to stomach, Alex Webber," she purred. "She only did it for you, Alex—she only came to me, whispering secrets, to save your life. Isn't that right, Ellabell?"

Alex turned to Ellabell, a look of bewilderment on his face, but Ellabell's expression showed nothing but rage as she tried to struggle free of her guard, wanting to lash out at Alypia. There was no shame, no guilt, just pure fury from the fiery, bespectacled girl as their eyes met.

"Liar! If you're going to tell tales, at least make them believable!" Ellabell smirked, her eyes burning brightly. "Alypia threatened to kill you if I didn't feed her little tidbits about your powers and secrets," she explained, turning from Alex back to Alypia, "but I knew it was a load of garbage! I would *never* betray him like that. You needed him too much! I knew you'd never lay a finger on him. It was all smoke and mirrors, and I'm not stupid enough to fall for a stupid trick like that. At least do your research if you're going to try and blackmail a person."

Jari looked at her with understanding, and Alex realized they must have been offered the same thing. Though Ellabell had taken the offer, it was clear she hadn't complied with what Alypia wanted.

"Yeah—you want to turn Alex against her. That's all this is!" yelled Jari. "None of us would betray him or anyone like this. You can try and pin it on any one of us, and we'll tell you the same thing—piss off!" He grinned triumphantly.

Ellabell leveled her gaze at Alex, but he didn't need any further assurance. He could see the truth in her strength as she defied Alypia's words, her face showing she would not be broken as she turned back toward Alypia, her mouth set in a grim line.

Alex looked slowly over his shoulder, seeing something strange out of the corner of his eye. Skulking behind the intimidating group of guards, a trail of frayed gray robes flashed between the gaps in the guards' bodies. Alex caught the glint of smug satisfaction in the black, dead eyes of the ghostly Renmark as his foul face appeared over the shoulders of the oblivious Stillwater soldiers. It was not Ellabell, or Helena, or Natalie, or Aamir, or Jari.

Renmark was the mole.

Alex realized he must have missed the phantom's presence, with Renmark managing to hide away, unseen, overhearing all of their conversations and watching their movements, witnessing everything and scurrying back to impart his knowledge to Alypia. At least that answered Alex's question about whether or not Alypia could see Finder-like creatures. It turned out she could not only see them, but she could use them for her own dastardly purposes.

And this Finder seemed uniquely designed to find Alex.

As understanding dawned on him, he found himself thinking back to the moments, so often recently, when he had felt his skin crawling with the heat of unseen eyes on him, prickling the hairs on his arms and shivering up the back of his neck. He thought back to the ransacked cottage, when he had simply shrugged the feeling off as a guard having seen him and passed on information. Having forgotten about it, he had not remembered the peculiar sensation it had made him feel, of how it didn't add up. He realized now that it must have been Renmark, in his phantom state, having arrived at Stillwater already— before Alex first saw him with the group from Spellshadow. Perhaps he had tipped off the guards to search the place. It could have been Renmark's first offering of inside information, gifted to Alypia, to make himself valuable to her.

Alex knew then that he had not been cautious enough. He had allowed himself to feel invincible, and that was the most dangerous, vulnerable place to be. Perhaps, Alex thought, in addition to being able to see him, Renmark had added skills to those of the previous Finder, Malachi Grey—something that made Renmark less visible to Alex. Or perhaps Alex just hadn't been looking hard enough.

All Alex knew was that he wanted to apologize to Helena with everything he had, for not trusting her. She had not been involved, that much was evident now. This affected her as much as any of them, if not more so; her chance to escape had been stolen too, by the ghostly espionage of Renmark.

Alypia had turned her attention to her daughter, the disappointment evident in her noble eyes as she glowered in the girl's direction.

"Take them away!" commanded Alypia.

"No! This was my fault—they had nothing to do with this!" pleaded Helena, her eyes gleaming with fear.

"Silence!" Alypia roared, her voice shaking the ground. "You have done quite enough."

Nobody manhandled Helena as the guards stepped forward to take the others away, sharing one prisoner between two guards to prevent them from wriggling free. It was evident that Alypia would be having private words with her daughter, away from the prying eyes of the guards and the would-be escapees. There would be no prison cell for the princess, though Alex knew he'd much prefer one to the wrath Helena was likely to face.

Once they had been dragged back through the belly of the school, Alex was thrown into a dingy, bleak cell, with Ellabell thrown in straight after. For a long while, she was very quiet, huddled against the far wall. But she wore a look of grim determination, even though Alex wasn't sure there was much hope left for them. He knew the terms of the offer he'd agreed to, and he was pretty sure attempted escape was a big breach in those provisos, if not the biggest breach they could have achieved.

He sat beside Ellabell, placing his arm around her as she leaned into the hollow of his shoulder. Looking up into his eyes, she smiled sadly.

"You know I'd never do anything like that, right?" she whispered, her face so close to his.

He nodded, resting his cheek against the top of her head. "Of course," he said softly, mumbling into her hair.

"What do we do now?" she asked, wrapping her arm around Alex's waist as she held him tighter.

"I don't know," he breathed, trying to tamp down the hopeless feeling that was threatening to swallow up his voice. "What *did* you tell Alypia?" he asked, curious.

She smiled against his shoulder. "I just told her useless information whenever I was called in—Alex prefers milk in his tea, instead of lemon. Alex likes to eat his cereal soggy. Alex doesn't like bell peppers. It was mostly food related."

He chuckled, holding her tightly. "Very observant."

"No, it's just weird," she giggled.

Tentatively, he placed the lightest of kisses on the top of her forehead, realizing that if this was the end of the road, he wanted her to at least have some inclination as to his feelings. He felt her smile again, against his t-shirt.

Anger trembled through him as he thought of everything the school, the Head, the Headmistress, Malachi Grey, Renmark, and all those magical forces had taken from him. Soon, they would take Ellabell and his friends too, and with them any hope he had left of returning home to his mother and a normal, teen-age existence.

Even as a ghost, Renmark had managed to crush them.

CHAPTER 39

A LEX WASN'T SURE OF THE TIME OR THE DAY WHEN THE guards came for him.

Ellabell was asleep in his arms when they threw open the cell door and demanded he follow them. Lifting his finger sharply to his lips, Alex was amused to see the guards stop mid-sentence, putting on a silent display of charades as he gently extricated himself from Ellabell's arms and lay her carefully down on the floor. She stirred, but did not wake, much to Alex's bittersweet contentment. It would be easier this way.

He followed them dutifully, keeping his head down and his thoughts sharp as he traipsed through now-familiar paths and hallways to the underbelly of the villa. To his surprise, he realized the guards weren't taking him to the glass-ceilinged office, but toward the gloomier, more desolate part of the school.

It was strange to admit, but he felt a pang of disappointment; he would have liked to have seen that room again, with the heady scent of citrus and flowers and the warmth of it enveloping like a comforting embrace. Funnily enough, he found he also had a desire to see the lake one last time, to say a goodbye of sorts to the ethereal specters beneath the water, knowing he would soon be joining them. He wondered morbidly if that was where Alypia would put him, once she had used him for whatever grim purpose she had in mind. Part of him hoped so.

Turning past an instantly recognizable corner, he understood he was being taken to the windowless study, with the grisly antechamber next door. Pausing beside it, one of the guards pushed open the door and gestured for Alex to step inside. There was no pushing, no shoving, just a civilized walk into the room.

Alypia sat in her chair behind the desk, impatiently tapping her long fingers against the sleek surface. The way she was sitting looked almost constructed, her body draped languorously, as if she had spent a long while trying to look as dramatic as possible. The idea made Alex smirk, causing a flash of irritation to spark across Alypia's eyes as she saw the insolent look, which only served to widen his discourteous smile. For a moment, the mask slipped, as Alex saw Alypia's beauty turn ugly, revealing the true, twisted face beneath. It was as Alex had suspected all along: her beauty hid a rotten core.

"Sit!" she barked.

He did as he was told, trying to wipe the smirk from his face. "You called?" There was a sing-song note to his voice that seemed to irk Alypia even more.

Her expression was icy. "I thought we had a deal, Alex Webber."

"I think we both knew that was never going to pan out," he grinned, challenging her.

"Be that as it may, a deal is a deal, and you broke your end of it," she replied, a threatening smile curving at the corner of her lips.

"Is it just me, or is it cold in here?" he mocked, knowing he was pushing his luck and finding he didn't care.

"You're trying my patience, Alex."

"Sorry—you were saying?" he encouraged, sprawling across his chair in much the same manner Alypia was.

"It's unfortunate, Alex, but thanks to your misconduct we are going to have to speed up proceedings. A broken contract cannot be tolerated, and you must be punished for your insolence," she began, her face devoid of humor. "You know, Alex, you might not believe me but I truly wanted to keep you and your friends safe here, away from those who might seek to use your powers for their own ends. I merely wanted to help you control and utilize them, in the hopes that one day you could use them for good."

He sniggered, gaining a sharp glare. "You were just the benevolent spirit-guide, helping me on my way?" He raised an eyebrow in disbelief, willing her to challenge him so he could rip her to shreds for it.

"It's not a joke, Alex. This is not a silly game you and your friends can play at your leisure," she hissed. "This is serious. This is life or death. I wanted to build you up, to be a formidable Spellbreaker, but you have squandered what goodwill I had toward you. I may not be entirely altruistic, but I am fair. With me, you would all have had a better chance at returning home. Now, you have zero chance—do you hear me?" She snapped her teeth at him. "Zero."

For the first time since entering the room, he felt fear. Not for himself, but for the others. Alypia was not a woman to be messed with, and they had caused her a world of trouble. The offers had been just, and they had flouted them. He began to wonder if, perhaps, they hadn't just made a huge, irrevocable mistake. The others might have been happy here, even.

"What are you going to do?" he asked, clearing his throat.

"I wanted you trained and coached, but I'm going to have to make do with the strength I've got," she muttered under her breath. "You understand I cannot permit you to remain within the school walls, after the way you have influenced my daughter? I could perhaps have forgiven an escape attempt, had you not tried to rope my girl into it, leading her astray the way you have. She's a fantasist, you know?"

Alex thought that was unlikely, musing that perhaps a lifetime under the same roof as Alypia was what had driven Helena to want to leave. He didn't dare say as much, though the words danced on the tip of his tongue for a moment, begging to be spoken. For the sake of keeping Alypia's temper as bottled-up as possible, he held the accusation back.

"She seems perfectly sane to me—saner than a lot of the people here, I'd say," he replied, skirting as close to his cutting comment as he could.

"You don't see what I see, Alex. Her mind is easily swayed. She is an idealist, with dreams of leading a life beyond the

magical world, beyond her royal duties, out in the 'real world.'"
Alypia laughed coldly.

"That sounds perfect to me," Alex retorted.

"Your mind is so small, you cannot see the gift right in front
of your eyes," she snapped. "You might have had your dream
too, had you stuck it out like a good little boy. Not now—now
I have but one option for you. You have forced my hand. Just
remember, you brought this upon yourself."

His blood ran cold. "So you're just going to waste me?" he
ventured, wondering if he could garner any information about
his fate.

She smirked cruelly. "Hardly. Your curly-haired friend was
right. I would never have simply killed you… You are much
too valuable," she said wistfully. "You are the key to stopping
this godforsaken plague hacking away at our numbers—it only
seems right, seeing as you are responsible for wasting so much
essence. You created an imbalance in the chain, Alex. Thanks to
your paltry little uprising and that foul, gray little man, we have
been cheated out of far greater numbers. You have sent us back
more steps than I care to count, so perhaps it is fitting that your
life is forfeit."

She scraped her chair back, getting to her feet. Running her
long fingers absently along the spines of the books upon the
bookshelf, clearly more anxious than she wished to let on, she
prowled around the room, twisting a strand of white hair between her fingers as she muttered to herself. Alex watched her
lips moving, trying desperately to figure out what she was saying. All he could make out was the word "unprepared" before
she rounded on the wall, slamming her fist against it with a flare

of anger in her pale eyes.

"But what choice have you given me?" she snarled at the air around her.

All the while, with Alypia visibly distracted, Alex had been forging anti-magic beneath his hands, hiding them beneath the desk as he felt the familiar twist and coil of the silvery strands bending to his will. Glancing at the perplexed Alypia, he knew he only had a slim window in which to do what he planned. Taking a deep breath, he let the cold energy sink back beneath his skin, feeling it snake through his veins and into the deepest, most enigmatic part of his being. Shivering, he touched upon the very edge of his own essence, feeling the searing pain of it as it burned rapidly through his body, bringing every cell and fiber to life as he utilized the smallest piece of his soul.

His whole body began to tremble and smolder with white-hot heat. He looked up toward Alypia, feeling the blaze of his eyes glowing at her, suddenly vibrantly silver and blinding with bright white light, flecked with sparks of black.

For the very first time, he saw terror on Alypia's face. Having only witnessed what he could do in the setting of the arena, Alex understood why. Poor, misguided Alypia had believed he need-ed anger to use those powerful anti-magical skills, the kind that made his eyes burn silver. What she didn't know was that his ha-tred for mages like her was always bubbling away, just beneath the surface, ready to be used when he needed it most—a verita-ble well of fuel for his silver fire.

Holding his palms steady, he fired the liquid silver directly at her, feeling the force of it tear through his skin as it surged for-ward, twisting around her beautiful face, clawing at her perfect form, trying to sink beneath her smooth, porcelain skin to get at the pulsing red glow within. She howled like a wounded, scared animal as it raked at her flesh, making her muscles spasm as it tried to feed upon her magic. In the mist of fine, glittering light, Alex could see Alypia's face had turned sour and demonic, the façade of perfection falling away against the grasping fingers of his anti-magic, which seemed to temporarily stall the effects of the strange magic all around them—the crackling air that appeared to have brainwashed all those within Stillwater, as well as made those within its influence more beautiful.

Alex knew this was his opportunity. He threw back the chair and ran for the antechamber, hoping his silver mist would keep Alypia at bay for long enough. Seeing the rows upon rows of smoky black bottles, he knew he didn't have the time or the space to take them all, and so he ran the length of the room, scooping as many as he could into the satchel still around his body, filling the bag until it was full to bursting.

Satisfied with his bounty, he reached for the first rack at the side of the antechamber door and wrenched it down as hard as he could, watching as it smashed into the next one, and the next, and the next, collapsing like dominoes, the countless bottles exploding into shards, releasing the long-trapped wisps of red-tinged life essence. He did the same with the other side, until the antechamber was a writhing mass of pulsing red light that had begun a mass exodus back into the earth, sinking into the ground where it belonged, never to be used for any unnatural purpose as it ebbed away.

Alypia was still screaming when he ran back into the study, slamming the antechamber door shut behind him. Her arms flailed wildly as she tried to fight the silver mist that clawed at her with hungry desperation, but Alex knew the anti-magic wouldn't hold her for much longer.

What would, however, was life magic.

He wasn't sure how he felt about using it, but there wasn't time to balance the morality as he picked up two of the bottles from his satchel, apologizing softly to the unknown people they had belonged to. Plucking out the stoppers, he poured the shivering vines of pulsing red light into his hands. The essences burned his palms as they met with the coiling silver twist of his anti-magic. He wasn't certain how to manipulate life magic that belonged to someone else, but he figured he had come this far by making it up as he went along. Trusting his instincts, he fed his own anti-magic into the glowing bands of red, watching in wide-eyed awe as they crackled into life, pooling liquidly from his hands toward the flagstones below.

Before they could reach the floor, Alex exploded the blazing pools into two gargantuan beasts of golden and scarlet-tinged magic. They charged in a surge of raw energy toward Alypia's trembling figure, their monstrous eyes glowing black like the clockwork mice he had so adored. As they crashed into the white-haired mage's body, a red miasma snaked from within the jaws of one and wrapped around her, squeezing tighter with every breath she took. The life magic retaliated against her, trying to claw and scrape at her inner essence, drawn in a frenzy toward it.

Golden jaws snapped and red-tipped talons tore within in the confined room. There was nowhere for Alypia to run. Tentatively, Alex withdrew his anti-magic from the roaring, snarling beasts, pleased to see that the monsters remained as he took his influence away. It was almost as if they had a mind of their own now, urged on by whomever they had once belonged to. They attacked Alypia with ferocious vehemence, and the shiver of the spilt, nearby life essence seemed to join with the monsters, fueling them, making them more powerful and more autonomous than Alex could ever have imagined.

Almost fearful for his own life, Alex scampered from the room, worried they might turn on him if he stayed too long. As he ran, the horrifying screams of Alypia followed him, echoing through the hallways. Had it been anyone else, he might have felt worse about how he had left her, but he was in no doubt that she would fend off the glowing golden creatures eventually.

Just not until we're long gone, he hoped.

The bottles clinked in his satchel as he sprinted toward the prison cells, his lungs burning with the exertion. On his way toward his friends, he almost took out Helena, who was running in the opposite direction, careening into her at full force.

"Whoa!" he yelled, grabbing her shoulders to stop her from going flying.

"Alex?" She seemed stunned.

"No time," he gasped.

"Who's screaming?" she asked, pointing the way Alex had come.

"Your mother." He shrugged apologetically, his chest heaving from the sprint. "I'm… keeping her… busy. We're leaving."

Understanding flashed in Helena's eyes. "The others?"

"Cells."

Drawing on his last stores of strength, he tore off down the hallways with Helena running beside him, not stopping until they reached the prison cells. Leaving Alex to regain his breath, Helena hurried along the passageway, removing the key from around her neck and unlocking the doors that contained Jari, Aamir, Natalie, and Ellabell. Alex saw that her hands were shaking, but whether from fear or excitement, he wasn't sure.

Alex ushered everyone out, yanking the doors open and helping them to their feet, assisted by Helena. It was a rushed affair with no time for explanations, and there was panic in the atmosphere as Helena led them all back through the labyrinthine school toward the door with the portal. With a gut-wrenching smack of dread, Alex realized, as they neared the room midway down the dingy corridor, that the portal itself could well have been removed, just as Natalie had removed the one that brought them to this place.

"Please still be there," he muttered, pushing open the door.

To his overwhelming joy, it was still there. He wasn't sure he'd ever been more thrilled about anything in his life. Whooping loudly, he scooped Ellabell into his arms, spinning her wildly around, and though her expression was one of total bemusement, she laughed as he set her down.

His delight was short lived as he heard the piercing sound of Alypia's screams, echoing into the room. The howling, animalistic sound could be heard from where they were, making Alex worry about the rapidly closing window of time they still had.

"What's going on?" Jari asked.

"I used magic to keep Alypia at bay, but it's going to wear off soon, so we need to get going!" explained Alex as quickly as he could. He would fill them all in on the minutiae later.

His ears pricked up as he heard the percussive beat of footsteps on flagstones, pounding beneath the shrill pitch of Alypia's pained cries, signaling that others were coming to her aid, drawn by the haunting sound. They didn't have long at all.

Kicking the door shut behind them, Alex grasped Ellabell's hand and dragged her toward the portal, squeezing it tightly as he pushed her through to the castle courtyard on the other side. It was as easy as stepping through a doorway, with no troubling drop to worry about. He urged the others through, watching anxiously as they all made the short leap, but Helena was hanging back.

"Come on," he insisted, trying to maneuver her toward the portal. "It's easy."

She pushed him away firmly, shaking her head. "I can't go with you," she whispered sadly, her eyes filling with bitter, frustrated tears.

Jari, hearing this, moved to the edge of the portal on the other side, sticking his head back through. "Please, Helena—come on. You have to come with us!" he begged. "I'll take you dancing! You can paint with my mom and listen to all my dad's terrible jokes!"

Helena smiled miserably. "I can't come with you," she repeated.

"Of course you can," encouraged Alex, wondering what had caused this sudden change of mind. He wanted her to be free, and the sight of her holding back was a sad one to behold.

"I can't—don't you see?" She brushed away a hot, angry tear. "Now that she knows about the plan, Alypia will move heaven and earth if I go missing. If I come with you now, I am dooming you all. You've got more chance without me."

Jari was beside himself, trying to get through the portal as the others dragged him back. "Alypia will kill you if you don't come with us—you *have* to come with us! You have to!" he pleaded. "Please, Helena… please come with us."

Helena smiled, with the look of a bittersweet farewell upon her pretty face. Of all the perfect creatures within Stillwater, Alex imagined that if the magic were completely removed, she would be the only one who still looked beautiful. He watched as she moved slowly toward the edge of the portal, leaning in for the briefest of moments to kiss Jari swiftly on the lips.

"My mother will punish me, but she won't kill her only daughter," she assured him, holding her hand against his cheek before stepping back into the room.

"You have to come, Helena," insisted Alex, trying hard not to look at Jari's dazed, heartbroken face peering through the portal.

Leaning close to his ear, she whispered her last words to Alex. "I know you will do what is right, no matter the consequences. Today, you'll save the few. One day, you'll save the many."

Alex wasn't sure what she meant, but he leveled his gaze with her strange gold eyes. He didn't know if he could bring himself to leave her to face the punishment surely waiting for her, once her mother disentangled herself from the glowing beasts.

"No," Alex said, shaking his head. "I can't just leave you to that woman. I don't care if she's your mother or not—we're not leaving you."

"Helena, come on!" shouted Jari.

"Please, Helena," Natalie added hopefully.

Helena sighed, sparking Alex's hope that she was relenting and they could get the hell out of there. She seemed deep in thought, and Jari's eyes went wide with adoring optimism.

"I'm sorry," she said with a sad smile.

And then Alex found himself staggering backward as Helena pushed a barrier of fierce, unexpected magic at his chest, the blast knocking him squarely through the portal and out the other side. Sprawling backward on the hard ground of the castle courtyard, he looked back up in time to see that Helena was lifting her hand in a tearful farewell. Giving one last sad wave, her hands crackled to life, thrumming with a pink-tinged coil of golden magic, before a shimmer of light blinded them all for a moment, forcing them to turn their faces away.

When they looked back, the portal and Helena were gone.

CHAPTER 40

S ITTING UP PROPERLY, ALEX CHECKED THE PRECIOUS
cargo in his bag, worried some of the bottles might have
broken on impact with the ground. Thankfully, they were
all in one piece, no life essence spilling out onto the courtyard.

Looking around, he could see they were, indeed, in a castle
courtyard, staring at the now-empty wall where the portal had
been.

Jari was in pieces. "She was the love of my life!" he wailed,
rocking inconsolably on the flagstones.

The others seemed equally sorry to see Helena go. Alex
knew they must have arrived at the same conclusion as him, realizing they had misjudged Helena at times, when she hadn't deserved anything but their trust.

"I can't believe she stayed," said Ellabell quietly, her voice croaky. "I hope she'll be okay."

Natalie nodded, her brow furrowed. "I will miss her... She was a good friend."

It was almost like a death, knowing they'd never see Helena again, and though Alex wondered if he could go back and get her, he knew there was no way to do it without figuring out portals. And that seemed more and more unlikely now that they didn't have the help of Stillwater's books.

Alex got up and dusted himself off, shifting the bag of bottles carefully around to a more comfortable spot. He had no idea where they were, and the uncertainty unnerved him.

Aamir moved nervously toward Alex, his eyes transfixed by the satchel Alex held onto.

"What's in the bag?" he asked.

The others looked toward Alex, their eyes showing surprise as they noticed the bulky satchel for the first time. Alex removed one of the bottles, holding it up to the light so they could see the dim red glow that burned in the middle of the black, smoky glass.

"Is that what I think it is?" Ellabell gasped.

He nodded. "It is. It's life essence. Bottles and bottles of life essence—the currency that is going to see us home," he explained with a hopeful smile.

"How did you get it?" Jari chimed in, his interest piqued though he was still snuffling slightly.

"I found where it was being kept. Alypia had the bottles in a little room, just to the side of her study." He shrugged, looking intently at the glowing pulse within the bottle.

"Whoa. How did you get them from Alypia?" pressed Jari,

really interested now.

"Using my powers. I just conjured a powerful spell that managed to keep Alypia at bay while I ran off into the chamber where they were stored and scooped up as many as I could. I kicked the rest over—they all smashed, and the essence drained away, back into the earth," he murmured, feeling bashful beneath the intense gaze of their eyes.

"Were you the one who caused her to scream that way?" Natalie flashed a look of concern, clearly suspecting some of what Alex had done.

"Sort of," he admitted. "I used two of the bottles and fed my anti-magic through the essence to make two of those beast things Derhin used against Aamir. They kept her occupied while I ran away."

His friends fell silent, looking at him with a sort of awestruck fear. It worried him—too many people were looking at him that way these days. He only hoped what he had done to Alypia would be enough to keep her from following them for a while. The Head had managed to restore the portal at Spellshadow, and Alex guessed Alypia would do the same as soon as she was able to, but he knew those beasts would stall her for a while. Her ungodly screams had been evidence of their destructive powers against her. Still, as ever, the ticking hands of time clanged above them.

Shifting his muscles, he tried to stretch, wanting to get the knots and aches out. His whole body felt tired and a little disjointed, making him wonder if it was because he had used a small speck of his essence in his anti-magical conjurations. He didn't feel any different mentally; he just felt shattered physically.

Silently, he made a note to ask Natalie later, if that was what happened when you used strong, dark magic.

Suddenly, he jumped to attention as he became aware of a shadow in the darkness of a hallway, a short distance away from where they were gathered. Shuffling along the tunnel, a figure stepped out into the muted light of the courtyard.

Seeing who it was, their faces lifted in surprise, their eyes going wide. Alex wasn't sure he could take many more surprises; his heart was still thundering from the panicked exit they had just made. Though, saying that, Alex had to admit this was one of the better ones.

"At last! I thought you'd never get here!" a voice bellowed from the shadows.

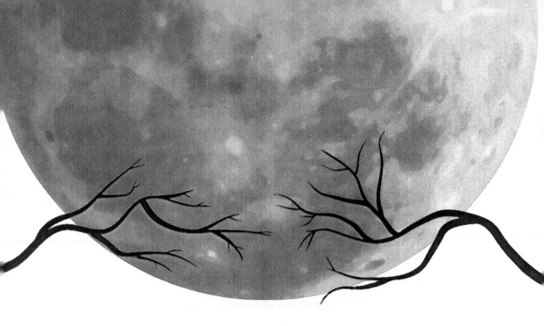

EPILOGUE

E LIAS LOLLED CASUALLY IN THE ROOM ABOVE THE PORTAL, picking stars from his teeth.

Seeing Alex leave had pleased him greatly—he was starting to grow tired of Stillwater. He'd always hated it, even when he'd come through to study as a teacher, with all the beautiful people preening and primping, all obsessed with beauty. That wasn't Elias's style at all. Elias was more into the interior, magical beauty of a person, rather than the false, ephemeral outer shell. After all, the mortal coil could be shuffled off at any moment, leaving shadowy strands that simply would not behave, when faced with the magic of Stillwater.

He had been watching Alex with keen intrigue, though he had been unable to do much thanks to his unruly, disjointed body snaking off to wherever it pleased, at any given time, within the magical otherworld of Stillwater House. He loathed it, thinking far less of the fearsome Alypia for using such trite techniques to control everyone. Manipulation was easy, he smiled—you just had to know how to pull the right strings. Puppet master extraordinaire, that was Elias, and he relished the position.

Sadly, and much to Elias's chagrin, the magic that affected everybody's state of mind, making them giddy, smiling zombies, also wrought havoc on his ability to hold his transient, shadowy form together. Finding and taking that book from Alypia's office had been no mean feat for a being that could barely keep his face from disappearing into the ether, and still Alex had dithered with it.

At least he rallied in the end, thought Elias smugly, slinking toward the windowless study, clapping the wispy fronds of what should have been hands together as he saw the royal mess Alex had made of the bottle chamber.

A royal *mess indeed*, chuckled Elias with starry-eyed delight, as he watched the scene playing out below from the safety of his dark corner. It called for popcorn, he mused with a grin, though he could barely remember the taste of such a paltry human snack.

The guards had arrived to assist Alypia, disposing of the great golden beasts with some difficulty. Elias struggled not to laugh aloud and give his position away as he watched them try to dissipate the creatures.

Child's play, he thought to himself. *And they call themselves the best—the best at mediocrity, perhaps.*

His shadowy mouth turned up in a pleased grin as he saw

the bruised, ugly shape of Alypia crouched on the floor, her pale face drawn and almost skeletal, her beauty yet to be restored by the crackling magic.

Ah, there's the family resemblance! Elias bristled with catty pleasure, enjoying the woman's suffering. He had never much cared for her, nor she for him. *Definitely showing your age, Alypia,* he thought smugly. She looked almost dead, but the frail twitch of her fingers confirmed she was not.

Bored with Alypia, he slunk away, moving deftly from shadow to shadow. His curiosity spiked when he saw Helena running back through the grounds of the school. The girl was of interest to him. He swooped close to her, marveling at the work she had saved him in trying to squirrel away a book on portals. The Leander book had almost finished him off, dispersing his wispy body to the four corners of the earth, but Helena had done the job just as well. It would do, for now. Nobody except she and Elias knew what she had done with the portal, but they would, and boy would she be in trouble then.

She was something of a mystery to him, this silver-haired waif who had failed to steal Alex's heart away from that curly-haired do-gooder. Elias still wasn't sure how he felt about Helena, though he did enjoy the powerful energy that emanated from her very being, feeding his weakened state. It was like drinking pure energy.

Elias's mood turned sour as he thought about Ellabell, which was what thinking about her usually did. Especially after the stunt she pulled outside the cottage—Elias was still seething about that. Ellabell was the girl who seemed to ruin everything, as far as Elias was concerned, always seeking to turn Alex against him in one way or another. One little smack to the head and it was curtains for Elias.

Well, I showed that troublesome little pest. He grinned, flashing his teeth, pleased that Alex still felt the need for him. It was addictive, Elias knew it was—he had made it that way. Knowledge was highly addictive, that little French girl was evidence of that, and Alex was just as hooked.

Alex's affection for Ellabell was an issue, Elias had decided. He felt a growing resentment toward the bespectacled saint, who could do no wrong in Alex's eyes. Elias wondered if, perhaps, it wasn't about time to do something about her, in such a way that Alex wouldn't suspect it was him. Alex would never stand for it if he knew Elias was responsible. That was a surefire way to lose Alex's faith, but he had a whole arsenal of devious methods up his wispy sleeve. All he had to do was take up the delicious task of choosing the right one.

Draping himself from the rafters of the bell tower, Elias felt like a proud uncle, thinking about the smattering of dangerous, dark magic Alex had used to attack Alypia. It was like seeing the quiet kid stand up in class and breakdance, an unexpected, if slightly amusing, pleasure. Alex had fumbled and gone at it in a haphazard manner, but the progress was remarkable. Elias shivered with pleasure as he recalled the liquid silver eyes, burning brightly, so similar to those of Leander Wyvern's.

For a while, Elias had wondered if he'd been betting on a tired horse, but Alex had shown there was hope for him still. He wouldn't be putting Alex out to pasture just yet. When pushed, his strength grew. When threatened, he showed his worth. Elias just had to keep playing upon that, which was what Elias enjoyed best in his fairly dull half-life. Alex was just about the only thing that kept Elias amused these days.

The boy was becoming a powerful Spellbreaker, finding his way through the spells and anti-magic with an instinctive surety that thrilled Elias.

It must be his heritage coming through, he thought wryly.

Even Elias had to admit he was impressed to see Alex using his essence for his own needs. It was promising—very promising. He felt the shadowy, starry crevasse of his chest swell with something akin to satisfaction as he thought about how far Alex had come, in such a relatively short span of time. Most of it was due to his tutelage, of course, Elias knew, but Alex had certainly done some of the footwork.

As much as Elias tried, he couldn't deny being fond of the boy.

Swooping down toward the glittering lake, beneath the cover of darkness, he relished the feel of the warm breeze rushing through his translucent form. He'd be leaving this place soon, much to his relief, but it didn't mean he couldn't do a lap of honor.

Skimming low across the water, the black, endless pools of his eyes caught sight of a body floating beneath the dark surface of the lake. It made him sad to see her brought so low. Well, as sad as Elias was capable of being. He had always been close to her, *before*, but that was so long ago now. He watched Gaze's body for a while, her rippling features decidedly peaceful, before quickly shaking off the feeling of melancholy, knowing that was not his way. Elias didn't do emotion, nor did he permit himself to get emotionally attached.

Elias answered to nobody and nothing.

Refusing to look back again, committing Gaze to the memory of long-forgotten life, he gathered his various parts together, knowing with intense pleasure that he was closer to his goal.

Vengeance was a dish best served cold, and it was almost freezing.

Ready for the next part of Alex's journey?

Dear Reader,

Thank you for picking up The Chain. I hope you enjoyed reading it as much as I enjoyed writing it!

The next book in the series, **The Keep**, releases **July 21st, 2017**.

Please visit: www.bellaforrest.net for details.

Until next time,
Bella x

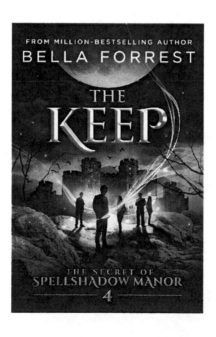

ALSO BY BELLA FORREST

THE SECRET OF SPELLSHADOW MANOR

The Secret of Spellshadow Manor (Book 1)
The Breaker (Book 2)
The Chain (Book 3)
The Keep (Book 4)

THE GENDER GAME

The Gender Game (Book 1)
The Gender Secret (Book 2)
The Gender Lie (Book 3)
The Gender War (Book 4)
The Gender Fall (Book 5)
The Gender Plan (Book 6)
The Gender End (Book 7)

A SHADE OF VAMPIRE SERIES

Series 1: Derek & Sofia's story

A Shade of Vampire (Book 1)
A Shade of Blood (Book 2)
A Castle of Sand (Book 3)
A Shadow of Light (Book 4)
A Blaze of Sun (Book 5)
A Gate of Night (Book 6)
A Break of Day (Book 7)

Series 2: Rose & Caleb's story

A Shade of Novak (Book 8)
A Bond of Blood (Book 9)
A Spell of Time (Book 10)
A Chase of Prey (Book 11)
A Shade of Doubt (Book 12)
A Turn of Tides (Book 13)
A Dawn of Strength (Book 14)
A Fall of Secrets (Book 15)
An End of Night (Book 16)

Series 3: The Shade continues with a new hero...

A Wind of Change (Book 17)
A Trail of Echoes (Book 18)
A Soldier of Shadows (Book 19)
A Hero of Realms (Book 20)
A Vial of Life (Book 21)
A Fork of Paths (Book 22)
A Flight of Souls (Book 23)
A Bridge of Stars (Book 24)

Series 4: A Clan of Novaks

A Clan of Novaks (Book 25)
A World of New (Book 26)
A Web of Lies (Book 27)
A Touch of Truth (Book 28)
An Hour of Need (Book 29)
A Game of Risk (Book 30)
A Twist of Fates (Book 31)
A Day of Glory (Book 32)

Series 5: A Dawn of Guardians

A Dawn of Guardians (Book 33)
A Sword of Chance (Book 34)
A Race of Trials (Book 35)
A King of Shadow (Book 36)
An Empire of Stones (Book 37)
A Power of Old (Book 38)
A Rip of Realms (Book 39)
A Throne of Fire (Book 40)
A Tide of War (Book 41)

Series 6: A Gift of Three

A Gift of Three (Book 42)
A House of Mysteries (Book 43)
A Tangle of Hearts (Book 44)
A Meet of Tribes (Book 45)
A Ride of Peril (Book 46)

For an updated list of Bella's books, please visit her website:
www.bellaforrest.net

Join Bella's VIP email list and she'll personally send you an
email reminder as soon as her next book is out:
www.morebellaforrest.com

CPSIA information can be obtained
at www.ICGtesting.com
Printed in the USA
LVOW12s2356290617

539815LV00005BA/803/P